Praise for The Lost Colony Series

"Packed with non-stop action, this SF adventure is sure
to keep readers turning the pages!"

—Maria V. Snyder, *New York Times* bestselling author
of *Navigating the Stars*

"If you like high fantasy style sci-fi, witty banter,
will they won't they vibes, and plenty of action
then definitely check this one out."

—Amber Torro, author of the Sentient Stars trilogy

"This fast-paced space adventure kept me turning pages right
up to the exciting conclusion. I wanted to run away on a spaceship and spend more time with the characters, especially the
engaging and relatable cyborg lead."

—Jordan Rivet, author of *Wake Me After the Apocalypse*

"...a fantastic sci fi adventure!"

—Emma Hill, author of *And Maybe They Fall In Love*

"...a very fun, easy read with lots of dark angles and
high-intensity action."

—Leah Jubilee, author of *Technically Not Dead*

"If you like Star Wars with a smidge of dystopian,
you need this book on your shelf. Now."

—Alli Earnest, author of the Gate Chronicles series

TO MADNESS AND RUIN

THE LOST COLONY TRILOGY, BOOK 2

EMILY LAYNE

OWL HOLLOW PRESS

Owl Hollow Press, LLC, Springville, UT 84663

To Madness and Ruin

Library of Congress Cataloging-in-Publication Data
To Madness and Ruin / E. Layne. — First edition.

Summary:
A devastating visit to Roanleigh sets Auri and the crew on a dangerous journey to the Federation's mysterious origin world, Earth—a planet no one has heard from in almost fifty years. What they discover there could be the key to saving their galaxy or the catalyst for the destruction of all they hold dear.

Cover Design by Les Solot

ISBN 978-1-958109-68-7 (paperback)
ISBN 978-1-958109-69-4 (ebook)

For Dad,
your bin of books was a portal to new worlds,
and your support gave me the courage
to create my own.

———

CHAPTER ONE

———

10 Sept 3319, 05:12:01
Ancora Galaxy, Planet 04: Babbage,
Distribution District

Aurelia Peri had forsaken her family and military career to discover the truth. So her current dilemma shouldn't come as a surprise.

"Trespassers, halt!" a man bellowed for the second time, now only meters behind her, his deep voice still hoarse with sleep.

Dragged from their bunks at, as Castor would say, "the *ketsu-*crack of dawn," the two guards would likely be more trigger happy than usual. A lucky blast from their fisted laser pistols would mark a disastrous end to Auri's first mission as a renegade.

Heart already slamming against her ribs, she forced her beleaguered legs to move faster. Sweat slicked her organic skin under the mesh mask designed to scramble facial recognition scans. She cut a glance toward the water sloshing beside her, searching in vain for the rescue shuttle.

The rising sun painted the expanse of ocean in hues of red and orange. Auri squinted into the brightness. Warehouses the size of luxury spaceliners floated in the distance, all property of the Ancora Federation. They were fixed to hulking platforms, identical to the one where Auri was currently trapped, and connected by a network of bridges.

The platform's narrow pestrian walkway hugged the exterior of the metal warehouse, the crashing, white-capped ocean centimeters below. Auri could barely hear the pounding footsteps of the pursuing guards over the notoriously choppy waters. Each wave sent a fresh spray of salty brine across the already slick path. Auri couldn't help wondering what happened if her boot, damp with salty spray kicked up by the waves, slipped…

She sucked in a breath through her nose to calm the panic, smelling ozone with an undercurrent of decaying fish. A stink wholly unique to Babbage.

Two other members of Auri's new crew, Katara and Malachi, sprinted a dozen meters ahead. Katara had twisted her long brown hair into a conglomeration of braids close to her scalp. She ran with a lithe grace that belonged to a cat of prey. Despite the massive rucksack on her shoulders, the assassin probably hadn't even broken a sweat.

The steady *bang-bang* of the guards' pursuit abruptly stopped. Before Auri could turn to see why, Malachi glanced back and his multi-colored gaze caught hers. From this distance, his eyes were the only recognizable feature underneath the mask.

"*Kuso*," he swore, mesh undulating as it shifted around his lips. "Drones!"

Auri's stomach dropped to her boots. Malachi jerked back around, adjusted his rucksack—filled with the contraband that had gotten them into this Charlie Foxtrot in the first place— and doubled his speed, catching up with Katara, both pulling even farther from Auri.

"Get to the bridge!" he shouted.

Auri risked a look to see how much time they had. She frowned at the sight of the hunched guards meters back, yanking off their hats to wipe sweat from their faces despite the chill of the early morning.

Above them, an army of flying black dots pocked the brightening sky. The dots grew larger with each second. Fear shot through Auri, layered with a detached, almost clinical, disappointment. Drone strikes were a lazy soldier's tactic. These guards weren't helping change the narrative of the Military Police Brigade (MPB) being the cushiest service branch.

Auri forced her mind to shutter against the thoughts stealing her speed. Public opinion of the MPB wasn't her concern.

Not anymore.

The drones were coming in hot, and they were armed with stunning devices that could go from bee-sting discomfort to lethal laserfire, depending on their operator's threat assessment.

Auri ignored her aching muscles, heaved her rucksack higher on her back, and increased her pace. She leaned into her robotic leg, using its extra strength to propel her forward.

A faint hum overlapped the rhythmic crash of the ocean against the platform. It reminded her of hundreds of insect wings flapping in unison. And it meant the drones were getting dangerously close. She gritted her teeth.

Thankfully, so was the bridge. Katara and Malachi were meters away from the metal structure just wide enough for a large hover-truck to cross. A cross-hatched safety barrier rose to knee-height on either side. The bridge connected this warehouse to the one almost five hundred meters further out to sea, currently a smudge on the horizon.

Movement inside an operator booth beside the bridge's entrance caught Auri's eye as she pushed to catch up. The platform trembled as if struck by an earthquake. A siren blared and strobe lights fixed atop the bridge's safety barrier flashed an angry red. Gears ground together, letting out a jaw-rattling screech that made it clear they were overdue for cleaning. The bridge split in the near distance, each end rising ever so slowly toward the bright dawn.

Malachi's distant curses echoed the *kuso, kuso, kuso* pounding through Auri's brain.

A female guard darted from the booth with a blaster gun clutched in both hands, raised at eye level. "Halt!" she ordered, her green fatigues perfectly pressed, the patch on her shoulder declaring her rank.

Katara accelerated, loping ahead of Malachi. The guard fired as the assassin hurled herself forward in a roll, the blasts scorching the platform. Katara landed on one knee while her other leg slammed into the guard's shins. The woman's head made a sickening *thud* as it hit the metal walkway.

Katara's eyes locked with Auri's as she stood. "Little Warrior, haul *ketsu*! You're falling behind!" Her voice was barely audible between the approaching drones and blasting siren.

Malachi and Katara clanged up the bridge, the incline growing steeper with each passing second. Auri raced after them, forcing herself to not check on the downed guard. The buzzing of the drones had increased in intensity, drowning out all sound, even the warning siren.

Auri had taken three steps onto the bridge when something yanked on her rope braid and hauled her backward. A fiery arc of pain roared along her skull.

She smacked against the platform. Air fled her lungs in a *whoosh*, her spine cracking against a hard object in her rucksack. The incessant buzzing quieted. All that remained was the siren's incessant wail.

The drones hovered a ball's toss above, quiet now that they weren't flying at max speed. Palm-sized, they had a single sensor in the center of their bellies. And the sensors were all fixed on Auri, likely running facial recognition scans while she lay there gasping like a landlocked fish.

Auri tried to roll onto her feet, but the weight of the rucksack stole her momentum. In a blink the guard's gun filled Auri's vision. Crimson coated the side of the woman's head where she'd hit the platform.

Auri's hand darted for her disc, only remembering she'd left it aboard the *Kestrel* when her fingers met air. The guard snapped, "Don't move."

Baka, Auri thought, curling her hand into a fist. She should have gone for the laser knife strapped to her hip.

The guard's gaze darted to Auri's barcode arm, covered by a green jacket and cuff. Then to Auri's face, more visible at a closer distance, the mesh only meant to confuse scans. Her brows drew together, and her finger shifted off the gun's trigger. "You look like—"

A rucksack slammed into the guard's back, and Auri scrambled to her feet as Katara hefted the bulky bag by its straps. The guard stumbled into the narrow booth before she toppled over the platform's edge.

Auri sucked in a breath, every molecule of her body demanding she dive in to help.

"*Move*," Katara grunted, shoving Auri toward the bridge. Rapid laser fire pelted the spot where Auri had been. The drones had just switched to attack mode.

"*Chikusho*," Katara swore, yanking her rucksack back on.

The guard was already swimming back to the platform. She held up her gun to get off a shot, but the blaster's trigger clicked uselessly.

"Go, go!" Katara pushed Auri again. The momentum propelled Auri up the bridge, now raised at a fifteen-degree angle.

Malachi balanced at the top; a coil gun raised. He shot at the drones, managing to knock a few off course. One screeched as it dropped from the air to disappear below the waves.

Half the drones shifted their attention to Malachi, unleashing more laserfire. He spared one glance at the growing gap in the bridge before he stepped off the edge.

Auri and Katara were heartbeats behind. Heat flashed just behind Auri, and she smelled the acidic tang of burning hair. She squeezed her eyes shut. Then she and Katara were lurching forward, falling, falling—

They toppled through an open hatch and slammed into the hard floor of a shuttle.

"Go!" Malachi was already on his feet, tearing off the sticky mesh mask. It made a disgusting squelching sound. He shoved it into a pocket of his leather jacket before he stumbled toward the front of the shuttle, supporting himself with one of the empty seats.

Loud pings reverberated as the drone's laserfire was absorbed by the shuttle's shield. Auri thanked the stars that Malachi had decided to refit the General-in-Chief's stolen transport for this mission. It was one of the few in the entire galaxy that would hold up against a barrage of high-intensity lasers.

Auri was just pushing to a seated position, shrugging off her rucksack with a groan, when the shuttle dropped into the water. She grabbed one of the handles set in the floor, positioned exactly for this purpose, and held on with a white-knuckled grip. Beside her, Katara did the same. Their bodies jerked up, then dropped back to the floor with a painful smack. Auri's abandoned rucksack made a loud *thunk* as it crashed into something at the back of the shuttle.

The pulse of laserfire and blast of the siren abruptly silenced. Water enveloped the craft in a deafening quiet. Auri suppressed a shiver at the expanse of midnight-blue darkness, only illuminated by the shuttle's headlights. Something long and lithe shot through the darkness beyond, scales flashing orange then gone in a blink.

They had approached the platform the same way, but this was only Auri's second time using a shuttle underwater. The concept made sense: if a ship was space worthy, it could be sea worthy too. With some modifications. But still. It felt unnatural. Auri fought the instinct to hold her breath.

Katara pushed to her feet, letting her bag slam to the floor. She yanked off her mask and tossed it behind her. It slapped onto one of the windows and stuck there. Then she aimed a razor-sharp glare at Auri.

"*Aho!* You absolute idiot. What was that?" She stabbed a finger at the ceiling above them. "Did that guard recognize you?"

"I-I don't think so…"

Ever since the Bleeders' attack on the Spire eleven days ago, the GIC had made it clear in multiple interviews that he believed Auri dead. According to her daily barcode scans, she'd officially been labeled missing in action. How convenient for him that everyone who witnessed the Bleeders' rampage was either deceased or easily bribed—like his son Ty.

Auri and Malachi had decided it best if Auri disappeared for the foreseeable future. The GIC's lie would be just another mark against him when they confronted Ancora Federation's citizens with the truth.

Auri had no idea what the GIC would do if he actually discovered her location. Would he have her arrested? Let her go? Or worse, toss her into Attica without a trial—which she now knew he had the power to do.

"But she *could* be notifying authorities about you," Katara muttered. "Great."

Auri glanced back at Malachi, who had eased into the co-pilot's chair. Marin sat next to him, studiously ignoring Katara and Auri. Her sightless gaze was straight ahead, one hand on the controls, the other in a sling.

Malachi crossed his arms. "One guard claiming she saw the GIC's adopted daughter won't start a bounty hunt. People aren't exactly mourning the loss of a cyborg." He shot Auri an apologetic glance.

Auri physically shrugged off the sting. She'd avoided watching news feeds and political commentary streams for that very reason. Many were relieved the GIC was no longer harboring a cyborg—or *clank*, as some dared call her—in his household. In fact, the GIC's approval rating had only improved since the Spire attack.

"I'll monitor the feeds to be safe," Katara said to Malachi, "and let you know if anything pops up." Then to Auri, "Exposure aside, you almost got yourself killed."

"I would've been fine," she countered, unpeeling her own mesh mask. Auri folded it into a small square as Tsuna had instructed before stowing it in one of the many pockets on her cargo pants. "I was about to go for my knife."

Katara sighed and dropped onto one of the benches lining the walls. "You're not a DISC agent tracking one target anymore. You aren't an untouchable MPB soldier protected from the rim."

Auri crossed her arms, ignoring the way Katara's words made her stomach twist. Her arm cuff shifted against her synthetic skin, a physical reminder. She never would've dreamed of covering her barcode before she crossed into the rim. Before she joined Malachi's crew.

"I *know*," Auri whispered. When she decided to help the crew of the *Kestrel* with their job on Attica—breaking Tsuna out of the infamous prison—Auri knew the ramifications.

But knowing and living them were two entirely different things.

Nothing had made the repercussions of her choice more abundantly clear than being chased by those guards. Auri didn't regret her decision, but a quiet part of her still ached—and almost missed—the life she knew.

"I don't understand why you brought her," Katara said, turning on Malachi now. "She's greener than Ferris when it comes to jobs like this."

"Exactly." The captain shifted in his seat. He glanced down at Katara's laser katar tucked in a thigh sheath, then at the other knives fixed at her hip and ankle. "Auri needed to see what life is like outside of the MPB, especially before we reach Roanleigh. I was hoping you could take her under your wing."

"I don't have *wings*." Katara crossed her arms, cocking a hip. "And *you*, Captain. Mind explaining why you let our job go to *kuso*? What in that warehouse was worth triggering the silent alarm? The gear, tech, and meds I *thought* we were taking weren't monitored. Which is why we risked this mission at all."

Malachi laid a protective hand atop the rucksack nestled between his feet. "A prototype. It's worth the hassle. Trust me."

"You know I do. I'd just rather that trust not get me shot by a drone. Embarrassing way to die." Katara looked back to Auri, but Malachi cut her off before she could dish out another criticism.

"Kat," he murmured. He watched Auri for a beat, and she felt the urge to tighten her arms over her chest, as if the captain peered past her bones and sinew into the depths of her soul. Did he see the ache there for a lost, familiar life? The fear of what lay ahead?

Maybe he did, because he shook his head. "I think she's been berated enough."

Katara opened her mouth as if she wanted to object, but she shut it with a growl. "Fine." She jerked her chin at Auri's singed braid. "If you go on future missions, you need to do something about that. It's too easy for an opponent to use against you. And next time I might not be around to help."

CHAPTER TWO

———

10 Sept 3319, 07:02:56
Ancora Galaxy, Planet 04: Babbage,
Free Airspace

The *Kestrel*'s rectangular kitchen table was barely visible beneath the haul from Babbage. Auri bit the inside of her cheek as she studied the contraband. Her stomach was a knotted mess of pride that she'd contributed to the crew…

And guilt that she'd stolen from the Federation.

A crack followed by a delicious sizzle drew Auri's attention away from her inner turmoil. Castor stood at the griddle set into the island countertop, frying eggs for breakfast. He clearly hadn't seen what had become of the dining area.

On one end lay temperature regulating winter gear for the crew going planetside, state-of-the-art medical supplies requested by Ferris, specific tech for Tsuna, and extra parts should something go wrong with the *Kestrel*. Each item would help the crew survive Roanleigh's known dangers, courtesy of the intel retrieved from the Spire: constant blizzards and potential Bleeders.

That same intel revealed 115 settlers, Auri included, had left Earth in 3276, over four decades ago, bound for Ancora Galaxy without the Fed's knowledge. After a year of space travel, they touched down on Roanleigh. The Fed's current propaganda claimed the planet was uninhabitable after it failed its terraforming. The presiding GIC had even given it the monicker the Toxic Planet. And both were now proved to be lies.

When the galaxy was first studied as an option for colonization, Earth's scientists declared the eighth planet capable of supporting life, though at great cost. With the planet's constant snowstorms, most food and livestock would need to be imported, not to mention the quality of life on the planet would have been dismal for those accustomed to life on Earth. Roanleigh had been prohibited. But something had happened, and 115 explorers attempted the impossible without hope of aid or rescue.

That *something* was one of the many things Auri was desperate to discover. The past she thought true was nothing more than spoon fed lies from her adoptive father. While she appeared nineteen, she was technically forty-five, accounting for her time trapped in cryo sleep on Roanleigh. But any memory of her time on the Toxic Planet, on Earth, even her rescue by an exploratory vid crew, was nothing but whisps of shadow and the occasional bloody nightmare.

But not for long. Not if Malachi's suspicions about the intel trapped on Roanleigh proved true.

"Are you sure this is enough?" Katara asked Malachi where she leaned over one of the high-backed chairs tucked under the table. "I feel like we should have gotten weapons too."

Malachi shook his head. "We already have weapons. We were short on time, and this gear was more important."

"As important as the prototype that almost got us caught?" She raised a brow.

"No wonder you made an excellent assassin," Malachi mused, not meeting Katara's eyes. "You never give up."

She grinned. "I'll cash in on your bounty one of these days."

Whatever prototype the *Kestrel*'s captain took, he clearly didn't plan on sharing it with Katara, let alone the crew. It remained tucked inside his rucksack, the one bag not folded for storage.

"I would still prefer some kind of explosive." Katara rubbed at her scalp underneath her tight coils of braids.

"Dead Bleeders aren't worth risking the mission. We need any intel fully intact."

She sighed. "Well, *alive* Bleeders are their own risk. Do you plan to land if our scans detect them?"

"Depends on how many," he murmured.

The captain had a tendency to play his cards close to the chest, which set Auri's teeth on edge. He had a purpose and plan for the prototype he took on Babbage, but for some reason didn't deign to inform the crew of that purpose. Even though they had all proved their loyalty and could likely offer insight and ideas that he might not have considered.

A familiar *woof!* made her turn, banishing her irritation.

A white poodle bounded into the kitchen from a connecting hallway. Birdie plopped onto her rump in front of Auri, long tail kicking up an impressive breeze.

The tightness in Auri's chest eased at the sight of her dog, partner, and best friend. "Hey, Bird." Auri dropped to her knees and wrapped her arms around Birdie's neck. The familiar warm scent of dog enveloped her.

It hadn't been easy leaving Birdie onboard, but DISC canine training focused on following direct orders and subduing a target. The crew's operating style was more evasive maneuvers and sneaking around. Auri had started building on Birdie's knowledge, but she didn't think the dog was ready for live missions yet.

Katara probably wishes I'd stayed behind too, Auri thought with an internal sigh.

Birdie wriggled, and Auri obediently released her. With a final scratch, Auri rose, and the poodle trotted around the table to

Katara, completely bypassing Malachi. The captain rolled his eyes.

"You're only paying me attention because Marin isn't here," Katara chided, giving Birdie an obligatory scratch behind the ear. Marin had gone to the bridge upon arrival to scan for pursuit.

Birdie's next target was Castor, and she kept pace with him as he meandered around the kitchen collecting final ingredients and sipping on a palm-sized cup of steaming green tea. He yawned, unaffected by the dog's pleading whine. "Wait until breakfast, you mutt."

Birdie dejectedly wandered over to a heating grate and lay atop it with a heavy groan.

Castor wrapped nori around the final *onigiri* and added it to the plate of twenty others. Then his gaze landed on the occupied table. "*Chikusho*, Malachi. Where am I supposed to put the food?"

Malachi deposited the folded rucksacks onto a free corner of the countertop before he picked up a coffee mug. There was a cartooned lucky cat on it, a speech bubble saying *meow* above its head.

"I don't think so." Katara snatched the mug, deftly avoiding sloshing coffee everywhere. "Go wash your own. I'm sick of you using my mugs."

Malachi studiously ignored her. "It'll be a buffet breakfast, Castor. Call the crew. I want to punch out of Babs's orbit directly after chowtime." He strode over to the coffee maker, which was always full these days. Instead of opening the mug cabinet, he just grabbed the entire pot. He held it up to Katara in a half-hearted salute. "Yours was the first I grabbed. *Gomen*."

"Funny how that always happens," Katara muttered. She moved over to the back of the kitchen and opened the pressurized air washer. "Was that so hard?" she asked Malachi after putting the mug inside.

"I'm not saying it's hard," he said. "It's that I misplace my mugs all over this ship."

Now it was Auri's turn to glare at Malachi. So, the mug that had almost sent her plummeting off the catwalk in the cargo hold yesterday had been *his*.

Castor sipped his tea and pressed his thumb against a small screen fixed on a wall by the fridge. "Breakfast." His voice echoed from the intercoms throughout the ship.

Ferris arrived seconds later with his blond hair and beard freshly trimmed. His hands were tucked in the pockets of his vest, and he whistled a cheery tune that made Castor groan.

"Mornin'," Ferris called to Auri and Malachi. He stopped next to Katara and ran the back of his fingers across her arm. "Glad you're back safe," he murmured. Katara squeezed his hand once before turning to flip off Castor, who had made a rude gesture.

Malachi took a swig of coffee from the pot, and Ferris eyed him with a worried frown.

"Cai…" Ferris began, but Malachi shook his head and the doctor trailed off with a sigh.

Tsuna arrived next, dressed in a khaki jumpsuit with a tumbler of iced coffee in one hand. Her eyes widened in excitement when she saw the tech on the table. She beelined for it and began rifling through, making occasional satisfied hums.

"Looks like you got everything I needed." She plucked a small chip from the table and held it between thumb and forefinger. "I was up all night tweaking my simulation to get our tech to talk with Roanleigh's."

"Any luck?" Ferris asked.

Each crew member had a specific role in the upcoming mission on the Toxic Planet. So far, Tsuna's proved the most difficult: copy a massive cache of intel stored on the planet's central datacenter. A task every archeologist sent to Roanleigh had failed to do because of its old, and therefore incompatible, tech.

After scouring what they'd obtained in the Spire, Tsuna decided to assume Roanleigh's computers were similar to Earth's. Which was a risk in itself since communication with the origin planet had been lost during General-in-Chief Krugel's command decades ago. Finding software and cable adapters that corresponded with the outdated tech had been difficult. Especially since most of Ancora Federation operated largely by near field communication—a term Auri recently learned courtesy of Tsuna.

The hacker shook her head in response to Ferris's question. "But I'll get there. At least I have a plan. The systems I'm trying to connect to are just painfully *old*." When that didn't earn her sympathy from the doctor, she added, "Imagine having to relieve pain with morphine instead of Tirflox."

"*Kuso*," Ferris muttered. "A nightmare."

"Exactly."

Marin padded into the kitchen on bare feet, so quietly Auri wouldn't have known she had arrived if she weren't facing the doorway.

"How we looking?" Malachi asked her.

"No signs of pursuit."

"And the…?" Malachi asked, trailing off suggestively.

"Clear as well."

Auri's brow furrowed. "What—"

Malachi addressed the rest of the crew. "Grab some chow and sit best you can. Time to talk Roanleigh."

Filing away her question for later, Auri quickly filled her plate, making sure to toss two fried eggs atop the dog food in Birdie's bowl. The poodle attacked her breakfast with relish while Auri returned to the table. She sat in her usual spot between Malachi and Marin, plate balanced on her thighs. Neither of her tablemates had bothered with breakfast.

Marin's droid body was incapable of digestion, but Malachi…

"Are you going to eat?" Auri asked him, pulling her chopsticks out from a small drawer under the table.

Malachi raised a brow. "Worried?"

Warmth prickled Auri's belly at his teasing tone. "You're so focused on Roanleigh, I want to make sure you're still taking care of yourself." She gestured to the pot in front of him.

"You're starting to sound like Ferris." He lowered his voice as the rest of the crew slid into their usual seats. "I'm finally close to real answers about the Bleeders, Aurelia. I'll sleep when I've had my revenge." Then louder he said, "I wouldn't need so much coffee if our ship's doctor would give me actual stimulants."

Ferris rolled his eyes. He and Malachi had known each other since childhood, but they bickered like an old married couple. "Those are liquid adrenaline, Cai. They could kill you. *Baka.*"

"Then let's all stop judging my coffee consumption," Malachi said. He clapped his hands together and everyone followed.

"*Itadakimasu,*" the crew murmured in unison.

While everyone ate, Malachi peered into his coffee, one finger tapping a beat on the pot's handle. The captain of the *Kestrel* was still an enigma. Auri had learned more about his past—how he had witnessed the Bleeders' rampage on his district and his little sister's death before being wrongly convicted of the murders and escaping Attica—but sometimes the present Malachi was as much a mystery as when they first met.

Finally, Malachi stood and his chair scraped across the floor. "*Kestrel* has been refueled, and we have all the supplies we need for Roanleigh." He gestured to the table laden with their stolen goods. "The very best the Fed has to offer."

Castor gave Malachi a toast with his third cup of steaming green tea.

When Malachi first proposed the plan to break into a Babbage warehouse, Auri argued that the crew should legally purchase at least some items. But Katara's accounting had made the truth abundantly clear: what they needed was high end, and no one had enough credits.

Even Auri was practically destitute since cutting ties with the GIC and the MPB. Her income came from the *Kestrel*. And they hadn't taken a legitimate transport job since their delivery on Attica two weeks ago.

Malachi shoved a pair of winter boots aside to turn on the table's hologram feature. A map of the galaxy flashed to life. A blinking blue dot illuminated their current location, still caught in Babbage's gravitational pull.

"This time of year," Malachi said, bracing his hands on the corners of the table, "planetary alignment works in our favor. The trip to Roanleigh will last about a week."

"A week of space travel," Katara murmured. She crossed her arms and leaned back in her seat. "This will be interesting."

Ferris split a fried egg with the edge of his chopstick. "Our current record is four days. And we all know how that trip went." He glanced at Malachi pointedly and rubbed his nose.

Malachi tilted his head toward the ceiling and released a longsuffering sigh.

Voyages between planets within the Federation were usually only a few days, even without using the Fed-controlled slingshots, but Roanleigh was the furthest planet in the galaxy. Auri wished she had the cred to accelerate their travel, which she didn't, but their mission needed to stay under the Fed's radar anyway.

"Don't worry, Cai," Tsuna teased from across the table. "I'll make it at least five days before flirting with you this time."

Castor's grip on his cup tightened. "Don't joke, Tsuna. You nearly got me kicked off the crew. All to play one of your little games because commitment terrifies you."

Tsuna's lips formed a thin line. Her usually warm voice was icy when she replied, "How dare you say that in front of everyone."

"You started it," he snapped back.

"I did *no*—"

Marin cut Tsuna off with a raised hand. "You two have the relational maturity of this body." She rested her slender fingers atop her chest, covered by a yellow *yukata* with blooms of flowers spattered across the fabric. "More adult behavior would be appreciated. Or might I suggest marital counseling?"

"Didn't work," Castor said.

Simultaneously Tsuna snapped, "We're *divorced*."

Auri rubbed her organic eye with her palm. A headache blossomed at her temples. She understood the confines of a ship straining crew relations, especially when danger lurked at their destination. The sooner they discussed next steps, the sooner she could get some much-needed sleep. "Malachi, what is the plan once we reach Roanleigh?"

Malachi swiped at the display, magnifying the Toxic Planet. Roanleigh orbited before them, cast in the blue-ish hue of the table's holo lens. It was the smallest planet in the system. Its single moon, Caesi, shifted around it in an endless loop. Images taken by the one archeologist who survived the last expedition, C.K.E., flashed in succession around the projected planet: endless snow, ice, and odd circular dwellings. They hadn't been able to ID the man beyond his initials. All that remained of the mysterious C.K.E. were the photos he saved to his c-tacts and uploaded to the Spire.

"Thanks to the Spire's intel," Malachi began, "we know that there were 115 original settlers on Roanleigh. They came prepared to start a habitable colony. Well, as habitable as it can be with all the snow." With a tap of his fingers, a flight manifest scrolled across the bottom of the hologram. Names and occupations flicked by ranging from botanist to engineer to doctor. Only a few names didn't have an attached job description. In its place were two possibilities: spouse or child. There weren't many of either.

Auri squinted at the children's names as if they might trigger a memory, even though she'd already studied them, and the others, for hours without so much as a flicker of recognition.

"What we don't know," Malachi continued, "is what happened to 114 of them."

Heat flooded up Auri's neck as everyone turned to look at her.

"As Cai already knows, I upgraded the *Kestrel*'s specs," Tsuna said, breaking the silence and lowering her chopsticks to her empty plate. Auri let out a relieved breath as the crew's attention shifted. "When we get closer, Marin can scan Roanleigh to ensure Bleeders aren't waiting in ambush." She shivered, likely remembering their time trapped in the vault while those creatures tore themselves apart to get at them.

Which brought them back to Malachi's evasive answer to Katara's earlier question, but the time for gray answers was over. Auri cleared her throat. "We never discussed what will we do if there are Bleeders planetside. Five or maybe ten we could fight off, but what if there are more? The storms make air support unreliable." Not that the *Kestrel,* a Class Four transport ship, even had exterior weaponry. Malachi gave her a knowing look. "The dead archeologists made it clear that Roanleigh seems to be the Bleeder's homebase. We just don't know how many of them are currently... *home.* We'll see how it plays out."

Auri doubted the captain would leave Roanleigh empty-handed. His desperation and single-minded focus to bring the GIC to justice for his lies about the Bleeders seemed to fuel him even more than coffee.

"Bleeders aren't our only problem." Ferris nodded at the cold-weather gear. "The blizzards could be even more dangerous."

"We can detect the storms from orbit," Tsuna said. "Worst case scenario, we wait it out."

"Unless it cuts too far into our fuel reserves," Katara added.

Castor snorted. "You'll be warm enough in this gear. I could poison a politician and still not make enough to buy just one of these suits."

"I would go planetside, if I weren't the pilot," Marin murmured too quiet for anyone but Auri to hear. "The cold doesn't bother me."

"Easy for you to say, cook," Ferris muttered. "You're staying cozy and warm on the ship. How long has it been since you shot a long-range rifle?"

Katara rolled her eyes and flipped one of her knife-shaped chopsticks across her knuckles.

"Enough you two," Tsuna scolded, giving Castor a slap on the arm that was more playful than painful. "Castor is a good shot, Ferris. Even I can vouch for that. I hate his guts, but I still wouldn't want anyone else providing cover if things go sideways."

Ferris sighed. "I know the whole *Toxic Planet*"—he made air quotes with his fingers—"is a lie. But the terraforming really did Roanleigh wrong."

"The Spire's intel proves it was never meant to be colonized," Malachi said, double tapping the display. The holo image of Roanleigh disappeared. "The first planet in Ancora Galaxy to be terraformed was Attica, back in 2225. Every twenty-five years, a new planet was made habitable and settled."

Castor groaned. "I did not sign up for a history lesson."

"If you'd actually read the intel, we could avoid it," Ferris stage whispered. Castor glared.

Malachi pointedly ignored the cook and the doctor, staring down into the darkness of his half-drained coffee pot. "Roanleigh would have been too costly to support, so settlement was banned. Not to mention Ancora Federation stopped immigration from Earth and declared itself a separate government in 3200."

"Except colonists still came," Ferris said. "Over seventy years after the border closure during GIC Krugel's command. Big time gap."

Malachi looked up, gaze locking with Auri's. "They left Earth to illegally settle an inhospitable planet, expecting little— if any—aid from the Fed. Possibly even retribution for breaking our laws. Krugel had quite the reputation, even before he cut ties with Earth in 3275. So much could go wrong. What would drive them to take such a risk?"

A leeching cold sucked at Auri's gut, but she met his gaze. "Something to do with the Bleeders?"

Her eyes shifted, releasing her from their multi-colored scrutiny. "I'm hoping that's one of the things we find out."

"And information on how to force the GIC into an early retirement," Katara added. The twist of her lips made it clear her idea of *retirement* was not the same as Auri's.

Malachi toasted her with his coffee pot. He swiped at his eyes, purple smudges dark beneath them, and faced Marin. "Once you're ready, punch out of orbit and set course for Roanleigh. I'll meet you on the bridge shortly." To the rest of the crew he said, "Find your gear plus any specially requested items, and get them stored. Tsuna, I expect updates on the tech situation."

He scooped up his rucksack, still filled with the contraband that had almost gotten them arrested and which he'd still not explained, and coffee pot. With a final nod to the crew, he disappeared through the engine room doors at the back of the kitchen.

Auri pushed to her feet, wanting answers, but nearly leapt out of her skin to see Katara standing beside Marin's now-empty chair.

"Stars, Katara," Auri breathed, placing a hand over her chest as she sat back down with a soft *thump*. "I didn't even see you get up."

Katara smirked as she lowered herself into the seat. "You were busy watching the captain."

Auri tensed as she glanced over at Tsuna, Ferris, and Castor. They had started cleaning up the remains of breakfast, oblivious to Katara's embarrassing implication.

Auri opened her mouth to protest, but the assassin waved away Auri's concern, then began untwisting one of her tight braids. The scent of lavender blended with the lingering smell of breakfast.

"I was too hard on you earlier," Katara said. "Nothing has popped up on the feeds about the GIC's renegade adopted daughter."

Auri's eyes widened. "Are you—"

"I'm not *wrong* for berating you, but the delivery needed improvement. Leaving the Fed's service is a hard transition. I want to train you to better fight the Bleeders, if you're willing."

"Train me?" Birdie trotted to Auri's side, the fur around her muzzle wet with water from her bowl. "I've already—"

"Not DISC agent *training*." The way Katara said *training* made it seem like Auri's time at basic had been a vacation. "I mean hand-to-hand combat, close-range weapons. If you're going to survive, Little Warrior, you need to know how to really fight." She glanced over Auri's shoulder where Tsuna and Ferris chatted while storing leftovers in VPRO bags. "I don't let people into my life easily." Her gaze cut back to Auri, sharp and intense. "But once I do, I'm sure as hell not going to let them be a *baka* and get themselves killed."

Auri's fingers knotted in Birdie's white curls as understanding moved through her. The poodle gave her robotic fingers a quick lick. The pressure of the movement registered, but not the warmth or wetness.

"Thank you," Auri murmured. "Thank you for caring about me enough to want to keep me safe." Saying the words aloud made tears prick at her organic eye.

Katara chuckled and shoved Auri's shoulder too hard to be entirely playful. "Don't get sappy. After a training session, you might not be so thankful."

Auri swiped at her eye. "When do we start?"

"I'll meet you outside your room tomorrow at 0600." Katara moved to stand, scooping her winter gear under one arm. "Get some rest. You'll need it."

CHAPTER THREE

A wooden baton hurtled through the air. Auri suppressed the instinct to dodge and rushed forward, arms raised. Her forearm struck Katara's neck, stopping the baton mid-strike. She heaved a breath and slammed her knee into Katara's stomach. Instead of malleable flesh, body armor absorbed the brutal force—Auri had learned not to hold back.

She struck again. The pad radiated the intensity throughout the material. In a real fight, Katara would be breathless on the ground, if not dying from a ruptured lung or spleen. Sweat beaded along Auri's hairline. A single droplet rolled down her temple. She shifted backward to retreat.

"Mistake," Katara hissed. Her hair was plaited close to her head, and her copper skin only glistened with exertion—unlike Auri's drenched tank top. Katara hefted the baton, snapping it out with a *crack*. It glanced off Auri's robotic leg. Her irritation flared.

Auri had forgotten to take the baton. Again.

Except this time, Katara didn't pause to explain how to correct the mistake. The assassin lunged.

The baton caught Auri's organic shoulder as she moved too slowly to intercept the blow. Pain crackled from her neck down to the tips of her fingers.

"Katara!" she hissed, clutching her throbbing shoulder.

"You won't forget again." Katara's eyes gleamed with a feral intensity. She shifted to attack. A bolt of fear shot through Auri.

Katara rushed forward, and Auri moved to meet her. Auri's chest slammed into Katara's baton arm, bent in anticipation of a strike, stopping the blow. With a twist, Auri wrapped her arm around Katara's in an overhook control. The baton was now useless.

This time Auri didn't stop. She slammed her robotic knee into Katara's belly, using the extra strength in the limb. Over the last five days, Katara had helped Auri use her cyborg components as tools to block or attack while protecting her weaker and more susceptible human parts. Auri had always subconsciously leaned into her cyborg limbs when tired or afraid, but now it was intentional.

The lessons offered her a new perspective of her less-than-beautiful machinery, though she would still sacrifice the cyborg "advantages" to be wholly human.

In quick succession, Auri slid her hand onto the base of the baton, jerked backward, and channeled the momentum to swing at Katara's throat, stopping only centimeters from contact.

For a beat, neither of them moved. Auri's chest heaved. The arm supporting the baton trembled, the fingers squeezing the smooth wood. Right when Auri thought she might drop the weapon, Katara raised her hands and stepped back, grinning wide.

"Finally!" the assassin cried. "Get consistent and we can start hand-to-hand combat."

Auri glared, putting hands behind her head as she fought to catch her breath. She dropped the baton and it clanged onto the cargo hold's metal floor.

Birdie's head jerked up from where she'd been dozing atop a heating grate. The dog's tongue rolled out in a yawn before she fell back asleep. So much for a DISC-trained canine. Auri's skull could've been dented by Katara's baton and Birdie would've slept through it.

"What was that?" Auri wheezed, wiping sweat and stray red hairs from her now-falling-apart ponytail. Her black tank top and camouflage cargo pants clung to her with a sticky discomfort. "You looked ready to kill me!"

Katara snorted. "If I wanted to kill you, Little Warrior, you'd be dead." She grabbed a water bottle off one of the cargo boxes and squirted a long stream into her mouth. "Toss me the baton. We'll go through it again."

Auri crossed her arms with a wince. "Not until we talk. You've been quiet and… and in a killing mood all morning." She rubbed her aching shoulder for emphasis. There would be an angry welt there tomorrow, worse than the others she'd accumulated the last few days. She'd been lucky the erratic woman hadn't broken her collar bone.

Katara's grip on the water bottle tightened. Auri tensed, ready to fend off another attack. But Katara sighed and muttered, "Killing would probably do me some good."

Auri shifted toward the abandoned baton.

"Not you, *aho*," Katara said with a shake of her head, placing the water bottle back onto the crate. She looked around the cargo hold, mostly empty except for extra food supply crates shoved against one wall and the shoe storage shelf. Two staircases led to twin catwalks that provided access to the second level. At the opposite end of the room were the ship doors, a small window in the middle showcasing the dark emptiness of space.

Four days of non-stop travel was wearing on the crew. The *Kestrel* had seemed like a decently sized transport ship—until seven people and one dog were trapped on it, their destination only offering more danger.

On day three, an argument between Castor and Katara over who had eaten the last of the nori crisps turned into a shouting match between Ferris and Malachi about some long-ago disagreement. Now everyone avoided each other except for the still-mandatory crew breakfasts.

"What's going on?" Auri asked Katara again. She caught a second water bottle Katara tossed her way.

Katara glared at her combat boots. "Ferris said he loves me."

Auri choked on water. Across the room, Birdie's ears quirked back, but the dog didn't rise. "He *what*?"

"My reaction wasn't much different from yours." She unclipped the body armor across her chest and tossed it atop the crate. "I think the stress, both from the Bleeders and the Fed, is loosening his tongue. Normally… normally he reads me better."

"You've only been together for, what, a few weeks?"

Katara nodded, running her thumb over a loose thread in the armor. "We've been crewmates for over a year. Though the man has been smitten with me for at least half as long."

Auri's brows drew together at Katara's softening tone. "Katara…" she began, struggling to find the words. Finally, she settled on, "Do you love him?"

Katara's voice dropped to such a low whisper, Auri had to lean forward. "I'm afraid of losing myself." Her hands curled into fists as if she could physically grapple with her emotions. "I was blinded by the Federation for so long, and they took so much. I'm terrified of losing myself to Ferris. But at the same time…" She let out a humorless laugh and shrugged almost helplessly. "I can't imagine losing *him. Kuso.* What's wrong with me?"

"The Fed only took," Auri said, squeezing Katara's hands with her own. "They kept you trapped and dependent, without any security that they wouldn't take what they'd given." She cleared her throat, realizing the words echoed her own complicated feelings toward her adoptive father. "What has Ferris taken that you didn't freely give? How much has he offered in return, without any expectations?"

Katara opened her mouth, but the cargo hold door slammed open.

Auri jumped and Katara whirled, pulling a laser knife from a hidden sheath. Birdie growled and bounded over to Auri.

"I don't need empty encouragement," Tsuna snapped as she stormed into the hold. Castor followed a few steps behind. "I *need* answers. We're a day out from Roanleigh and our tech still can't communicate with Earth's in my sims." She stomped up to a crate labeled *extra rice,* yanked off the top with a grunt, and leaned over the edge.

Castor crossed his arms as he watched her, wearing a long, loose shirt and baggy pants. A few gold bands encircled his braids, clinking together when he shook his head. "Don't be dramatic, woman. The simulations show an almost 99.9% compatibility."

"Uh-oh," Katara murmured to Auri, sheathing her knife. "This won't end well." When Auri opened her mouth to ask, Katara shook her head. "Just watch," she whispered.

Castor and Tsuna were so focused on their argument, they didn't notice Auri and Katara a few meters away.

"That doesn't matter!" Tsuna cried, jerking her head out of the crate to glare at the cook. "I need 100% or the tech won't communicate and we won't get *anything.*" She leaned back over the edge of the crate to rifle through the contents. "Where is it? I know you bought some at our last supply stop."

"Bought what?" Castor asked, eyeing Tsuna's plump backside while he fiddled with the tattooed chain around his left ring finger.

Heat warmed Auri's cheek. This was not something she wanted to witness. "Katara," she hissed, "shouldn't we—"

Katara held a finger to her lips. "*Damaru.*"

"Whiskey, *busu.*" Tsuna let out a grunt. Something heavy toppled over in the crate and Castor winced. "I can literally feel your eyes on my *ketsu.*"

"I'm watching you tear holes in my rice bags."

"The bags are *fine*. Our two vices were always whiskey and pipes. I kicked the pipe, but… ah-ha!" She emerged from the crate with a glass bottle filled with amber liquid.

Castor reached for it, but Tsuna stepped back. "I won't drink more than a finger's worth. You—" Her gaze shifted over Castor's shoulder, finally landing on Katara, Auri, and Birdie. "Oh, hello."

Castor's gaze followed hers. "*Kuso.*"

Katara gave him a finger-filled wave. "Does the captain know you've smuggled hard liquor onto the ship?"

"Not unless you tell him." Castor snatched the bottle from Tsuna, who crossed her arms with a flirtatious pout. "Tsuna, you know I'd do almost anything to help you. *Except* letting you guzzle my last bottle. Finger's worth my *ketsu.*"

"You need a full night's sleep." Ferris's voice echoed from the catwalk above. Katara tensed. Auri looked up to see Malachi moving down the far staircase beside Ferris.

"Not artificially," the captain said. "It's worse than the few good hours I get."

Ferris paused a few steps above the floor, his gaze finding Katara. Red darkened the back of his neck, and his hand tightened on the metal railing.

Malachi took in the room. He raised his brows at Auri as if he expected a sitrep. She shrugged in a helpless way. All these onboard romances were making a simple week-long journey unnecessarily complicated. She was understanding more and more why Malachi didn't like them. Castor shifted toward the still-open crate, stowing his whiskey back inside it.

"Since when did my crew become a bunch of bickering space rats?" Malachi asked, crossing his arms. When no one responded, he ran a hand over his jaw. "*Maitta na.*" He hopped down the final steps and pressed an intercom on the wall. "Marin, set this boat on autopilot. You're needed in the cargo hold."

Silence held the crew captive as they waited for Marin. When she stood among them in a deep purple *yukata*, her hairless head cocked under the fluorescent lighting, she broke the quiet. "Well, what is it, Akki-tan?"

Malachi leaned against the wall by the intercom. "I think it's time we put our energies toward something a little more… fun."

Auri's eyes widened. The last word she had ever expected to come out of Malachi's mouth was *fun*. Even Birdie huffed in a dog version of surprise.

"What do you have in mind?" Auri asked.

He crossed his arms, flashing a rare smirk. "Volleyball."

"Volleyball?" She'd only watched a few games on the Fed's streams with Ty. When they'd lived with the GIC, Ty's bedroom walls were plastered with holos of his favorite players. For Ty's tenth birthday, the GIC purchased presidential seats for one of the championships.

Now that Auri recalled the trip… Ty had thrown a fit when Auri tagged along. He proceeded to pretend she wasn't there the entire game.

The memory made her stomach twist in knots. She swallowed hard, shoving thoughts of her traitorous first love and her lying adoptive father from her mind.

"Aurelia!" Malachi called.

Auri straightened, the muscle memory of basic taking over. "Sir—!" She caught herself with a grimace and relaxed her rigid spine. "I mean, yes?"

Castor snickered.

Malachi crossed his arms. "You're team captain."

Her mouth popped open in surprise. "Me?"

He nodded. "I'll be the other. Let's choose our players."

Malachi offered Auri first pick, and she chose Marin, knowing what it was like to be routinely picked last. To Auri's surprise, Malachi's mouth gave the slightest twitch downward, as if he were disappointed by her choice. Marin adjusted her arm sling as she stood next to Auri.

"Have you played volleyball before?" Auri asked. Marin was technically blind and communicated with the technology encompassing the *Kestrel* through the soles of her bare feet. In turn, the tech provided a distorted vision of the surrounding room. Or that's how the girl had explained it.

"Many times," Marin said, shortening the *yukata*'s hem to allow her pale legs more maneuverability. "Though this will be the first time with only one operable arm."

Auri's final team was comprised of Marin, Ferris, and Tsuna. Malachi chose Katara and Castor, conceding Auri the extra player.

"Where's the net?" Auri asked, resting a hand between Birdie's shoulder blades. "And the ball?"

Tsuna flipped open a panel fixed above the shoe rack and pressed a few buttons. The lights in the cargo hold dimmed and then brightened. A holographic net rose from the floor at their feet, projected by tiny lenses Auri hadn't noticed before. Within moments, the hologram solidified so it looked tangible.

Malachi strode to the crate hiding Castor's whiskey. Castor straightened as if ready to explain, but Malachi simply reached into the one beside it. He scooped out a white volleyball with a small sensor in the middle, likely so the holo net could track points. Birdie trotted over to the sidelines and her favorite vent.

"Marin!" Malachi called and tossed the ball to the girl. She caught it easily with one hand. "You get first serve."

Both teams lined up along their sides of the court. Marin stood in the back right corner while Auri, Ferris, and Tsuna were in front. This close, Auri could hear the holo's soft hum.

Malachi stuck out his hand under the net across from Auri. "Good luck, Aurelia."

His palm was warm in her own, callouses rough against her skin. A spark of competitiveness lit inside her. "You too."

Auri stepped back and nodded at Marin. A rare smile curled the girl's lips. She tossed the ball and then leapt upward. Her palm made contact and the ball hurtled through the air, almost faster than Auri's organic eye could follow.

Katara dove low, her palm catching the ball centimeters from the floor. The ball shot back up into the air, and the game began.

Marin was inhuman on the volleyball court. She moved with a grace and speed that left Auri speechless. Whenever Auri, Ferris, or Tsuna missed a volley, Marin seemed to appear out of nowhere.

The score between the two teams was projected on either end of the net. A loud buzzer announced the end of the first set: 25 to 16.

Auri grinned, fresh sweat slicking her skin. The victory was mostly thanks to Marin, but still. They had won.

By the second set, Auri understood the flow of the game. Even though Malachi's team won by two points, she could feel tension melting out of her body. They were locked in a tie with one more match to go.

Auri shifted at the back of the court, ball in hand. Everyone's faces—except Marin's—were slick with sweat. Ferris raised his arms with a quick *"Banzai!"*

Across the net, Malachi's team hunched low, ready for her serve. Auri shifted into position.

Tsuna straightened with a cry. "That's it!" She bolted off the court. A buzzer sounded as she crossed into out-of-bounds and rushed from the cargo hold.

Malachi looked to Castor as if seeking some kind of translation.

"That woman," Castor muttered, wiping his forehead with a sleeve. "I bet she just solved the problem with her simulations."

"Without any help from your whiskey," Malachi said with a nod.

"Yes. Thank—" Castor cut himself off with a curse. He glanced at Malachi, who raised a brow at him.

Malachi looked to the rest of the crew. "Great game, everyone. Get cleaned up, and I'll see you at breakfast." He strode through the holo net as the rest of the crew dispersed, staking claims on the shower. Malachi held his hands out for the ball and Auri tossed it to him as he came to stand beside her.

"Are you ready?" he asked, looking down at her. "For Roanleigh?" His thumb stroked the small sensor in the ball, the gesture hinting at his own nerves.

Auri wiped a bead of sweat rolling down her cheek. "Are you?"

For a moment, Malachi didn't answer. His gaze seemed to see past Auri, as if a ghost hovered just out of sight. Then he said, "I hope so, Auri. I hope so."

CHAPTER FOUR

The crew had squeezed onto the bridge. Impressive, considering the semi-circular room was barely larger than Auri's quarters. Marin sat erect in the pilot's chair, the dashboard controls and screen curved in front of her. Buttons and switches in various sizes littered the low ceiling.

Malachi had claimed the co-pilot's seat, a dark brown leather chair that looked practically brand new compared to the rest of the *Kestrel*. It squeaked whenever he shifted.

Katara and Ferris huddled near Malachi, shoulders touching. Castor hunched behind Marin with Auri squeezed between him and Tsuna. Judging by the scowl on Castor's face, he didn't enjoy the close quarters. Even Auri felt the itch of intensifying claustrophobia. Birdie was banished to the hallway, much to the dog's displeasure, judging by the occasional groans that penetrated the steel door.

Beyond the pilot and co-pilot controls were panels of reinforced glass. Barely visible seams connected them to form a massive hexagon spaceshield. A tiny dot of light appeared in the center, growing rapidly larger.

"There it is," Malachi murmured, leaning forward. The seat squeaked as if to punctuate his words.

"Is that really…?" Tsuna whispered. She shifted for a better view of the still growing ball, using her height to her advantage. Her arm brushed Auri's shoulder.

"Akki-tan is correct," Marin answered, running a finger along the readout screen. The *Kestrel* slowed its rapid approach, and the artificial gravity levels adjusted to ease the transition. Even still, the crew lurched forward. Auri caught herself on the back of Marin's seat. Castor whacked his head against a panel of switches and swore. "We have arrived at our destination."

Auri straightened, her heart pounding a deafening cadence. Days of infinite blackness pocked with far-off stars and the occasional meteor…

And now, before her… A planet.

She sucked in a breath at the sight.

A white-frosted orb engulfed the spaceshield. Swirls of clouds indicated active surface blizzards—Auri counted at least four. She wasn't sure what she expected to feel when seeing the Toxic Planet in person. Maybe a sense of belonging? Or an awakened memory?

But the world before her felt as foreign to Auri as her forgotten past.

"Roanleigh," Malachi breathed. He pressed both hands on the console before him as if to stop himself from touching the untouchable. "Are we close enough to start the scan?" He looked to Tsuna.

Everyone turned to the hacker.

"How far are we?" Tsuna asked, shifting from her spot beside Auri. "Excuse me." She sidestepped Castor, brushing his chest with hers as she drew behind Marin.

Marin pointed to the readout on her screen. "Exactly one hundred ninety klicks from the surface."

Tsuna released a slow breath. "Yes." She gave Malachi a firm nod. "We're close enough."

"Our moment of truth," Malachi breathed. "Marin, start the scan."

Marin ducked under the console and flicked a switch secured with duct tape. The tech had been jerry-rigged through a series of thin wires that snaked into an open floor panel between the pilot and co-pilot consoles.

Marin righted herself and tapped the screen to open another menu. A gentle vibration radiated from the floor under Auri's slippers. Almost like the *Kestrel* hummed a lullaby.

"That's it," Malachi murmured. "Come on." He ran his fingertips across the console before him. The touch was surprisingly gentle.

"Ready momentarily, Akki-tan." Marin pushed a button above her head. The hum abruptly silenced, followed by a steady beeping. The *Kestrel*'s forward propulsion halted.

"The scan is in progress," Marin said. "Searching for settlement and lifeforms. Currently at fifteen percent."

Auri held her breath as her eyes swept the darkness for other space vessels. The archeologists who visited the Toxic Planet under the GIC's orders had suffered catastrophic losses at the hands of the Bleeders. The *Kestrel*'s crew wouldn't follow in their footsteps—if they could help it.

Auri glanced at the men and women around her, wondering if their nerves were on fire too. Could they hear the panicked race of her heartbeat? Or were their own hearts beating just as loudly?

What would Malachi do if more than a handful of Bleeders were waiting on Roanleigh? The thought of turning around made her stomach churn even as her toes curled in her slippers. Even just ten or fifteen was no small number. Not when it came to Bleeders.

The creatures were capable of physical regeneration. That, combined with their inhuman strength and insatiable hunger for flesh, made them near titan-worthy opponents.

As the steady beeping picked up rhythm and the percentages climbed, Auri's fingers drifted to her ear where a flower earring once hung. She hadn't worn it since Harlequin, where Malachi had ripped its twin from the lobe of a dying female Bleeder.

Both earrings were currently stowed in a drawer in her quarters. Their significance was one of the many answers she hoped waited on Roanleigh. Yet a childlike part of her trembled at learning what the earrings meant. Even though she already suspected the truth. That they had belonged to someone important. Like her—

A high-pitched *chirp* abruptly ended the steady beeps. Auri craned her neck to catch a glimpse of Marin's screen, but Tsuna's slender back blocked her view. Marin's face was expressionless as she processed the read out. She looked up, gaze finding Malachi's.

"The lifeform scan is complete," she said. "No other life forms have been detected on Roanleigh's surface or in surrounding space."

Everyone on the bridge released a collective breath. Auri relaxed her hands, unaware she had even curled them into fists.

"What about air quality?" Ferris asked, resting a hand on the back of Malachi's chair. "Will we need suits?"

Marin shook her head. "The Spire's intel was correct. The quality is comparable to that of Medea or Kaido, though the temperature reading of the entire planet is currently minus 12 degrees Celsius and dropping. A storm is brewing."

"That's cold." Malachi gave a preemptive shiver before looking to his crew. "But we might not have this opportunity to explore Bleeder-free again. We need to move. Katara, Ferris, Tsuna, and Auri, get your gear on. I want us planetside as soon as Marin pinpoints where that discovery crew found Auri."

Castor straightened to stretch his back. He knocked into a button on the ceiling and grimaced. A countdown began in a computerized woman's voice.

"I'm too tall for this piece of *kuso*," he grumbled.

Marin calmly pointed at the button that had begun flashing. "Castor, unless you want all our oxygen going out the airlock…"

Castor swore again.

"Beanpole," Katara muttered, crossing her arms.

"Go back to snuggling your doctor," Castor retaliated. He jammed his thumb into the button to stop the countdown and looked to Malachi. "I should come with you. I'm useless without any Bleeders to shoot."

"You're to stay with the ship," Malachi said, watching Castor's gaze dart to Tsuna. He continued before Castor could object. "I want you ready for anything."

Castor frowned but didn't argue. "My rifle is cleaned and prepped. Haven't had a chance to really use her since that mess of a job on Delfan."

Ferris winced at the memory. "We swore never to speak of that again."

Malachi rolled his shoulders. "Let's move."

———

An hour later the crew gathered in the cargo hold, those going planetside yanking on winter boots over black temperature-regulating pants and coats. Despite the warmth both garments provided, they weren't bulky. The lining was comprised of synthetic fibers and thin wires that heated the interior. The tech would've been very pricey—if they had paid for it.

Auri tightened the buckles of her last boot with glove-covered fingers. Beside her, Birdie nibbled at the coverings on her paws. The poodle attempted a few steps, looking as if she tiptoed across ice. Auri bit back a laugh.

Birdie looked over her shoulder, covered with a padded vest for extra warmth, and bared the whites of her eyes. She even whined.

"You need to protect the pads of your feet," Auri said, then stood with a grunt. Sweat already pooled at the base of her spine. When Birdie continued to pout, Auri added, "They're staying on, so get used to it, Bird."

The dog let out an annoyed *huff.* She continued her comical tiptoe walk around the cargo hold, eliciting smiles from other crew members.

Katara and Ferris stood close together, the assassin checking that Ferris's jacket was secure. He grinned as she yanked him this way and that, then murmured something only the assassin could hear. Katara smirked in response.

Tsuna crouched in front of a thin tactical backpack, sorting through the different tech inside. She chewed her lower lip and muttered to herself.

A door slid open, and Castor stepped into the cargo hold, a long black case gripped in one hand. Castor nodded at the gathered crew, moving closer to the outer doors. He lowered the case to the floor and opened the two heavy-duty clips, revealing a long sniper rifle. The cook seemed oddly sober despite Tsuna's scans coming up clean. A shiver of unease scuttled down Auri's spine.

Auri busied her nervous hands by re-checking her own weapon harness. The weight of her disc felt both alien and comforting on her back.

By the time Castor finished setting up his rifle, Malachi appeared at the top of the catwalk. The captain hurried down the steps, boots clanging with each step. At the sight of him, Birdie finally stopped trying to kick off her booties. She trotted over to Auri and plopped onto her rump.

"Ah, so you *are* coming," Ferris teased Malachi, pulling at the collar of his coat. "You took so long, I thought you changed your mind once you saw the snow."

"Not even snow would keep me from getting planetside." Malachi's mouth was a thin line amidst the stubble coloring his cheeks. "Marin located the settlement where Auri was found and made a rendering better than what we got from the Spire." He reached into a pocket of his coat to reveal a palm-sized holo projector. He squeezed the rounded sides, and a 3D rendering of Roanleigh's surface appeared, rolling out before him until it was as long and wide as Auri was tall. Everyone gathered to examine the map.

Buildings half obscured by snow were rendered malicious in the holo's green light. The structures resembled a strange architecture that Auri had never seen before the Spire's intel: half circles cut into the snow with long tubes in front.

Malachi shifted the holo and the image spun. The *Kestrel* trembled simultaneously, the thrusters flipping to slow their descent. Auri braced herself to avoid falling onto her rear end. Ferris groaned and clasped a hand over his mouth.

"Cai," Tsuna grimaced, looking away. "You're making us motion sick."

Malachi steadied the projector. He pointed to a large rectangular building. It sat in the center of the small settlement like a general amongst privates. "Katara and Tsuna, you'll come with me for reconnaissance. According to the Spire's intel, this is the central hub." He looked up.

Tsuna nodded her agreement while Katara studied the rectangular building. She leaned forward and pinched the holo to zoom in, then cursed.

Malachi voiced her disappointment. "We couldn't scan the details. Too much snow in the air."

She sighed. "Well, it's better than what we got from the Spire, but without building schematics, the job was always going to be interesting."

"Interesting's one word for it," Castor grumbled.

Katara hesitated a beat, then shifted closer to Castor. Standing beside the cook, Auri caught Katara's whispered promise, but doubted anyone else did.

"I won't let anything happen to her."

Malachi squeezed the sides of the projector and the holo vanished. He dropped the tech into a coat pocket. "Aurelia, Ferris, and Birdie, you are free to explore the settlement, *staying on comms the entire time.*" He tapped his ear where a small communicator was tucked inside. Auri checked hers to ensure it was positioned properly. "You have an hour," he finished.

Her mouth popped open. "An hour? That's not enough time to even search half the settlement."

"It's all you've got," Malachi said with a tone that belayed argument. "A blizzard will hit the settlement in a little over an hour. We don't know enough about the storms on Roanleigh, and I don't want to risk stranding the *Kestrel.* After it passes, maybe…"

But Auri already knew Malachi wouldn't leave them vulnerable in Roanleigh's orbit for long. Not when Bleeder ships could approach at any moment. Not when they only had enough supplies for the return trip to Medea.

"Cai," Katara said, moving over to him and resting a hand on his shoulder. "Can I talk to you?"

The captain's brows rose in surprise. "Keep it quick, Kat. We're on borrowed time."

Katara drew him far enough away to avoid eavesdroppers. Auri glanced at Ferris, but he seemed as curious as the rest of them.

"Absolutely not!" Malachi cried moments later, making Auri and Tsuna jump in surprise. "*Kuso*, Katara," he said, lowering his voice. "I made that promise a long time ago. How dare—"

Katara grabbed his arm and yanked him closer, glaring at the watching crew. Auri quickly turned around, the others doing the same. After a few moments of intense whispering, the conversation came to an abrupt halt with Malachi's "Fine."

And Katara's "Thank you, Captain."

"Castor?" Malachi called, striding back to the center of the group. Katara had her arms crossed as she followed. Ferris raised his brows in question, but she waved him off. "You set to cover a retreat?" Malachi asked.

Castor nodded. "Yes, Captain."

The ship shook beneath them as the *Kestrel* touched down on the surface. Nervous excitement thrummed through Auri's veins.

Malachi hurried toward the cargo hold doors, the windows only revealing a blinding whiteness beyond.

Auri knotted one gloved hand in the fur at the base of Birdie's neck. The poodle seemed to sense Auri's nerves and leaned her warm bulk against Auri's leg.

Malachi pulled his hood over his head. He gestured to Auri, then the button that opened the doors. "You do the honors."

She straightened her shoulders, released her death grip on Birdie, and stepped forward.

Auri stopped beside Malachi and yanked her hood up. It framed her view of the captain in black on either side. "To Roanleigh," she murmured.

"To Roanleigh," he repeated.

Auri raised her hand and slammed it against the button.

The cargo doors opened with a hiss.

CHAPTER FIVE

---

17 Sept 3319, 11:01:11
Ancora Galaxy, Planet 08: Roanleigh,
Owari Colony

An icy wind gusted through the open doors, carrying the scent of crisp air and the heaviness of a coming snowstorm. Auri's hood flew back. Her rope braid whipped over one shoulder. Renegade snowflakes kissed her cheeks, almost in welcome. As they melted against her organic skin, it felt like tears rolling down her face.

Malachi wiped one away with a thumb. The unexpected touch and roughness of his glove made Auri gasp, but by the time her gaze jumped to meet his, he was already turning away, pressing a hand to adjust the comm in his ear.

"Can everyone hear me?" he asked.

Malachi's voice echoed through Auri's earpiece, crisp and clear of static. Her heart tripped a disjointed rhythm. She could still feel the press of his thumb.

"I can hear you," Castor said.

"Loud and clear," Katara added. She scooped up Tsuna's tactical bag, her face flickering with surprise. "This is heavy, Tsu. What's in here?"

Tsuna shoved her arms through the straps and adjusted the bag so it hung in the center of her back. She gave Katara a tense smile. "Literally everything. I want to be prepared."

"Marin?" Malachi asked, checking the comm-to-ship feed. "You hear me?"

"Akki-tan." Marin's voice relayed over the speakers in the cargo hold. "Cease procrastinating entering Roanleigh's cold temperatures. You already know the comm-to-ship feed is fully operational."

Ferris chuckled at Malachi's grimace. "Kaido-born through and through."

Malachi flipped a rude gesture at the doctor. "Okay, let's go. Balls to the walls, ladies and gents."

"I hate that phrase," Tsuna grumbled.

The *Kestrel*'s captain strode down the ramp leading out of the cargo hold. Auri followed a few steps behind. Already a thin layer of snow covered the rubberized metal, making each step treacherous. Cold air bit into any exposed skin, and Auri pulled her hood tight around her face. She was so focused on her footing that she didn't notice the landscape until her feet crunched into a half meter of snow.

Auri gasped in surprise while Birdie lowered her nose to sniff the whiteness. Her tail wagged.

"No," Auri hissed as the rest of the crew followed behind. "We're on a mission. *Heel*, Bird."

"*Chikusho*." Malachi's curse made Auri's head jerk up. "That's a lot of snow."

A blanket of white stretched before them, barely discernible from the sky laden with heavy clouds. Meters from the ship, a wooden signpost stuck out of the snow. Words were engraved at the top, but ice coated the letters, rendering them illegible. Auri trudged toward it, boots breaking through the top crust of snow into the fine powder beneath, Birdie at her heels.

A gust of wind buffeted her as she reached the sign. She caught her hood before it slipped again. Auri brushed a thin layer of ice off the wood, her fingers finding the grooves of long-ago carvings.

Owari Colony
Population: 115

Owari roughly translated to *end* or *final* in English. Auri's brows drew together at the odd name choice not mentioned in the Spire's intel. Snow crunched behind her as the rest of the crew joined her in front of the sign. She started to turn when something at the lower corner caught her eye.

She brushed away the snow and ice only to recoil. Her back bumped into Malachi and he caught her before she toppled over.

"Malachi," she rasped, pointing. "What is that?"

Carved by what looked like fingernails and splattered with long-ago dried blood were five letters: A-M-B-R-O.

"Ambro?" Malachi murmured, moving around Auri for a closer examination. "Anyone know what that means?"

Tsuna stopped beside Malachi. "It wasn't in the intel." She had tightened the cords of her hood so only her eyes were visible. "And we don't have the luxury of finding out." Her voice came out muffled. "I need as much time on site as possible."

"Right." Malachi peered into the snow ahead. "Katara, Tsuna, let's go." He turned to Auri and Ferris. "Keep on comms. Meet us at the Hub"—he pointed to the rectangular building in the distance—"at 1200. Radio if you find anything…" He trailed off.

"Or if anything finds us," Ferris finished. He reached over and squeezed Katara's hand where he stood beside her. "Be safe, ay?"

"Don't worry, Doctor. I'll rescue you if you get into trouble." She started to turn, but hesitated. With a muttered curse, she grabbed the front of Ferris's jacket and captured his mouth in a kiss. She pulled away moments later, snow caught in her long lashes.

Ferris cupped her cheek with his gloved hand. "See you back on the ship."

Malachi, Katara, and Tsuna trudged down the main road—if it had been a road. Auri couldn't tell underneath the snow. Kilometers east of the colony, the sky was heavy and dark with the approaching storm.

"Ready?" Auri asked Ferris.

He nodded. "You lead. See what you can remember. I'll take guard duty."

Auri followed the others' tracks at a slower pace, scanning the buildings on either side. The circular structures were comprised of a thick red material that made them stand out amid the snow drifts.

And something about the crimson set against white made a deep sense of unease nestle between her shoulder blades.

Birdie lowered her nose to the ground, huffing into a mound of snow and then sneezing. Auri grabbed the handle attached to the dog's insulated harness, giving it a gentle tug to remind the poodle they were on a mission. Birdie's ears quirked at the silent reprimand, and she drew her head back up.

They passed two, then four, then six structures, each of them perfectly spaced a few meters apart. As they ventured farther into Owari Colony, a sour taste grew at the back of Auri's throat and a familiar dread hollowed out her stomach.

Something horrible had happened here. She could feel it in the remnants of her human bones. Memories, hazy and just out of reach, clustered at the back of her mind. But each time she tried to bring them into focus, they flitted away.

Far ahead, visible only because of their black snow gear, Malachi, Katara, and Tsuna had stopped outside the large rectangular building.

"We've reached the Hub." Katara's voice came over the comms, startling Auri out of her cluttered mind. "We're searching for an entrance now. Stand by."

"Recognize anything?" Ferris asked Auri, voice hushed as if he sensed the pall over the colony.

Auri reached for Birdie's reassuring warmth but froze. Across the street stood a structure identical to the others, one side covered by a particularly deep snow drift. But something about the door…

Auri slogged through the snow toward it, squinting against the gusts of wind. A meter away, she realized why the door looked different. The other structures had deep inset handles. But this one was outfitted with an old-fashioned doorknob. The metal had oxidized to the point it was entirely green, the elaborate curlicues of the rectangular base barely visible.

A memory detached itself from the shadows of Auri's mind, rising to the forefront. No images accompanied the recollection. Just sound. Voices…

"Are you sure this will last outside?" a man called out; words slightly muffled by fabric—snow gear? "Maybe we should…"

The voice and memory began to fade.

No, no, no! Auri grabbed the doorknob as if to physically hold on to the memory. An icicle broke off and dropped into the snow at her feet.

A woman's voice, sweet as honey with an odd accent, grew louder and louder. "…look like everyone else. It's a piece of home." Then a chuckle. "Granny would roll in her grave if she saw the knob now."

The man's tone turned serious, laced with the ache of loss and regret. Almost hopelessness. "How did we get here? How did it go so wrong?"

"Shush," the woman whispered. Her voice grew fainter as the memory slipped from Auri's grasp. "She can hear you. She's been through enough…"

Then the memory faded entirely.

Auri tightened her grip on the doorknob. A deep ache scoured her middle as if she had lost something—someone. Birdie gave Auri's glove a comforting lick.

"You remembered something," Ferris said with certainty. Auri turned to see him standing just behind her, gaze panning the snow. "Katara reported that they made it inside."

Auri swallowed, her throat suddenly dry. "I didn't even hear."

"You were lost in your own mind," he said. "I wasn't going to say anything until you came back. This structure must have some meaning for you." He inclined his head at the building.

"I think…" She let out a slow breath. "I think this was my home."

CHAPTER SIX

———

17 Sept 3319, 11:25:09
Ancora Galaxy, Planet 08: Roanleigh,
Owari Colony

Auri tapped the comm in her ear with a trembling hand. "Sitrep," she began, eyeing the snow-covered street marred by mounds of snow every few meters. "Ferris and I are entering the seventh dwelling on the right side of the street, facing away from the *Kestrel*."

"Roger that," Malachi replied.

Auri turned to Ferris, who offered a reassuring smile. "I've got your six."

"Let's see if I can even get this open." She shifted her grip on the doorknob. The oxidized metal scratched against her glove. She gave a hard yank. The door didn't budge.

"Maybe there's a lock."

Auri shook her head. Somehow, she knew none of these homes had been locked. The people in Owari Colony had trusted each other implicitly. This door was more likely stuck from decades of harsh temperatures.

Ferris shifted to monitor the street, one hand on the coil gun at his hip. The serious expression on his face was so different from his usual easy smile. Maybe Owari Colony was pressing on his nerves too. Like they all balanced on the precipice of something life altering.

Auri gripped the knob with her robotic hand, rolled her shoulders, and staggered her stance. She pulled on the door as hard as she could. The sound of ice cracking echoed from the seal. Birdie let out a startled yelp. The doorknob snapped off in Auri's hand, and she gasped in surprise. She gawked at the broken pieces of metal, unable to shake the feeling she was in trouble.

"Everything okay?" Ferris asked.

"I…" she started, looking up at the door. A smile twitched at the corners of her mouth. Where the door had been firmly sealed, there was now a narrow opening just big enough for her hands.

Auri tucked the broken knob into her coat with the utmost care. "Ferris?" she called over her shoulder. "Can you give me a hand?"

He shifted away from watching the street to stand beside her. Birdie sidestepped out of his way. Her nose had been deep in the snow. She sneezed twice as if she smelled something unpleasant.

"On three," Auri told Ferris. He slid his fingers into the gap just above Auri's. His herbal scent drifted over her, so different from Malachi's musk and lavender. "One… two… *three!*"

The door slammed open with a grating force. The metal runners securing top and bottom screeched so loudly Auri felt it in her bones. Panic swept through her as both she and Ferris whirled to the street behind them.

But the snow remained unperturbed save for the occasional flurries kicked up by gusts of wind blowing over the mounds. Above, the sky had darkened, the inbound storm growing closer with each passing second.

"Birdie, guard," Auri instructed, pointing to the door opening. To Auri's surprise, the poodle didn't attempt to wheedle her way out of it. She plopped onto her rump and stared out at the snow. Even when they'd been fresh out of basic, heady with training and purpose, Birdie hated being left behind. The prickle of unease in Auri's belly turned into a spike of concern. She glanced at the street one last time. But all was quiet.

Auri and Ferris stepped through the doorway and onto a rectangular woven mat that said *so happy you're here*. On reflex she reached for the flashlight tucked into a cargo pocket of her pants, but stopped, realizing she didn't need it. The interior of the structure provided an unencumbered view of the landscape outside, tinted by some kind of overlaying screen.

"I've never seen anything like it," Ferris murmured.

"Me either."

The temperature inside matched that of the planetscape outside, but the air smelled musty. As if whatever machinery kept the dwelling heated had broken long ago.

Ahead stretched a short rectangular hallway ending with a door made of the traditional Japanese rice paper, some of the panels shredded or spotted with mold. Next to the door was a shelf that had been knocked over, scattering shoes across the rubberized floor. Auri looked away from a small pair of boots that likely belonged to a child.

"We've located the main server." Tsuna's voice came through the comm. Auri clenched her jaw to stop herself from jumping in surprise. "We're extracting the data now."

Katara spoke next. "Ferris, any sign of hostiles?"

"Negative, Kat," Ferris answered. "We've just entered the residence. I've got an eye on the time. We'll be there by 1200."

"Over and out," Katara said.

Auri stepped over the scattered shoes and pushed the door aside. One of the panels disintegrated at her touch. The motes fluttered down, so much like the snow outside, to land atop Auri's boots.

The room beyond was cut in a half circle. A narrow hallway led toward the back of the structure. Familiarity rippled along Auri's nerves.

To her left was a kitchen with bare necessities: a shallow sink, narrow fridge, stovetop, and table with three chairs—all covered in layers of dust. A memory rippled over Auri's vision. A hazy shadow of a woman stood at the stove, red hair piled atop her head, humming as she stirred something in a pot.

Auri blinked and the specter vanished.

The right side of the semi-circle was a living room. Or what would have become a living room. The remains of a broken couch, its cushions torn to shreds, was the only furniture. Stacks of knocked-over books were strewn about, and corpses of plants and shattered pots littered the floor at the room's edges.

Someone—or some*thing*—had ransacked this place.

Ferris was silent as Auri moved through the main room. She felt more like a ghost than a girl, treading down the same hallway as the dwelling's inhabitants.

Before they'd mysteriously disappeared.

The dim hall branched off to four doors, two on either side. Auri peeked into the shadows of the first to see a bare-bones bathroom: a micro shower, a toilet and sink. She turned her attention to the rest of the hall, eyes adjusting to the darkness.

Along the wall toward the second door was a bloodied handprint followed by a long crimson smear. Auri sucked in a slow breath. In through her nose, out through her mouth. It did little to ease the panic building in her chest.

"Well," Ferris whispered, "that adds some pucker factor, ay?"

Auri forced a tight smile.

The second door revealed a dark bedroom with a queen-sized bed and large suitcase on the floor, still closed. Unlike the main living area, these rooms weren't afforded a floor-to ceiling view of the outside. Their walls were slate gray and curved, barely discernible from the shadows. Auri clicked on her flashlight, Ferris following suit, and slipped away to the next room.

As Auri's fingers curled around the inset handle of the first door across the hall, a memory slammed into her like a crash-landing shuttle.

A male voice spoke in a low tone. "It's all we have. It's *more* than we had back home. So maybe you'll change your mind while you sit in your room, hungry."

Auri shoved the door open. A smaller room lay beyond, a cot situated against a back wall. A worn bunny, one of its button eyes missing, lay on the pillow of the made bed. Auri started to reach for it by reflex, but recoiled, nausea pressing at the back of her throat. She hated the thought of disturbing anything here. This was less a home and more a tomb.

"I think this was my room," Auri murmured, only realizing she said it aloud when Ferris replied.

"Clearly you hadn't been here long when…" he gestured at a suitcase beside the cot with his flashlight beam, "when whatever happened, happened. No time to unpack. No real furniture."

She nodded in agreement, fighting to remain detached, distant. "Owari seems only half established. I don't understand." She gripped her temples. "I'm not getting solid memories. Just random voices and pangs of familiarity." Her gaze sought Ferris's, eager for a medical explanation. For him to say that she *would* remember everything, she just needed time.

"Cryo bite is literal brain damage, Auri. Not to mention you obviously survived something traumatic. Under the best of circumstances, you might not remember from that alone. Your brain wants to—" He cut off and cocked his head. "Hey, look at this." He strode toward the wall at the opposite end of the room.

Auri followed, skirting around the shut suitcase at the foot of the cot. Ferris crouched in front of the curved wall, aiming his beam on a child's drawing of a field of flowers. Below in a messy scrawl was an English name with the *kanji* translation underneath.

Auri ran her gloved fingertips over the letters, breathing aloud, "Elodie Dayre."

They started as whispers. Different voices calling the name in a variety of tones: happy, angry, yelled, whispered.

Then the voices grew in pitch, overlapping each other until Auri couldn't tell them apart. Her skull felt ready to burst with the pressure. She squeezed her eyes shut, gripping the sides of her head.

"Elodie, Elodie, Elodie."

Then a final scream—a screech of terror. "*Elodie!*"

Auri's eyes snapped open. She staggered backward, fleeing the room before Ferris was even upright. She ran to the final door in the short hallway, this one fully ajar. Another bloodied handprint marred the wall. Below the print was a square keypad. It looked like it had once been functional, but the wiring beneath was pulled out and blackened at the tips. The discovery crew who rescued her years ago must've done it.

Auri wavered at the threshold. Her chest tightened, and she struggled to breathe.

A cryo chamber sat in the corner of the closet-sized room. The lid was still propped open. Auri sucked in a breath. It felt like icicles sliced down her throat, leaving it raw and bleeding.

Flashes of memory hit her: being carried down this hallway, cradled close to someone's chest. The world was a blur of pain. She was barely conscious, barely breathing. The rapid flutter of a woman's heart—her mother's heart—and panicked breaths were the only thing that had grounded Auri. Then suddenly she heard the start-up sequence of the cryo chamber, a computerized female voice relaying instructions.

Fear overpowered her pain. Raw panic surged through her.

While most passengers bound for Owari Colony used the cryo chambers, Auri's parents had been forced to stay awake because their daughter had adamantly refused to even get near one.

But now—

Her mother forced her inside the chamber. One hand pressed down on Auri's chest, keeping her fixed in place. Auri grabbed for her mother's face but caught her earring instead. The last words Auri heard before the lid closed and icy liquid rushed in, forcing its way into her nose and mouth, had been *I love you.*

"I love you."

"I love you."

"I—"

"Auri!" Ferris's hand clamped down on Auri's shoulder, dredging her up from the assault of memories. She'd had flashbacks of the moments leading up to her time in the cryo chamber each time she encountered the Bleeders.

But then she hadn't known, not really…

"Oh, *Kami*," she breathed, realizing she had fallen to her knees at the open cryo chamber. She reached out for Birdie only to remember the poodle was still guarding the entrance. "My mother. She…"

Malachi had shot Auri's mother—no. Not Auri's mother. The Bleeder. The Bleeder who had attacked Auri, who would've killed her, *eaten* her…

If Malachi hadn't shot first.

Auri shoved her palm into her organic eye to stop the tears from falling. Not here. Not now. When she was back aboard the *Kestrel*, when they were safe. Then she could let go. She could let her brain travel down these new pathways.

Right now, she was on borrowed time.

She pulled up her c-tacts to see the current time on Roanleigh. 1152. *Kuso.* They had to move if they wanted to meet up with Malachi's team.

"You were screaming," Ferris said, uneasily glancing over his shoulder.

Auri cleared her raw throat. "Sorry. I was remembering…" She gestured to the cryo chamber, a shiver skittering along her spine.

"We have just enough time," he murmured to himself. He knelt beside the cryo chamber and tapped the controls. Auri shifted to give him more room. The readout gave a soft *chirp* that died halfway through. Ferris muttered under his breath then shifted a dial and pressed a small button in the center.

While he coaxed a response from the control panel, Auri forced herself to rise and examine the rest of the room. Two small lumps caught her eye, wedged behind the cryo chamber. Auri tilted her head, moving to examine them: a blood-stained *Hinamatsuri* doll and a camera drone like the ones Fed newscasters used. Except this one was larger, bulkier, and had a cracked lens.

"I can't get much off the cryo's memory," Ferris said, drawing her attention away from the drone and doll. "It's barely got enough juice to show me the last program." He shook his head. "It was set by an Elinor Dayre. Programmed for a six-year-old child. Without a withdrawal date. Between this program and the drawings in that bedroom..."

"I was—*am*—Elodie Dayre," Auri whispered, finally admitting it to herself. "And I am the only survivor of the Owari Colony."

CHAPTER SEVEN

17 Sept 3319, 11:59:16
Ancora Galaxy, Planet 08: Roanleigh,
Owari Colony

As Ferris and Auri approached the Hub, Katara radioed instructions for entering. They trudged around the side of the building to two double doors, shut against the constant barrage of wind. Birdie kept close to Auri's side, still dropping her nose to the ground at occasional intervals.

Auri held a hand up to block a particularly strong gust while Ferris shoved a door open.

A large main area greeted them, empty except for a few toppled chairs and dark stains on the tiled floor. Hanging on the wall directly across from the doors was a person-sized map of the building. Two hallways branched to the left and right, disappearing into the shadows beyond. As the door banged shut behind them, what little light the white planetscape provided vanished. Birdie whined.

"It's okay, Bird," Auri soothed as both she and Ferris turned on their flashlights. Auri started to move over to the map.

Ferris caught her arm. "Katara said it's the hall to the left." He cast his flashlight's beam in the same direction.

He led them down a hall lined with doors every few meters. Auri followed, doing her best to stay alert, but her mind kept drifting. Over and over again, she mentally walked through the rooms of her family's dwelling, replayed the newly awoken memories.

More than ever, Auri hated the GIC's lie—that her biological family abandoned her on Medea after a wild animal attack.

Though, she supposed he had slipped a grain of truth into the story. A *wild animal* attack. But were Bleeders to blame for Auri's fate? The fate of Owari Colony?

If so, where were the settlers' bodies? Auri had seen Bleeders fight and kill. And they weren't creatures that cleaned up after.

Unless…

Auri thought of her mother—the Bleeder Malachi shot in the Spire weeks ago. Were there no settler corpses because they had all become *Bleeders*? But if that were true, why wasn't Auri a Bleeder too? An ache blossomed at her temples. Answers only led to more questions.

Auri bumped into Ferris's back with a startled gasp. She opened her mouth to apologize, but a whispered curse cut her off.

Katara stood outside an open door a meter away, her coil gun level with Ferris's chest. "I almost shot you." She lowered the weapon and jerked her chin toward the opening. "They're almost done."

"And, final question." An unfamiliar male voice drifted into the hall.

"Can I…?" Auri started, gesturing to the doorway.

Katara shrugged. "They're just killing time until the transfer completes."

Auri stepped around Katara into the room, Birdie following.

"What did she find?" Katara whispered to Ferris.

"More questions, I think," Ferris answered, his voice laced with pity and concern.

"She'll need time to process…"

Then Auri was out of earshot. Two figures hunched in chairs placed before a wall of screens, their brightness the only source of light in the room. Hulking shadows splayed against the walls, shifting as the image on the screens changed. Malachi watched while Tsuna remained focused on the controls.

Auri opened her mouth to announce her presence, but the next image tightened her throat.

A woman perched on a white stool in an entirely white room. Her red hair curled over her shoulders, brown eyes intent on someone beyond the camera. She wore a white jumpsuit with white socks, her toes curled around the stool's lowest rung.

"The sooner you ask it," the woman began, tucking a strand of hair behind her ear. Flower earrings swung below both lobes. "The sooner you can interview the next candidate and decide you want me instead." She quirked an eyebrow.

Auri reached for her own flower earring but brushed air.

The interviewer chuckled. "I know your time is valuable, Mrs. Dayre. I just want to be thorough."

Mrs. Dayre.

Auri sucked in a ragged gasp, throwing her hood back. Her rope braid sprung free, the fiery hue so similar to the woman's hair on the screen.

My mother.

Malachi whirled, raising the gun that was resting in his lap. Tsuna started to duck behind him only to relax at the sight of Auri.

Malachi swore. "Auri, you know better than to come up behind us." When Auri didn't react, his gaze followed hers, and he swore again. "*Kuso.* Tsuna, cut the video."

Tsuna's brows drew together. "Why? We have time."

Malachi studied Auri's expression, mouth a thin line. "Just *cut it.*"

"Yes, Captain," she muttered and turned. The video blinked out a second later. The room plunged into darkness except for Auri's flashlight. Tsuna flicked on one of her own. "Just another two minutes on the transfer."

Auri stared at the black screens. Her mother's face hovered over them like a ghostly vision, permanently ingrained in Auri's mind. On those screens she was alive. Human.

Stars, she had been so *beautiful*.

"Turn them on," Auri ordered and she strode toward the controls. Malachi caught her shoulder. Birdie growled a warning, and Auri jerked her chin to glare up at him. "You just heard Tsuna. The transfer has another two minutes."

Malachi's grip was like iron. "You're not *ready*, Aurelia."

"Who are you to decide what I'm ready for?" she snapped. "I can handle this." But her voice broke. Shame washed through her, leaving her body cold and hollow.

Auri lowered her head, pressing her forehead against the slick material of his jacket. His nearness somehow warmed the chill that had crept into her bones. Birdie whined in concern.

"Au—" Tsuna started, but Auri felt Malachi shift as he shook his head.

Malachi lowered his mouth, his words meant only for her. His lips brushed against the sensitive skin at the curve of her ear. "I will show you everything we found. But not here. Not now. You don't realize it, but you're in shock. I can see it on your face." He squeezed the shoulder he still gripped. "Trust me to take care of you until you can take care of yourself."

Auri released a trembling breath. She loathed admitting it, but Malachi was right. She barely felt tethered to her body. Even hearing the name *Aurelia* felt like it would send her spiraling into uncharted space. Who was she?

Was she Aurelia Peri, adopted daughter of the GIC and renegade DISC agent?

Or was she Elodie Dayre, orphan and lone survivor of Owari Colony?

"I'll wait," Auri rasped, pulling back to meet his steady gaze.

But he wasn't looking at her anymore. She followed his stare to realize Katara had entered the room.

"Ferris?" Malachi asked the assassin.

"Guarding the door," Katara answered, eyes fixed on Auri. "Everything okay, Little Warrior?"

Auri cleared her throat, refusing to let her voice waver. "Yes."

"Akki-tan." Marin's voice cut in through the comms.

Malachi frowned, hand reflexively going to his ear. "What is it?"

"There is an inbound ship, about five hundred klicks out from Roanleigh. I wouldn't have noticed were I not looking." She hesitated as if reading the scans. "It's a Komodo class."

Auri's body went rigid. Malachi swore.

"Is that the same…?" Tsuna started to ask, pressing a hand over her lips as if she might vomit.

Katara shifted as Ferris entered the room beside her. "The same ship from the Spire," he said with a frown. "Seems odd it would get here shortly after us." Ferris glanced at Malachi.

"Not the time, Ferris." The captain's tone was laced with warning. "Marin, how long until the Komodo is in range for planetary scans?"

"Ten minutes. Unless they have long range scanners."

"That class wasn't outfitted with long range planetary scanners," Malachi said. "But that's no comfort. I want us off this rock before they even prep for landing." He looked to Tsuna. "What's the status of the transfer?"

A computerized chirp sounded behind them, and Tsuna let out a very uncharacteristic squeal, given the circumstances. "Transfer is complete!" The bulky holo computer perched on the table in front of her showed a bright blue 100%. The wires connecting it to the control panel hung from a port like a waiting noose.

Malachi nodded in approval. "Then let's get the he—"

Birdie let out a rumbling growl that made the hairs on Auri's neck stand up.

"Birdie?" Auri asked, kneeling. "What is it?"

The poodle's ears quirked and this time she whined, her tail shifting between her legs. Realization rippled across Auri's skin. Horror settled like a weight in her belly. She opened her mouth to warn the crew when Marin's voice came over their comms.

"Additional life forms have been detected planetside." Her tone grew in pitch. In panic. "They're… I believe… Crew, you need to return to *Kestrel* immediately."

Everyone was already drawing their guns, Auri reaching for her disc. Tsuna yanked the wire from the holo computer and powered it off. She slipped it into her bag with the utmost care before zipping it shut.

"Follow me," Malachi murmured, leading the way out the door. Over the comms, he asked, "Marin, how close to the Hub can you get the *Kestrel*?"

"Winds have increased," Marin answered. "I can get her airborne, but I can't guarantee landing accuracy. The probability of injury to *Kestrel* is high."

"*Kuso*," Katara hissed.

Malachi faced the gathered crew. "Looks like we're running."

CHAPTER EIGHT

---

17 Sept 3319, 12:06:56
Ancora Galaxy, Planet 08: Roanleigh,
Owari Colony

They clustered at the Hub's only exit. Even through the thick steel door, Auri heard the wind howl as the blizzard descended.

"Why," Katara hissed beside Auri, "did these people not install windows. We have no idea what we're walking into."

"Multiple life forms five meters from your location," Marin announced over comms. "Komodo class is three minutes from close range planetary scans."

Malachi didn't meet the crew's gaze as he asked, "How many meters between us and the *Kestrel*? How many hostiles?"

In the silence between question and answer, the wind released a mournful keen. Birdie shifted closer to Auri, and Auri knotted her fingers in the poodle's hair.

Fleeing across the narrow walkways of Babbage was one thing. But through knee-high snow? During an approaching blizzard? Auri swallowed hard. She tightened her grip on Birdie, palm meeting the ridge of the poodle's rounded shoulder blade.

"One hundred. *Kestrel* detects upwards of twenty life forms." Katara cursed and Tsuna whimpered.

"We could…" Tsuna rasped. "We could always bunker down in here. Wait it out."

Malachi shook his head. "It would be like the Spire all over again once they see the *Kestrel* and find out we're here. And we can't leave Marin and Castor."

"Well," Ferris murmured, "this mission just earned a hell of a lot more pucker factor." Even his usual light-hearted humor sounded forced.

"There's no other choice." Malachi took a slow breath. "We're going to run." He activated the comms. "Castor, I want those cargo doors open and you covering our retreat."

"Copy," Castor said, tone military-rigid in a way Auri had never heard before.

Malachi looked to the rest of them as they huddled together, gripping weapons and flashlights. The shadows cast on Malachi's face gave him a malicious air. "Ferris and I lead. I want Tsuna and Auri in the middle. Katara?"

She nodded. "I'll bring up the rear."

Ferris shifted. "I don't like—"

Malachi cut him off. "That's the plan, Ferris. Katara is our best fighter."

Ferris glanced at Katara as if he wanted her to argue. She gave his arm a squeeze. The doctor frowned but checked his blaster's charge.

Malachi drew both of his coil guns. Auri tightened her grip on her disc and used her c-tacts to strengthen the electricity barrier to full capacity.

"Run hard," Malachi whispered. "No matter what you see out there. One hundred meters. Don't stop until we hit the cargo hold."

Everyone nodded their agreement. Auri and Tsuna positioned themselves on either side of the double doors.

Malachi held up three fingers, counting down. At zero, Auri and Tsuna hauled the doors open. Wind and snow gusted into the Hub, momentarily blinding Auri. Ferris and Malachi broke into a run. Blinking snow from her tearing eye, Auri darted after them, Tsuna and Birdie on either side.

A pummeling gust slammed into Auri as she left the Hub, stealing her breath. Her hood flew back and her rope braid slapped against her face. The sheer chill froze the particles of sweat beading on her cheek.

Snowflakes swirled around them as they fled, and the sky had gone from a soft gray to an ominous slate. There were no signs of the Bleeders, but Auri didn't have time for relief or even confusion. She could barely take a breath, barely make out the shadow of the *Kestrel* a hundred meters away.

She forced herself to keep moving, working her knees up and down to get through the deep snow. Her heart thudded painfully against her ribs, then a spark of pain as a stitch formed in her side.

Birdie kept pace, loping through the drifts, her ears quirked back, her nose sniffing the air.

Marin's panicked cry came through the comms, "Katara, six o-clock!"

Katara screamed. Auri whirled, disc ready. Katara's laser katar sliced through something caught around her calf. A *hand*.

A hand that had shot from the snow. Katara kicked off the severed appendage that still clutched at her leg. Crimson splattered across white.

"They're under us!" Auri cried over the wind.

That was why the scanners hadn't registered the Bleeders when they first landed. Auri had thought the creatures were monsters only capable of hunger and savagery. But they had somehow lowered their body temperatures beyond what normal humans could survive. With their regenerating abilities, they were virtually invisible to all ship scans.

The mounds of snow that had seemed so harmless before, began to shift and crack apart as forms emerged from their frozen depths.

"Run!" Malachi roared.

Auri took off at a sprint, but between the descending blizzard's haze and the rush of adrenaline, she felt as if she barely moved. Two Bleeders burst from the snow meters ahead. Flakes clung to the blood that seeped from their eyes and noses. Malachi raised his coil guns, firing off quick rounds. The wind sent the bullets off course, and they lodged into shoulders and chests or missed the creatures entirely. The Bleeders howled as they charged.

"I've got them!" Auri cried. Malachi and Ferris reflexively broke apart to give her room. Auri hurled her disc, angling it with the wind. The rounded edge slammed into one Bleeder, then ricocheted to hit the other. They both went down, convulsing with the strength of the lightning barrier.

Fifty meters now. Just fifty meters between them and the *Kestrel.* Auri recalled her disc before it vanished beneath the snow, catching it midstride.

"You're in range of Castor," Marin said into the comms. *"Keep running."*

Auri barely heard Castor's rapid cover fire. Guttural growls carried on the wind, melding with the storm's howl. A copper tang coated Auri's mouth. She could barely feel her face. Her legs. Even with cyborg enhancements, her heart seemed ready to burst.

Twenty-five meters. Twenty. Fifteen.

The open cargo doors became visible through the grayness and swirls of white. Castor lay on his belly, sniper rifle swiveling between targets. Marin had raised the *Kestrel* so it hovered off the ground. They would have to jump, but they would also be airborne in seconds.

Go, go, go! pounded in Auri's head. *Almost there.*

Malachi and Ferris reached the *Kestrel* and leapt, hands grasping for the lip of the ramp. Tsuna and Auri would be next—

Pain lanced across Auri's skull as something yanked her backward by her braid. She had the absurd thought, *Katara's going to say I told you so.*

Just as quickly, the painful pressure released, and Auri slammed into the snow. Katara stood over her, katar flashing as she fended off a Bleeder. The creature flung a severed red braid into the snow before lunging around the assassin for Auri.

She rolled on reflex to remain a moving target, even while Katara attacked. Birdie barked in a panic.

Auri lurched to her feet moments later, disc blades extending. Another Bleeder was there, teeth bared, spittle flying. Auri whipped her disc in a crescent. The blades cut into the Bleeder's chest. Blood sprayed across Auri's face and coat.

Birdie popped from the snow, darting between the Bleeder's legs, throwing it off balance. The Bleeder snarled as it fell to one knee. It grabbed for the poodle's tail with a meaty hand, but its reflexes were delayed, as if hiding beneath the snow had slowed its nervous system.

Birdie dodged. Already the deep gouge across the Bleeder's chest was merging, replaced by bubbled scar tissue.

Auri swept her disc in another arc. Her blades sliced through the Bleeder's neck, tissue and tendon. The creature's head toppled to the ground. Gore splattered the snow. The body hit seconds later.

Birdie barked in warning, ears quirking. Auri blinked snow from her eyes, trying to find her crew. She could barely see her outstretched hand, let alone the *Kestrel*. Panic flared.

"Run!" Katara suddenly appeared at Auri's side. She caught Auri's jacket and tugged. "This way."

They ran.

Dark shapes coalesced in front of them, turning into a howling Bleeder as they drew closer. Katara shifted course, only for more to appear, first to the left, then to the right. As the wind howled and the snow blinded them, Auri and Katara backtracked, managing a few meters before five more creatures lurched to block them. Birdie snarled, foam and blood dripping from her mouth where she'd bitten one of the monsters.

"We're surrounded," Auri wheezed. She and Katara stood back-to-back, circling, as Bleeders stalked around them, just far enough away that their features were hazy, but close enough to make their threat clear: Auri and Katara were trapped. Birdie pressed against Auri's leg, snarling. The faint sound of panicked shouts reached her, but she couldn't tell what direction they came from. Or if they were even real. She had lost her comm in the scuffle.

Then, as one, the Bleeders charged, jaws unhinged as if to devour her whole.

Auri hurled her disc, lower this time, knowing she couldn't manifest enough power to sever their heads long range. The blades sliced deep gouges in three pairs of legs, sending their owners howling into the snow, before the disc swirled back to Auri.

Katara hurled dagger after dagger. Many hit flesh, but the Bleeders didn't slow unless the blades sunk into vulnerable tendon or eye sockets.

Katara reached for her final dagger, looking to Auri, her face splashed with blood. There was a crazed look to her eyes, as if she wasn't really seeing Auri.

"When I tell you, you throw your disc to clear a way ahead. Then you run and don't look back." She pointed in the direction she wanted Auri to go. The *Kestrel* was invisible in the storm, so Auri had to trust Katara as the Bleeders lurched toward them.

Katara hefted her blade. "Now!" she screamed.

Auri hurled her disc. It cut a lethal arc ahead of them. Bleeders fell, creating a bloody path in the snow. The disc cut into the snow and disappeared.

Auri ran, trying to recall the weapon at the same time, but a warning flashed across her c-tacts: *Battery depleted—90 second recharge commencing.* She reached for a knife only to fumble with an empty sheath. From the depths of her jacket pocket, she grabbed the only weapon she had left: her parents' broken doorknob. Her gloved fingers curled around the handle.

Birdie bounded just ahead, and the hulking shape of the *Kestrel* loomed out of the swirling snow. Hope flickered in Auri's chest. The dog barked a warning as a Bleeder stepped onto their path. Auri sidestepped, slamming the sharp base of the doorknob into the creature's throat. Blood gushed across Auri's fingers. The Bleeder gagged and staggered back, taking the knob with it.

"Go!" Katara shouted, right behind her. "Go!"

The snarls grew louder, but ahead gaped the open cargo hold of the *Kestrel*, a couple meters off the ground. Castor jerked his sniper rifle around as Auri and Katara came into view and began laying down heavy cover fire. The *tat tat tat* of his bullets discharging kept pace with Auri's racing heart.

Three meters… Two…

"Jump!" Ferris cried. He and Malachi waited at the end of the ramp.

Auri leapt, propelling herself higher using her robotic leg. Birdie followed. For a terrifying moment, Auri thought she would miss the ramp.

Then Ferris caught one of her arms, and Malachi secured her other. Together, they hauled her up and onto the rubberized metal. Birdie's claws scrabbled as she found her footing.

Auri turned to see Katara jumping, her arms flung forward. A gust of wind shook the *Kestrel.* Malachi and Ferris fell onto hands and knees beside her.

Auri rolled onto her belly, reaching out.

Katara's hands closed around hers. Pain lanced through Auri's shoulders like a hot poker.

"Nice ca—" Katara cut off in a scream, and Auri cried out in terror and agony as the weight she held doubled.

A Bleeder hung from Katara's calf, its nails sunk deep, snarling as it tried to tow her back down to the handful of creatures swarming below.

Even with the textured ramp, Auri began to slide forward. Birdie's jaw clamped around Auri's waistband, jerking backward. Ferris and Malachi grabbed at her shoulders to support both of her arms.

"*Chikusho,*" Malachi hissed. More Bleeders were running for Katara.

"Castor!" Ferris shouted, and Auri realized the cook had stopped firing. "Shoot it! Shoot it!"

"One bullet left!" Castor warned. He slid onto his belly at the ramp's edge, swiveling his rifle to shoot the Bleeder now clawing at the ramp, using Katara's shoulders as a foothold. It leapt toward Castor with a snarl. Tsuna caught Castor's hips and towed him backward as the Bleeder crashed against the ramp where he had been. The Bleeder scrabbled at the metal, nails ripping, feet dangling off the ledge, then slid back with a howl into open air.

"Don't let go," Malachi snapped at Katara. The Bleeder's howl of rage turned to a scream when it crashed into the snow. Auri reflexively squeezed her eyes shut.

Malachi's grip tightened on Auri. "Marin! Get this boat in the sky!"

"Hold on, Katara," Auri hissed through clenched teeth as the ship wobbled and lifted another meter, then two.

Katara let out another howl of pain, and Auri watched in horror as another Bleeder appeared, clawing up Katara's thigh. More Bleeders latched onto the woman's legs, using her body as a living ladder. They began to climb.

Something in Katara's left arm snapped at the weight pulling against her body. She whimpered.

"Katara!" Auri cried.

"Little warrior," Katara rasped, her voice so quiet Auri could barely hear her.

"Don't let go," Auri wheezed. "Ferris wouldn't forgive you. We'll get you up. Just *hold on.*"

"I'm not going to let the Bleeders get on the ship." Tears pooled in Katara's eyes and ran down her cheeks, leaving a clean trail through the blood. "Tell him I loved him," she choked. "I always did."

Katara's hands slipped from Auri's grasp.

Auri screamed. She lurched forward, desperate to catch her friend. The tips of their fingers brushed, and then Katara fell. Only the combined grip of Malachi and Ferris kept Auri from following.

Katara slammed back-first into the snow, the Bleeders who had been climbing her falling around her. In a blink, she had rolled into a crouch, her useless arm dangling at her side, her final dagger raised. The Bleeders swarmed. She fought one-handed, a beautiful, lethal whirlwind, despite her leg wounds. But their sheer number pinned her down, and in a few heartbeats one bit into her arm, ripping away her coat sleeve. Then another ravaged her leg with its nails, shredding the pants and skin beneath. Hot crimson turned the snow pink and slushy around her. Katara slumped to her knees.

"No!" Ferris bellowed. He staggered upright as if to jump. Auri slid back, out of his way.

"Move!" Malachi shoved Ferris hard, sending him sprawling back toward the cargo hold. He snatched the sniper rifle from Castor and positioned himself on the ramp.

"Damn you, Katara." Malachi's voice broke. He eased back to wipe his eyes then returned to the scope.

Ferris was on his feet again, running. But too slowly.

"Rest easy." Malachi pulled the trigger and Castor's final bullet sliced through Katara's forehead.

CHAPTER NINE

18 Sept 3319, 00:01:47
Ancora Galaxy,
Free Airspace

Something heavy immobilized Auri's chest. Darkness swallowed her in its embrace, and a deep cold seeped into her bones. She flailed in a panic. Fighting, reaching, searching—

Her hands slammed against something hard.

Auri's eyes snapped open. She stood outside a floor-to-ceiling tube lit with inset lights. The surrounding room was darker than the deepest reaches of space and colder than even Roanleigh. So cold, the tube's glass had frosted over, cloaking a shadowed, backlit, figure. Auri crept forward and scraped at the ice with her fingernails until she could peer inside.

Familiar blue eyes watched her. Long red hair swirled in the opalescent water that filled the tube, eddying like seaweed on Babbage. Suddenly the body jerked. Muscles bulged under skin. Nails grew long and jagged. Blood seeped from the eyes, nose, and mouth, dying the water crimson.

Auri stumbled back, a hand clasped over her mouth.

The Other Auri snarled and slammed her hands against the tube. It cracked under her palms. She struck again. Glass shattered and the murky water crashed into Auri. She let out a gurgled scream as the Bleeder pounced.

Auri's eyes snapped open. The ceiling of her dark room came into focus, illuminated by the light creeping under the door. Pin-pricks of distant stars were visible through her window. Her heart was a drum in her ears, her breaths heaving in and out. Sweat slicked her back and behind her knees as she tried to recall her dream.

But then she remembered the pieces that hadn't been a dream at all, though they felt like a nightmare.

They had visited Roanleigh.

They had been attacked by Bleeders.

They had *lost Katara.*

A sob caught in her throat. She clenched her jaw as a tear rolled down her cheek. Auri shifted to sit up, but something held her down. It was then she realized she wasn't tucked in her bed but twisted underneath her *kotatsu.* Birdie lay curled beside her, the poodle's warm head resting atop Auri's heart.

It must have been a particularly bad dream. Even now, it grew hazy in her mind. Something about being trapped, unable to move.

"Bird," Auri rasped as she finally sat up, jostling the dog. Birdie's tongue rolled out as she yawned, and the stink of fish-breath saturated the air. "Sorry to wake you," she whispered.

Birdie's fish-breath was nothing compared to the stale stench of sweat and blood covering Auri. Auri pulled up the ship time on her c-tacts, relieved to see it was just past midnight. Hopefully the rest of the crew would be asleep.

"I'm going to the bathroom," she told Birdie as she stood. "Stay."

Birdie blinked sleepy eyes and yawned. The sweat on Auri's skin had cooled and she shivered in the chilly air of her room.

Birdie stretched and yawned again. Then she hopped onto Auri's still-made bed and spun in three quick circles that turned the fresh sheets into a messy ball. Satisfied, the dog plopped down with a groan, her tail curling around her. She was asleep in seconds.

Auri stopped to slide on her slippers where she'd left them under the *kotatsu*. Then she shuffled out of her room.

The hallway was mercifully empty, the lights dimmed to their overnight levels. She stopped outside the bathroom door at the end. Her gaze darted to the other wing of the *Kestrel*, to the captain's quarters. She had only been inside once, when Malachi was having a nightmare of his own. She wondered what the captain was doing now. If he was even able to sleep after…

No. She shook her head, curling her toes. Not now. Not yet.

Auri tapped on the bathroom door, the steel cool beneath her fingers. When no one answered, she slid it open.

Auri avoided the long mirror fixed above a row of sinks. Instead, she faced the tub, stripping off her damp tank top and linen shorts. Stray hairs clung to her neck as she pulled down her ponytail. The odor of singed hair made her crinkle her nose, but she didn't pause to examine the red tangles.

She padded along the heated tiles to a handheld shower where she knelt to crank the dial as hot as it allowed. The heat seared her organic skin, and steam floated up in a cloud. She sighed as taut muscles loosened. Red swirled down the drain until, finally, it became clear.

She lathered her hair with the lavender shampoo, also using it to clean her battered skin. The suds clung to her, sliding down her breasts, her thighs, rolling off her knees where she knelt on the tile.

Memories of the *after* flashed through her mind as she rinsed her hair, eyes squeezed shut.

Malachi had shot Katara, and no one dared move in the aftermath. No one except Malachi. The *Kestrel*'s captain had slowly pushed to his feet, abandoning the rifle to the floor.

"Marin, break atmo," he ordered into the comms, voice almost robotic.

As the cargo hold door slammed shut and the thrusters went to full power, realization finally settled on everyone.

Ferris moved first.

He approached Malachi, tears running down his face. He stared at the captain.

"Go ahead," Malachi murmured.

Ferris punched Malachi in the face. Malachi staggered back. Blood gushed from his nose and pattered onto the floor.

Auri gasped and stood. Birdie sniffed Auri's legs, as if checking to ensure she wasn't injured.

"Ferris—" Tsuna started, only to cut off in a wince as Ferris landed an uppercut to the underside of Malachi's jaw.

Malachi reeled back but kept his feet.

Auri swallowed hard, uncertain. It almost looked like Malachi *wanted* Ferris to beat the *kuso* out of him. She glanced at Castor, but he was staring at the closed cargo doors as if waiting for Katara to suddenly appear.

Katara.

The only one who could've handled the two men. But Katara was...

Malachi slowly raised his head. He didn't bother staunching the flow of blood from his nose. Already, purple tinged the right side of his jaw.

Ferris punched Malachi in the face again. This time the captain hit the ground, hard. One of his coil guns fell from an unhooked holster. It spun in a chaotic circle until it slowed to a stop, barrel aimed at Auri.

Ferris grabbed the gun and stalked over to Malachi who had pushed himself onto hands and knees.

"Stop!" Auri yelled, imbuing her voice with as much of Katara's commanding tone as she could.

Ferris paused. His shoulders shifted as he turned to look back at Auri. Flecks of Malachi's blood stained his beard.

Auri slowly stepped between the two men. Ferris's hands tightened into fists, and Auri realized it looked like she was protecting Malachi. As if she thought what Malachi had done was *right*.

Right or wrong didn't matter. Ferris had just lost the woman he loved. They had all lost a woman they loved.

Auri took one step and then another toward Ferris. When he didn't move to strike her or raise the gun, she wrapped her arms around the doctor's chest, her head reaching his jaw.

Tension radiated from his body. Panicked. Feral.

Then, without warning, he crumpled, nearly taking Auri to the floor. She grunted and braced her legs as his arms came around her, borderline painful. He buried his head in her shoulder as he released a heart-breaking sob.

"Oh, *Kami*," he cried. "Oh, *Kami*. She can't be gone. She *can't be*."

Marin's voice came over the intercom of the cargo hold instead of their comms. "Scans show the landing Komodo class is attempting pursuit."

Ferris stilled against Auri. She wasn't sure he even breathed.

"Marin, burn thrusters as much as we can spare." Malachi's voice sounded a nasally and choked with blood. "Everyone else, got to your quarters until the all-clear."

The *Kestrel* bucked underneath them. Auri staggered, and Ferris released her. She hit the floor on her rear end. A lance of pain went up her spine and nestled in her skull.

Ferris stumbled back a few paces. He grounded himself and then watched Malachi. Auri tensed, ready to intervene again, but Ferris only tossed the gun to the floor and fled the cargo hold.

Tsuna and Castor gave Malachi a wide birth as they followed, tears still wet on Tsuna's face.

"Malachi…" Auri started, rising to stand. His face looked horrible. It would be a miracle if he didn't have a concussion.

"Go," he rasped, retrieving his weapon without looking at her.

When Auri didn't move, he turned, his face expressionless. "As your captain, Aurelia Peri, I am ordering you to your quarters. Are you going to disobey a direct order?"

Past his façade, pure agony glittered in his eyes. It belayed the sharp command. The subtle threat. Auri wanted to stay, to hold him so tight his fractured pieces knit together. To grieve with him. But that wasn't what he wanted.

So, she had turned and left him alone in the cargo room, Birdie on her heels.

In her quarters, Birdie and Auri hunkered on the bed. Two of the wall panels around it opened to reveal a pair of safety harnesses. Auri had jerry-rigged Birdie's to fit, and after strapping her dog in, she secured herself. The *Kestrel* jerked and rolled as Marin attempted to evade the Komodo ship and break atmo.

When the openness of space glistened through her window, relief weakened Auri's taught muscles. Soon after, Marin gave the all-clear. She didn't offer details on where the Komodo ship was now, but Auri found she didn't care as long as it wasn't following.

Auri considered venturing to the bathroom to clean herself up. Or to the kitchen to fill her empty belly. Or even to check on Malachi and the rest of the crew.

But she couldn't summon the strength to open her door. Instead, she changed clothes and yanked her singed hair into a messy ponytail. At Birdie's insistence, she filled a spare bowl with water and gave the dog a bone.

Auri turned on the heater of her *kotatsu,* a table with a large blanket attached around the edges, and tucked herself underneath. She leaned against the table, resting her head atop her folded arms. The vastness of space lay beyond her window, the same as it always was. Yet it would never be the same again.

An ache hollowed out her insides. Ty's face rose unbidden and she wanted to laugh at herself. She was an absolute *baka* of a girl. Ty didn't care about her. But the desire to talk to someone outside her circle of grief was so tempting. To talk to someone who she remembered as having cared for her, even if it had all been a lie.

Her heart raced as she found his last ping in her messages screen.

09 Aug 3319 – 0923

Mind grabbing me some takoyaki?

Auri remembered opening the ping and rolling her eyes. Ty always thought of his stomach.

But secretly she'd been happy.

Happy that he remembered walking around Babbage together during his leave the previous year and finding the *takoyaki* vendor.

What a fool she had been. What a fool she was now.

Auri composed a ping that she altered multiple times. At first it was too long, then it was too short.

Finally, she settled on a message unrelated to her present circumstances.

Hey, Ty. Get any good takoyaki *lately?*

Auri bit her lip as she contemplated sending it. She checked her connection to the *Kestrel*'s grid.

The ship's cyber security rivaled that of some of the Fed's intel bases. She had to change her personal password twice a week. It was annoying, but at least advertisements no longer barraged her c-tacts.

All that security would be for nothing if Auri sent this ping to Ty. The likelihood of Ty telling the GIC, and those who could track the communication, was high.

Kuso. As much as she needed the distraction, she couldn't risk it.

With a halting sigh, Auri lowered herself onto the floor, feeling achingly alone even with Birdie now curled up under the *kotatsu* with her. She stared at the message to Ty and let herself imagine what his response might be.

At some point during her made-up conversation, she must've fallen asleep, trading one nightmare for another.

Auri gave her head a hard shake to bring herself back to the present. She turned off the shower and wrapped herself in a towel.

She padded over to the sink, surprised to see the mirrors fogged over. Modern tech usually kept them clear. Apparently even anti-fogging mirrors couldn't withstand a shower set to maximum heat for who knew how long.

A loud *scraaaatch* came from the other side of the bathroom door.

"I'm fine, Birdie," Auri choked out.

Birdie whined.

Auri tightened the towel around her only to realize she'd forgotten a brush. The wet strands of hair clung to her shoulders and back. She tapped a panel in the mirror to open the storage compartment behind it, intending to borrow one of the male crew's spare combs.

As she selected a black wide-toothed one, her gaze caught on a pair of scissors. She picked them up without thinking. The metal was surprisingly cool against her palm.

She closed the panel and wiped away the mist. A ghost of a girl stared back at her in the glass. One eye bloodshot, half her skin red from the heat of her shower, her body showing the stark contrast between organic and robotic. Her once waist-length hair was now up to her elbow in some places.

Auri looked at the comb in her left hand and then the scissors in her right. Katara's warning echoed in her mind.

"You're either going to get thrown around by it or strangled. And I might not be around to help you then."

She should've listened. But because of Auri and her star's-cursed vanity, Katara was dead.

Because of Auri, Malachi had been forced to—

A sob broke her. The comb clattered to the floor. She grabbed a chunk of hair with a trembling hand and raised the scissors. The sharpened blades sliced through with a loud *snip*. Auri threw the hair into the sink and picked up another section.

Katara's face flashed in Auri's mind. "Little Warrior," she said with a smile.

Cut.

Katara's face shone with sweat, offering praise after a successful sparring session.

Cut.

Katara's promise to Castor that she would keep Tsuna safe.

Cut.

Katara as she fell, Auri unable to catch her, to save her.

Auri keened in agony. She dropped the scissors. They barely made a sound as they fell atop the damp curls of hair. Tears rolled down her cheek and she wailed.

"I'm so sorry," she wheezed. She gripped the countertop, knuckles white. "Katara, I'm so sorry."

The door to the bathroom slid open. Auri gasped, her eyes jerking to the mirror. Her gaze met Malachi's in the glass. His nose was a swollen mass, even more crooked than before. Dark purple splotches stained his skin underneath the days-old scruff on his jaw. He turned to murmur through the narrow opening, "I've got her, Birdie."

There was a worried whine and then the sound of padded feet moving down the hall.

Malachi eased the door shut but didn't approach. His multi-colored eyes studied her face in the mirror. Auri met her reflection's gaze, finally seeing her butchered hair. She'd chopped it just below her jawline in an asymmetrical bob that would've been comical in any other circumstance.

Auri let out another sob, clasping her hand over her mouth.

Malachi caught her wrist, turning her to face him. His skin was warm on hers and something about it undid her further. She crashed into his chest. He winced and then sighed, wrapping his arms around her. The dark material of his fresh shirt smelled of the engine room.

"Let it out," Malachi murmured. "You're safe. Let it out."

Auri sobbed until there were no tears left to spill. Malachi held her quietly, not murmuring promises or useless platitudes.

Because what words could possibly fix the ache inside her? The ache and loss and guilt they both felt.

Auri sniffled, relaxing against Malachi's chest. Her racing heart slowed to match the steady rhythm of his. The captain shifted to look down at her. He wiped a stray tear from her cheek with his thumb.

Auri cleared her raw throat, suddenly aware she stood pressed against him in just a towel. She moved back to tighten the fabric under her arms. "H-how did you know?" Her voice sounded hoarse from crying.

"Birdie found me." He gestured to the sink with a nod. "Why the haircut?"

Auri fingered the butchered ends of her hair. "A Bleeder grabbed my braid. Katara…" Auri's throat closed around the words, and she lowered her hand. "After Babbage, she warned my hair would get me in trouble. But I didn't listen."

"You have beautiful hair," Malachi said. "And Katara says—" He caught himself with a staggered breath. "*Said* a lot of things. Not all worth listening to."

"How can she be gone?" Auri whispered. "It doesn't feel real."

Malachi picked up the scissors she'd abandoned in the sink and held them toward her hair with a quirked brow.

She shrugged. "I doubt you'd make it worse."

"You do have a way with scissors, Auri," he murmured with a weary smile, drawing closer. His warm breath on her neck made her shiver, and her skin puckered with goosebumps.

Malachi raised the scissors, the soft *snip snip* the only sound between them, until her hair rested at her jaw, just long enough to tuck behind her ears. As it dried, the waves made it look even shorter. The haircut gave her a wild, feral look. Auri appeared less and less like the structured DISC agent every day.

She turned to Malachi. "What do you think?" She tucked a curl behind her ear. "Do I look okay?"

The intensity in his multi-colored eyes made her breath catch. She leaned back, pressing into the lip of the counter. Heat blossomed in her belly as he looked at her in a way no one, not even Ty, had ever looked at her.

"Aurelia," he said, voice rough, stepping forward so his hips pressed against hers. One of his hands came up to her cheek, and she pressed into the warmth of it. She tilted her chin up. Yearning filled her. How would it feel to forget the pain? To push away the loss of both Katara and a family that she barely remembered? It all felt like too much.

But Malachi… He was enough. And so much more. She shivered.

The captain leaned down, and his arm shifted from her cheek to loop around her waist.

"Malachi," she whispered. The heat of his skin chased away the chill in her bones. She rose to meet him, but he stilled.

"No," he choked out. He released her waist and purposefully stepped back. "Not like this. You deserve better." He pulled open the bathroom door and left without another word.

And Auri was alone, staring after the *Kestrel*'s captain with a mixture of disappointment, longing, and relief.

CHAPTER TEN

When Auri woke the next morning, her eye felt swollen and dry. She probed the skin with gentle fingers before running a hand through her hair. It fanned out over her pillow in short waves of red. The length was still startling.

Auri closed her eyes, remembering the feel of Malachi's arm around her waist, the want in his eyes. Her heart skipped a beat. Had what she felt been attraction? Or just weakness from grieving?

And what about Malachi? What did he think she deserved? A better situation? Or did Malachi think she deserved a better *man*? Was she just an escape for him?

Auri bolted upright to free herself from the memory. There were more important things than romantic entanglement with the captain. She had seen firsthand that onboard romances did not end well.

"Oh, Ferris," she breathed. She couldn't begin to fathom his agony.

Her own was still raw, but Katara would be furious if Auri wasted more time crying. Katara would want Auri to act. To make her death mean something.

And that's what Auri intended to do.

Auri dressed in a pair of khaki cargo pants and a black t-shirt. As she yanked her boots on, Birdie slunk from under the *kotatsu*, yawning.

The two of them stepped into the hall only for Auri to stop at the sight of Katara's open door. Ferris sat on the assassin's narrow bed, Castor's whiskey bottle in one hand.

As if sensing her gaze, he looked up. Then he stood, stepped over to the door, and closed it soundlessly.

Auri swallowed, trying to stamp out the sting of rejection. Ferris was drowning in grief. She had no right to be hurt over his need for privacy. She would understand if Ferris never spoke to her again.

Hushed voices drew Auri down the hall and into the warm lights of the kitchen. There were no delicious scents sizzling on the stovetop. Just the smell of freshly brewed coffee.

Tsuna and Malachi sat at the table in different seats than their usual. The rest of the crew was absent. Auri guessed Marin was on the bridge and Castor was probably still asleep.

Steaming coffee sat in front of Malachi—in one of his mugs, she noticed. His bruises looked even worse this morning. Auri doubted he bothered treating them with something from the infirmary.

Tsuna munched on a protein bar, wearing a simple blue tank dress belted at the waist. Her braids were tied back in two thick ponytails down her back. She swiped at a large screen in front of them.

"How much have you gotten through?" she was asking Malachi.

He let out a humorless chuckle. "About a quarter."

Tsuna's eyes widened. "But there were petabytes of data." At Malachi's blank look she sighed. "In other words, a normal person would've barely made a dent even after I ran a defrag and sorted files by keywords."

He tapped the side of his head. "I couldn't sleep last night."

"I, uh," Tsuna ran her thumb over the edge of the screen, accidentally swiping to another page. "I couldn't either." She bit her lip and glanced at Malachi to gauge his reaction. "It may complicate things, but I ended up—"

Malachi held up a hand. "How you grieve is your affair, Tsuna. As long as it doesn't interfere with my ship and what we're doing here. I already have one problematic crew member."

"He lost the woman he loved, Cai," Tsuna murmured. "Show some sympathy."

"We all lost a woman we loved," he countered. "And I showed sympathy when I let the piece of *kuso* nearly break my skull in two."

Auri cleared her throat to announce her presence. They turned.

"Good morning," Tsuna said. Her dark eyes were bloodshot but warm.

Auri felt Malachi's eyes on her, but she wasn't brave enough to meet his gaze.

"Your hair looks lovely," Tsuna said with a tired smile. "When did you…?" She glanced at Malachi, who still studied Auri. Tsuna's brows rose.

"Are you looking at the intel from Roanleigh?" Auri quickly asked. She strode past the table to fill Birdie's food and water bowl.

"Sections of it," Malachi said. "Tsuna ran a program to sort everything by keywords." He sipped his coffee, wincing as the mug's rim bumped his broken nose. At least he had taken time to splint it with tape. Ferris could probably have done better, but Auri doubted the ship's doctor would help heal the nose he'd broken. "If you think you're ready," he said, "she found something you'll want to see."

Auri grabbed a protein bar from the pantry, more because she knew she needed to eat, not because she wanted to. "Is it related to the video log I saw on Roanleigh?" *Moments before our world shattered?* The thought crept in, unwelcome and just as unhelpful.

"Yes," Tsuna said. "You caught a glimpse of an interview with Elinor Dayre."

Auri mouthed the name. It didn't feel familiar on her lips, but she wouldn't exactly have called her mother Elinor. Though *Mom* felt just as foreign.

Tsuna pulled a smaller screen from the tactical bag at her feet. "I've loaded Elinor Dayre's video logs for you. It might take a while. There's a lot of footage."

Auri accepted the tablet, her grip delicate, as if the military-grade tech were as breakable as non-tempered glass.

"Thank you," she murmured. "I think… No, I *know*. Elinor Dayre was my mother."

Malachi's gaze shifted to Auri's mostly synthetic ear, still devoid of the flower earring. He looked like he wanted to say something, but Auri spoke first.

"I know, Malachi. I know we killed her back on Harlequin."

Tsuna's eyes widened. "She was a *Bleeder*?"

"Yes. And it wasn't just her. The entire colony became Bleeders—save one." Malachi lowered the mug to the table and shook his head.

Auri had suspected the same thing. He must've seen something in the intel to prove that beyond a doubt.

"What I don't know," he continued, "is *how* the transformation occurred. The reports, video logs, manifests—everything just stops after some kind of in-fighting." He glanced at Auri and pain flickered across his face as if he'd witnessed something horrible.

"Did you see anything about me?" Auri asked, shifting her grip on the tablet. "How I stayed human?" She planned to go through every scrap of intel, but this information seemed crucial to how they would proceed. "Or why the Bleeders seem interested in me?"

"Another mystery," he whispered, frowning into his now-empty mug.

Tsuna squeezed his shoulder. "We didn't find the Bleeders' origins, but the little we've seen in the video logs and crew manifest are proof that Roanleigh isn't toxic, contrary to the GIC's propaganda. With the archeologists' logs we retrieved from the Spire, we have enough to prove Bleeder existence and compile a case against him."

Malachi steepled his fingers over his lips. "I want to go through all the data from Roanleigh. Even things that don't match our keywords. Every little scrap of ammunition needs to go into our report against the GIC."

Tsuna nodded. "I'll try to get the other crew members involved. More eyes will help. Though I think Ferris should be left to his own devices."

"And Marin hasn't left the bridge," Malachi added. "See if you can convince Castor, but it might just be us three."

"How is Marin?" Auri asked.

Malachi shook his head. "She's grieving in her own way."

"I'll go take a look at the video logs," Auri said, tightening her grip on the tablet. "And let you know when I'm finished. I want to see everything."

"It will take days, if not weeks," Tsuna warned. "And not all of it is useful. There are plenty of uninteresting day-to-day reports."

"Owari Colony was my home." Auri blinked away the sting of tears in her eye. "I want to know everything about it. I want… I want everything we sacrificed to mean something."

"I hope you find some answers, Auri," Tsuna said. "And some comfort too. I only watched a few clips, but it was clear that Elinor loved her daughter very much."

Tsuna's kindness only resurfaced Auri's final memories of the Bleeder Elinor had become: her blood pooling on the floor after Malachi tore apart her brain with bullets.

She would've killed you, Auri scolded herself. *Not just killed you, but eaten you alive.*

Auri realized an uncomfortable amount of time had passed. "Thank you." She forced a smile. "Bird, you've got free range of the ship."

Birdie gave a huff of understanding, her nose still buried in her bowl.

Auri strode to the spiral staircase in the corner of the kitchen and hurried down. The sitting area below was thankfully empty. Someone had even cleaned the low table in the center of the room, which was always littered with coffee rings and bits of dried rice. The bookshelves were even tidied, every knickknack shoved to the upper shelves, the lower ones filled with wires, tablets, and naked motherboards.

Auri snagged one of the blankets folded in a neat pile atop the larger of the two couches. She lowered herself onto a loveseat and turned on the tablet. As soon as it powered on, the tech synced with her c-tacts, and controls appeared in the corner of her vision. Auri opted to transfer the files to her cloud c-tact storage so she could view them without the tablet.

While the tablet transferred the video files, Auri forced herself to nibble on the protein bar. The promised chocolate and strawberry flavor tasted like chalk. Every time she tried to swallow, nausea rose, but she forced down every bite.

Data transfer complete flashed against the lower left of her vision. Auri took a slow breath and skimmed the contents. They were saved in a video diary format using simple dates for file names.

Auri opened the first video. As it loaded, the paused thumbnail showed a smiling woman caught mid-sentence, her wavy red hair held back in a claw clip, her hands a blur.

"Hello," Auri whispered to the image. "Mom."

ELINOR ꟼAYRE
VIDEO LOG #01

February 14, 3277
Location: U.S.J.S Nozomi

"No one calls me Elinor." A fiery-haired woman leans to adjust something just above the lens. She shifts back into frame. Her arms cross over a white jumpsuit. A nametag at her shoulder reads *Dayre Elinor, Botanist III.*

"You can call me Marnie," she says. "Whoever you are, watching this video. Probably just future me."

A loud crash comes from off camera. Marnie releases a slow breath and closes her eyes as if summoning the dregs of her patience. She stands in front of a circular window, the vastness of space visible through the glass.

"Everything okay?" she calls.

Another crash makes her pinch the bridge of her nose between thumb and forefinger. "I could be in cryo sleep right now," she mutters.

"We're fine!" a male voice is quick to call.

Marnie frowns, but she clears her throat and continues. "I am a level three botanist. That skill got my surviving family seats aboard the *Nozomi*." She places a hand over her heart, thumb and forefinger out like a gun and the others curled.

"It's the last ship bound for the New World, and our commanding officers ordered some of us to record video logs. While inconvenient, maybe I'll be glad to have them in the future. A *future* wasn't something I was brave enough to even pray for back on Earth.

"Earth…" She trails off as if searching for the right words, only to shake her head. "Earth doesn't matter. Not anymore." Her gaze meets the camera. Her brown eyes are determined, her hands tight fists. "Roanleigh is a new start. A saving grace. We land tomorrow, and I—"

A blur enters the room. The camera shifts to follow, revealing a corner with two chairs and a table. The lens settles back on Marnie as the blur slams into the woman's legs.

A child wraps her arms around Marnie's knees. "*Mooooommy,*" the little girl whines. Her red hair is a shade darker than her mother's vibrant copper. "You promised we could go to the greenhouse."

Marnie sighs as a man enters the room. His brown hair is buzzed close to his head. A large scar runs down the left side of his face where one of his eyes is covered with a patch. His white jumpsuit reveals his name as *Dayre Aldin.*

"Sorry, Marn," he says, playfully crinkling his nose at the young girl. "This rascal escaped."

Marnie smiles at him. "It's okay, love. I was wrapping up anyway." She kneels in front of her daughter. "Looks like you've been playing in my soil samples. I knew I should've waited to take them out." She swipes at a smudge of stubborn dirt on the child's jaw, then seems to remember the camera. The woman doesn't look back to the lens, now wiping the child's cheek with her white sleeve, rendering it dirty. "Camera, stop recording."

CHAPTER ELEVEN

Auri watched Elinor Dayre's video logs over the next few hours. At first, she recoiled every time she saw her younger self, especially in the final video, but soon her parents consumed her attention. She studied the graceful way her mother moved, the tender way her father loved his wife.

It became abundantly clear that Auri—Elodie—was adored. Which made the GIC's lie even more abhorrent, painting her parents as people who would abandon their dying child.

After her third rewatch, she realized one of Roanleigh's colonists looked strangely familiar. She pulled up the crew interviews from the other intel Tsuna had added to the tablet. The man she recognized was named Othniel "Niel" Davis. She didn't recognize the name, but the longer she watched his video interview, the more she felt like she knew his mannerisms. The way he straightened his white jumpsuit and ran a hand over his hazel eyes. Maybe it was a surfacing memory?

Auri tried to ignore the sense of familiarity, but it became like an unreachable itch. Malachi had been through more of the intel. Maybe he could point her in the right direction.

She threw off her blanket and stood, nearly face-planting onto the carpet. Her organic leg tingled with pins and needles. She grimaced as she limped up the spiral staircase. By the time Auri searched the kitchen, cargo hold, and stifling engine room, the sensation had worked its way out of her leg. Malachi could only be one other place.

Auri squared her shoulders and ventured to the captain's quarters. She knocked, and a muffled voice said something like *come in*.

She slid open the door.

The captain hunched at the low *kotatsu* in the center of his room, a holo projected before him. It looked like the schematics of an engine, but as the door opened, he tapped it clear and whirled around. His hand curled around the coil gun resting on the floor beside him. Then he saw Auri.

"What are you doing here?"

Auri swallowed, fighting the heat rising on the back of her neck. "I… I thought you said come in."

"That was my holo talking through a simulation." He lowered his gun back to the floor.

"*Gomen*," she apologized, raising her tablet. "But I think… I know you've gone through my mom's video logs…"

"I have. Almost halfway through the other keyworded intel." He reached for the holo disc and pocketed it before standing.

"I—" She cut off, realizing he only wore a pair of tight sleep pants. Warm light glistened on his broad shoulders and chest. Muscles flexed as he crossed his arms, watching her. The tattooed names curling around his arm stood out on his skin. Heat rushed to her organic cheek. She took a step back. "I didn't realize you'd be in your pajamas—"

"It is after 2300, you *aho*," he teased, moving closer to take the tablet she offered.

Auri swore. "I'm sorry. I had no idea it had gotten so—"

"What did you find?" He led the way back to his *kotatsu* and sat down. Auri followed, sliding her legs under the warm blanket.

Auri loaded the video where she first saw Othniel. "Watch this." She studied Malachi's expression as the footage played. When the section she wanted him to see finished, she paused the log.

Malachi's brows drew together, and he winced. The bruising around his face looked even worse in the dim light of his room. "This looks like a colonist helping your parents assemble furniture."

Auri rewound the clip and paused it over Othniel's face, slightly blurred and out-of-focus. "Does he look familiar?"

Malachi zoomed in. He studied Othniel for a beat, but then shook his head. "Why would I recognize him? You're the only Owari survivor."

"I thought that too, but..." Auri pulled up the man's interview. "His name is Othniel Davis. He goes by Niel. The Roanleigh mission recruited him for his mechanic skills. He was a Level Two Fixer."

"A Renaissance man of the ship," Malachi murmured as he skimmed through the interview. "Do you think he avoided becoming a Bleeder?"

Even the man's voice sounded vaguely familiar to Auri. The timbre of it, if not the strange accent that elongated his vowels. She wanted to yank at her short hair in frustration.

"Well," Auri began, recalling the final video with a pang of loss, "he, of anyone, could've gotten off planet. Not transformed, somehow."

Malachi lowered his voice to a more sympathetic tone. "I doubt he made it. If he did, why didn't the truth about Roanleigh come out? There aren't any records of him anywhere I've seen."

"I do have a living brother," Niel replied to one of the interviewer's questions, drawing Auri's and Malachi's attention back to the tablet. "But it won't be a problem, if I'm selected."

Malachi finished the video and then leaned back. "*Maybe* he gives me some déjà vu. But nothing concrete." He shook his head and handed the tablet to Auri. "How are you feeling after watching Elinor's logs?"

Auri swallowed. "It's a lot to take in."

Malachi cleared his throat, bruised eyes meeting hers. "Aurelia, I know it won't change anything, but I am sorry for your mother. Back on Harlequin. If I had a do-over, maybe I could've made another choice."

"She was going to kill me, Malachi," Auri whispered. "I know that the woman—the Bleeder—in the Spire was not Elinor Dayre. I just wish I knew how they became Bleeders. And why I'm *not*."

"Every settler seems eager to forget Earth," Malachi mused. His gaze moved to the large window above his bed, unslept in and still sporting the hospital corners drilled into every recruit in basic. Auri doubted there were many citizens of the Ancora Federation who *didn't* make their bed with hospital corners.

"El—" Auri caught herself. "My mother's brief mentions of the planet made it seem like they were running from something."

"The colonists became Bleeders," Malachi said slowly as if thinking aloud. "And they came from Earth—without Ancoran approval or even knowledge."

"I can't believe no one in Ancora knew. That Earth didn't at least send a warning." Auri shook her head. "In school, we were taught Krugel cut off communication after the origin planet demanded we share resources, even though we'd been a separate entity for decades. But that comm silence happened only a year prior to the settlers' ship leaving Earth." Auri tugged at a loose thread at the hem of her shirt. "Do you think Krugel received word of their coming and ignored it?"

Malachi's brows drew together before his eyes slowly widened. He turned to her. "What if… what if Earth didn't want our supplies at all?"

Auri licked her lips. "What do you mean?"

"What if the people from Earth needed help? What if they were trying to escape and only a few reached Roanleigh?"

"Earth," Auri whispered. "You think the Bleeders originated there."

Malachi's eyes grew distant, lips curved down in a thoughtful frown. Then he cleared his throat and looked away from the window. "Get some sleep, if you can. We'll reach Medea soon for Katara's funeral."

Her lips parted in surprise. "A funeral on Medea?"

"Katara has a connection there. In an ideal world, I'd wait until this mission was complete, but Ferris needs closure."

"Mal—"

He cut her off with a raised hand. "I'll see you in the morning. Good night."

With that, Malachi walked her to the door and shut it behind her. Auri stood in the hallway, staring at the whirls and grains in the rice paper. For a moment she considered bothering the captain again out of spite for being kicked out. But then the soft glow of light through the paper clicked off. Auri let out a puff of air before she slowly made her way back to her own room.

———

The next time Auri saw the captain was at breakfast the next day. Malachi had declared the return of the mandatory meal over the *Kestrel*'s intercom system.

Dragging herself from bed had been an act of will. Auri's head and neck ached from being fixed in one position while going through Roanleigh's intel.

She and Birdie entered the kitchen in time to watch Castor tow Ferris across the room and shove the doctor into his chair.

Castor snorted in disgust. "Next time, fetch him yourself," he muttered to Malachi, who was already seated.

Ferris still wore the thermals they'd had on under their winter gear days ago. His beard was unkempt, his hair sticking up as if he'd run his hands through it over and over again. The stench of alcohol seeped from his skin.

With an unintelligible grumble, Ferris slouched with his arms crossed over his chest. He watched Castor toss a variety of protein bars on the table. Under normal circumstances, Ferris would've joked that Castor was outliving his usefulness.

Auri looked away from the doctor only to find she was passing Katara's empty chair. Her organic eye burned.

Malachi watched Ferris with a concerned frown. Auri took her usual chair between the captain and Marin. The girl didn't even turn to look at Auri. She looked distant in a way Auri hadn't seen before. As if she'd detached the human part of herself to hide from the agony of Katara's loss.

Tsuna was busy pouring green tea and bringing the small cups over to the table. She was so consumed by the task, she even gave Marin a mug.

"I don't wanna be here," Ferris slurred as Tsuna placed the tea in front of him. "I don't wanna be with *him*." He spat in Malachi's general direction, but it only dribbled down his chin, disappearing into his beard. He wiped at his face with a stained sleeve.

"Ferris," Malachi said, a warning tone in his voice.

"*Damare konoyaro*," Ferris grumbled under his breath.

Auri's eyes widened. *Uh-oh...*

Tsuna froze beside Castor, halfway through lowering his mug. "Ferris," she hissed.

"Disrespect me again," Malachi said, voice sharp as steel, "and you'll spend the rest of the journey bound in the pantry."

Ferris picked up his own cup, glaring into its contents. He raised it to his lips and took a tentative sip, only to drop the cup to the floor. He gagged once, twice, then leaned over the side of the table and vomited. After several violent heaves, he groaned, leaned over the table, and passed out.

"What did I just witness?" Castor asked, mouth contorted with one hand over his nose.

"Ferris never learned his limit with alcohol," Malachi muttered. His gaze shifted to Castor. "I'm guessing you never got around to dumping your liquor?"

Castor cleared his throat, suddenly intrigued by the steam coiling from his cup.

Tsuna started to move toward Ferris, but Malachi shook his head. "Let him sleep it off. We'll clean up after we eat."

"If any of us have an appetite now," Castor murmured, eyeing the bars with a grimace.

The chalky taste of the over-processed protein stuck to the back of Auri's throat. Her stomach knotted around what little she managed to swallow.

"We're enroute to Medea." Malachi broke the silence that had settled over the crew. "We'll hold a funeral for Katara when we get there."

Tsuna's gaze shifted from the still-unconscious Ferris to Malachi. "Thank you, Cai. He needs it." She glanced at the unwrapped but uneaten bar in her slender fingers. "We all do."

"Auri?" Malachi asked.

Auri swallowed hard and grimaced at the chunk of protein scraping her throat. "Yes?" She sipped at a mug of green tea.

"I'd like you to collect a few of Katara's belongings to bury." *Because we don't have a body.* His unspoken words haunted the empty seat where the assassin should have been.

Auri's fingers trembled around the mug. The warmth emanating from the ceramic did little to ease the chill of panic. She finally managed to squeak out, "*Me?*" Her eyes cut to each of the other crew members, almost beseeching. "You have known Katara longer than I have."

At that, a flicker of humanity stirred in Marin's eyes. The small girl turned to face Auri. "*Onee-chan*, Katara would want you to do it. She admired your warmth and how you loved so easily."

And how could Auri say no to that?

CHAPTER TWELVE

20 Sept 3319, 20:12:33
Ancora Galaxy, Planet 07: Medea,
Lot #33116

I t had been ten minutes since Malachi summoned the crew for Katara's funeral. And Auri still hadn't summoned the courage to open the door to the assassin's room.

Birdie huffed as if to say *Just open it.* The dog even raised a paw and scratched at the door.

"I know," Auri hissed. "It's just…"

Auri had never been inside Katara's room when the woman was alive. She hadn't even known her that long. Ferris should've been given this task, but something vital had fractured inside the doctor. The crew had given him space after the fiasco at breakfast, but someone needed to talk to him soon.

Auri let out a long breath and grabbed the handle. In one quick motion, she slid the door open.

The layout of Katara's room was identical to Auri's. There was a small window overlooking the dark planetscape of rural Medea. A *kotatsu* sat in the center, the blanket a patchwork of black and gray designs. Katara's built-in bed was still freshly made, the cabinets set into the wall beside it shut tight. On a small table beside her bed was an old-fashioned lucky cat clock. The secondhand made a comforting ticking sound in the quiet room.

On a large wall that was empty in Auri's quarters, Katara had mounted weapons. Knives, guns, staffs, even the practice batons had their own dedicated spaces. A particular weapon drew Auri's attention. It looked like a large boomerang at first, but on closer examination, the center had small prongs along it, as if they could unhook to become close-combat weapons.

An alert popped up on her c-tacts, informing her of a ping from Malachi. She opened it.

Get distracted? Or still in the hallway?

Auri pursed her lips and sent a reply. *Neither.*

She has an amazing weapon's cache.

Auri glanced over her shoulder, half expecting Malachi to be lurking in the hall. But only Birdie looked back at her. *Wrapping up. Ferris show up?*

A few seconds elapsed before Malachi replied. *Yes. Hurry.*

Auri dragged her attention away from the boomerang and scanned the rest of the wall. Katara would want to be buried with a weapon, that much was obvious. Auri moved to the far-left side where the wall was marred by scuff marks of frequent use. A laser katar rested in a set of hooks, black grip worn to reveal the metal underneath.

The katar was surprisingly heavy in her hand, but the weight was perfectly balanced along the grip. She laid the weapon on the bed, and it sunk into the tufted comforter.

Auri turned to the cabinets. She opened one and a scent that was all Katara wafted out: dried flowers and weapon polish. One side of shelves was dedicated to clothes: shirts, jackets, cargo pants, multiple pairs of boots.

A leather-bound journal rested on the opposite row of shelves. She picked it up, surprised at the thickness. Dried blooms and messy handwriting decorated the pages. Katara had detailed the name, meaning, and when she'd received each flower.

"Oh, Ferris," Auri breathed, flipping to the last page. A small peony, the light pink bloom now browned with age, was taped to the upper right corner. Under the date and flower name, Katara had written,

Means luck. Though it could also mean romance, which Little Warrior didn't mention. Mission: Attica prison-break.

Auri swallowed hard and closed the book. When the time was right, Ferris needed to see this journal. If only to catch a glimpse of how much Katara cared for him.

Auri slipped the book into an inner jacket pocket, then turned back to the closet.

Behind the journal Katara had wedged a small pink box. Auri stood on tiptoe to slide it out. Dust coated the top, disturbed by her tugging. Her rapid sneezes elicited a snort from Birdie.

Inside the small box a rattle nestled in a bed of white fabric. It looked like a family heirloom, unpainted and made of a polished metal. There were dents on the sides as if generations of infants had sent it clattering to the floor. Auri lifted the rattle and took one of Katara's cat t-shirts from a neatly folded pile.

A katar, a shirt, and a rattle.

Auri wanted to laugh and then sob. How could a complex woman like Katara possibly be simplified into three objects?

But she had already spent enough time choosing. Now she needed to join the rest of the crew and say her goodbyes.

———

Evening wrapped the planet of Medea in a cool embrace. The *Kestrel*'s running lights elongated the crew's shadows where they waited meters from the ramp. Beyond them, the occasional flashes of green interrupted the darkness of the rural planetscape as lightning bugs searched for their destined mate.

Auri and Birdie hurried down the ramp to join the others. The stars above her were breathtaking, the waning moon painting everything in a silvery glow. A breeze caught the loose waves at the nape of Auri's neck. It carried the smell of warm earth and fresh rain. She stopped at the end of the ramp to breathe deep. After so long on the ship, and then on the icy planet of Roanleigh, the scent of fresh, living air was a balm to her soul.

Even if it was wind that blew across Medea. It had been a month ago on this planet where she first learned about Bleeders and been hunted by them—courtesy of Malachi's scheming.

The captain turned as if sensing her thoughts. He was almost all shadow, but she was able to see his arm move as he waved her over.

Auri stepped off the ramp. Her boots sunk into the overgrown yellowed grasses of the field surrounding the *Kestrel*.

"Find what you needed?" Malachi asked as she approached.

Auri nodded, offering the items to him.

But he shook his head. "Give them to Ferris." He spoke loud enough so Ferris could hear a few meters away. Then he lowered his voice for Auri alone. "He needs to be the one to do it."

"How about you give them to him?" Auri countered, nerves fluttering in her stomach.

Castor scoffed beside Malachi. "He wants to survive to see sunrise, I think."

Auri sighed. It was probably best to keep the two as far apart as possible. "Fine."

She moved down the line of gathered crew until she reached Ferris where he stood next to Marin.

"Hi, Marin," Auri murmured, resting a hand on the girl's shoulder. Marin reached up and laid her fingers atop Auri's in a touch as fleeting as a butterfly's wings.

"Don't blame the messenger," Auri said when Ferris raised his head. In the dim light, she could see shadows under his eyes and in the hollows of his cheeks. At least his hair was clean, face washed of the grime that had coated it at breakfast yesterday.

"I don't blame you," he said, voice rough with disuse. "You didn't shoot her."

Auri bit her lip. She dropped her gaze to the objects in her arms. The venom in Ferris's usually friendly eyes clawed at her insides. "I have some of her things. What do you think?" She offered them for examination.

Ferris hesitated. Then he pulled his hands from the pockets of his dark green pants and took the items. His thin linen shirt shifted as he moved, rendering the fabric almost transparent. Toned muscles shifted under his skin, and Auri caught a glimpse of a tattoo just above his heart.

Katara had caressed Ferris's skin with her fingertips, kissed his lips, *loved* him.

The assassin's final words rose in Auri's mind. Katara hadn't explicitly said so, but Auri knew they had been meant for Ferris. Auri just didn't know if sharing the words would help him…

Or break him further.

Ferris looked at the three items and his entire body seemed to shudder. He raised a trembling hand to wipe at his eyes. "They'll do. But I'm not—"

"Ferris." Marin's soft voice made the doctor turn. Her face was its usual expressionless mask, but there was a rawness to her tone. She clutched at her unusable arm. "If you refuse to do it for yourself, do it for me. For *us*. We loved her too. As capable as I am of such feeling."

"Marin," Ferris murmured. "I…" Auri prayed he finally realized he wasn't the only one hurting. That he could share his pain and together they could carry it. "All right."

Malachi strode up to a small holo stake in the ground. It projected *Lot #33116, Sold,* followed by an image to scan for further inquiry. Around the stake grew purple wildflowers, their bell-shaped blooms almost luminescent in the holo's light.

Malachi clasped his hands behind his back, standing at parade rest. "When Katara first joined the crew, she saved from each cut. After a year of being the biggest *kechinbou*—"

"Cheapskate," Castor cut in. "That woman tricked me into buying her a weapon at the Flesh Market." He shook his head, arms crossed, face turned toward the sky. "Still can't believe I fell for it." His voice cracked.

Tsuna laid a hand on his arm.

"She saved all the money she tricked *us* into spending on her behalf," Malachi continued, "and bought this piece of land."

"She wanted to raise a family here," Ferris rasped. His gaze was fixed on the holo. "It should be where she's laid to rest."

"I hoped you would agree," Malachi murmured. He straightened as Ferris approached and gestured at a small hole by his feet, a shovel beside it.

Ferris knelt. He took a trembling breath and wiped at his eyes before lowering the items. The only sound was the wind tickling the surrounding grasses and the cascade of pebbles as Ferris filled in the hole.

"I miss her," Marin murmured.

"It's my fault," Auri choked out. "She saved me."

"Katara made her choice," Marin countered. "But if you want someone to blame, look to Akki-tan. He'd be happy to take the responsibility for the entire galaxy's ailments."

"Was the Komodo ship following us?" Auri asked.

Marin's mouth twitched as if she wasn't sure of the correct response. "Yes. Since the Spire," she finally answered. Auri's jaw clenched at the revelation. "Akki-tan didn't want me to worry you or the crew, so we kept it quiet." Marin paused, then added, "Our landing didn't awaken the Bleeders on Roanleigh. The Komodo sent an electronic burst to the planet moments before the attack."

"And that alerted the hibernating Bleeders," Auri murmured, her eyes widening. Her gaze cut to Malachi. The captain offered a hand to help Ferris stand, but Ferris ignored it. "Even if he kept the Komodo from us, Malachi isn't to blame for Katara's death. What he did was a mercy. I wish Ferris could see that."

"Katara asked Malachi to kill her," Marin whispered.

Auri's head turned toward Marin so sharply, pain shot down her spine. "*What?*"

"Akki-tan forgot to turn off his ship comms. So I heard her request. She asked him to shoot her if she fell victim to the Bleeders." Marin's tone shifted to imitate Katara's rougher way of speaking. "I don't want to go out being eaten alive, Cai. *Promise me.*"

Auri thought back to Malachi's and Katara's whispered conversation in the cargo hold before Roanleigh. "Does Ferris know?"

"No. Akki-tan wants it to remain that way."

Ferris grabbed a fistful of dirt from the ground and stood. He looked down at the clumps of earth in his hands. "To Katara, the knife in the dark and ruler of—" His voice broke and he took a steadying break. "Ruler of my heart." He tossed the dirt atop Katara's buried belongings and stepped back into the shadows.

Auri approached next, scooping up her own fistful. The dirt was cold and damp in her organic hand, but rich and full of life-giving potential. Atop the pile, as if by fate, lay one of the blue wildflowers that populated Katara's small piece of land. This close, Auri realized they were harebells. A quick grid search confirmed her suspicion.

"I didn't know Katara long," Auri began. "But this land speaks of her." With her free hand, Auri plucked a harebell, twisting the stem in her fingers. Through the living thing, now slowly dying in her hands, she felt a connection to those lost: her botanist mother and Katara, on whose land the flower grew.

"Harebells have a special meaning," Auri continued, her voice wavering. "Constancy and everlasting love. Once you worked your way into Katara's heart, she gave you both things." She cleared her throat to regain her composure. "Goodbye, Katara," she whispered and tossed the dirt.

The rest of the crew took turns saying their farewells. Tsuna recounted the times she and Katara had gone adventuring off ship.

Castor admitted he would miss their one-offs. Marin quietly described the way she *saw* Katara.

Malachi was the last to approach.

"Katara could have done anything after leaving the Dispatchers," he mused. "When she showed up outside my scrapheap of a ship for the second time, I thought she was finally going to kill me. Instead, she became the second member of the crew." His grip on the dirt tightened. "Rest easy, Katara. Your wit, your knowledge, and your aim will be missed." He let the soil fall.

Silence settled heavy on the crew. Auri's chest felt raw and exposed, but no tears gathered in her eye. It felt as if she had cried herself dry.

After a few moments, Malachi spoke. "There is one last tribute to Katara on the ship." He led the way back to the *Kestrel*, bringing the shovel. The crew followed soundlessly. Ferris was the last to leave the burial site, but then he too fell in step behind Auri and Birdie.

Once they exchanged their shoes for slippers and were gathered in the living area outside the infirmary, Malachi fished an item out of his pocket. It was another holo projector, obsidian black with a luster to it, and a name engraved along the top in gold letters.

In Memory of Katara, 3296-3319.

Malachi squeezed the sides and an image of Katara appeared in a three-dimensional rendering. Ferris gasped. Tsuna covered her mouth with a hand. Katara had been caught mid-laugh, hair curling around her shoulders, her eyes almost squeezed shut, mouth open. The joy on her face was breathtaking.

Malachi placed the holo on an empty shelf. "Castor?" he called over his shoulder.

Castor approached and pulled an item out of his pocket: Katara's sword-like chopsticks. Malachi took them from the cook and laid them beside the holo.

"We will have our own memorial here," Malachi said as he turned. "The image," he added, voice soft, "is one Tsuna caught when Katara was talking to you, Ferris."

Auri glanced at Ferris to see color creeping over his ears. But it wasn't an embarrassed flush. His hands were curled into fists.

Malachi cleared his throat. "I'm sure you're all wondering what's next. Most of you have looked through the important pieces of Roanleigh's intel. Combined with what we learned from the Spire, there is enough to prove the Bleeder's existence and launch an inquiry against the GIC."

"Finally." Castor clasped his hands together. "I thought we would never—"

Malachi raised a hand to silence the cook. "I want to see the man burn for the lies he's spread, the lives he's destroyed. And he will. Tsuna has helped me assemble a report she's going to pass off to one of her contacts."

Auri's stomach twisted at the thought of the citizens of Ancora Federation turning on her adoptive father. She gritted her teeth against the guilt. Whatever his fate, he deserved it. If Malachi hadn't escaped Attica, he would be dead now, executed for allegedly killing the members of his district. Just one of many of the GIC's attempts to cover up the Bleeders.

"I would love to hack into a mandatory broadcast," Tsuna said, drawing Auri's attention. "But I'm the best there is, and even I can't touch it. My contact does have an opening in a news' network's firewall. It will take him some time, but he can get it out there and locked in on repeat for an hour."

"What intelligence are you going to share?" Marin asked.

Tsuna glanced at Auri. "Video logs that show the destruction of Owari Colony, how Auri was found and came to be in the GIC's care, the murders falsely blamed on Ancorans. I've managed to shorten it all into a three-minute clip to ensure more views. From the clip, people can jump to a forum where I've made all the intel public."

Castor's brows drew together. "*Kuso*, Malachi. You've gotten everything you've wanted. Why do you look so unsatisfied?"

Malachi tilted his head. "We have a plan to expose him, and hopefully, the GIC will be brought to justice. Unfortunately, I'm not going to be here to witness it."

"What do you mean, Akki-tan?" Marin asked.

"Was there even a point?" Ferris interrupted, gesturing to Katara's memorial. "To any of it? These years spent chasing your revenge? A purpose to all we've lost?" His voice was loud, and the last question was punctuated by his hands raking through his hair, a hopeless, desperate gesture. In the silence after, he slowly lowered his hands. He stared at Malachi, tone low and intense. "Who cares about a rogue GIC who's going to retire in a decade?"

"You joined this crew because you cared about justice." Malachi's voice hummed with a dangerous edge. Ferris shifted back a step. "*Justice,*" Malachi continued, "is the purpose to all we've lost. Justice and the pursuit of *truth*. Which is why I'm not content to just see the lying *bakayaro* brought down. I want to stop the Bleeders."

"That's very noble and all," Castor said. "But just how do you propose to do that?"

Malachi took a slow breath. "Combining the intel from Roanleigh with what we know about Earth… I believe Bleeders originated on Earth."

The statement was met with shocked silence.

"I've pinpointed the city where the Owari colonists departed," he continued. "I propose we land there, discover how Bleeders are created and how to stop—"

Ferris cut him off. "It's always the *next thing* with you!" He yanked at the black band that covered his barcode. "Consider my contract terminated. I'll be off the ship first thing in the morning." He tossed his arm band to the floor.

Cold swept through Auri. She turned toward Ferris, trying to force words past her frozen tongue. *This can't be happening.*

"Ferris," Tsuna gasped, reaching for him, but he jerked away. Pain flashed across her face, and she looked to Malachi as if she expected him to do something.

"I'll see you're given any backpay owed," Malachi said, voice deadpan, as if they all weren't watching a vital member of their crew leave.

Ferris gave a sharp nod and disappeared down a hallway. Auri stared after him, her lips parted in shock, stomach twisting in knots.

"Should someone go after him?" she asked.

"Probably not wise," Marin murmured.

"Well, *kuso*," Castor swore. "I was expecting him to do a lot of things. But leave?" He looked to Tsuna and then Malachi. "You don't really think…?"

"He's done," Malachi answered Castor's unspoken question. "I've been waiting for him to grow enough balls to say so." He prodded his still-healing nose. "It's best he's not on the crew anyway. After Roanleigh, he's a liability."

Malachi's reasoning was military logic. If Ferris lost control like that once, it could happen again. And in less ideal circumstances. But Ferris wasn't just some hired crew member. He and Malachi had grown up in the same district, were *friends*.

Malachi studied the remnants of the crew. "Anyone else? Hopefully Roanleigh reminded you of the dangers we face. If you have any doubts, I want you out. Marin, that means you too. You're not trapped here."

Marin frowned. "Stop being self-deprecating, Akki-tan. It doesn't suit you."

"I'm staying," Auri said. "What is the point of trying to expose the GIC if we can't put an end to the Bleeders' threat? We need to go to Earth. Katara… I want her loss to mean more than the GIC's removal."

Castor glanced at Tsuna, who raised her brows as if to say *Well, I'm not going anywhere.* The cook sighed and nodded at Malachi. "How do you propose we even get to Earth? It took the

Roanleigh settlers, what, a *year*? I'm all for causes, but a year of my life just sitting on this ship—"

"I stole engine schematics from a warehouse on Babbage," Malachi said, straightening. "I've been studying them. They detail a prototype improvement to Falcon class ships that would shorten the travel time to Earth by at least tenfold—about two months travel time."

"Sounds pricey," Tsuna mused.

He nodded. "We can sell the winter gear and anything else we don't need. I'm hoping that will be enough to get all the parts. We'll need to refit the *Kestrel* to help her handle the increased speed. Should take me a few days."

Tsuna ran her fingers over her braids. "If Earth advanced past Roanleigh's fossil of a computer system, I might need time to get up to speed."

"I'm hoping what you used for Roanleigh will work," Malachi said. " I doubt Earth technology improved much after the Owari colonists left." He sighed. "Of course, we have no way to know for sure, so get whatever you need to feel prepared."

"Are we..." Auri glanced back the way Ferris had gone. "Are we going to hire another doctor?"

"No," Malachi said.

Castor's eyes widened. "*Chikusho*, Malachi, what if we get hurt?"

"Pray it isn't life-threatening," he said, voice hard. "I'm not bringing anyone else onto this crew, and we don't have time to vet a new candidate anyway. Take the next few days in Medea to get the supplies you need. Castor, stock up on MREs for the crew. Get four months rations and a two-week surplus in case things go to *kuso*. And make sure you all have extra weapons." His gaze met each crew member's. "Earth hasn't been contacted in over fifty years. Who knows what we're walking into."

CHAPTER THIRTEEN

20 Sept 3319, 22:58:06
Ancora Galaxy, Planet 07: Medea,
Trade District

"What's on the list?" Auri asked. She hurried down a long flight of stairs bolted to the exterior of a six-story building. Malachi strode an arms-length ahead, his broad shoulders covered by his brown leather jacket.

They had taken the *Kestrel*'s shuttle to Trade District, one of Medea's bartering ports. Castor and Tsuna had visited earlier in the day and successfully sold the winter gear and stocked up on weapons and MREs, per Malachi's instruction. Now all they needed were supplies to refit the engine—a task best done under Medea's darkness, according to Malachi.

They touched down on a small roof lot where Auri had been shocked to learn the exorbitant cost to park.

But Malachi explained that this was one of the few lots with security monitoring and an owner that didn't auction off the parked ships—or their contents—to the highest bidder.

Auri tried to reign in her disgust. They *were* on Medea, though she only knew the planet by its reputation. Other than a Bleeder-infested FOB, all she'd seen was an out-of-date transport terminal and the crowded city beyond it.

Much like that other city, Trade District was comprised of two-story buildings, all walls and windows without a tree or even a potted shrub in sight. There were a few taller buildings, but they capped at six stories, parking lots fixed on their roofs.

Even at the late hour, the district was lit brighter than the running lights of the *Kestrel*. Pedestrians hurried across narrow streets just wide enough for hoverbikes or trucks hauling cargo. Shuttles zoomed overhead, blotting out the starless sky and half-moon, the air thrumming with the sound of their passing. The district smelled of fried bread mixed with the odor of rotten garbage.

When they reached ground level and Malachi still hadn't answered her question, she caught his shoulder before he stepped into the crowd.

"What is on our list?" she asked. "Or did you want me to come just so I can follow you around like some clueless pinion?"

"A *pinion*?" Malachi raised his brows. "I'd like to meet the man brave enough to call you that." He tugged her aside as a lanky boy darted past. Three broad men pursued, blasters clutched in their hands.

Auri turned to stare after them, wondering if she should intervene, but Malachi spoke. "I'll worry about the list. You watch my six. Medea's districts are unpredictable." He led her into the crowd. Everyone stood so close she could smell their dinners. The crowd shifted to the left as a hovercycle rushed by. Malachi's back pressed against her chest, and the warmth of his body sent a rush of excitement through Auri. Her mind flashed back to their stolen moment in the bathroom, her hair wet on her shoulders, his hips against hers—

Then the vehicle passed and the crowd spread out again.

Auri and Malachi followed the current of pedestrians along the sidewalk. Blue lights set into the streetlamps above deepened the purple bruises under Malachi's eyes and along his jaw. He caught her hand as they moved down the main thoroughfare.

Auri glanced down at their linked fingers. Butterflies flitted about her stomach. *It's not romantic,* she chided herself. *He doesn't want me swept up by the crowd.*

They stopped at a crosswalk as more vehicles sped past. There had once been an automated barrier to keep pedestrians from jaywalking, but someone had stabbed a rusty machete into the solar box that powered it. People crossed whenever they wanted, regardless of signals.

Malachi chuckled at Auri's gasp when a jaywalker nearly collided with a hovercyclist. The two paused mid-lane and shouted at each other. The cyclist reached for a gun strapped to her thigh and the pedestrian fled.

The crossing signal flicked to green, and they hurried across the street. Malachi led them down a side alley lined with brown and orange awnings. After a few minutes, he stopped at outside a door labeled *Pieces & Parts – All Machine Engines.*

"This is it," he said, releasing her hand. Auri felt a pang of loss at the severed connection. To hide it, she reached for the door, but Malachi caught her arm.

"Put away your DISC background for this one," he warned. "Harold, the owner, will sniff it out faster than Birdie on a target's trail."

Auri's brows drew together. "What're you talking about? I lost my disc on Roanleigh." She gestured to the laser dagger sheathed at her hip, the only weapon she had left.

His brows drew together. "You lost...?" Then he shook his head. "I meant the way you view the world." He nodded at the building's second story. "Harold owns this whole block. He runs a fight ring upstairs. They pit militia POWs against each other. Whoever walks away earns their freedom."

Auri knew renegade militias were a common problem across the Ancora Federation, especially on the rim planets like Medea and Delfan. Dishonorably discharged soldiers, or those who left the service with no clear direction, usually ended up a militia member. Which was just a soldier's term for interstellar gangs who terrorized those unable to fight back.

"Don't let him get a reaction out of you," Malachi said. "Katara hated Harold, but he'd never know it."

A pang went through Auri at the reminder of the assassin. Auri schooled her features into a mask of what she hoped was indifference.

It must've passed muster because Malachi shoved open the door. An old-fashioned bell rang as they stepped through. The room beyond was bright but surprisingly small given the exterior. A single counter waited just ahead with a young boy sitting behind it. His gaze was far away, likely watching something on his c-tacts. To their immediate right, a single staircase spiraled to the floor above, a small barcode scanner fixed on the wall beside it.

"We're being watched," Malachi whispered as they strode up to the counter. He tapped the small bell that had a sign next to it reading *ring for service.*

The soft *ding* made the boy jump as if a gun had gone off. He nearly toppled off his stool.

"*Gomenesai, gomenesai,*" the boy mumbled as he bowed, rubbing at his flushed neck.

"Hey, kid. Harold around?" Malachi asked, crossing his arms and leaning against the counter.

"He's in the back" was the mumbled reply. The boy had a buzz cut with the beginnings of a moustache on his upper lip. He couldn't be much older than twelve. Probably hadn't even taken his high school entrance exams yet—commonly known as the ASVAB—which eventually determined his service branch and role.

"You know I'm always around for you, Captain Malachi!" came a deep voice.

Behind the boy, a door slid open and a hunch-backed man in a tailored suit hobbled out. Even bent nearly in half, he stood almost as tall as Malachi. The man leaned on a cane decorated with an eagle's face carved mid-scream. His dark brown, almost black, gaze shifted from Malachi to Auri. A gleam lit in his eyes. It made her want to cross her arms over her chest and glare. Instead, she took a slow breath and offered him a cold smile.

"Well, yer new," Harold said, returning her smile with his own, showing too many teeth. He clapped a hand on the boy's shoulder. The kid tensed and looked down at the worn wood floor. "Lucky I was watching the feed," Harold continued. "Or I might've missed my favorite customer." His grip tightened and the boy winced.

Auri slid her tongue between her teeth to resist clenching her jaw. *Calm*, she thought. *Be like Katara. Katara wouldn't care about some stranger. Kid or not.*

"Good to see you, Harold," Malachi said, straightening with a nod. "I'm looking for something specific. High end."

Harold shoved the boy aside to approach the counter. He rested his cane on the polished mahogany. "If I don't have it, I can find someone who does."

Malachi inclined his head. "That's why I always come to you first."

"Who is your pretty lady?" Harold asked. "Or should I say…" His brows rose toward his white hairline. "*Clank?*"

Auri nearly bit her tongue in two. Malachi laid a hand at the small of her back. "She's not for sale, Harold. Are we going to do business or not?"

Harold held up his hands. "What are you looking for?"

While Malachi described the part, Auri watched the boy. His gaze remained on the floor, mouth a thin line, hands fidgeting in his lap.

He's scared, Auri thought. And her heart ached. How had such a young child gotten tangled up with Harold? Where were his parents?

"That's an awfully fancy piece you're looking for," Harold mused, drawing Auri's attention. She started to find him watching her. His gaze cut back to Malachi, and he caressed the eagle head atop his cane. "Rare to see it on this side of the Curve."

"I came to you for a reason," Malachi said. "So can you get it or not?"

"Boy, get the boxes in section E, numbers 483, 594, and 596." Harold snapped his fingers and the boy hurried behind the door. He turned his attention back to Auri. "Your legs aren't as nice as the other woman's, but I've always had a weakness for clanks." He slid around the counter and drew closer to Auri, stopping half a meter away. His smell washed over her: copper and vanilla. She locked her knees and refused to step back. Harold only grinned and turned to Malachi. "I'll give you my best offer for the cyborg."

Malachi cocked his head in a friendly way, but the look in his eyes was icy. "I already said—"

"Everything's for sale," Harold cut in, baring his too-perfect teeth. "For the right price."

Auri had been bullied. She'd been beaten. But she had never been made to feel like an object. Anger pulsed hot under her skin.

The door behind the counter opened, and the boy returned carrying three stacked metal boxes, the load reaching to just beneath his nose. His forearms flexed as the boxes wobbled.

"Took you long enough," Harold snapped. "Bring it around so the captain can get a good look."

The boy scurried around the counter as the front door slammed open. At the sudden sound, the boy stumbled—just a step, but enough for the lighter top box to slide off and hit the floor. The metal lid remained secured, but something inside clanged in a likely broken way.

Harold rounded on the boy. He unsheathed his cane, baring a thin, sharp blade. "That's your last accident, boy." He raised the weapon. The boy threw his arms up with a whimper.

Auri slammed into Harold, her arm going up to stop his from descending. She caught the eagle handle and yanked it free. Then she leapt back into a protective stance before the child.

"Don't touch him," she hissed.

To her surprise, Harold's face remained expressionless. He pulled a kerchief from his blazer and wiped his brow. "Impressive." The single word carried a threat that made Auri's grip tighten on the cane.

"Aurelia," Malachi said, voice tense.

Auri blinked as the haze of adrenaline receded. Small red dots covered her chest. She followed the beams of light. Automatic defense guns had popped out of the ceiling, detecting her as a threat.

She swallowed but didn't drop the weapon.

Harold folded and pocketed his kerchief. "Captain," he said, an edge of controlled fury lacing his words, "you better get a hold of your *yariman*."

Someone snorted, and Auri realized another person was in the room. A hulking man in an oversized trench coat, damp at the shoulders, waited at the door. He looked vaguely familiar, and Auri realized he had been part of the trio chasing the other boy through the streets not an hour ago.

Malachi crossed his arms. "You were about to splatter blood all over your inventory, Harold. That's no way to do business. My *partner* saved you the hassle of cleanup. But…" He eyed the boxes and shook his head. "You and I both know these are too big to be what I need. Why are you wasting my time?" He turned to Auri. "Give Harold back his pointy stick. We're leaving."

At first Auri didn't move, afraid the guns would activate. But when Malachi cleared his throat, she relented.

"Here," she said, voice steely. She held out the weapon to Harold, hilt first.

He snatched it, and the edge sliced into her organic skin. Auri hissed, clenching her hand into a fist to dampen the pain.

Harold grinned at the sight of her blood oozing down the blade. He sheathed it. "Safe mode, activate," he called. The dots on Auri's chest disappeared, and the guns retracted back into the ceiling. Harold watched Auri for a beat longer before facing

Malachi. "One strike is all I allow, Captain. I don't want to see you in my shop again. No matter how much cred you toss around."

"Understood." Malachi grabbed Auri's arm and led her toward the doors. At the sound of a hard object hitting skin and a pained cry, Auri tried to turn around.

But Malachi yanked her past the burly man and into the night. He didn't release her until they were a few streets over from Harold's shop.

Auri jerked away and leaned against a building, her palm burning, blood dripping between her fingers. Her heart hammered in her chest and that sickening *smack* echoed in her mind.

Malachi whirled on her. "What were you thinking?"

"*Thinking?*" she snapped. "I wasn't going to let a boy get murdered in front of me. How could you just stand there?"

"I just *stood there* because now that kid is likely to get double what Harold was originally going to dish out." He ran a hand through his hair, took a few steps away from Auri, and then strode back to her. "This was a mistake. You're not—"

"You're right. I'm *not*." Auri finished the sentence for him, ignoring the hurt coiling inside her. "I'm not *Katara*." She shook her head. "*Kuso*, Malachi. No one is Katara. Have you even let yourself mourn her?"

"Mourn her?" he hissed. "I miss her just as much—"

"*Missing* is not the same as *mourning*. As grieving." She held out her hands, wincing as she uncurled her palm. "The weight of your losses is going to break you. You aren't thinking straight. You can't just replace Katara. Especially with me. I'm… I'm not her." She ignored the catch in her voice. "I'm not just some cheap alternative to *cover your six*. I shouldn't have come with you. I'm not meant for this. I'm not good enough—"

He grabbed the front of her jacket, pulling her away from the wall, closer to him. "Don't you dare say that. You are *better* than this."

Auri swallowed hard, his face cast in the warm glow of the cafe across the street. Her mind flashed back to the bathroom on the *Kestrel*, remembered the warmth of his hand in hers as they navigated the crowded streets. The fire of her anger turned into something else. Something deeper. "Malachi…"

He stared at her for a moment, and heat blossomed between them until Auri radiated with it. Awareness buzzed under her skin, and she mentally begged him to do something. To break this agony of waiting.

"You're dangerous," he murmured, stepping back. He took a strip of gauze from a jacket pocket and caught her palm, bandaging the wound with military efficiency. "I'll head to the other two shops on my own. I'm almost thankful Harold didn't have what I needed. I'd be *kuso* out of luck right now." He pointed to the cafe. The patrons inside were visible through a large circular window at the front. The sight was a stark contrast to the darker section of the street where Auri currently stood. A holo sign glowed just above the awning: *Hole in the Wall: Coffee, Teas, and Refreshments.*

"Go in there," he instructed. "Get yourself dinner. I know you haven't eaten yet. I'll be back in an hour."

When she didn't move, Malachi added, "Ferris is inside. I'm sure he could use your company. He actually likes talking about his feelings."

Auri shifted to scrutinize Malachi's innocent expression. "Did you know he was here the whole time?"

Malachi shrugged. "I saw him inside as we came down the alley. He's at a corner booth in the back."

"Am I really here to watch your back? Or did you drag me along to keep Ferris company so he doesn't do something stupid?"

"You're not the one I'd choose to keep Ferris from doing something stupid," Malachi said, his tone teetering on teasing.

But Auri was too frustrated to find anything humorous after what happened at Harold's. "I'm getting tired of your chess playing, Captain Malachi Vermillion. Stop hiding things from me." Her voice lowered. "Marin told me the truth about the Komodo ship. Next time something like that comes up, *you tell me.*" Auri refused to escape the GIC's control only to be led around by a renegade captain. No matter how much she liked him.

Malachi's lips twitched as if an angry reply teetered on his tongue. Instead, he shoved his hands into his jacket pockets, flashing the coil guns secured at his hips. "I'll be back in an hour."

"And if you're not?"

"Wait for me."

Before Auri could argue, he strode from the alley onto the main thoroughfare and disappeared into the crowd.

CHAPTER FOURTEEN

20 Sept 3319, 23:30:06
Ancora Galaxy, Planet 07: Medea,
Trade District

Ferris didn't look up as Auri slid into the booth across from him. The cushion creaked and a split in the middle gaped like a grinning mouth. She lowered the pastry she'd bought at the front counter—a chocolate croissant—onto the table.

"Curse you, Tsuna," he muttered, glaring into the cup of tea nestled between his palms. "You went and told Malachi." An ambient violin and piano medley played, overlayed by the murmur of conversation. The place smelled deliciously homey: fresh pastries, brewed coffee, and frying bacon.

"What are you talking about?" Auri asked.

Ferris finally looked up and gave her a tired smile. "She gave me the third degree when I left the ship, so I admitted I was coming here. She must've told Malachi, and Malachi—"

"Sent me to check on you." *When I couldn't handle the mission,* Auri silently added. She broke her croissant in half and attempted to banish the frustration still burning in her chest over the *Kestrel*'s captain. "This looks amazing." She held out one end. "Try some."

He hesitated before he took the other piece and took a bite. His eyes widened. "That is really good." Auri had only managed a few mouthfuls of her half before his was gone. The doctor must've been hungrier than even he realized.

A waitress stopped to check on Auri's food. Auri didn't bother asking Ferris before she ordered them both a breakfast platter.

"You didn't need to do that," Ferris said, eyeing her remaining croissant half.

"When did you last eat?" she asked.

He opened his mouth then shut it with a shrug.

Thousands of responses crowded Auri's lips. From expressing concern to apologizing for his loss.

Instead, she asked, "Why come to a café if you weren't going to eat?"

He looked out the window to the dark street beyond. "It's where I fell in love with Katara," he whispered. Auri leaned forward to hear him over the music, clink of cutlery, and chatter. "I accompanied her when she bought her land. She thought my upstanding look would help sway the owner. And I have experience with land purchases." His hands came around the cup again, as if trying to draw warmth from it. "We didn't know each other well. I had only recently joined the crew. Afterwards, she took us here."

Ferris pointed to an empty booth beside a holographic fireplace. The flames flickered in and out of focus like a bulb hovered on the verge of death. "We sat there. And for once I was nervous. *Speechless.* This gorgeous, powerful woman was sitting across from me, and I forgot how to breathe." A phantom smile curled his lips. "Thankfully this old woman came by. She was peddling these miserable, half-dead weeds."

Realization made Auri's eyes widen.

"I bought her a wilted daffodil, vaguely recalling my mother telling me they meant *new beginnings*. Katara seemed surprised, like she'd never been given flowers. After that, I studied flower symbolism, and when I could, I gave her a bloom before she left on missions. It was a beginning. Our beginning."

"That's beautiful," Auri murmured, forgetting, just for a moment, that Katara was gone.

"But I ruined everything." Ferris slammed his fist on the table, rattling the silverware and startling the waitress as she approached with a plate the size of Auri's torso. *Onigiri*, fried eggs, bacon, sausage, and butter-slathered toast were piled high. The waitress dropped two pairs of disposable chopsticks before fleeing.

Ferris didn't seem to notice the food. "I told her I loved her too soon," he rasped. "I knew better. Knew *her* better. I was just afraid I wouldn't have the chance…"

"She loved you," Auri murmured.

Ferris shook his head. "Don't lie to me, Auri. She—"

"I'm not." Auri caught Ferris's hand. It was different from Malachi's, devoid of calluses and cooler to the touch. "Before… Before she let go, she told me to tell you that she loved you, she always did."

Ferris's fingers closed around hers, the grip borderline painful. "She said that?" His voice cracked with emotion.

"I'm sorry I didn't tell you sooner." She slid her hand free to reach into her jacket. "But you were so…"

"Drunk?"

"Anguished," she corrected with a gentle smile. "I found this in her room." She pulled out the small leather-bound journal and handed it to him.

Ferris flipped through the pages, and tears pooled in his eyes. Auri looked away to give him privacy. She picked up her chopsticks and made a show of eating, though the food that had looked so delicious moments ago made her stomach clench.

"Thank you."

Ferris's voice made Auri look up. "For what?"

"For giving this to me." He clutched the journal against his chest. Then, to Auri's surprise, which she was careful to keep from her face, Ferris broke his chopsticks apart and began to eat.

While he polished off the *onigiri* and took a sip of his green tea, Auri finally got the courage to ask, "Are you really going to leave?"

"I can't stay," Ferris said, matter of fact. "The memories alone are enough to drown me. I know Malachi did the merciful thing, but I can't let go of my anger. At him. At the Bleeders. It's the only thing I can cling to. I'm what an officer would call a loose blaster. You and the crew don't need that kind of liability. There are already enough unknowns."

Auri understood, but still wished things were different. "Where are you going to go?" she asked. "How can I find you if we get back?"

He shrugged. "I'll volunteer at a clinic on the rim. I've got enough creds saved up to last me a few weeks until I get on my feet. And *when* you get back, I'll be a ping away."

Auri tucked a curl behind her ear. "I wish I shared your confidence about surviving Earth."

"You've got that AB blood type," he teased, showing a glimmer of the old Ferris. "You'll be fine. I like your hair, by the way." He gestured to her short curls. "Katara… Katara would approve." He cleared his throat and glanced out the window, blinking quickly. "Captain coming back for you?"

"He said he was," Auri answered, toying with the ends of her short waves.

"I'll stay until he does."

They fell into an easy conversation, talking about the planets they had visited. Ferris had traveled in similar circles to Auri, serving in the Air Command as a field doctor. His luck had gotten him out of a lot of scrapes. The stories he shared from basic and beyond had her laughing.

Malachi eventually returned, proud owner of the illusive engine part. He offered Ferris a ride, which the doctor agreed to. As the trio walked back to the shuttle, Auri hoped what Ferris had said during their meal was right.

That whatever dangers awaited them on Earth, they would be *fine*.

ELINOR JAYRE
VIDEO LOG #02
February 15, 3277
Location: Planet 08: Roanleigh, Owari Settlement

A blurred figure leans into the camera, fiddling with switches on the drone. She tongues her cheek, and her breath fogs the air. The image focuses to reveal a hazy Marnie, standing in the snow and frowning at a watch on her wrist, the skin underneath reddening with cold. After she taps a few buttons, the camera drone chirps in response.

A thick crimson braid hangs over a shoulder of her white jumpsuit. Snowflakes glitter on the strands. The video becomes even clearer. Marnie leans back, satisfied.

Behind her, Aldin trudges into a dwelling, tapping the outer rim of the door and murmuring, *"Ganbatte."*

"We'll need all the luck we can get to finish set up before dark," Marnie calls over to him with a smile.

"Get in here and help then, ya minx."

"Sorry about that," she says, breath misting from her lips as she turns back to the camera. "Or I should say *gomenasai,* to start acclimating. My husband is well on his way to being a native speaker." A shiver rakes her body as she gestures behind her to a swath of snow pocked with circular dwellings. "This is video log 002. We've officially landed on Roanleigh and dropped our prefabbed houses. Welcome to the Dayres' home sweet home." Marnie gestures for the camera to follow and does an about face.

She approaches the round structure where Aldin disappeared. In the front is a short tube with an inset door and porch. Using the antique doorknob, she pulls the door open and steps inside. The camera lens fogs with the temperature change. Marnie pauses to wipe it with her sleeve.

The camera follows her down a narrow hallway lit with fluorescent bulbs. Curved walls show a tinted version of the snowy landscape outside.

Marnie stops near a shoe rack and unlaces her boots. "All of the temporary housing on Roanleigh is built to specific requirements for each family. We hope to get help from the other planets once we alert them to our arrival. Though I doubt they'll be pleased at first."

She shuffles in her stockinged feet through the next door.

The circular room beyond is a myriad of biodegradable boxes. Aldin hurries about the kitchen, storing cutlery and MRE packs while simultaneously checking that the fridge and other electrics are powering on.

One of the larger human-sized boxes shifts and reveals a young man behind it. A knife gleams in one hand as it slices through tape.

"Thank you for helping!" Marnie calls to him, shoving up the sleeves of her white jumpsuit. The young man wears a matching outfit, except his shoulder patch says *Fixer II.* Marnie squints at the nametag above it. "Othniel Davis?" she asks. "Is it Othniel or do you prefer a nickname?"

His hazel eyes crinkle in a smile. "Niel. Always thought Othniel was a mouthful, but I was named after my grandfather."

"Understand that. I wanted to name our daughter Aurora, after my mother, but we decided on Elodie instead." Marnie holds out a hand. "Nice to meet you, Niel. And, again, thank you for helping."

Niel hurries to shake it. He seems eager to please with an almost nervous intensity. His brown hair falls in front of his eyes. "I'll have your couch assembled in a few minutes," he says to Marnie, gesturing at the box in front of him.

"Don't you have your own furniture to put together?" Aldin asks, closing the final cabinet in the kitchen. There is a quiet hum as the machinery begins to pull energy from the dwelling's power source. "Not that I mind your help."

Niel shrugs. "It's just me and my—just me. I can tackle my furniture any time. Might as well help people with kids. There aren't many families in the colony anyway."

"That's very sweet, Niel," Marnie says. She places her hands on her hips. "Speaking of kids, where is our daughter?" She directs this question at Aldin.

Aldin emerges from the kitchen. "I think she's unpacking her room." He helps Niel pull cushions from the box, followed by wooden slats that comprise the couch.

Marnie gestures to the camera drone. The image wobbles as the drone catches a current of hot air from the vents in the floor. Then it rights itself and follows Marnie down a narrow hallway.

She stops at the first door on the right. It's already open. She taps on the doorframe, calling, "El? Can I come in, little love?"

"Yup!" a child's voice responds.

The only items in the room are a pop-up cot and a suitcase, thrown open with a few pieces of clothing scattered about. Unlike the main area, the walls are solid, not offering a view of outside. The only light comes from a bulb fixed in the center of the ceiling.

Marnie rounds the cot. On the other side, Elodie sits cross-legged on the floor, her hair twisted into two braids down her back. She has just finished drawing something on the wall with a broken crayon.

"Oh, Elodie," Marnie sighs. "You know better than—" She stops as she shifts closer. Marnie tilts her head and kneels beside her daughter. The camera hovers just behind them, unable to capture the drawings.

"Is that…?" Marnie begins to ask.

"*Kanji*," Elodie answers, lowering her crayon. "I wanted to practice but couldn't find paper." She turns to look at her mom. "It's taken me so long to learn, I didn't want to forget."

Marnie rests a hand on her daughter's head. "The best way to learn is through doing. I'm proud of you. Though…" She tugs on one of Elodie's braids. "Let's try *asking* Mommy and Daddy for a tablet next time, yeah?"

Elodie giggles. "Yeah."

Marnie stands. "Go see if Daddy and Mr. Niel need any help. I'm going to wrap up this tour and then join you."

"But—"

"You can practice your *kanji* later. On *paper* or a tablet," Marnie says. "Now shoo."

Elodie purses her lips but drops the crayon and dutifully hurries out the open door.

Marnie pauses before leaving, running her fingers over the drawings, her brows drawn together almost in grief. Then she clears her throat and leaves the room. She strides down the hall, stopping outside a door with a keypad. After entering a code, the door unlocks with a cheerful chirp.

"We were all allotted one locked room for the sake of privacy," she explains, entering the small room. "I asked if I could take an unused cryo chamber." She approaches the long coffin-like tube and leans against the glass lid. "Since none of us cryo slept on the way here, the higher ups didn't mind giving me one allotted for our family. Maybe I can use it to test plant growth." She tapped the reinforced lid with her knuckles. "Either way, I have a feeling it's going to come in handy."

CHAPTER FIFTEEN

The wooden baton pressed against the hard calluses on Auri's palm. She tightened her grip and darted toward Tsuna, who watched with a bottom lip between her teeth.

"Arms up!" Auri called. She slowed her attack to allow Tsuna time to react.

Tsuna stepped forward, mirroring the technique Katara had spent days teaching Auri. The same technique Auri had used on Medea to disarm Harold.

Sometimes she wondered what became of the shop boy, but mostly her thoughts wandered to Ferris. He had snuck off the ship early the next morning, not saying goodbye to anyone. Auri had sent him a few pings, but he hadn't replied by the time they passed Roanleigh and she lost grid access.

Less than a week into the almost two-month journey, many of the crew started suffering withdrawal from the lack of vids and streams—Tsuna in particular. Which was why Auri suggested they train together.

During the long, dark days, the crew formed a routine. Auri worked with Tsuna in the mornings, sometimes with Castor and Marin watching. Afterwards, they went to the mandatory crew breakfast: protein bars and the occasional bowl of steaming rice. The bars had started sticking to the roof of her mouth, and Auri forced them down with swigs of green tea.

Afterward, everyone drifted apart. Tsuna and Castor spent most of their time in Castor's quarters. Malachi usually went to the engine room or his quarters. Marin would alternate between the bridge and the infirmary, where she read Ferris's abandoned medical tablet.

Auri spent her days breaking and reshaping her body with physical exercise: running the cargo hold with Birdie, learning more hand-to-hand combat, and doing target practice with a blaster gun she'd taken from the crew's weapons cache.

Once physically exhausted, she poured over the Roanleigh intel and the limited documentaries about Earth she'd downloaded before they left the grid.

When the Owari settlers left, the old planet was more populated than the entire Ancora Federation, but condensed into such a small space. She wondered if, among the high-tech cities with their skyscrapers and legally mandated patches of countryside, the people on Earth felt boxed in. Maybe the desire for space had been what enticed the early settlers to travel beyond the Milky Way.

She tried to imagine what Earth looked like now. Had the society advanced along with the Ancora Federation? Were the Bleeders obliterated? Or maybe kept in tight prisons where they didn't bother the populace? Did the people know what became of the final colonists sent to settle Roanleigh? Had they sent colonists to other galaxies?

Most nights she fell asleep watching her mother's video logs, memorizing Marnie's face. Aldin's voice. Trying to tease more memories from her locked mind. But that only resulted in bloody nightmares turned hazy terrors that left a sour taste in her mouth when morning came.

Tsuna's arm slammed into Auri's shoulder and Auri's focus returned to the fight.

"Sorry," Tsuna winced, pulling back. "Too hard?"

"Tsu," Castor snorted where he leaned against a wall, mortar and pestle in hand. Small vials had been laid carefully around him in a semi-circle. "She's your attacker. Don't apologize for hitting too hard."

"But…" Tsuna glanced at Auri, arms still up to block the baton.

Auri nodded. "He's right. You didn't hurt me, promise."

"Katara put her through worse," Marin said. She perched on a large crate, peeling potatoes, one of the vegetables they had in plentiful supply thanks to their long shelf life. "You need to learn to defend yourself beyond a keyboard, Tsuna. Earth will not be like the planets we know."

Birdie, curled at the base of Marin's cargo box, sneezed.

Marin had spoken the words that they had all been thinking. The *Kestrel* hurtled them toward another unknown danger, and after Katara, Auri feared not all of them would make the trip home. That thought made her gaze cut back to Tsuna. She stepped back.

"Fight like you mean it, Tsuna," she said. "You've been holding back since we started. I know your gifts are in hacking, but…"

"No amount of practice is going to help," she snapped. "Not when even Kat—"

"Just try again," Auri interrupted. "Every edge counts. If not for you, do it for me so I can have a sparring partner." She gave the taller woman a tight smile.

Tsuna sighed and lowered her arms. "Okay. Let's go through it again."

This time, Tsuna snatched the baton and swung for Auri's head. Auri ducked under the clumsy thrust, bringing her arm up in a block. Tsuna retreated when Auri reached to steal the weapon.

Distantly, Auri heard the clang of boots on the catwalk above. She blocked another blow from Tsuna and brought her elbow toward the woman's face. Tsuna dodged again. Auri rushed forward, allowing herself to pick up speed. She slammed into Tsuna, and the woman gasped. Auri caught the baton and yanked it free from Tsuna's grip as the woman swore.

Awareness prickled along Auri's sweat-dampened skin. She glanced up and locked eyes with Malachi where he stood on the metal staircase.

He wore his usual fitted pants and boots, but today he had on a dark tank top. A sheen of sweat still coated his skin, a sign he had been working in the engine room. The swirl of tattoos on his left arm stood out under the warm lighting of the cargo hold, disappearing underneath his glove. His stubble had thickened into a coarse beard.

His mouth twitched a smile, and Auri's heart skipped. She frowned. The last person she'd felt like this around was… *Ty*. She couldn't make the mistake of loving the wrong person again. The *Kestrel*'s vengeful captain with his shady morals seemed textbook "bad guy." Even if he was warm and understanding and—

A sharp bark had Auri jerking her gaze from Malachi's. Tsuna's fist slammed into the side of Auri's face. Auri grunted in pain and staggered back, dropping into a defensive stance.

Unlike Katara, Tsuna didn't rush in for another attack. The hacker's hands flew to her mouth. A few of her tiny braids had escaped their low pig tails.

"*Kuso*," Tsuna cried. "Auri, are you okay? I thought you were going to dodge!" She hurried to inspect Auri's face. Auri straightened with a wince. Her cheek throbbed with every pump of her racing heart.

Birdie loped over, sniffing at Auri's knees and licking her hand.

"I'm okay," Auri assured the poodle and Tsuna. "My own fault."

"That is definitely going to be a black eye," Malachi said.

Auri looked over Tsuna's shoulder at the source of her distraction.

The captain approached, arms crossed. "You'll want to ice that." Then he looked to Castor and Marin. "Here's the rest of my misbegotten crew." He gestured to Marin who had finished peeling potatoes. "Castor, should I pay Marin your share now?" Malachi's voice sounded sharper than usual. Auri wondered what was bothering him enough to emerge from the engine room before breakfast.

"I'm prepping poisons," Castor said, already moving the vials and dried plants into a large wooden box. "Marin offered to help."

"Have you had your coffee yet, Akki-tan?" Marin ventured, hopping down from the box.

Malachi cleared his throat at Marin's subtle rebuke. "I'm trying to cut back." He inclined his head to Castor. "*Gomen.*"

Castor shrugged, tucking the box under one arm. "Tsuna, you want to help with breakfast? Might as well try to enlist you too. I'm making a hash. Give us a break from those awful cardboard bars."

"You know my specialty is instant ramen," Tsuna said. "I'm going to clean myself up." She turned to Auri. "Are you sure you're okay? Maybe we should go to the infirmary—"

Auri held up her hands. "I'm fine. It serves me right."

Tsuna gave Auri one last concerned look before she followed Marin up the stairs to the catwalk. Castor trailed a few steps behind, letting out a low whistle of appreciation. Tsuna flipped him a rude gesture, but her mouth quirked in pleasure.

Auri caught Malachi rolling his eyes.

Onboard romances? she mouthed, tightening her nub of a ponytail that threatened to come lose.

"Destined to end in failure," he said as he approached. The rest of the crew had disappeared onto the second level.

Birdie huffed in Malachi's direction but lowered her head for a pat.

Malachi frowned. "Is this a ploy to bite me?" he asked the dog.

Birdie growled and Malachi held up both hands. Auri realized he carried a curved black case about the size of her arm.

"I have something for you," he said, noticing her gaze.

"What is it?"

"See for yourself." He held out the case, and Auri took it. For its size and bulk, it was surprisingly lightweight. Her mind flickered to the disc she had lost on Roanleigh.

Auri moved over to a cargo bin, Malachi following. She lowered the case and flipped the two latches in the middle.

"Oh." She sucked in a breath as she raised the lid. Inside lay a familiar obsidian boomerang with *kanji* engravings on one end. Auri squinted, trying to read the difficult symbols. *Hiragana* was an easier way to write and read the Japanese words but was rarely used since English was the primary language in the Federation. *Kanji* was usually written because of the calligraphy style.

Malachi moved closer. She could feel the heat of him through her sweat-soaked tank top. Smell his usual scent of lavender and engine room metal.

Auri tensed. Her entire body seemed attuned to his presence.

"It's pronounced *ganbaru*," he said, pointing at each symbol as he said the word. "It means *to persevere*. Katara changed the name from *ganko* after she won the weapon." Malachi chuckled and his hot breath fanned Auri's cheek. "That in itself is quite the story."

"I remember seeing it on her wall. Why give it to me?"

"Katara never touched it. She only won it to prove a point. Long distance wasn't her thing. But you?" He shrugged. "I think you're going to be good at both."

"Both?"

Malachi lifted the boomerang and pressed a switch at the base. The boomerang split into two identical pieces. "Batons," he said. "And then…" He pressed another switch with his thumb and a serrated blade emerged from a curved end.

"Wow," Auri breathed.

"I thought you would like it." He deactivated the blades and reconnected the batons. "It isn't powered by technology, so you can't recall it. Which is why I recommend you also practice with these." He patted a coil gun in one of the holsters at his hip.

"You're giving me one of your guns?"

"*Chikusho.* No." He chuckled. "Only way you'd get these was if you took them off my dead body. You have the blaster gun from our cache you've been practicing with. I can't stand those; they always jam at the worst times. Castor and Tsuna love them though. I suppose you can still beat someone with it." At Auri's aggrieved look, he added, "If necessary."

He lowered the boomerang back into the case and clicked the lid closed. Going into Katara's room clearly hadn't been easy for him, facing that wall of weapons and the memories hung there.

"Thank you," she murmured, taking the case when he offered it. She pressed it against her chest. With *Ganbaru,* her old life and her new had fused into one weapon.

"Now go get some ice on that eye. I wasn't entirely teasing earlier. It's going to be a shiner."

As if his words had reawakened her nerves, the throb along her cheekbone returned. She winced. "Right."

Malachi started to leave, but Auri caught his arm. He turned to look at her and she glimpsed the agony twisting inside him before he shuttered the pain away.

"I'm here," she said quietly. "When you're ready to talk. Or not talk. Just sit. Whatever you need."

Malachi huffed a humorless laugh. "I'm not grieving, Aurelia." He looked up at the ceiling, the curved dome that made up the back half of the *Kestrel*. "There is sadness. A loss of a partner and occasional friend—when she wasn't threatening my life." He shook his head and returned her gaze. "But my hatred has swallowed the sadness, the loss. I'm *angry*. Angry at the choices I've made because of the GIC's lies. But he will be made to pay for it, when Tsuna's contact publishes our intel. Who knows, he could already be reaping the seeds he's sown." His eyes sparked with malice. "All that will remain are these Bleeders and whoever the hell created them. I'm going to stop the monsters. They'll never harm anyone ever again. Whatever happens, I promise you that."

Auri could feel that anger radiating off him, the cool, indifferent mask he wore cracking at the corners.

"It's my burden." He gently tugged his arm free. "But if it ever gets to be too much…" His multi-colored eyes, so much like a splash of green and brown paints across a canvas, were clear. Determined. "I'll come and bear my soul to you." His mouth twitched in a broken-hearted smile before he disappeared through the sliding door a few meters away.

Auri's grip tightened around the case. The hinges dug into her palms. She could almost imagine Katara standing beside her, arms crossed and rolling her eyes.

"Men," Katara would grumble. "He either needs to bed or shoot something."

Auri felt heat wash over her aching cheek, as if Katara had really said it.

"I miss you," Auri whispered, praying Katara's spirit was listening. "But I think he misses you even more."

CHAPTER SIXTEEN

14 Nov 3319, 09:03:56
Milky Way Galaxy, Earth,
Free Airspace

Two paws slammed into Auri's chest and her eyes snapped open. Something thick covered her face, suffocating her. She shoved it away in a sweaty panic, only to realize it was her blanket.

Auri heaved in a breath as Birdie eased back onto her haunches. The dog let out a plaintive whine, her head cocked.

Auri swallowed, throat raw. She placed a hand atop Birdie's head. "I'm okay, girl," she rasped. "Just a bad dream."

Her heart still thrummed a rapid pace in her ears. Sweat slicked her skin and her short hair clung to her face and neck. She shoved it back with a trembling hand.

"I'm sick of these nightmares," she said around a sob. She shoved her palms into her eyes and took a slow breath.

There was a knock on the door and Auri jumped.

"Auri?" Tsuna called from the other side of the rice paper. "Auri, are you okay?"

Auri swiped at her eyes. "Yes. Hold on." She swung out of her bed and Birdie pranced away so she could open the door. Auri slid it open to reveal Tsuna on the other side.

"We're in orbit," the hacker said.

Auri's stomach dropped. Tsuna didn't need to say what planet. They'd been only a few hundred klicks away from Earth at breakfast, Marin missing the mandatory meal to stay on the bridge to monitor their approach. No one had been up for talking, even though Castor had pulled out all the stops.

He'd made fried eggs, brought out the dried fruit, bacon, and actually made *onigiri* instead of the usual rice. Auri had appreciated the effort, but it felt like a last meal. Which had dampened her appetite.

Afterwards, she'd come back to her room to rest, but only managed to get caught in another nightmare.

"Malachi sent a ship-wide announcement," Tsuna was saying. "But when you didn't show up, he asked me to get you." She squeezed Auri's arm, her skin soft and warm. "Are you okay? I thought I heard screaming."

Auri shook her head, tucking her hair behind her ears to try to make it look like less of a red tumbleweed. "Just a bad dream."

"You're not the only one with nightmares lately." Tsuna inclined her head down the hall and Auri fell into step beside her. Birdie's claws click-clacked on the floor as she followed. "If you ever want to talk, my door's always open."

"And if you're not in your quarters?" Auri couldn't help but tease.

Tsuna pursed her lips around a grin. "Cheeky, aren't you?" She raised her brows. "What about you? You and Malachi are quite the pair, hm?"

Auri froze midstride. Birdie's head bumped into the back of her knees. "*What?*"

"I've seen the simmering intensity between you two." Tsuna resumed walking. She was quiet for a moment before she spoke again, tone no longer teasing. "Be careful. Though I'm not one to talk given that Castor and I don't have a real future, but I'm still leading him on." She paused as they reached the kitchen. "Cai is one of the better men I've met, but he makes hard choices. Choices he can live with, but you might not be able to." She bumped Auri's shoulder. "Just some big sister advice."

Heat burned Auri's cheek at Tsuna's implications. Her boots clanged on the steps as she climbed up to the bridge, the cargo hold empty below her.

The limited experience Auri had with relationships had been catastrophic. Falling in love with a made-up version of her adoptive brother was embarrassing. And the ship-board romances she'd seen so far? Auri couldn't imagine experiencing the level of loss Ferris had. Or knowing her feelings had a specific timeframe like Castor and Tsuna.

"Don't worry," Auri told Tsuna as the bridge came into view, the door open and the rest of the crew clustered inside. "I've made mistakes in love before. I don't plan to repeat them."

Tsuna gave Auri's arm a final squeeze before they stepped through the door.

Castor sat in the co-pilot seat, knees knocking into the control panel. Malachi leaned around Marin in the pilot's chair, pointing at the display and asking questions. Tsuna slipped behind Castor and laid a hand on his shoulder. He looked back and smiled.

Auri stopped in the middle of the bridge. The space seemed so much bigger now. Emptier, with Katara and Ferris gone.

But the ache of their loss was pushed to the back of her mind as her gaze swept over the spaceshield. Beyond the glass loomed a planet similar in size to Aurora. But the colors… Every hue of green and blue with swirls of white.

Auri drew closer, lips parted. Her soul slipped between bones and muscle, taking flight at the beauty swirling in the darkness before her. She had approached every planet of the Ancora Federation this way. But she had never been speechless or awed by their beauty. A sense of familiarity woven into her very sinews beckoned her closer.

"Beautiful, isn't it?" Malachi asked. He watched her, one arm on the console, the other behind Marin's chair. A warm smile quirked the corner of his mouth.

He makes hard choices, Tsuna's voice replayed in her mind. *Choices he can live with, but you might not be able to.*

"*Gomen*," she said. "I missed the announcement. Fell asleep."

"Maybe you can talk sense into the captain," Castor said. "None of us have been able to." He shifted in his seat, trying to get comfortable.

"Likelihood of success is low," Marin added, an edge of petulance to her voice.

"What do you mean?" Auri asked Malachi, wondering what made him the target of Marin's ire.

Malachi ran a hand through his beard as he straightened. "Marin is upset because I'm keeping her on the ship."

Auri frowned. "What do you mean, *keeping her on the ship*?"

"I don't want to repeat Roanleigh." He crossed his arms. "We're going to take the shuttle down to the city the Owari colonists departed from and get a lay of the land from the air. The surface scans are concerning."

Tsuna slipped away from Castor. "Mind if I take a look?"

Malachi nodded and shifted closer to Auri. Tsuna looked down at the scans. Her eyes narrowed and she leaned closer. She let out a slow breath. "*Kuso*. How…?"

"Is someone going to say what the problem is?" Castor snapped. "Or do we all need to look at the display?"

"There's barely a flicker of electricity on Earth," Malachi said, gesturing to the planet looming beyond the spaceshield. "Likely failing systems or old solar power, as far as our scans can detect. That aside, the planet is completely dark."

Castor snorted. "What are you saying, their society collapsed?"

Tsuna bit her lip, expression grim. "It's a possibility."

The cook sobered. "*Chikusho.* I was joking. How could that have happened?"

Malachi's determined gaze cut to Earth where it orbited in the stillness, a beautiful behemoth. "We're going to find out. Castor, Tsuna, Auri, get geared up for a flyby to do some recon of the city."

———

An hour later, with the *Kestrel* tucked into a closer orbit of Earth, everyone gathered in the cargo hold. The scans showed their intended section had a climate similar to Rokuton: fairly warm, though thankfully not as muggy. They had dressed in hot weather gear: cargo pants and tank tops or loose-fitting shirts.

When Auri looked at the scans, she'd been amazed at the mass of vegetation combined with the very few lifeforms. What had happened to all the people before Earth went dark? Maybe it was for the best, especially if the lifeforms weren't humans at all—

But Bleeders.

Even with the advantage of the scans, they were going in blind.

She tugged at the thick strap of her high-necked tank. It had gotten caught underneath the strap of the disc holster she had refitted for *Ganbaru.* Her fingers brushed over the mottled scars at her shoulder. Auri paused to rest her palm against them.

The rest of the crew readied their own weapons. Castor slung a bandolier of pouches across his chest, each outfitted with a different poison. A brace wrapped around his right wrist hid a dart gun.

Tsuna tucked an oversized blaster gun in a holster around her hips. It tugged on the jumpsuit she wore so the already low V-neck was even deeper. Her tactical bag hung from her shoulders, stuffed with tech and MREs, "just in case."

Marin radiated nervous energy, openly staring at Malachi with sightless eyes, who was checking the spare mags for his coil guns.

Auri approached the girl. Birdie trailed behind, her working vest a dark green to blend in with their new planetscape. "You okay, *Imouto-chan*?" Auri asked.

Marin kept her gaze on Malachi. "I'm not technically human, so I don't have a sixth sense, but I fear I will not be with all of you again."

"We're going to—"

Marin cut Auri off as she spun on her bare feet and hurled herself against Auri. Auri gasped in surprise, stepping back to brace herself from falling.

The girl buried her head against Auri's chest, eyes squeezed shut. "May I listen to your heartbeat, just for a moment?"

"Oh, Marin," Auri murmured. "It's going to be okay." She hugged Marin back and rested her cheek against the cool skin of her friend's head. It felt too thick somehow—inhuman. Much like how Auri imagined her synthetic skin felt to others. Birdie butted her nose against Marin's knee in her own show of affection.

Marin pulled back moments later, one hand atop Birdie's head. "You are the heart of *Kestrel*, Aurelia. Without you, we would not be the same. Return to us."

A lump formed in Auri's throat, and she swallowed hard. "I think that's one of the sweetest things anyone has ever said to me, Marin."

"Everyone ready?" Malachi called, striding over to Auri and Marin. "You okay, kid?" he asked Marin, genuine concern in his eyes. "We won't be gone long."

"I'm not pleased to be left behind," she said. "But I under-stand why. I won't be alone. *Kestrel* will keep me company."

"Remember," he began as Tsuna and Castor joined their clus-ter. "If—"

Marin cut him off. "If you don't return within three hours, I'll put life support on low to preserve fuel. I will be fine. I only need minimum oxygen to retain brain function."

Malachi nodded. "Let's just hope it doesn't come to that."

"It's just a reconnaissance mission," Castor said. "What could go wrong?"

The captain raised his brows. "Have you ever actually been on a reconnaissance mission?"

"Well, I…" Castor cleared his throat. "I've seen things."

"By *things* he means those dramatic war movies." Tsuna elbowed Castor. "He was a mail courier for the MPB back in the day."

"Which led me to you, you backhanded woman," Castor muttered.

"We'll see you soon." Malachi rested a gloved hand on Marin's shoulder and gave it a tight squeeze. Marin laid her hand atop his, the skin almost translucently pale against Malachi's.

"Come back safe, Akki-tan," she whispered.

"No promises, no regrets," he murmured. A smile flickered across Marin's lips before she released Malachi's hand.

Castor and Tsuna said their goodbyes and headed toward the door that connected to the *Kestrel*'s docked shuttle. Tsuna pressed a button on the panel and the door whooshed open.

Auri paused at the threshold and raised four fingers to her lips. She pressed a quick kiss to their tips then touched the metal rim. "*Ganbatte,*" she murmured. *Good luck.*

"Where'd you learn that?" Malachi asked behind her.

"I saw my dad do it in one of my mom's video logs." She stepped inside. "We need all the luck we can get." She guided Birdie to one of the spots on the floor where they had installed a belt for her. Auri knelt, gave the dog a kiss, and then secured her harness to the buckles.

"A good captain makes his own luck," Malachi countered, sliding into the pilot's chair.

"Always so contrary," Auri muttered. She slipped off her holster with the boomerang and secured it under one of the bench seats.

Malachi jerked a thumb at the co-pilot's chair. "Take your seat, Co-Pilot Peri."

Auri hesitated. "Malachi…"

"I'm asking *you* to be my co-pilot. Not expecting you to replace someone else."

With that, Auri eased into the chair. The leather was cool against her organic skin. As she buckled her belts, she imagined she also secured her jangling nerves.

Castor and Tsuna settled onto a bench along one wall. Tsuna had secured her tactical bag under her seat along with Castor's bandoliers. They were clicking buckles across their chests and waists, talking in low voices.

Malachi flicked switches and initiated the startup sequence. The front headlights flicked on, doing little to illuminate the starlit space visible through the spaceshield.

He flipped a small rectangular button in the center of the console beside the u-shaped steering wheel. Static crackled through the speakers of the ship. Malachi cleared his throat. "Shuttle *Purloin* to F.T.S. *Kestrel*," he said, leaning close to the mic.

"You named the GIC's stolen shuttle *Purloin*?" Auri teased, unable to stop a grin from tugging at her mouth. "Since when?"

"It's been *Purloin* since we kept it after the Spire," Malachi replied with a wicked smile. "Ferris's idea." His smile faltered and he turned back to the mic. "Shuttle *Purloin* to F.T.S. *Kestrel*, over."

After a few seconds, Marin's voice replaced the static. "F.T.S. *Kestrel* responding. Radios are operational. Be safe, crew."

"Over and out." Malachi flipped off the radio and curled his fingers around the steering handles. "To finding answers," he said, looking ahead as the shuttle trembled around them, preparing to pull away from the *Kestrel*.

"To finding answers," Auri echoed.

CHAPTER SEVENTEEN

———

14 Nov 3319, 10:53:16
Milky Way Galaxy, Earth,
Free Airspace

Shuttle *Purloin* broke Earth's atmosphere, and a wall of white slammed into the spaceshield. The shuttle bucked. Malachi swore. Auri's grip on her chest straps went white-knuckled.

Wisps of cloud hurtled past, tinted red at the heat from their rapid descent. The floor vibrated under Auri's feet, stabilizers activating as the turbulence increased. Malachi shifted the controls, and the shuttle's sharp descent eased into a wider angle.

"Almost there," he murmured. The shuttle bucked again, and Auri slammed into her restraints with a grunt.

"Pocket of air!" he called to Tsuna and Castor. "Hold on!"

Tsuna dry-heaved.

"Don't puke on my boat," Malachi ordered. "Or you'll clean it up this time."

Purloin gave a final lurch and, as if a hand had swiped across the spaceshield, the cloud-cover vanished. Auri gasped, her chest aching from where she'd hit her harness.

Greenery engulfed everything. Auri had never seen so much green, and she had spent years on the rainforest planet of Rokuton. The closer they came to the surface, the more details emerged. At five hundred klicks, Auri could see that the surface wasn't all vegetation, as the scans showed. The plants had *grown over* man-made buildings familiar from the vids Auri had watched.

They dropped to three hundred klicks and flew over what must've been the remnants of a large city. Skyscrapers' windows were blown out, the metal supports exposed like bones jutting from skin. Long grasses covered most of the asphalt street below. Cars, foreign yet familiar in design, were parked or toppled over. A massive yellow vehicle lay upside down, deep grooves slashed along its side.

"Is this where the Owari settlers originated?" Auri asked, breaking the tense silence. Everyone stared out the windows, expressions grave.

"Yes," Malachi answered, adjusting the shuttle's trajectory. "Though they left from a base called Fort Caddel. That's where we're headed." He nodded at the spaceshield. "Scanners are detecting life readings, but there aren't many. If anyone is down there, I can't see them this high up."

"Bleeders?" Tsuna croaked. She clapped a hand over her mouth and groaned.

"Should've brought vomit bags," Castor grumbled.

"The scans can't differentiate between humans and Bleeders," Malachi said. "I'm hoping for humans."

The shuttle left the city behind, gliding over a fast-running river. A massive bridge spanned the gap between the two pieces of land. Ivy tendrilled up the curved supports and a giant oak tree sprouted from the middle. Its roots spread across the bridge to delve into the land on either side. The plant life gave the structure a fairy-tale look at odds with the post-apocalyptic city.

"What do you think happened?" Auri asked. "Could all this be why we lost communication with Earth during Krugel's term?

Maybe you're right, and the people here really were asking for help."

Krugel had been the most bloodthirsty, borderline insane GIC in the history of the Ancora Federation. But could he and his subordinates have really ignored a plea for help from their home planet?

The shuttle flew over grassland intermingled with thick patches of trees. A building appeared amidst the overgrowth. Auri would have missed it if she wasn't looking out the spaceshield. The structure was square with an inner courtyard overgrown with trees, tall grasses, and ivy. Not far away was a detached hangar that could've held at least three full-sized transport ships. A massive chain-link fence encircled the two structures. Constantia wire curled across the top.

"This is the base where the colonists departed," Malachi said.

"Whatever happened," Castor murmured, "it wasn't sudden. People had time to flee, to move around or settle in." He pointed to a bulky-looking aircraft parked on a large landing pad. The body was missing multiple slats of metal that revealed the innards, as if someone had scavenged it for supplies. "Fort Caddel looks abandoned."

"It might be a good homebase for the *Kestrel*," Malachi said. "Let's get a closer look." He steered the shuttle downward, executing a slow turn as they dropped closer to the structures below. A flock of birds exploded from the foliage growing atop the square building's roof. A blue light flashed in one of the broken windows.

"Did you see—?" Auri started.

A female voice emitted from the shuttle's speakers. "Aircraft, you are in illegal airspace. Immediate landing requested."

Malachi's hands stilled on the steering. "Marin?" he ventured. "Marin, is that you?"

"I am an automated flight warning system," the voice replied. "You may call me Betty. You have fifteen seconds to land or I will commandeer your aircraft."

"This seems like working technology," Auri said, eyes wide. Whatever blue light had turned on inside the building was dark now.

"*Maitta na.*" Malachi's grip went white-knuckled. He increased the shuttle's thrust, flipping switches. "Let's get—"

"Automated piloting initiated." Betty's voice came through the speakers again. The entire shuttle vibrated so intensely that Auri rattled in her chair like she was on a flight simulator. "Error, error, error," Betty said. "Cannot compute."

Malachi battled with the steering. No matter how hard he pulled, the mechanism wouldn't move. He opened his mouth just as a screeching keen exploded from the speakers as if someone held two walkie-talkies together. Birdie howled. Auri clapped her hands over her ears.

As suddenly as it started, the sound stopped. The shuttle went still. Auri watched in horror as the *Purloin*'s display went dark. The shuttle dropped from the sky.

The pressure of their rapid descent slammed Auri into the back of her seat.

"Hold on!" Malachi cried.

The shuttle crashed into the ground with an agonizing force, barreling straight through the side of the dilapidated hangar. The restraints dug into Auri's chest and waist. Pain radiated across her body and her spine popped. Birdie yelped and Tsuna screamed. Metal and glass exploded across the spaceshield.

The shuttle bounced once, twice, then rolled onto its side as it skidded to a stop in the center of the hangar. Auri hung out of her seat at an angle. Her head pounded, and copper filled her mouth where she'd bitten her cheek.

The sound of dry-heaving echoed through the shuttle. Auri was distantly thankful that Tsuna hadn't vomited yet. The last thing they needed was it sliding across the shuttle. The thought almost made her gag too.

"Get moving," Malachi ordered, unbuckling the harness across his chest. He dropped down, landing on what had once been a wall. "Make sure you have everything you need. We need to put distance between us and this useless piece of *kuso*. Then contact Marin somehow."

"Wait…" Castor held up a hand as if trying to clear his mind of the rush of adrenaline. He looked almost comical, tilted sideways in his seat. "We're going to leave the shuttle? What about Betty? We have no idea what we're walking into. Our scans were obviously wrong."

"Listen closely," Malachi hissed, checking that his coil guns were still snug in their holsters. "Betty or whoever engineered her will be coming to claim our bird. Not to mention we just announced our presence and our tech to whoever—or whatever—else is prowling around."

Images of Bleeders racing across the overgrown landscape toward the shuttle flashed through Auri's mind. She could already hear their claws scraping against the metal exterior.

Auri released her harness. Gravity took over and she fell, smacking her robotic knee on the console.

Birdie scrabbled against the floor, trying to find purchase with her extended claws. She hung so the full weight of her body pressed on her chest. The position did not look comfortable.

Castor helped Tsuna undo her straps. He looped an arm around her waist as she lowered herself to the floor.

"Hang on, Bird," Auri grunted. She caught Birdie's front legs as she unbuckled the belts. The poodle's weight slammed into Auri's already beleaguered chest and she grunted, dropping to one knee.

Birdie leapt out of Auri's arms. She gave a full body shake before moving to sniff at the shuttle wall that was now their floor. Her tongue flopped out the side of her mouth, but otherwise she seemed fine.

Tsuna dropped down beside Auri, followed by Castor, and they retrieved their stowed belongings. The weight of the boomerang on Auri's back eased some of the panic buzzing under her skin.

"*Chikusho*," Castor swore. He was peering out the spaceshield. "We've got company." He pointed at a group of people approaching the empty hangar from the hole made by the *Purloin*. The four moved with military precision, splitting apart to enter at the edges of the hole, weapons down, backs against the wreckage.

Malachi swore. "Can you see their weaponry? How advanced is it?"

Castor raised his arm where the dart gun was fixed. He tapped a button on it and a scope unrolled itself. He peered through.

"They all have some kind of crossbow," Castor murmured, squinting. "No electromagnetic bolts or computerized scopes. All wood and reinforced string. They also have machetes. Just the blade. Nothing fancy." He pulled back, awaiting Malachi's next order.

"We stand a chance," Malachi murmured. He looked up at the remains of the crew. "Let's see if we can avoid a firefight."

CHAPTER EIGHTEEN

14 Nov 3319, 11:46:58
Milky Way Galaxy, Earth,
Fort Caddel

Auri fingered the trigger of her blaster gun. She leaned against the open hatch of the shuttle, Birdie and Castor on her left. Her heart thudded as she looked across the ramp to Malachi. Tsuna stood just behind him. The hacker's eyes were wide as she gripped her own oversized blaster with both hands.

"We just want them to surrender," Malachi hissed, his voice drawing Auri's attention. "Don't shoot unless they give you reason. We don't know they're an enemy."

Castor snorted. "They just shot us out of the sky with technology they're not supposed to have, and you don't think they're an enemy?"

"Save the snark for when we question them." Malachi glanced beyond the open shuttle door before quickly drawing back inside. He made two quick motions with his hands: two combatants approached on either side.

The captain raised three fingers. Sweat slicked Auri's organic palm. She clenched her jaw. A breath in through her nose, out through her mouth.

Malachi slowly lowered each finger.

Three.

Two.

…One.

Auri spun from the shuttle, blaster gun raised. The two combatants on her side—one woman and the other a dark-skinned man—were a few meters from the ramp. Their gazes were on the shuttle, so by the time they saw Auri and Castor hidden by the shadows of the hangar, their crossbows were only halfway raised.

Auri allowed herself an instant to be surprised at their clothing—a strange conglomeration of metal and leather plating—before she called, "Drop your weapons and surrender."

The woman, her blond hair braided in a series of cornrows to her neck, tilted her head. She murmured something to the man, nodding at Auri's weapon. Matching expressions of confusion drew their brows together.

"I don't think they know I'm holding a gun," Auri whispered to Castor. "Or if they even know what a gun is." She pointed her blaster at the floor and pulled the trigger to show them the threat, but the weapon jammed. "*Kuso*," Auri muttered.

"Eyes on me," Castor yelled at the pair before they realized Auri's threat had diminished substantially. "Do you understand?" He raised his arm. The scope on it glowed green. "If not, I can make you. Weapons on the floor."

They glanced at each other, then looked back to Castor. The man sighed then nodded at his companion. They both dropped their crossbows, and they clanged against the cement.

Auri gawked at the weaponry, comprised of mismatched wood and metal gears. They looked… *handmade*.

"Kick them over here," Castor said, gesturing to the crossbows with his dart gun. "No sudden movements."

The woman looked like she wanted to argue, but the man shook his head. They obeyed Castor's demand and slid their weapons over.

Motion caught at the corner of Auri's eye, and she turned as Malachi came into view. The other two male combatants had their arms clasped behind their heads. Tsuna trailed just behind.

Malachi herded the men over to join Auri and Castor's captives. "It's clear you understand our language," he said. "Maybe one of you can explain why you shot our bird out of the sky."

No one moved to answer his question. The woman's eyes widened at something over Auri's shoulder. Auri frowned, cocking her head. Malachi whirled as a crossbow bolt shot through the air and sliced his forearm. Blood spattered across the cement. Malachi's coil gun clattered to the floor as he let out a gasp of pain.

"Birdie, retrieve," Auri ordered, spinning around and simultaneously raising her blaster at the unknown adversary. It might've been useless, but they didn't know that.

The poodle darted forward, snatching the gun. Castor and Tsuna kept their weapons fixed on the captives.

Malachi drew another coil gun, raised it, and called, "Show yourself!"

A shadow moved atop the shuttle. Auri blinked, realizing a woman crouched there. She held a crossbow propped on her knee, the already loaded bolt aimed at Malachi. She slowly straightened to her full height.

"Maybe," she called, voice surprisingly husky. A heavy accent made her next words harder to understand. "My people can first explain why they didn't *wait* to enter the hangar like I *told them to.*"

"Drop your weapon," Auri demanded. "Or I'll shoot." Anger boiled under her skin. In her peripherals she could see blood dripping from the gash on Malachi's forearm. It didn't look deep enough for stitches, thank the stars. But the could-have-been's crowded her mind.

"I was about to say the same," the woman countered. Her midnight black hair was tied in a tight bun atop her head, a dingy red bandana around her neck. "You may have fancy weapons, but I can still get off a shot before you shoot me dead. Are you really willing to lose this man?" She arched a brow.

Auri glanced at Malachi, who watched the woman with narrowed eyes. After a beat, his lips twitched in a pained smile. "Lower your weapon, Auri." He knelt to place his gun on the ground, pulling the third, smaller one from the holster at his thigh. "You too, Castor, Tsuna. This piece of *kuso* slicing my arm hurt enough. I don't need one in my chest."

"Captain," Castor argued, not lowering his dart gun. "We could easily—"

"Just do it," Malachi grunted.

Auri flashed back to the last—and only—time she had surrendered. Pirates attacked her shuttle, and she had her first glimpse at the darkness that lurked beyond the inner planets. Months later, the words still tasted sour in her mouth when she relayed Malachi's order.

"Surrender, Birdie."

Birdie cocked her head as if she thought Auri misspoke. Auri didn't blame the dog. Yes, they risked the woman getting off another shot, but their weapons were faster. More advanced. She wouldn't be a threat for long.

But Malachi had his reasons. Reasons he'd hopefully explain sooner, rather than later.

"Surrender," Auri told the poodle again. Birdie whined but obeyed. She lowered Malachi's gun on the ground and dropped onto her belly, head resting on paws. Auri followed with her blaster gun and knife. Tsuna was next. Castor was the last one to unbuckle his dart cuff and drop it.

"Bags too," the woman said, gesturing at Tsuna and Auri. "Or whatever's on your back, Red."

Auri bit back a grimace. She had hoped the woman wouldn't notice the boomerang. Auri and Tsuna moved at the same time, dropping bag and holster.

The woman grinned, revealing a chipped canine tooth. "Consider yourselves captives." She frowned at the other members of her group. "Grab your weapons and theirs. Maybe follow an order this time?" She waited until her people had secured their crossbows and the crew's weapons before she slid her own crossbow into a brace on her back. In one graceful motion, she dropped down the side of the shuttle and landed on her feet.

Unlike the others, the woman wore more metal than leather: two metal shoulder pads, chest plates, and thigh guards. That, combined with her attitude, made it clear. Whoever this woman was, she was their leader.

The crew was searched for more weapons and then herded into a tight circle. Malachi studied the leader as she watched the proceedings, arms crossed. "What're you going to do with us?" he asked. "Did you even have a plan when you shot our bird out of the sky?"

"That wasn't us," she said. Up close, Auri realized the woman wasn't much older than herself.

One of the men coughed and the leader glared at him.

"Stuff the sass, High Top," she grumbled. Then to Malachi, "It wasn't us *intentionally*. All you need know is that you're Scavenger captives and are coming with us."

The dark-skinned man, High Top, spoke. "Arms to spine." He had a buzzed head except for a thick tuft of hair at the top that ran from forehead to neck. A chunk was missing from an ear, and scar tissue bubbled over what remained of the cartilage. White, mottled skin gleamed around the edges of an eyepatch over his right eye. Despite his rough exterior, waves of laugh lines creased his remaining eye and mouth. "Arms to spine," he repeated.

It took Auri a moment to understand what he meant. The rest of the crew must've struggled too because he dramatically mimed putting his arms behind his back.

Once the crew's arms were bound, their ankles were tied to a long lead rope. Birdie snarled when one of the Scavengers approached.

"Surrender," Auri hissed a reminder. Birdie tucked her tail between her legs and whined. The dog allowed a rope to be tied to her harness and attached directly to Auri's ankle. There was just enough slack to allow Birdie room to walk.

With the crew secured, the leader drew her crossbow again.

"Greenie and Misshot," she called to the other woman and one of the men. Based solely on the names, Auri wasn't sure who was who. "You two stay with the vehicle. I'll send someone back for you after we talk to Chieftain. High Top and Knuckles, you're with me."

High Top clasped a hand on the blonde woman's shoulder. "You got this, Greenie. Just stick with Misshot. He'll have your back."

"I want a new nickname," the woman—Greenie—muttered, hefting her crossbow. "I won't always be new to the group."

"The names remind us of our mistakes," High Top said. "If I were you, I'd hope that Greenie was my nickname until I was old and gray. Or I transferred." He tugged on one of her braids playfully. Color flushed across Greenie's freckled cheeks.

"High Top," the leading woman called. "Let's go. I don't want to run out of daylight." She adjusted her grip on the crossbow and led the way out of the hangar. Auri walked in front while Malachi and Tsuna followed with Castor tied at the rear.

After so long in the dimness, the bright sunlight burned Auri's organic eye. She ducked her head with a wince.

While her vision adjusted, she noticed the smell first. The only way she thought to describe it was *green*. A verdant, lush, effervescent *green*. She breathed in earth and dirt with the underlying odor of a woodfire. When she could see clearly, the sun shone in a nearly cloudless sky, creating shadows of the massive square building ahead. Asphalt covered the ground, but grass, trees, and wildflowers flourished in the many cracks.

Birds fluttered across the blue, trilling songs to one another. For once, Birdie didn't follow them with her gaze, eager to give chase.

Other than the birdsong, the military base was quiet except for the crunch of boots on pavement and the rustle of their leg rope.

The leader remained in front while High Top assumed middle guard. Knuckles kept a few paces behind Castor. The Scavengers radiated a tension that made Auri's jaw clench.

High Top jogged to catch up to the woman in front. "Oz," he murmured, just loud enough for Auri to hear. "You think it's tight to leave Greenie and Misshot here, after what happened?" He looked over his shoulder at the square building on their right, mouth a thin line.

The leader, Oz, hefted her crossbow into a more comfortable grip. "Whatever we accidentally turned on is off now. I think it ran out of power. Either way, I don't want the Walkers getting their hands on that vehicle. Chieftain needs to know about it."

"He won't like that we were here." High Top scratched at the skin under his eyepatch.

"He *will* like having an advantage over Merks and Walkers," Oz argued.

"Is it really an advantage? I have an itchy feeling about it all."

"Better warn Greenie about that itch," she teased. High Top snorted and Oz continued, "Now shutter it, we've got extra ears." Oz's gaze cut back to the crew. Auri quickly lowered her head.

Oz and High Top remained silent as they approached the chain link fence that encircled the base. A large gate lay across the remnants of an asphalt road that snaked into the tall grasses beyond.

"Stop," Oz called, holding up a hand. "Blindfold the captives."

"*Chikusho,*" Castor muttered from the back of the line. "How do you expect us to walk bound and blindfolded?"

"I suspect you'll find a way," High Top said, prodding him with the edge of his crossbow.

"Castor," Tsuna warned. She gave a slight shake of her head.

Auri's eyes caught on a sign affixed to the chain link fence. Deep gouges marred the lower part of the metal, rendering the words illegible. But the name of the base was easy enough to read: *Fort Caddel.*

Auri sensed someone watching her and turned to lock eyes with Oz. The woman pursed her lips as if in thought. The way Oz watched the crew reminded Auri of the disconcerting way she felt about Malachi when she first met him.

But Auri didn't get to study Oz further. High Top approached with a black bandana. Pressure built Auri's chest at the thought of being bound and trapped in the dark. Her breaths came faster.

Sensing her fear, Birdie snarled.

High Top froze and the others in his group trained their crossbows on Birdie. Auri forced herself to calm. "It's okay, Bird. I'm okay," she lied.

High Top leaned forward, smelling of sweat and dirt, and tied the blindfold tight across Auri's eyes. The world, already unfamiliar, went dark.

———

Smells changed first. From fresh earth and air to human: metal, cooking fires, and life. Birdie's bulk bumped into Auri's thigh as if something had spooked her. The heat of the sun vanished from Auri's face. Her boots went from grasses and hard-packed dirt to the smooth floor of some interior place. It sloped downward before leveling out.

The temperature continued to drop as Oz led the crew deeper into… wherever they were. Voices murmured around her. She felt the heat of bodies on either side and clenched her jaw against the desire to dislocate her robotic arm and free herself.

"Stairs," said a voice, and it took Auri a moment to recognize it as Oz's. The steady tug on the rope attached to her ankle lessened as if someone had given the crew more leeway to navigate.

Auri counted each step she descended. Her boots clanged on the metal. One flight. Two flights. By the fourth flight, goosebumps prickled across Auri's organic skin as the air took on an uncomfortable chill. She fought the weight of claustrophobia. It felt like she was wandering through some void or in the cryo chamber again.

Trapped, alone, and desperately afraid. Only the tug on the rope at her ankle and Birdie's warmth kept her from spiraling.

At the fifth landing, Oz mercifully called out, "A little farther."

Auri was led a few meters before High Top called a halt. The warmth of a human body heated the air in front of Auri. Callused fingers brushed her skin and the blindfold slipped away.

After so long in the darkness, the dim hallway around her was a relief.

Oz stood before Auri, her arms crossed, blindfold dangling from a finger, crossbow back in its holster. A narrow hallway stretched out behind the woman. If Auri's hands were free, she could've reached out and easily touched either side of the smooth walls. Fixed at even intervals were thick metal doors with a small slot at the bottom and a square window with a metal grating toward the top.

"Welcome home," Oz said, drawing Auri's attention. She unlocked one of the doors using a large metal key. "Only the finest comforts await you."

"Nice to see sarcasm is universal," Malachi muttered. Auri glanced back at him. The blood on his arm had dried across his gray t-shirt, leaving flecks of black across the fabric.

High Top stood just behind Castor. Unlike Oz, he hadn't put away his crossbow. The other man in their group had disappeared.

Oz ushered them into the cell. As she did, she sliced the ropes binding them with a small pocketknife. Auri rubbed the tender skin of her organic wrist as she squeezed toward the back corner.

The room was smaller than the *Kestrel*'s bridge. There were two wooden bunks bolted to the walls, a bucket tucked under each. Other than that, the room was swathed in shadow, and it took Auri a moment to realize there wasn't a light source.

Whatever this place was, it made the maximum-security cells on Attica look like a luxury spaceliner suite. At least Attica's cells had running water and electricity.

Auri ended up sitting on one of the beds with Birdie to make room for the rest of the crew. Despite the straw-stuffed mattress, Auri's bones could feel every inch of the wood frame underneath. Tsuna perched on the opposing bed while Castor and Malachi stood side by side in the center of the cell.

Oz surveyed the crew from the doorway, High Top at her side. "You clearly aren't Walkers," she said. "Where are you from?"

Malachi crossed his arms. "An answer for an answer."

Oz snorted. "You might want to reconsider that strategy. You'll be talking with Chieftain soon, and he isn't as open-minded as I am." She turned to leave, but her eyes shifted over Birdie and she paused. "Red, what's with snuggling up to the walking steak?"

It took Auri a second to understand. First, that Oz was addressing her. And second, that she was referring to Birdie.

Auri frowned, resting a protective hand atop Birdie's head. "She's a *dog*."

"I know." Oz stared at Auri, as if waiting for further explanation. When Auri didn't elaborate, Oz looked back at High Top. "She says *dog* like it's supposed to mean more than a filling meal."

Auri gritted her teeth and her fingers knotted in Birdie's curls.

High Top nodded. "Frack if it's not making me hungry though."

"Let's see if there's any leftover stew meat from dinner."

The pair turned and left. High Top slammed the door shut behind him, and the tumblers clicked into place. Footsteps echoed the Scavengers' retreat before a deafening silence settled onto the hall.

CHAPTER NINETEEN

---

14 Nov 3319, 13:01:24
Milky Way Galaxy, Earth
Scavenger Territory

Time passed, but Auri couldn't tell if it had only been hours or a full day. The only other sound beyond the cell was the faint toll of a bell every so often. No one brought food, so she assumed they hadn't been imprisoned long. Unless Oz had decided to starve them.

Auri huddled on a bed, back pressed against the cold stone wall, Birdie curled beside her. In the opposite bed, Tsuna had retreated into herself, staring into the shadows, expression haunted. Auri watched the hacker, brow furrowed with concern. This place was cruder than Attica, but maybe the Fed's prison had more of an impact on Tsuna than Auri realized.

Castor kept himself busy probing every centimeter of the cell as if he expected a trap door to spring open. Malachi leaned against the door, staring through the narrow grating to the hallway beyond.

When the silence finally got too oppressive, Auri broke it with a question. "What now?"

Malachi turned to face her. "If you were hoping for a brilliant plan, you're going to be disappointed."

Castor snorted and finally abandoned his search of the cell's walls. He slid down to the floor. "Your plans have never been brilliant. We always just got lucky."

"Seems that luck has run out," Tsuna murmured, resting her chin on her knees.

Someone's stomach growled, and Auri belatedly realized it was her own. She grimaced.

"Look," Malachi said, holding out his hands. "This isn't ideal. Would I prefer to have radio contact with Marin right now? Yes. But we saw from the air what happened to their society. What did you expect? The people on Earth would welcome us?" He looked to Castor with a raised brow. "Worship us for our advanced technology?"

"Maybe theirs is advanced," Auri countered. "Betty wrecked the shuttle pretty easily."

"I'm not sure that was intentional," Malachi said. "Before the power in *Purloin* cut out, I felt the thrusters shift, the steering dip. Whatever Betty was, she was trying to land us."

Auri rubbed at her arms as she shivered. Birdie leaned into her with a whine. "I overheard Oz mention she accidentally turned something on. Maybe that *something* was Betty."

"That's slightly reassuring," Tsuna said, perking up at the mention of technology. She dropped her feet to the floor and leaned forward. "If they don't know how to access that tech, maybe we have leverage." She turned to Malachi. "If we can get *Purloin*'s radio, maybe I could find a way to recharge it. Contact Marin."

Malachi started to reply, but the echo of footsteps filled the silence.

Everyone tensed. Malachi reached for a coil gun that wasn't there. The footsteps paused as a key slid into the lock outside.

"If this is our summons from Chieftain," Malachi hissed, stepping away from the door, "let me do the talking. I'll make sure we get what we need."

No one had time to disagree before the door creaked open. Two broad-shouldered men stood outside. One held a curved machete with linen wrapped around the handle. The fabric seemed to be the only thing keeping the split wood together. The other man held more blindfolds. He gestured for the crew to step into the hall.

"Mutt stays," the man with the machete huffed, nodding at Birdie.

Auri opened her mouth to argue, but the man shifted his machete in warning.

Auri looked to Birdie, who hovered at the threshold. "I'll be back. Take a nice nap, okay?" She tried to sound relaxed, but Birdie had already picked up on the undercurrent of danger. The poodle whined as the crew was blindfolded, bound—this time hands in front with no ankle rope—and led out of the cell. Only when the door slammed shut did Birdie's whine go quiet.

As they ascended the stairs, the air grew warmer and the dank smell of the prison hall was replaced with woodsmoke and sizzling meat. Auri's stomach growled again.

Murmurs reached her ears, and Auri's skin prickled with the discomfort of being watched by unseen eyes. She wondered if this was how Marin felt all the time. The thought of her friend made Auri's heart ache, but knowing the girl was safe on the *Kestrel* was a comfort.

The murmuring coalesced into loud conversations laced with lively debate. Someone shouted, "That's fracking stupid!" close to her ear, making it ring and throb. Auri stumbled, righting herself before face-planting on the floor. Or worse, into someone she couldn't see.

"Stop," one of the men ordered. Auri came to an abrupt halt. So abrupt that one of the crew ran into her back. Bound hands bumped against Auri's rearend and an embarrassed flush warmed her cheek.

"*Maitta na*, sorry," Tsuna whispered.

She was just relieved it hadn't been Malachi or Castor.

Moments later, Auri's blindfold was yanked off, strands of her hair going with it. She winced and squinted into a bright room illuminated by four skylights. In front of her spread a large table carved from live oak. Men and woman sat behind it, studying her and the rest of the crew. A beautiful woodland forest mural, dappled sunlight filtering through the lush trees thick with summertime leaves, covered the wall behind them.

Shifting at the edges of the circular room, upwards of thirty people all seemed to be talking at once. They wore clothing familiar in style—sweaters, pants, shirts—but made from a combination of hides and homespun fabric. Their discussions grew louder and louder as they fought to be heard. The two men from the cell positioned themselves at either end of the lined-up crew.

"Muzzle up!" a deep voice bellowed. Auri's gaze cut away from the crowd to the source of the command. The man seated at the center of the table stood. "Muzzle up, Scavs. Muzzle up!"

Auri gaped at the sheer size of the speaker. The man stood two heads taller than Castor, who was one of the tallest Ancorans Auri had met. But unlike Castor's willowy build, this man was all muscle. He wore a long-sleeved robe, but the fabric strained around the bulk of his arms and chest. Two braids split his thick beard, skirting the belt around his navel.

Someone broke through the quieting crowd to stand beside the giant man. Auri's brow furrowed at the sight of Oz. She had changed out of her leather and metal getup and now wore a simple pair of patched cargo pants and a knitted sweater, long black hair curling to her waist and crossbow still slung over her back.

When Auri could finally hear her own intake of breath, the man spoke again. "I am Chieftain," he bellowed, "leader of the Scavengers. Who speaks for your people?"

Malachi inclined his head. "I'm Malachi Vermillion, a transport captain from the Ancora Federation."

Chieftain raised his brows as he eased into his seat. The chair was carved from the same wood as the table with elaborately curved legs and back. The others around the table also sat. Oz remained standing but rested one hand on the side of the seat. Her brown, almond-shaped eyes and dark hair was identical to Chieftain's. Even her height hinted at her parentage.

"Ancora Federation?" Chieftain asked. He worked his tongue around the words, his thick accent making it into *Ah-cure-eh*. "That's vaguely familiar. Is that beyond the sea?" he continued. "Or further inland? Has anyone heard of it?" He looked to the others at the table, then at the gathered audience. No one spoke.

Malachi cleared his throat. "We aren't from across the sea or further inland. We've traveled from beyond the Milky Way. We're from another galaxy entirely—*Ancora* Galaxy."

The crowd murmured in recognition. Those seated at the table turned to each other to whisper their own commentary. Snippets of "the ones who abandoned us?" and "that's what the legends say" reached Auri's ears.

Chieftain frowned. Beside him, Oz's lips parted and excitement burned in her eyes. She leaned down to whisper into Chieftain's ear.

Chieftain sighed and shifted in his seat. He raised a hand to silence the grumbling audience. To Malachi he asked, "Where did your vehicle come from? The one you crash-landed."

Malachi tilted his head, raising his brows at Oz. "*Crash-landed?*"

Oz glared at him but didn't speak.

Malachi continued, "From the same place we came from. We have many different kinds of boa—vehicles there. We also have Bleeders. Which is why we're here. To learn where they came from."

"Bleeders?" Chieftain ran a hand over his beard, tugging on one of the braids. "What kind of creatures are those?" The expressions of those at the table matched Chieftain's confusion.

Malachi paused. "You might call them something else. Blood-thirsty creatures with increased strength and regenerative abilities."

Chieftain's fingers stilled on his beard. "Merks."

"Merks," Malachi repeated, nodding affirmation.

Chieftain glanced at Oz, who had clasped her hands behind her back. She stood rigid and emotionless, but Chieftain must've seen something in her eyes. He gestured to Malachi. "Ask the man your questions before you burst from them, daughter."

Daughter.

Oz was more than a patrol leader who had wandered into forbidden territory. As Chieftain's daughter, would she be in charge of the Scavengers one day? Auri knew some societies worked that way. Ancora Federation's General-in-Chief commanded until his voluntary—or not so voluntary—retirement. A new GIC was then promoted by an advisory board. If Tsuna's contact had been successful, the current GIC would be retiring sooner rather than later. Or assassinated.

Oz moved around the table to stand before the crew. Her gaze flicked to each of them before she settled on Malachi. "You called yourself a *transport captain.* Did you fly the vehicle that crash-landed?"

Malachi's lips twitched in almost smile. "I did."

"Clearly he needs flight lessons," Chieftain said with a belly laugh. Some onlookers joined in, a few clapping in agreement. Others rolled their eyes at Chieftain's sense of humor.

Oz's face remained impassive. She stepped closer to Malachi until they stood almost nose to nose, though Oz was a few centimeters taller. The Scavenger's proximity to Malachi made Auri's throat tighten.

"Is it fixable?" Oz asked, voice a whisper.

"Fixable?" Malachi countered, raising his brows, goading her to say more.

"The vehicle," she ground out, moving back a pace. "Can you fix the vehicle?"

"Not alone." He nodded at the crew. "We are each an expert in different areas. Even the dog."

Oz quirked a brow. "I know what you're doing."

He just gave us all value, Auri realized.

"What use is a vehicle to us?" Chieftain asked, resting his forearms on the table. "Don't tell me you really believe they are from this... *Ancora Galaxy*? They're nothing more than a legend."

"You're the one who taught me legends have truth to them."

"Ah, and this legend tells of a heartless people who abandoned our grandparents and great-grandparents when we most needed help. This is the truth you want to believe?"

"No," Oz hedged, studying the crew before she looked back at her father. "But the vehicle would give us an advantage over the Walkers."

"Oz," Chieftain warned. His mouth tugged into a worried frown.

"Chieftain," she began, striding over to him. She braced her hands on the tabletop, and her hair tumbled around her in a wave. "You've tasked me with looking toward our future. I ask that you consider my proposal: allow me to oversee the repair of this air vehicle so that it may work for the protection of our people."

"True. But this isn't a decision I can make alone." Chieftain looked to the men and women gathered on his left and right. "What say you?"

"From a defensive standpoint," a man answered, his hair cropped close to his scalp. A four-lined scar started behind his ear and disappeared under his shirt. "Oz's reasoning is sound. It would make other tribes reconsider attacking us. And you know the Nightwalkers have grown bolder as our treaty ages."

"I agree with Sarge," a woman on Chieftain's other side added. "From an education standpoint, it would allow us to replace knowledge we have lost." She gave Oz a reassuring smile, but Oz didn't see it, her gaze fixed on Chieftain.

"What does my Farming Head say? Medical?" Chieftain asked. "Aye or nay?"

A man wearing worn coveralls and missing his middle finger didn't speak. Just gave a thumbs down. The other woman, her long gray hair twisted away from her face, shook her head. "I'd rather put effort into making more supplies that actually save lives, here and now. It's a nay from me."

Chieftain whistled. "Daughter, you've cut us down the middle. Which means I am the deciding vote."

Oz straightened, tilting her chin. "I await your decision, Chieftain."

He raised a brow. "But will you follow it?"

Oz's rigid posture shifted with uncertainty. Auri could almost see the GIC in the way the Chieftain moved, but unlike the GIC, there was a warmth about Oz's father. He seemed to truly care about the welfare of his daughter and his people. And wasn't afraid to show it.

"I will allow this venture on two conditions," he said, holding up thumb and forefinger. "First, that vehicle is to stay at the black site. I'm not as superstitious as your grandfather, but that place has a cloud over it, and I don't want it near our people."

"Understood." Behind her back, Oz's fingers twisted around each other. It was the only hint at the woman's nerves. Auri didn't like Oz, but she understood the weight of a powerful father and wanting to make him proud. And it seemed Oz was the only one keeping the crew from a likely death. "The second condition?" Oz asked.

"These captives need to add more value than just fixing up a vehicle if they expect to eat our food. I want them on rotation, even if they only serve as bait."

Oz started to speak, but Malachi interrupted, "We would be more than happy to help, but I have conditions of my own."

Chieftain's brows rose toward his hairline. He laughed. "The stones on this one. You sure you're no Scav? What are your conditions?"

"We came for answers," Malachi said. "We want to know more about the Merks, about the previous society, and what Earth is like now."

"Reasonable enough," Chieftain said. "Anything else?"

"We aren't to be treated like prisoners." Malachi purposefully tugged at his bound wrists. "And you will release us when the vehicle is repaired."

The humor in Chieftain's eyes vanished like light during a mandatory blackout. As he studied Malachi, an uneasy quiet descended. Auri practically saw the man's mind shift away from Oz's idea. He wasn't going to let them walk freely. He probably never even planned to let them go.

"I will speak for them," Oz said, breaking the silence. "I vow it."

Hushed whispers broke out. Chieftain's face paled. "You can't look toward the future of your people if you're dead."

Oz didn't back down. "I said I *vow* it."

The whispers turned to gasps.

Somewhere in the crowd, Auri heard High Top's familiar mutter. "Frack it, Oz. You dit."

Whatever Oz had just done, it seemed important. In the heavy silence, a bell tolled, louder than it had been in the cell. The low *bong* sounded four times.

"Change of watch." Chieftain took a slow breath and stood. When he spoke again, eyes on Oz, his tone was icy. "These prisoners are in your care." He looked to his gathered people. "These four Outsiders are Oz's guests. Treat them well." His gaze cut to Malachi. "But do not trust them."

Chieftain gestured to Oz as he moved away from the table. "Get their blood tested and find a place for the Outsiders to sleep.

And double them up. When that's complete, find me. We need to have words."

CHAPTER TWENTY

14 Nov 3319, 15:11:06
Milky Way Galaxy, Earth,
Scavenger Territory

After Chieftain and his advisers departed, the room quickly emptied. Only a few people spared a glance back at the "Outsiders." Everyone else had already dismissed them, as if they wouldn't be around long enough to warrant even the faintest curiosity.

Oz faced the crew, arms crossed. High Top melted away from a wall where he'd been waiting and joined her. He had changed into a worn waffle-knit shirt and cargo pants with frayed hems.

"That went better than expected," he commented, grinning at Oz.

Oz thumbed her chin at him before she turned to the crew. "I know his name," she pointed at Malachi, "but what about the rest of you?"

Castor raised his bound wrists with a toothy scowl. "Free us first."

"Fair enough." Oz slid a knife from the sheath at her waist and approached Castor. He maintained eye contact as she sliced the rope at his wrists. It fell to the floor where it lay like a coiled snake.

"Castor," he huffed as he rubbed his wrists.

Oz freed Malachi's hands then moved to Tsuna.

"I'm Tsuna," Tsuna said as her ropes were cut.

Oz grabbed Auri's robotic arm to steady her strike. Her fingers touched the synthetic skin exposed around the barcode cuff and her gaze shot to Auri's.

"What…?" she breathed. She looked back down to examine Auri's arm.

"My name is Aurelia," Auri said to draw Oz's attention back to her face. "I go by Auri."

Oz cleared her throat, but suspicion burned in her eyes. "Awree," she said and cut the rope. She sheathed her knife and stepped back. The hand that had touched Auri's synthetic skin flexed once before Oz rubbed it over her pants.

"Everything tight?" High Top asked her, studying Auri, fingers curled around his own knife.

Oz didn't answer, but instead nodded at Malachi. "Are you really from this other galaxy? You and your people?" She gestured to the crew.

"You already know the answer to that," Malachi said. "Otherwise, you wouldn't have forced your father to meet my terms." He looked to High Top. "What about you? What's your play in all this?"

"I'm Oz's second," High Top answered as if it explained everything. He turned to Oz. "Let's get them to the lab. There will be time for questions later."

The crew fell in behind Oz and High Top as they left the circular room. There was only one exit: a curved archway shaped from concrete with a thick wooden door. Beyond was a large hall, open to the lower levels on one side. A massive skylight made of what looked like reinforced plastic comprised half of the ceiling.

Ivy and long grass had grown over some of the edges, but it provided just enough light to illuminate the space.

Oz led them down the hall. Auri peeked over the side of the safety railing to see the lower levels. People moved about as far down as she could see. She wondered what kind of building this had been before the Scavengers claimed it. The space reminded her of the parking garages for hovercars and bikes she had seen on Babbage.

Movement caught Auri's peripherals. To her left, a large ramp led to a reinforced steel door. The doors were opened at the middle just wide enough for a pair to walk side by side. Through the gap, Auri glimpsed sunshine and a flash of green. Two guards stood at either side of the opening, and at the sight of the crew, their hands went to their machetes.

So, that was one way out of the Scavengers' base. Not too heavily guarded. The guards themselves only seemed to have what looked like standard issue gear: crossbow, knife, and machete. Not ideal, but better than a blaster or taser.

Oz led them further down the hallway until it opened into an oval gathering area. A massive stone fireplace was fixed in the center of the opposite wall. One giant iron pot hung above dying embers, a woman coaxing them back to life with a long poker. At least fifteen picnic-style tables were positioned around the fireplace in neat rows. A few tables were occupied by other Scavengers hunched over wooden bowls.

Beyond the dining hall, the corridor dead-ended in a metal staircase that led to the lower levels. They descended into the echoes of their own footsteps while each level grew darker and colder. The bulbs fixed in the walls around the stairwell only lit the space to a dull glow. It seemed the skylight was the main source of illumination.

They reached the third level, and Oz escorted them down one of four branching hallways. Bulbs hung from the high ceiling, though they only seemed to create shadows instead of banishing them. Woodsmoke from the fire above overlapped the scent of iodine and herbs.

Auri tried to peer through the open doors interspersed at even intervals, but each was pitch black. In the one lit room, she only managed to glimpse a table bearing rows of seedlings under a sun lamp before she was led forward.

Oz and High Top finally stopped at a set of double doors at the hall's end. These doors were simply labeled *lab*.

High Top pushed open a door, letting out a bright stream of light, and Oz strode through. "Time to test your blood," she said by way of explanation.

Auri hadn't expected a high-tech lab like those on Aurora or Rokuton, but this was even more rustic than the cyborg doctor's on Delfan. The room was comprised of cement walls, floor, and ceiling. The bulbs here burned at full brightness.

Five gurneys were covered with gray sheets that may have once been white. An array of cabinetry and shelving spanned one wall, ending in a cluster of I.V. poles. On a shelf in one corner sat a yellowed fern halfway through its death march.

It looked clean, but Auri didn't like the thought of anyone pricking her or testing her blood. She shot Malachi a look where he stood beside her, but he only shrugged as if to say *We don't have a choice.*

A woman with short gray hair wearing a crisp gray lab coat approached, already pulling on medical gloves.

"Welcome to the lab," she said with a smile, the lines around her eyes crinkling. "I'm Gomery. Though I prefer Mery." Her skin looked even paler than Auri's, without a sign of freckles or sunspots. When was the last time this woman had been beyond these cement walls? If ever? "This won't take long," she promised.

"I have kitchen duty," High Top said to Oz as Mery moved to a cabinet. She withdrew a rectangular device the size of Auri's palm and four rectangular cartridges. "Come find me after you get the Outsiders settled."

"Sure, as long as one of them doesn't jump me in the halls," Oz teased as High Top moved toward the doors.

He paused, one hand on the handle. "Just make sure your ghost visits to help me hunt them down."

Oz snorted. "Have fun."

High Top gave her a thumbs-up before disappearing into the hall.

"It seems pointless to do these tests," Oz said to Mery, watching the woman load a cartridge into the rectangular device. "Merks are attacking anyone these days, Ambrosium-rich or not. They don't bother sniffing us out."

Ambrosium. The word stuck in Auri's mind. A sense of déjà vu hovered before her like a cobweb caught in an updraft. The more she tried to grasp the familiarity, the further it slipped away.

"Roanleigh," Malachi murmured.

Auri turned, eyes widening. "Ambro," she breathed. "Do you think…?"

He nodded.

"Ambrosium?" Castor asked the Scavengers. "What is it?"

"It will decide if you're suitable for patrol or not," Mery answered without really explaining. "Hop on this gurney, and we'll get you tested."

Castor peered at the rectangular device Mery held. "I'm not letting you stick anything in me."

"Care to change your mind?" Oz asked. She drew her machete and angled it so light glinted on the serrated blade.

Castor crossed his arms. "I'm not afraid of your pointy stick, little girl."

Oz arched a brow, but Tsuna stepped in front of Castor, resting a hand on his arm. "Try a little less confrontation," she said, glaring at him, "and a little more *self-preservation*." She turned her charming smile on Oz, tilting her head. Oz lowered her machete slightly and blinked as if she wasn't sure how to respond.

"I'll go first," Tsuna said. "Since you're so scared of a little needle, Castor."

"I know what you're doing, woman," Castor muttered. He grumbled under his breath as he slid onto the bed. The sheets rustled and his long legs hovered a centimeter off the floor.

Mery moved over to him and squeezed the fleshy side of his bicep. Her gaze lingered on the cuff around his forearm, but instead of commenting on it, she said, "This won't hurt." She raised the rectangular object and pressed one end against Castor's skin. There was a soft *click* followed by a chirp.

Oz leaned closer to the doctor to see the tiny screen light up yellow.

"Slightly higher than our average," the doctor said, "but if rumors are true—" she glanced sideways at Oz—"then it would make sense." She dabbed at a bead of blood on Castor's dark skin with a clean cloth. "Who's next?"

"What do you mean?" Tsuna asked as she slid into Castor's vacated seat. She eyed the rectangular device and the screen, curiosity brightening her face. "How does it work?"

"This is a reader," the doctor explained as she loaded a new cartridge. She jabbed Tsuna's arm and the screen flashed green. "Lucky you. Your levels are exceptionally low." She helped Tsuna off the gurney and explained, "The reader draws a drop of blood and scans it for Ambrosium, the Merks' favorite snack."

"The more Ambrosium you have," Oz continued, "the more of a target you are. Usually."

"And mine…?" Tsuna asked, biting her lip. "Was green?"

Doctor Mery nodded, motioning for Malachi. "If you come up green and get cut in the field or it's between you and someone else, you'll probably survive a Merk attack. Unless they are desperate."

"I don't understand," Malachi said, taking Tsuna's place. "Blee—Merks attack based on the amount of Ambrosium someone has in their blood?"

"We don't know why," the doctor said. "A lot has been lost. Without Oz's mother, we wouldn't know half of what we do now. It took us a long time and a lot of sacrifices to discover the correlation. Even longer to develop this." She tapped the reader's screen. "Some people have less Ambrosium in their bodies. And some…" The machine chirped as it finished processing Malachi's blood. The screen lit up yellow. "And some have more. It's genetics."

"You next, Auri," Oz called, jerking her chin at the gurney.

Auri swallowed as she slid over the rough gray blankets, staring at the reader gripped in Mery's palm. Malachi drew closer to the doctor so he could more easily see the screen, as if he expected Auri's result to be different. Mery reached for Auri's robotic bicep, but Auri shifted her other arm forward.

"*Gomenesai*," she said. "But could you do my other arm?"

Oz cracked her knuckles, mouth pulling in a frown. "Gah-meh-si? What does that mean?"

"*Go-men-a-sai*," Malachi corrected. "It's a formal way of apologizing in our galaxy."

Oz snorted. "I've never heard a word like that before."

"I have a few others I'd be willing to share," Castor muttered, which earned him an elbow jab from Tsuna.

The doctor obligingly took Auri's other arm. Malachi's eyes locked with Auri's as the doctor pressed the reader against her skin. There was a quick prick, like someone had pinched her. After a few moments, a chirp sounded. The doctor gasped. Auri broke Malachi's gaze to look down. The screen was lit an ominous red.

CHAPTER TWENTY-ONE

---

14 Nov 3319, 15:36:41
Milky Way Galaxy, Earth,
Scavenger Territory

"Frack," Oz hissed, eyes widened to their limits. "We've never—"

"H-how is so much Ambrosium in your blood?" Mery stammered. "How are you still alive?" Her fingers trembled around the reader, and she turned to place it on the counter before she dropped it. A droplet of blood ran down Auri's arm to stain the gurney sheets.

"I…" Auri started, looking to Malachi. She had been the Bleeders' target ever since their run-in on Medea. They had wanted her so badly that they hunted her from the rim, all the way to Harlequin where they had killed so many Ancorans. Then back again to Roanleigh where Katara…

Auri swallowed around the sudden lump in her throat.

All that loss of life was because Auri had more Ambrosium in her blood? But why? How?

"You can't leave," Mery rasped, whirling around. Her pale face looked almost blue with panic. "If you so much as get a *paper cut* and they smell you, they'll go into a feeding frenzy."

Oz approached Mery and rested a hand on her arm. "Gomery," she whispered. "Let's not get carried away. The reader could even be malfunctioning. It's pulled me up as red once or twice when you know I'm a green. It's getting old."

Mery shifted to meet Oz's eyes. Oz stood almost a head taller than Mery. "But we…" she started. "I'll test her again. Just in case."

Oz shook her head. "Don't waste the cartridges. I need her to be able to leave the Hole. You believed in my mother, believe in me. What I'm trying to do. We can't keep living like this." She took a deep breath. "I love Chieftain and understand the leeway he's given me, but that alone took years of convincing after my mother's death. With these Outsiders, I don't have time. I need to act."

Oz started to pull away, but Mery caught her wrist. "I'll report her reading to Chieftain as yellow. But don't let the girl near any Merks. Or she'll die along with anyone near her."

The words pierced Auri's chest like coil gun bullets. The doctor's warning rang with a painful truth. A trail of bodies littered Auri's past. Owari Colony, those in the Spire, Katara…

"Aurelia," Malachi whispered. He caught the back of her neck to make her look at him. "Stop." The warmth of his hand fought back the chill. "Don't go there. Don't *ever* go there."

Auri blinked, realizing Tsuna and Castor were watching her. And so was Oz, her gaze intent and analytical.

"I…" Auri shook her head and looked at her crew. "I'm so sorry. I didn't realize…" Her voice broke.

"You're not to blame for Katara," Tsuna said. "Bleeders are."

"We'll figure it out," Malachi promised, hand moving to squeeze her shoulder. "That's why we're here."

"Enough," Oz said, striding up to them. "Thank you for your time, Mery. I'm going to escort my *guests* to their rooms."

They left Mery in the lab, the doctor's trembling hands shoved into her coat pockets, and Oz took them down another level. The hallways here were narrower and more maze-like. Sconces stuck out from the walls, the wiring visible as if it was accessed often. Doors were painted with a myriad of colors and symbols, each given an individual feel in a place where everything looked the same.

"These are the living quarters," Oz explained as she started down one of the five corridors. They passed women escorting children and men in groups with weapons slung casually over their shoulders. Auri couldn't help but notice Mery, not more than fifty, had been the oldest Scavenger she'd seen so far.

Oz turned down another hall. It dead-ended and she stopped at the last door. "Welcome home," she said without warmth. She jerked her thumb at the door on the left. Two latch locks were bolted at the top and bottom of the door. It looked like the Scavengers had had other *guests* before. "Malachi and Auri, you bunk here. Castor and Tsuna, you're across the hall."

"I don't think—" Malachi started.

"And I don't *care*," Oz said. She swung open Tsuna and Castor's door. "In."

"Don't treat me like a dog," Castor snapped.

"If I did," Oz said, "I'd have you up in the kitchen over a fire. Be grateful I'm calling you by your given name." She appraised him with a wicked smile. "Or would you prefer Lanky, you old mutt?"

Castor glared.

The strange names of Oz's group—High Top, Misshot, Greenie, and Knuckles—started to make a little more sense.

"Is Oz your nickname?" Auri asked, partly from curiosity and partly to keep Castor from getting a machete through the gut.

Oz glanced at her, lips a thin line. "No, it's not. I only give nicknames to my patrol. Makes it easier when they die. Also helps them remember their first mistake—that way they don't repeat it. So, maybe," she glanced at Castor, "I should call you Big Mouth instead."

Tsuna laid a hand on Castor's chest. He looked ready to tackle Oz. "Self-preservation," she hissed.

"Nice to know everyone is expendable," Malachi said. "Except you."

"I'm just as expendable," Oz countered. "Even Chieftain can be replaced. Hopefully by me, one day. Now *in*. Or do I need to start cutting throats?"

"Come on, Castor," Tsuna said, catching Castor's wrist and tugging him inside.

Oz shut the door behind them and fixed the locks on the top and bottom. She opened Auri and Malachi's door. A white blur shot out with a happy bark. Auri sucked in a relieved gasp as Birdie leapt up, paws on Auri's chest.

"Bird!" she cried. Birdie gave Auri's cheek an affectionate lick. "Thank you," she rasped to Oz, "for bringing her here."

For a moment, it looked as if there was a flicker of warmth in the Scavenger's eyes. Oz blinked and the spark vanished.

"Down, Birdie," Auri said. "In." She pointed back to the room. The poodle dropped to all fours and led the way inside.

It was a narrow space with two wooden bunk beds shoved against either wall. Between the bunkbeds was a wooden dresser with two drawers, one of which was tilted in its frame and missing a knob. Tucked under one of the beds was a metal bucket. A flush swept over Auri at the thought about using it with Malachi in the room.

Oz slammed the door shut without so much as a goodbye. Auri jumped at the loud *bang* and Birdie growled. In the silence, the locks clicking into place sounded ominous.

Malachi stared at the door, arms crossed. "So much for guests," he muttered. "This is a Charlie Foxtrot of epic proportions."

"We'll find a way out," Auri said. The words sounded more confident than she felt. "You've given us an opportunity to fix the *Purloin*."

"That's not what I meant." Malachi continued to glare at the shut door. "Do you understand what Oz did?"

Auri's brows drew together. "What do you mean?"

"She's picked up on the relationships between us," he murmured under his breath. "*Kuso*. She's good."

Auri's stomach twisted at the appreciation in Malachi's voice. She shoved the sensation aside. "She's hoping Castor and Tsuna's feelings for each other will distract them?"

Birdie nudged Auri's hand with her nose before she hopped up on one of the bunk beds. Judging by the mess of the scratchy-looking wool blanket, Birdie had already made herself at home.

"Yes, Castor and Tsuna," Malachi repeated, his tone almost teasing. He turned to look at Auri. Now that it was just the two of them, his shoulders slumped as his mask of composure peeled back. He took a slow breath and raised a shaking hand to his eyes. "Oh, *chikusho*. Auri, I hope I've done the right thing."

Auri watched the weight of their fate settle over him. Coupled with his grief over Katara and Ferris's abandonment, Auri feared he would break.

Malachi stumbled backward onto the opposite bunk. He dropped down, forearms on knees, head hanging. "I didn't see another way to get the information we need. Maybe we could have captured a Scav? Asked them questions? Used them as a trade?" He scoffed and shook his head. "But these people clearly view themselves as expendable. They wouldn't trade." He continued to mutter to himself, almost as if he'd forgotten Auri was still in the room.

Auri sat down beside him, close enough so her shoulder brushed his.

His rambling quieted. He clasped his hands together and pressed them against his forehead almost in prayer.

Silence stretched between them. Auri's stomach growled and she tensed with embarrassment. To her surprise, Malachi chuckled. It broke off in a ragged breath that propelled Auri to speak. To be the first one vulnerable.

"I'm afraid, Malachi," she admitted, looking down at her hands, at the cuff dark against her synthetic skin. "I'm trying to mourn my mother, but I can't seem to connect the woman she was and the monster she became. I half hope my father is already dead, just so I don't have to kill him myself. Which is such a horrible thing to think." Her voice caught as tears threatened. "I'm afraid that Mery was right, that I've caused all this death. That one day I'll be as monstrous as the Bleeders. I sometimes even miss the GIC and Ty and my old life and I—" Auri cut off as her throat became too tight to speak.

Birdie whined. She pattered off the opposing bed and jutted her nose against Auri's knees.

Auri hid her face in her palms as the tears rolled down her organic cheek. Shame filled her. She was crying in front of Malachi. *Again.* All she'd intended was to encourage him to share his fears by exposing her own.

"I haven't been sleeping," Malachi rasped.

Auri forced herself to quiet her sobs. She peeked at him between her fingers. He was staring down at his hands. The slice in his arm had scabbed over, the other a swirl of tattoos ending in his usual fingerless glove.

"I see Katara's face whenever I close my eyes," he continued. "My choices killed her. Killed the people in the Spire. All those deaths are on me, Aurelia. Not you." He shook his head. "I knew the Bleeders were following us after Medea, but I went to the Spire anyway. I *led* them there, thinking it would make it easier to reach the vault."

Tsuna's warning drifted back to Auri, but she shoved it aside. "They would've found me at some point."

"But you and I both know if you'd had the same information, you would've waited. You would've tried to lose the Bleeders before you approached the Spire."

Auri didn't answer. He chuckled and reached out to brush his thumb across her cheek, wiping away the trail of tears. "That, among a million other reasons, is why I need you."

Her breath caught. Her gaze jumped to his.

"Don't lose your light, Aurelia," he murmured. "You're my sun amidst all this darkness."

"Malachi," she rasped, swallowing, aching. "I want…"

But what did she want, really? To be with him? Or just drown her sorrow with his warmth. Auri cared for Malachi. She wanted to want him for more than just an escape. To love all he was, not someone she made perfect in her own mind. And even more so… She didn't want to love him only to lose him.

Before Auri could decide what to say next, the sound of approaching footsteps made them both turn. A shadow creeped through the bottom of the door. The locks unclicked and the door opened. High Top stood on the other side with a tray of food in hand.

Auri's stomach was immensely grateful.

But her burdened heart? Not so much.

ELINOR JAYRE
VIDEO LOG #03

February 18, 3277
Location: Planet 08: Roanleigh, Owari Settlement

Marnie sits at a curved desk, the white material so thin it almost looks transparent. A monitor is positioned before her, projecting a bright blue holographic keyboard. The room is lit by fluorescent light that shines on fifteen other desks. Most are vacant.

Marnie taps a command into the keyboard. A *beep* comes from the monitor as it powers down. The holo keys flick off a moment later. Marnie tugs an identification card from a slot on the monitor's right side. She slips it into a pocket of her white jumpsuit and turns to the camera with a sigh.

"Won't need cards soon," she says, patting her pocket. "Apparently computerized contact lenses are used here. Or something like that." She crinkles her nose and stands. "I'm not fond of having a computer in my head." Her back pops as she stretches.

"Not that we've been able to get in touch with the other planets to get the lenses or even learn about more advancements." She picks up a half-empty glass of water. "The constant snowstorms have—" As if summoned by her words, the wind whistles outside. The lights above flicker. Everyone looks up uncertainly.

"Hub was made for this!" Marnie calls to reassure them. "Don't worry. Finish your work so you can get back home before the snow picks up again." To herself she mutters, "Thank the Lord we got the Hub up before the first one hit." She clears her throat and gestures for the camera to follow.

"See you tomorrow," someone calls as Marnie moves down a row of desks, bound for the door at the back of the room.

"Have a nice night," says another.

"Tell Aldin I said hello."

Marnie relays her own farewells and steps into a dark hall. It is empty save for another woman who hurries past. They give each other a friendly nod.

"We've established the Hub," Marnie says to the camera as she moves down the corridor. "Water supply is up and running and planting is underway. Which is why we are pulling such odd hours."

Marnie turns into a small alcove of lockers with a single bench cutting down the middle. She opens the locker with her name on it, pausing to empty the contents of her glass.

"Water could use some tweaking," she says with a grimace. She deposits the cup inside her locker. "It's oddly sweet."

Marnie chuckles as she slides off her slippers and tugs on a pair of snow pants and boots. "I can't get Elodie to drink it." Next is a puffy coat with florescent patches along the back and shoulders. "She's plowing through the apple juice we brought from home—from *Earth*. I've been diluting it with a little water to help it last. And to get her used to the taste, but…" She shakes her head and yanks up her hood. "That girl has a stubborn streak a planet wide." Her mouth twitches in a smile. "Just like her mother."

CHAPTER TWENTY-TWO

15 Nov 3319, 05:59:45
Milky Way Galaxy, Earth,
Scavenger Territory

A loud *bang* tore Auri from sleep. She bolted upright as the sound repeated. Birdie groaned and rolled off the pillow she'd made of Auri's chest. Across the narrow walkway, Malachi was already out of bed. Auri wondered if he'd slept at all. She'd tossed and turned through broken nightmares as bells rang throughout the Scavengers' base—the Hole, as they called it—every hour. After what she guessed was midnight, the pitch had changed to a higher tone.

As if on cue, somewhere a bell let out a chipper peal that rang six times. Auri swallowed back a groan and rubbed at her bleary eyes.

Seconds later, the door swung open. Oz stood at the entrance with Castor and Tsuna behind her. Castor's eyes were half-lidded as if he was still asleep, and Tsuna tapped at her face as if trying to wake herself up. Indents from a pillow or blanket marred her cheek. Both of their clothes were rumpled.

"Rise and shine," Oz called. "Time to visit your vehicle."

"It's called a shuttle," Malachi muttered. He rubbed at his temples. "You don't happen to know what coffee is?"

"Or tea?" Castor added.

Oz cocked her head. "Never heard of it."

"*Chikusho*," he and Castor groaned at the same time.

Oz led them through the maze of hallways back to the main staircase. More people were out and about. Some were clean and fresh-faced, likely headed to start their tasks for the day. Others looked ready to collapse into their beds. No matter their state, they all called out greetings to Oz, which she returned.

The main level of the Hole swarmed with Scavengers. Adults escorted lines of yawning children to the dining hall for breakfast. Men and women chatted in tight clusters, while others lugged weapons and rustic farming equipment up the exit ramp. The busyness made Birdie press closer to Auri, and she rested a hand on the poodle's head.

Auri couldn't help but gawk at the scythes and rakes. The Fed's farming was mostly automated, and she'd only ever seen such tools in old vids. She couldn't imagine the amount of work it took these people just to fill their bellies, let alone protect themselves from Bleeders.

They followed the exiting Scavengers toward the ramp. The doors were open wider than yesterday, letting in glimpses of an overcast sky. Two guards stood at the top, crossbows in hand. Off to the side waited three figures Auri recognized. They smiled as Oz approached.

"Where's Knuckles?" Oz asked High Top.

"Got called in as a floater for a hunting expedition." High Top lifted his eyepatch, revealing an empty socket underneath. He scratched at the pale skin around it.

"That's not ideal," Oz grumbled.

"Looks like you're stuck with us," one of the men teased.

"It's too early for you to be this annoying, Misshot," the blond woman muttered, tugging at the bandana tied around her neck. "I stopped by the dining hall like you asked," she said to Oz, raising a cloth sack.

"Thanks, Greenie." Oz took it and rifled through its contents. She pulled out a small object wrapped in thin fabric with frayed edges and tossed it to Malachi, before passing a similar bundle to Tsuna, Auri, and Castor.

Auri unwrapped the fabric. Nestled inside was a long brown log of… *something*. Birdie sniffed at it eagerly. Which didn't say much. The dog used to eat her own poop before Auri nipped that habit.

"Here," Auri said. She broke her bar in half and gave one piece to Birdie. Birdie snapped it up in one bite.

Auri felt the heat of someone's gaze and looked up to see Oz's eyes on her.

"What use is the dog?" Oz asked without malice, just genuine curiosity. She handed the bag back to Greenie, who tucked it into a backpack. "We have goats, rabbits, and chickens. But we eat them. What do you do with a dog?"

All eyes were on her. Auri opened her mouth, trying to think of a way to explain Birdie's worth in a way they could understand. "She's my partner. She protects me and I protect her. I've known her since she was a puppy."

Oz's lips twitched as if she wanted to ask more, but she cleared her throat. "Very sentimental. Let's get moving."

"Hold up," Castor said. "You can't expect us to go unarmed. Where are the weapons you stole from us?"

High Top raised his brows, the expression borderline mocking thanks to his eyepatch. "You don't trust us to protect you?"

Castor crossed his arms. "Would I have asked for my weapon otherwise?"

"You go weaponless," Oz said. "I'd rather not end up with a knife in my back. Let's go."

Castor looked like he wanted to argue, but Malachi stopped him with a quick shake of his head.

At the top of the ramp, the guards scrutinized the crew before one nodded at Oz. "You let Chieftain know you're going out with them?" he asked. Streaks of gray colored his beard and hair where it was pulled back in a slick ponytail.

"You let your wife know you were playing cards last night?" Oz asked.

The guard grunted and spat a black wad out the side of his mouth to land on the ground outside. "Little blackmailer."

Oz gave him a toothy grin that was all shark. "Wouldn't work if you'd win for once. Besides, Chieftain knows. We don't have time to spit in the breeze. I need to get my guests to the black site and then do a check-in on the Block Towers."

"*Guests*," the other guard snorted. He adjusted the bandana tied around his head, already damp with sweat. He curled three fingers in so his forefinger and thumb stuck out like a gun. He pressed his hand against his chest. Oz and the Scavs did the same.

They murmured something to each other, but Auri didn't hear over the memory surfacing in her mind. She'd seen her mom make the same gesture in the vids from Roanleigh.

Tsuna's hand on Auri's shoulder brought her back to the present. Oz and the others were already walking up the ramp. Auri caught up to the Scavengers as they stepped through the open doors.

They emerged amid dense trees that seemed to brush the clouds with their upper branches. Long grasses had been cut into walking paths that branched off in different directions. Groups of people hurried along each, some leaving and others returning. The air was more humid than the day before, and the glimpses of clouds Auri saw through the foliage seem to hang heavy, promising rain.

"Oz," Auri started, following the woman and her people down the path that led straight ahead. "Where did that gesture come from?"

"What gesture?" Oz asked.

Auri imitated the motion, her skin buzzing with the memory of seeing her mother do it. Maybe Auri herself had even done it once.

"It's a greeting," Greenie explained. She fingered the back of her head where her hair was wrapped into a tight bun. "And a farewell." She hesitated, glancing at Oz before asking, "What do you do?" She nodded at the crew. "Where you're from?"

Ahead, the trees thinned, revealing more sky and land beyond.

"We shake hands," Tsuna said. "Or we bow."

High Top stopped at that. "You do what?"

Tsuna gave him a sly grin. "Are you asking for a demonstration?"

High Top blinked, lips parted as if he wasn't sure how to respond. Auri felt Castor's hackles rise. Greenie's jaw clenched.

"Enough chatting," Misshot muttered. He was shorter than High Top, but judging by his broad shoulders and thick neck, his leather and metal armor hid corded muscle. "We're wasting time. I'm due for a transfer at Block Tower One during Oz's check-in."

"Misshot is right," Oz said. "Shutter it and pick up the pace."

They broke through the trees moments later, and Auri got a clear view of the surrounding space. A squat structure was tucked behind at least an acre of farmland. Barbed wire extended from the house to an identical one kilometers away. Auri couldn't see every structure because of the trees, but it looked like they spread out in a circle, likely encompassing the boundaries of the Scavengers' territory.

Men, women, and children were already at work in the fields. They moved down the rows, plucking weeds, watering, and fertilizing. Some were even harvesting what looked like potatoes into a large basket. They called to Oz when they saw her at the tree line.

Oz waved and then turned to the crew. "This is where you're blindfolded again."

Castor opened his mouth to protest, but she cut him off. "Only until we are a safe distance away. We work hard to keep our location a secret from rival tribes. I'm not blowing it on you." She raised a brow. "Unless you'd rather die at the end of our arrangement?"

Castor muttered a curse.

Once the crew was blindfolded, they were escorted forward. After what seemed like hours of stumbling over every rock and stick, their eye coverings were removed. They stood amid grasses that tickled Auri's knees. When she looked closely, she noticed black asphalt peeking through the overgrowth.

"Here we are," Oz said, drawing Auri's attention upwards. In the distance, through the haze of humidity, waited a familiar fence and rectangular building.

High Shot led and Oz covered their rear. Greenie and Misshot weaved through the tall grasses, monitoring their flanks. When they reached the fence, Misshot peeled away to guard the path while the rest of them hurried onto the base. He fell back in step with Oz moments later.

"This isn't part of your territory, is it?" Malachi asked as they hustled across the asphalt toward the hangar. Everything looked the same as before: skid marks along the grass-infested tarmac, the giant hole the *Purloin* created.

The crash had only been yesterday, but it already felt like a lifetime ago. Auri thought of Marin, alone in orbit, trapped on the *Kestrel* with no idea what had become of them.

"You're observant," Oz said. "And correct. It's technically part of no-man's-land. The area between us and the Nightwalkers."

Malachi looked like he wanted to ask more, but two figures emerged from the hangar. "Stay here," Oz ordered before hurrying over to greet the other Scavengers. The three shared a whispered conversation.

"She said Nightwalkers?" Tsuna asked the other Scavengers. "Who are they?"

"You don't want to meet them," Greenie said, glancing over her shoulder with a shiver.

High Top nodded. "If you think we're bad, they're in line with the Merks as far as hospitality goes."

"A bolt to the head is the best way to greet them," Misshot added, flexing his fingers.

Oz beckoned them over. The two Scavengers reassumed guard duty outside the hole in the hangar.

"Status?" Misshot asked Oz.

"Undisturbed," she answered. "The faster we get this thing running and parked on Scav land, the better. It's only a matter of time before the Walkers come looking. They are stupid, but not stupid enough not to see something flying through the sky."

"Your people must be a special kind of dit," High Top chided, side-eyeing the crew. "Don't they have like, invisibility cloaks where you're from? You're supposedly so *advanced*. That's what the legends say about the traitor galaxy. You know, the one that abandoned Earth after our people starting eating each other." He turned to showcase a toothy grin in a poor replication of a Bleeder.

"Enough poking at the Outsiders." Greenie elbowed High Top, which earned her a gentler, more genuine smile. "We are on borrowed time. I doubt the Chieftain is going to waste resources guarding this thing for long."

"Greenie's right." Oz gestured to Malachi. "Get to work."

Greenie and Misshot positioned themselves on either side of *Purloin*'s spaceshield. High Top and Oz stood at the bottom of the still-open ramp.

Castor clamored inside with Birdie loping after him. The poodle's tail wagged, and Auri had the guilty realization the dog thought they were going home.

Oz watched the crew enter the shuttle with a frown. She ran a finger across a scar along her jaw before drawing her crossbow. "I'm watching," she called. "If you try to escape in this… *shuttle*, I'll shoot you dead."

"Noted." Malachi said. He moved toward the control panel. As he passed Auri, he hissed, "You and Castor block Oz's line of sight best you can." He stopped before the controls and started tapping buttons and flicking switches. Tsuna came up beside him and knelt under the console.

"Castor," Auri called. "Should we check the…" She trailed off. Auri knew next to nothing about shuttles or engineering. Her abilities were limited to minor piloting if autopilot failed.

"Power panels," he finished for her. "We can start on this one." He pointed to a spot that had once been the floor but was now a wall.

Castor slid a panel open, using his lankiness to block Oz's sightline. Auri gawked at the myriad of wires that crisscrossed one another. She leaned closer as if to examine them, peeking under her arm at Malachi and Tsuna. They both crowded under the console, whispering to each other.

Malachi popped open a compartment and began rooting through thick cording. He yanked a square object from underneath, the mechanism itself only the size of Auri's thumb, a tangle of wires sprouting from it.

Tsuna's gaze darted out the spaceshield to keep an eye on Misshot and Greenie. "I might be able to charge that radio if we can find a power source. Think you can convince Oz to give us access to one?"

He nodded.

Castor cleared his throat. Auri turned to see Oz shifting closer to the *Purloin*'s ramp in an attempt to see Malachi and Tsuna.

"Oz," Malachi called as he straightened. He passed the radio to Tsuna who slid it down the front of her shirt. "Our shuttle is in pretty good shape, all things considered." He nodded to Castor and Auri as he stopped at the top of the ramp. "But I can only tell so much with a dead bird. I need a power source to wake her up and run a system diagnostic."

Oz blinked once, twice, three times. "Frack, *what?*" she said, tone edged with annoyance. "I have no idea what you just said."

"An AI took over…" Malachi started, but when Oz crossed her arms, he trailed off. "Do you have a power source that could charge this ship?"

She pursed her lips in thought, but then shook her head. "Nothing that powerful. Even if we did, we'd need to get this thing back to the Hole. There's no way we'd manage that. No way Chieftain would allow it."

Auri thought back to the light before Betty seized *Purloin*'s controls and the hushed conversation she'd overhead between Oz and High Top.

"What about in there?" She pointed through the hole in the hangar to where the other building loomed against the gray sky. She turned to Malachi. "Before Betty took over our controls, I saw a light in one of those windows. Maybe her power source is in there."

Oz's tanned skin had paled at Auri's mention of the building, but her voice was steady when she spoke. "It's drained. We turned it on by accident while exploring. It shut off when your shuttle crashed."

"Let me see about that," Tsuna said.

Oz whistled and Greenie and Misshot hurried over.

"What's up?" Misshot asked.

Oz crossed her arms. "We're going to head into the main building."

"Again?" Misshot swallowed. He glanced over his shoulder as if he expected to catch a ghost hovering in the shadows. "We said we wouldn't go back after—"

"*I know*," Oz said. "But their shuttle needs a power source."

"We've already come this far," High Top added with a nod at Oz.

Misshot glanced at Greenie, but she shrugged her agreement with the others. He sighed. "Let's just not take too long. I don't want to be late for my shift. Again."

"Got it." Oz gestured for everyone to follow.

They moved across the cracked asphalt toward the building. Four double doors—a pair on each side—were still locked despite the claw marks denting the metal. Auri shivered as her mind played out the likely Bleeder attack.

Oz led them to a side nearest the chain link fence. After a glance at the landscape beyond—empty except for an eagle launching itself after prey—she shifted a loose board from a shattered window. The opening was just big enough to slip inside.

Auri entered behind Oz. Her boots crunched on broken glass, and she called out a warning to Birdie. "Castor, can you pass her through to me?"

Seconds later, Birdie's snout slid through the opening. She gave Auri a pitiful look.

"Don't look at me like that," Auri chided. She looped her arms under Birdie's chest and belly, then set her down away from the glass.

Once everyone was inside, the Scavengers pulled rectangular objects from their backpacks. A bulb was on one end with a palm-sized lever on top. They cranked the lever and light shone from the bulb. The beams weren't as strong as the flashlights Auri was familiar with, but they eliminated some of the gloom.

Greenie's light shifted as she adjusted her backpack. When it stilled, it landed on the scattered remains of a skeleton. Auri's heart shot into her throat. She grabbed Birdie's harness.

"*Kuso*," Tsuna whimpered. She shifted closer to Castor.

The Scavengers ignored the skeleton and set off down the hall. Their flashlight beams moved in a constant sweep, illuminating the path ahead and behind.

"Do you think Bleeders killed that person?" Auri whispered to Malachi as they kept pace.

High Top answered, "Merks? Maybe. But humans fight too. Merks aren't the only villains when it's survival of the fittest."

"We don't know much about this place," Greenie explained as Oz led them around a corner. A fake tree emerged from a pot beside a cushioned bench stained black.

The further they went, the more the air smelled of damp and death. The rare shafts of sunlight illuminated dust motes dancing through the air and made contorted shadows out of the toppled furniture and other skeletons littering the halls. This place reminded Auri so much of the Hub on Roanleigh that her skin itched with a phantom panic.

"I've explored as much as I've dared," Oz said. "Chieftain, and the one before him—"

"And the one before him," High Top added.

Oz shot him a look. "Obviously, our life expectancy isn't high. The more superstitious Scavs think this site is cursed. Strange light used to come from here when Chieftain was a boy. But no one has seen anything since before I was born."

They hurried up a flight of steps covered with papers that crunched under their boots. Auri bent down to pick up a sheet, thinking it might pertain to the Owari colonists, since they had departed from this military base. Droplets of dried blood splattered across the bottom of the page. She peered at the mathematical equations far beyond her experience with simple algebra.

"Anything interesting?" Malachi asked.

"Nothing I can understand without the grid."

"There is something about this place," he murmured as they reached the landing. "It reminds me of where Marin took us on Rokuton." He frowned but didn't continue.

Auri shivered, remembering that horrible underground lab.

"Through here." Oz jerked her chin at the open door before them. "That's where we turned on… whatever you said landed your shuttle."

"Light?" Malachi asked. Oz handed him her flashlight. He cranked it again before he turned to Tsuna. "You ready?"

She nodded and followed him into the room with Castor, Auri, and Birdie bringing up the rear.

The room encompassed the entire side of the building. A circular workstation was fixed in the center, ten physical monitors evenly spaced atop it. There were no keyboards, which meant they were likely holos. At least some technology Auri was used to. In the ceiling was a large lens that reflected the light from Malachi's borrowed flashlight.

Unlike the rest of the building, this room seemed relatively untouched, as if there had been nothing to scavenge. Or they had been too afraid to try.

Tsuna ignored the workstations and instead explored the far corners where servers were racked from floor-to-ceiling. Squeezed in the center was a bulky workstation with a monitor and physical keyboard. Wires of varying thicknesses ran underneath into the wall and servers.

"Oz," Tsuna called. "Is this where you turned on the machines? Can you show me what you did?"

Oz entered the room, gaze darting to the ceiling above the circular workstations, as if she expected someone to be standing there.

"All I did was this," she said. She pressed the power button on the monitor. Light blossomed on the screen.

Oz retreated to the circular workstation and raised her crossbow.

Numbers flashed across the screen. Then a series of prompts. Tsuna's eyes scanned them in rapid succession, muttering under her breath, "Okay, okay. *Wow*. Okay."

Without warning, the screen went dark.

Tsuna waited a beat before she turned to Oz. "Did it do that before?"

Oz nodded, not shifting her gaze from the workstations. "Then a ghost appeared and threatened us. Then it started talking, telling someone to land."

"Fracking terrifying," High Top said from the doorway. Neither Greenie or Misshot had dared move from the hall.

"It wasn't a ghost, but I get why you would think so." Tsuna rested a hand against one of the dark servers. "Luckily, there is a functioning power source. Likely solar. The only reason the monitor turned on was because it had the last day or so to refill. I need to take a look around. See what these wires connect to." She looked to Malachi. "It may take more than a few hours."

Which meant they wouldn't be getting in touch with Marin any time soon.

Oz was silent a beat as she thought through Tsuna's revelation. "Do the best you can. Greenie, you stay with Tsuna and Castor. I'll send one of the other guards up here with you. High Top and I are going to escort Misshot to Block Tower One for duty."

"What about us?" Malachi asked. "Auri and I have knowledge of—"

"Shutter it," Oz said. "I'm keeping the four of you separated. I won't have you overpowering my people." She gave Malachi a snide grin. "Besides, our deal included answers to your questions. It's time for you to see what happened to Earth."

CHAPTER TWENTY-THREE

15 Nov 3319, 08:26:02
Milky Way Galaxy, Earth,
No-man's-land

They cut a quick pace through the landscape. Trees and grasses quickly gave way to a barebones town, the buildings and vehicles torn apart for scraps. There were no signs of life other than a few birds tittering atop the hole-infested rooftops and the occasional insect's droning.

Even still, Oz and Misshot moved with a guarded air, as if they were primed for attack.

They called a halt in front of a narrow four-story building positioned between two squat structures missing their doors and windows—one even had a tree growing in the center. Movement atop the building caught Auri's attention. She squinted as three figures scrambled over solar panels bolted to the roof. From up there, the Scavengers could probably see for kilometers, until the town eventually bled into the much larger city across the river.

A male voice called down to the group, "Ey, Misshot, late again? Watch Commander's got your stones in her fist already. She'll love when I report to her tonight."

Misshot threw Oz an exasperated look. Beside her, High Top snorted in amusement.

"I'll talk to her," Oz promised. They stopped outside the tower, and Misshot put away his crossbow to knock on a thick plank of wood, the only place on the lower part of the building not wrapped in clapped-together metal and barbed wire.

"Password?" a raspy female voice asked from the other side.

Misshot leaned closer to murmur something Auri couldn't hear. Moments later, a door appeared amidst the wood, metal, and barbed wire. It opened soundlessly, revealing a Scavenger on the other side. Her long hair was twisted into two braids down her back. She nodded at Misshot, Oz, and High Top. Her eyes widened at the sight of Malachi and Auri.

"You brought them with you? Really, Oz?" she chided. "And a mutt? Where'd it come from?" She pointed at Birdie who huffed in indignation.

"It belongs to the red-haired Outsider," Oz answered. "We're just here to drop off Misshot and see how Block Tower One is faring. We're taking these two on a loop of Tower One through Four."

The woman hesitated. "Just you and High Top?" She shook her head. "I don't think so. I've got an extra body here taking up space. I'm sending Grubs with you." She looked over her shoulder. A flight of steps behind her curved in an upward spiral. When she noticed Auri peering inside, she shifted to block her view. "Grubs, get down here!"

"Frack, it had to be Grubs. He gives me the creeps," High Top muttered. "The man spent too long living among the sewer Merks." He glanced sideways at Auri. "They're more animal-like. Above-ground Merks have human reasoning and intelligence. Well, until someone starts bleeding."

"He's a tad touchy," the woman agreed. High Top grimaced at being overheard. Oz elbowed him in the gut. "But he's got a sixth sense for bloodlust. And backstabbing." She looked pointedly at Malachi and Auri. "Misshot, you head up. You're late enough as it is."

Misshot dutifully hurried up the steps, squeezing against a wall as someone else came down. With the name *Grubs*, he didn't look how Auri had expected. He was a few centimeters taller than her. His hair was buzzed close to his scalp except for a portion on the top that was long and tied back in a bun. In addition to the standard issue crossbow, machete, and knife, he had a spiked baseball bat strapped to his back.

"Grubs," Oz said with a nod.

"Oz," he replied with a deep voice. A few of his teeth were missing.

"Watch yourselves," the woman warned. "Tower Two has reported increased Merk and Walker activity since yesterday."

Auri glanced at Malachi, who was already frowning. Increased activity since they crash-landed couldn't be a coincidence.

"When is the next rolling squad?" High Top asked.

"Not for three days."

"Stones," Oz muttered. "That's too long. The Merks will take root like weeds. And Walkers creeping closer to our territory… They give us any excuse to go on the offensive?"

"Nah," the woman said with a shake of her head. "Just scoping things out. They can do what they want here as long as they don't invade our towers or intentionally shoot us."

Oz clucked her tongue. "I still don't like it. We'll be cautious," she promised the woman. "See you for Harvest."

The woman grinned, the wrinkles around her eyes deepening. "Looking forward to your fiddle playing. Be safe."

"You as well."

They repeated the familiar Scavenger farewell gesture before the door shut and locked behind the woman.

High Top took a slow breath. "Any chance we just skip the Tower loop and head to the Hole for a late breakfast?"

"Not a chance," Oz said, pulling her crossbow from her back and sliding a bolt into place. "With the roll-out not happening for three days, we're going to make our presence known. Remind the Merks to stay away."

"Figured," High Top sighed, preparing his own crossbow.

Auri's fingers itched for a weapon. "Can you at least give us a knife?" she asked. When Oz shook her head, Auri added, "You plan to walk into an area reporting Walker and… *Merk* activity and still want to keep us vulnerable?" The term tasted strange in her mouth.

Ignoring Auri's concerns, Oz said, "Malachi wants to learn more about Merks. The best way to see them is in action." She moved away from the tower and headed down a street where the sky hung heavy and dark above the derelict buildings.

The street was overgrown with tall grasses, interspersed by flipped cars and homes with gaping holes where windows or doors used to be. Auri had the uncomfortable sensation that she was being watched.

"Do you know how Merks were created?" Malachi asked, keeping pace with Oz.

"Not yet," Oz murmured. "But I know something more important."

"What's that?" Auri asked.

"How to kill them before they regenerate."

High Top retreated to take up rear guard. "A few shots to the head and they're actually dead," he rhymed in a sing-song voice. "Their numbers are greater than ours, but thanks to Oz, we've been living in relative safety for the last year. With Chieftain's support, she instituted a rolling kill squad once a week. We've cleared our territory and this outer area of no-man's-land around our Block Towers."

"It's not enough," Oz muttered. "Chieftain is trying to convince the council to approve sending us out twice a week, but medical and farming don't want us to pull their people. The Merks are growing braver. Hungrier. This isn't the first time they've been seen creeping around. We're growing predictable."

"And predictability means death," Oz and High Top said at the same time.

"Your kill squads are worth shat unless you go in the sewers," Grubs whispered, almost as if he were talking to himself.

Oz glanced at him, but didn't reply.

"How did things get this bad?" Auri asked, gesturing to the street around them. "What happened?"

Ahead, the road split in a four-way intersection. A massive steel beam lay across one street, the pavement cracked underneath it. Old-fashioned stoplights lay scattered near the beam, the green, red, and yellow shards of plastic bright against the asphalt.

"Legends say people went mad," High Top said. His voice dropped as if he was relaying a ghost story. "Eat enough people and you become a Merk. Stay up past bedtime and blood seeps from your eyes. Ignore any of Oz's orders and—"

"Why did I bring you again?" Oz grumbled. She glanced at Auri. "The *real* legend says millions of people got sick, and whatever cure the scientists came up with made the sick people heal from anything, become three times as strong, and start eating other people. They outnumbered the normal humans, so it didn't take long for things to go to shat. When we asked our inter-galactic friends for help, we were told to screw off. And still the government sent one last ship of us to you.

"The details, we don't really know, but obviously some Scavs like to add their own twist." She raised her brows at High Top who grinned.

"We've got five blocks until Tower Two." She pointed down the street to their right and moved onto the cracked sidewalk. The sky above hung heavy, almost black. It cast the buildings in a hazy darkness as if evening had already descended. Auri breathed deep the scent of an approaching storm, feeling the electricity in the air. "So muzzle up in case there are Merks or Walkers lurking in the shadows."

Auri, Birdie, and Malachi were ushered into the group's center. Oz led while High Top kept his position at the rear. Grubs took middle guard. They skirted around derelict structures, which had transitioned from homes to multi-story buildings covered with glass windows. Debris lined the sidewalks and spray-painted graffiti marred most surfaces. Auri tried to read some of it, but the elements and time had rendered them illegible.

A gust of wind rushed across the street, stirring up stray bits of paper and garbage. Auri's hair lifted off the back of her neck and whipped about her face. Birdie paused and raised her head. She sniffed, then turned and sniffed again. A low growl rumbled in her throat. She stepped off the sidewalk onto the street.

Auri froze, watching Birdie's behavior with growing concern. Malachi paused beside Auri, drawing Oz's attention.

"What's going on?" Oz hissed in annoyance. Her gaze moved to Birdie. "Ugh, that fracking *dog*. Let's go."

But Auri didn't move. She watched as Birdie raised her front paw, her black nose pointing straight at a high-rise building directly across from where they stood.

"What's going on?" High Top asked, moving closer to stand beside Grubs. Grubs had cocked his head, his mouth a thin line.

"Something's off," Grubs murmured.

"Malachi," Auri whispered. He drew closer. One of the hanging traffic lights swayed in the breeze. A single raindrop pattered onto Auri's nose. "Something is wrong."

Oz took a step toward Auri and Malachi. She looked ready to knife both of them. "We can't stop—"

Something shot from one of the upper windows of the high rise. Auri whirled as a thick, black bolt buried itself deep in High Top's thigh. He grunted and staggered back, dropping his crossbow.

Birdie barked and darted to Auri. The darkening clouds made it hard to see, but Auri's robotic eye picked up at least five figures moving at the window above.

Grubs raised his crossbow and shot at their attackers. High Top broke off the end of the bolt protruding from his leg with a hiss before retrieving his crossbow.

"Cover this way!" Oz called.

Grubs looped an arm under High Top's shoulders. They raced down the sidewalk as another bolt struck the concrete centimeters from Malachi. The nerves in Auri's back hummed as if an electrical target blazed atop her head. She ached for her disc. Even the untested *Ganbaru*, confiscated somewhere in the Hole.

Oz disappeared around the side of a building. Auri followed, only to come to an abrupt halt. Ten men and women held their crossbows fixed on Oz. Birdie hunched low, her chest rumbling in a growl. Malachi's shoulder bumped into Auri as he slid to a stop beside her. Grubs was heartbeats behind Malachi, and High Top's rasping cries of pain turned to colorful swearing that ended with "Nightwalkers."

The name for the Scavengers' enemy was startlingly accurate. Where the Scavengers' skin was tanned golden from the sun, the Walkers were ghostly pale. As pale as Mery had been. Their hair was buzzed close to the scalp, even the women. They were slender in a way that hinted at childhood starvation. Despite gaunt faces, their clothes were in good repair: fitted pants and jackets with a plethora of weapons at their belts.

Oz raised her chin. "This is no-man's-land," she said. "You've broken the treaty by attacking my people. I'll let you keep your lives if you leave now."

One of the men let out a rasping chuckle. "You don't look like you're in a position to *let* us do much of anything. Tell us where that spaceship is, niece, and we'll make your deaths quick."

Auri glanced at the Scavenger in confusion, but Oz was focused on the threat ahead.

"My mother cut blood ties with your people," Oz spat, "the day she married my father."

"Look what good that did her," the man said. The rain picked up, fat drops plopping onto the sidewalk. "We still had to rescue her in the end. Well, her corpse, anyway."

Oz's body trembled. "How dare you," she ground out.

"As much as I love good drama," High Top cut in, "rehashing the past is a waste of time. Just shoot us because we're not giving in to your demands."

The man's gaze cut to High Top then down to the Scavenger's injury. He clucked his tongue, swiping rainwater from his eyes. "That looks fatal."

"So does this." High Top shifted, hurling a knife he'd hidden against his palm. It flew through the air, sinking deep into the man's throat. He dropped to the ground with a gurgle.

Oz shot a bolt into another Walker and charged forward, machete flashing. Grubs eased High Top onto the ground under an awning. Then he let out a savage battle cry, swinging the spiked baseball bat into a Walker's face.

"Outsiders," High Top's voice drew Auri's attention. He tossed Malachi his sheathed machete and handed Auri his last knife. She nearly dropped it, hands slick with rain.

Malachi's gaze met Auri's through the downpour. She saw the thoughts in his eyes as clearly as if he said them aloud: *We could run.*

Auri shook her head ever so slightly. Malachi's lips twitched in a grin of approval. "Be careful," he murmured. Then he turned and joined Oz and Grubs.

"Birdie," Auri called. "Attack!" Birdie lunged, intercepting a female Walker poised to stab Oz in the back. The Walker screamed as Birdie's jaw clamped around her shoulder and towed her down.

A thick blade sliced through the air toward Auri, and she leapt back. One of the female Walkers approached, an axe clutched in both hands. Auri gaped at the crude weapon. The

Walker swung again, droplets flying from the blade. Auri side-stepped. Fear pulsed hot in her blood, but so did adrenaline.

The Walker raised the axe, but Auri was already darting forward. The woman's arm slammed into Auri's robotic shoulder. Auri shoved her knife into the Walker's belly, hilt deep. Warm rainwater—or was that blood?—ran down Auri's hand. The Walker hit the ground. Eyes wide, she coughed up a stream of blood.

Arms looped under Auri's armpits and around the back of her neck. The stench of sweat and fear washed over her before Birdie's jaws locked around the attacker's ankle and tugged. Auri twisted at the same time, damp hair slapping against her cheek, and slammed her elbow back. It cracked against jawbone. A quick uppercut with her knife and the man fell.

Walkers lay scattered across the sidewalk and street. Half of them were motionless; the others bled out in silence or whimpered for mercy. Oz had sustained a scratch along her cheek and Grubs's knuckles were bloody. Malachi's hair was damp with rainwater. He shoved it out of his face, shirt clinging to his chest and stomach. His gaze met hers through the torrent. Fire burned hot in his eyes. Blood smeared his neck, but as Auri drew closer, the rain washed it away to reveal unmarred skin.

"More will be coming." Oz spat a wad of red onto the ground. The rainwater merged with the blood on street, turning it a dusty pink "We need to get to safety." Her gaze shifted to where High Top still leaned against the building where Grubs deposited him earlier. His head was rolled back, crimson a pool beneath him. Fear crept into the edges of her voice. "We need to get him back to the Hole."

"Oz…" Grubs started, but she silenced him with a glare. Instead, he changed tactic. "I know somewhere we can hide."

"Close by?"

"A block."

"Let's go. High Top, I've got you." Oz hurried to help him stand.

"Are you okay?" Auri asked Malachi, shoving tendrils of wet hair from her face. The rain eased, shifting from a downpour to a steady drizzle.

He nodded and swung his machete in a loop. "Haven't used one of these in a long time."

Her eyes widened. "You had machetes in the Renegade Sevens?"

Birdie trotted over. The rain had washed most of the blood from her coat, but pink still stained her underbelly and muzzle. Auri's gaze caught on a man on the ground behind the dog, his throat cut half open, a gash in his cheek revealing a clenched jaw of broken teeth.

The enormity of what had just happened, the brutality Auri had unleashed on other humans, barreled through her. A sour taste spread across her tongue. Pressure built in her chest, then throat. Birdie sidestepped as Auri dropped to her hands and knees. The half-digested remnants of that horrible protein bar reappeared.

Auri blinked tears from her eye only to see more corpses meters away. She gagged and then vomited again. "*Kuso*," she rasped.

A warm hand rested on the back of her neck. *Malachi.* She dry heaved again. Raindrops trickled down her cheeks, down the back of her neck, cleansing the blood from her skin. Her stomach slowly settled. She squeezed her eyes shut and took a slow inhale through her nose. Then she spat the taste of bile from her mouth.

Malachi helped her rise. Birdie sniffed at the pile of vomit and Auri grimaced. "No, Bird. Gross."

"Outsiders!" Oz called. She supported High Top with an arm, the sidewalk beneath him already red. "Follow or we're leaving you behind. I don't have time for your otherworld sensibilities."

CHAPTER TWENTY-FOUR

15 Nov 3319, 10:06:42
Milky Way Galaxy, Earth,
Scavenger Territory

Oz and High Top ducked after Grubs through a broken shop window, Malachi and Auri steps behind. Auri nearly slipped on the tiled floor inside thanks to her sopping boots. Malachi steadied her with a hand while Birdie bounded into the abandoned store. The stench of wet dog made Auri sneeze.

Oz guided High Top around fallen beams, metal shopping carts, and heaps of garbage. Grubs gestured to a counter at the back. High Top grunted as Oz eased him down behind it. She shifted to peer over the edge of the counter and out the window where they had entered.

The pelting rain drowned out most sounds, but Auri heard the faint hum of voices outside. A fresh wave of adrenaline made her arms and legs tremble. She shivered as her damp clothes clung to her. Wet tendrils of hair stuck to her cheeks and the back of her neck.

Oz swore under her breath and shoved hair out of her eyes. "More Walkers." She reached into her pack and pulled out a long belt. She prepared a field tourniquet above High Top's wound. He hissed as she tightened it.

"They were waiting for us," Grubs said with certainty. The bat lay across his lap, and he worked chunks of flesh and hair from the spikes with the edge of his machete. Auri looked away before she started dry heaving again.

"The stones on them," Oz growled. "This is supposed to be a noncombative zone. We haven't had an invasion like this since…" She trailed off and swallowed.

"Can we make it to Block Tower Two?" Malachi asked.

High Top shook his head with a grunt. His brown face had gone ashy with blood loss. "We probably wouldn't make it and—"

"And the sentries aren't allowed to abandon the tower," Oz interrupted. "They're a small contingent meant to protect the solar panels and provide early warning in case of attack. I'm not going to make them choose between duty and their future chieftain."

"Then what?" Malachi asked. "Are we going to sit here and hope they don't find us?" He peeked over the counter, taking the position of guard.

Oz watched High Top, concern flickering across her face. "Hope is pointless. They're not idiots. We could've only gone so far, and we have information they want."

Auri ran her fingers over Birdie's clumps of wet curls. Anger burned through her veins, helping to banish the rain's chill. After everything Auri had done, everything she had lost, she refused to die at the hands of *baka* humans targeting their own kind.

Grubs cleared his throat. "This building has an entrance to the sewers."

High Top rasped a shaky laugh. "You'd rather d-die by Merks?" He shook his head. "At least the Walkers would make it quick."

"No, they wouldn't," Oz countered. "You heard my *uncle*." She spat the word. "The Walkers want the shuttle. It's not about a territory anymore. They're starving. We're not. Their resources are finally drying up. *Frack*. The shuttle is probably just an excuse." Resolution hardened her voice. "They'll torture us until we give up the location of the shuttle and the Hole. And one of us will break."

High Top fingered the remains of his scarred ear. "So, we get gobbled up by Merks or we're tortured to death. Hell *and* high-water."

Oz let out a slow breath through pursed lips. She turned to Grubs, who had returned to de-fleshing the spikes on his bat. "Can we avoid the Merks in the sewers?"

Grubs paused. "As long as I stayed quiet, the Merks didn't bother me. The stench and darkness of the sewers will hide us. Mask the scent of blood too." He inclined his head at High Top.

Oz glanced at Auri. "Even better."

Malachi dropped back behind the counter so suddenly, Auri nearly jumped out of her skin. "We need to go," he hissed. "The Walkers just entered the neighboring building. We'll be next."

"Let's move." Oz looped an arm under High Top's armpits. "Deep breath," she told him. "And… *up*."

High Top strained, gritting his teeth to muffle a cry. Auri tried not to stare at the pool of blood left behind. Going into the sewers with an open wound like that…

Grubs led the group to the back of the shop. In a corner, behind a few toppled stools, were a pair of metal doors that had buckled inward. A broken padlock hung from a latch in the middle, the numbers on the dial stained with old blood.

Grubs eased one of the doors open. The rusted hinges released a squeal that set Auri's teeth on edge. Birdie's ears quirked tight against her head. Malachi glanced back the way they had come, muttering curses under his breath. Auri half expected to see a group of Walkers waiting at the doorway, crossbows aimed, rain pelting the street behind them. But the hallway was empty. *For now.*

The open door revealed a narrow closet, empty except for a cast iron manhole in the floor. *Property of the City of Archillean* was stamped around the rounded sides.

Grubs slid his machete blade along the metal seam. He pried the cover upward with a grunt and slid it noiselessly aside. A stench wafted from the opening that sent Auri's empty stomach rolling. Birdie sneezed.

Oz grimaced, palm over nose, as she stared down into the dark maw. She took a slow breath through her mouth, pulled out her flashlight, and cranked it. The beam illuminated a rung ladder that ended in murky, stagnant water.

High Top sucked in a breath. Sweat or rainwater had gathered underneath his eyepatch and trickled down his cheek. "Leave me here, Oz," he pleaded. "You and I both know what's going to happen. At least let it be above ground."

"I'm not abandoning you to the Walkers," Oz snapped. Before High Top could reply, she added, "And I'm not letting you die alone. So, tuck it in." Her voice cracked around the last words, and Auri felt a pang of pity.

"Grubs," Oz said, turning to the other Scav, "you go down first. High Top will follow. Then Auri, Malachi, and the dog. I'll bring up the rear."

Panic built in Auri's chest as she watched Grubs disappear into the hole. The scuff of his boots against the metal rungs reached the group as they waited for the telltale splash. When Grubs gave the all clear, High Top followed, using his good leg to move down the ladder.

Oz gestured for Malachi to go next. He glanced at Auri and must've seen the panic in her eyes. "Count the rungs as you go," he murmured before looking at Birdie. "I'm your best bet for getting down the sewer. Auri could carry you, but..."

"Don't try to reason with her," Auri choked out. "She's not going to like it no matter what."

Auri commanded Birdie to stay while Malachi picked her up, the dog's belly against his chest. Birdie wriggled, but then wrapped her paws around his shoulders. Her tongue lolled out as she panted.

Malachi grunted at the extra weight before he slowly made his way down the ladder. At some point Birdie released a sharp bark of fear, and Auri rushed to the opening.

Malachi called up, "She didn't like getting wet, Auri. Everything's okay."

Oz cranked her flashlight again to illuminate the ladder. "Go," she said to Auri.

The clatter of something falling, followed by a whispered rebuke made Auri whirl around. She couldn't see the front of the shop, but judging by Oz's clenched jaw, they had just run out of time. Auri shifted over the edge. They rung was icy cold against her organic skin. And damp, even this far up from the water.

Once Auri was far enough down, Oz swung herself over the side. Auri thought she could hear the faintest sound of unfamiliar voices above, but then Oz slid the manhole back in place. The motion sent Auri's mind reeling back into the cryo chamber, watching her mother close the lid. Air fled Auri's lungs in a rush. She couldn't breathe. Couldn't think. Couldn't *move*.

"Auri," Oz hissed. The tip of a boot nudged Auri's cheek. "If you don't go, I'm going to kick you off the ladder."

The threat brought her back, the organic parts of her trembling with barely contained hysteria. She gripped the rung more tightly with her robotic hand to keep from falling and forced herself to move. Oz didn't seem the type to make idle threats.

The gritty sides of the walls scraped against Auri's elbows as she moved down the ladder. The stink of decay grew more pungent the lower she went. Oz's flashlight beam bounced off the darkness with each of the Scavenger's movements.

Auri counted the rungs as she descended. *Sixteen, seventeen, eighteen...*

At twenty-two, Auri's boots splashed into murky water. Birdie bounded over with a whine. Sewer water splashed over Auri's already soaked pants.

A tunnel stretched to Auri's left and right, only a few meters of it illuminated by Oz's and Grubs's flashlights. Malachi kept High Top upright while Grubs moved a few paces ahead, creating ripples in the stagnant water. The liquid only reached Auri's mid-calf, but with the rainstorm above, it wouldn't remain shallow for long.

"Grubs," Oz murmured, recalling the Scavenger. Even her soft whisper echoed.

Grubs eased through the water, barely making a sound. "I was looking for my old markings," he said. "If we head straight down"—he pointed with an open hand—"we'll reach a four-way intersection. We take two lefts, and we should hit the outskirts of no-man's-land. From there it's only a twenty-minute, above-ground walk back to the Hole."

Oz opened her mouth to speak, but a loud *bang* followed by a splash reverberated down the tunnel. Auri froze, holding her breath, trying to guess where the sound originated.

Oz's gaze darted to Grubs as they both smothered their flash-light beams in their jackets.

Grub's gaze swept the curved ceiling as he listened. The sound grew quieter. "Moving away," he breathed. "Merks don't bother being stealthy. We use that to our advantage."

"Malachi, you help High Top," Oz finally dared whisper. "Stay behind Grubs." She looked to Auri. "You're on rear guard with me."

The group moved slowly. About halfway down the tunnel, High Top toppled forward. Malachi managed to catch him and sling the Scavenger across his back in a fireman's hold. Auri could feel the hum of Oz's barely suppressed panic.

"Move" was all the woman said.

When they finally reached the intersecting tunnels, Malachi was drenched with sweat and High Top was unconscious. Malachi eased High Top from his back into Grubs's arms and tried to catch his breath. Oz strode over to High Top, trying to rouse him back to consciousness with a rough shake of his shoulder.

Birdie sniffed at the entrances of three other tunnels. She paused at one, taking a few steps inside. A growl rumbled in her throat. Auri shifted closer to Birdie to see what had caught the dog's attention. Oz followed, catching Auri's arm in silent warning that she had ventured too far.

"Birdie," Auri hissed. This was no time for the poodle to get curious. "Birdie, come." Oz took another step forward, cocking her head as if she saw something in the shadows of the tunnel. "Don't wand—"

The Scavengers' flashlights blinked out at the same time. It was so dark, even Auri's robotic eye couldn't pick out any details from the blackness. Somewhere behind her, Malachi whispered, "*Kuso.*"

The sound of cranking followed as the Scavengers powered their lights. Water sloshed against Auri's knees. Birdie was finally coming back, thank the stars. The dog's curiosity was going to get them killed.

Oz's light flashed on, illuminating a Bleeder towering over her, blood smeared across a scar-ravaged face.

CHAPTER TWENTY-FIVE

15 Nov 3319, 17:02:14
Milky Way Galaxy, Earth,
Scavenger Territory

The Bleeder lunged.

Auri drew her knife and leapt in front of Oz, robotic arm raised, organic one crossed behind it. The Bleeder's jaws clamped around the synthetic skin above her barcode cuff. Auri heard its teeth glance off her metal bone underneath. Confusion flickered across its face.

Auri flicked her knife and buried it in the side of the Bleeder's throat. The creature gurgled. Auri yanked the weapon free, and blood gushed across her face. The sticky warmth made her want to gag. But even as the creature choked on its blood, its jaws didn't release Auri's arm. It drew a hand back, nails long and blackened.

Birdie dove from the shadows, sinking her teeth into the creature's leg.

Air whooshed beside Auri's cheek. A crossbow bolt buried itself deep in the Bleeder's forehead. The creature jolted. It grabbed for Auri again. But before it reached her, another bolt slammed into its temple, the point protruding out the other side. The creature went limp. Its jaws went slack. Birdie barely managed to dance out of the way before the creature's corpse splashed into the water. It floated just under the surface, dark hair eddying over the ripples caused by its fall.

Auri tucked her robotic arm against her chest. She flexed her fingers and rotated her wrist. Thankfully the Bleeder's teeth had missed the vital circuitry underneath. Oz still had her crossbow half-raised, flashlight gripped in her teeth. Behind her, Grubs supported a half-conscious High Top. Malachi had a crossbow in one hand and was sloshing toward them, face shadowed.

He kicked the Bleeder. "Look away, Auri." He handed Oz the crossbow and raised his borrowed machete. Auri turned as he brought the blade down. The squelch of skin splitting and the *clang* of the machete hitting cement made her grimace.

"The Merk was dead," Oz said to Malachi as Auri turned back to look at the decapitated Bleeder. "Overkill."

"When it comes to these pieces of *kuso*," Malachi said, spitting on the corpse, "there's no such thing as overkill." His gaze shifted to Auri, taking in what he could in the light. "Are you okay?" He caught her arm to examine the injury.

Auri jerked back, but the damage was done.

Oz's eyes landed on Auri's arm. The synthetic skin had been torn away in the shape of human bites. Underneath, the steel of her manufactured bone glistened in the light.

Realization washed over Malachi as he hissed a curse. He closed his hand over the wound on Auri's arm. His gaze cut to Oz. "Just a scratch. She should be fine."

Oz opened her mouth. Hundreds of questions flashed behind her eyes, but she settled with "We'll talk later."

"More will be coming," Grubs called. He shifted under High Top's weight, making High Top groan. "We need to go."

"Arm still functioning?" Malachi whispered.

Auri nodded.

"Good." He strode past her and took High Top from Grubs before returning the crossbow to the Scavenger.

They had just reached the opening of the next tunnel when a sound reached Auri's ears.

Bang, bang, bang.

At first, she mistook it for her own heartbeat. But in seconds it grew louder and more distinct.

Bang, bang, bang, bang!

Footsteps. *Running* footsteps. Realization lodged Auri's stomach in her throat. She tightened her grip on her knife.

Bang, bang, bang, bang, bang!

The howling started. It came from every direction, rebounding off the walls, the water. The sound chilled Auri's blood and woke a primal fear. Death was racing toward her. Toward all of them.

"Run!" Grubs cried.

They bolted down the tunnel, churning up dark water as they fled. The footsteps and shrieks of the Bleeders were disorienting. They sounded close and far away at the same time. Auri's organic palm ached from clutching her knife.

"Merks, left!" Grubs shouted as he made a sharp turn.

Auri glimpsed hulking shadows rushing toward them before she was inside the next tunnel. Malachi began to lag, drawing closer to Auri and Oz's position at the rear. High Top's head smacked against Malachi's back with each step, arms limp and lifeless. He must've passed out again.

The growling snarls grew in volume. When Auri risked a glance back, she saw at least five Bleeders chasing after them. One noticed her look and let out a cackling laugh.

"Almost there!" Grubs called. "I see the ladder. Go, go!"

A shape burst from an opening on the left. It slammed into Malachi. He and High Top tumbled into the water.

Auri rushed forward, knife raised, but Malachi shot to the surface with a gasp. He stumbled back, machete flashing as he prepared to strike.

"No!" Oz's cry drew Auri's attention to the Bleeder. It pounced atop High Top's half-submerged body. The Bleeder tore into the Scavenger with a howl. Anguish contorted Oz's face, but she caught Auri's shoulder, hauling her forward. "Go!"

Auri moved around the feasting creature, fatigue rippling through her muscles. Malachi's hand caught hers and they fled, Birdie at their heels.

They reached the ladder as the other Bleeders discovered High Top's corpse. A few broke off to fight over the remains but a handful kept chase.

"Up!" Grubs called. He drew his crossbow and began firing.

Oz went first. Then Auri, followed by Malachi with Birdie.

Oz struggled with the manhole lid, and she let out a heart-breaking whimper. Auri came up beside her and used the strength in her robotic arm to help shift it up and over.

Daylight broke into the hole. Spots danced before Auri's organic eye, but she kept moving. She and Oz launched themselves over the opening. Auri rolled onto her belly and caught Birdie as Malachi handed the dog up. Malachi heaved himself over next, followed by Grubs.

The howls of the Bleeders changed from hungry to enraged. They swarmed the ladder. The face of a male, eyes swollen and bulging, sprang for Auri as it reached the top rung.

Oz and Auri slid the grate in place. The bang of metal muffled the crunch of bone.

ELINOR JAYRE
VIDEO LOG #04

February 22, 3277
Location: Planet 08: Roanleigh, Owari Settlement

arkness consumes the camera lens. A familiar voice mumbles, "Flash on, low." There is the sound of rustling before the drone's light flicks on. Marnie winces and holds a hand up to her face.

She is propped on her elbow in bed. Tangled gray sheets rest at her hips. A baggy t-shirt covers her torso with a sport team's name written across the front. There is a small hole in the armpit of one sleeve. She tugs at the hem in an almost shy way.

"My husband's," she murmurs. Her voice is raspy as if she has recently woken from sleep. Beside her someone mumbles, snorts, then rolls over. The camera can barely make out the form of Aldin. His eye is closed in sleep, lips slightly parted. Marnie shifts to look at him. She tucks the blanket over his bare shoulder before facing the camera.

"I can't sleep," she explains. "It's two—I mean, 0200. I keep thinking about work." She runs a hand over her face. One of her cheeks is wrinkled from her pillowcase. "We've been busy. Crops have been transferred over to the greenhouse dome inside the Hub." Her expressions become less sleepy and more animated as she explains the process to grow food. "We are using soil brought from Earth, but hopefully we can find some way to work with

Roanleigh's climate. Use the soil here as well. There wasn't much time to prepare before we left."

The wind howls outside and Marnie pauses, listening. It turns into a keen as it whistles over the dome of her home. When it quiets, she sighs. "We could use help from the other planets, but storms are still interfering with comms. Worst of all, they've damaged our main ship. It wasn't built for this kind of weather. It's something of a miracle it carried us all the way here. They never planned on launching it. Until our world fell apart…" She clears her throat. "Now our only way off this planet is a one-man emergency shuttle."

Marnie sighs again and looks down at her open palms. Her brows draw together. She shifts upward in bed and leans closer to the camera to use the light from its lens. A small pink scar covers the tip of her finger.

"Strange," Marnie murmurs. "I cut myself with a spade a few days ago. It was deep enough that I needed stitches." She chews the corner of her cheek. "The terraformed air must be really good for our bodies. Not as polluted as…" She stares at her finger a moment longer before shaking her head. "No. We left that behind."

Aldin mutters in his sleep and reaches for his wife. He loops an arm around her waist and drowsily opens his eye. "Everything okay, love?" he mumbles.

She shifts closer to him and closes her fingers against her fist. "Yes, sweetheart. Just can't sleep."

"C'mere, Marn." He eases her down beside him. "I'll hold you until your worries melt away."

CHAPTER TWENTY-SIX

15 Nov 3319, 20:31:51
Milky Way Galaxy, Earth,
Scavenger Territory

The sewers had spat them out in the middle of an alley. Moss covered the buildings on either side and grasses sprouted from cracks in the asphalt. A curious squirrel watched them atop a rusted fire escape choked by vines.

Auri's limbs quaked with exhaustion and adrenaline. She stared, gasping, at the manhole cover, expecting it to fly off and a Bleeder to emerge. Seconds passed without incident, but she didn't relax. The darkness of the sewers clung to her like a sticky second skin she longed to shed. She ached to collapse onto the soft moss nearby and close her eyes, but they couldn't stop. The Bleeders weren't their only problem.

After a brief respite to catch their breath, Oz led the group from the alley onto a main road, keeping close to the shadows of the buildings. The rain had stopped while they had been in the sewers. Evidence of its passage lingered: damp pavement, potholes filled with rainwater, droplets clinging to glass. The streets were silent, devoid of both Walkers and Bleeders—thank the stars.

To the west, the horizon had swallowed the sun. Red and orange hues splashed across the darkening clouds as if the sky shared Oz's grief.

Auri's painfully empty stomach twisted over High Top's fate while a quiet part of her was thankful Malachi hadn't fallen under the Bleeder's jaws.

They abandoned the suburbs for a thick cropping of trees that quickly turned into a forest. The occasional raindrop spattered onto Auri's nose as they trudged through mud. Her hair and clothes had dried to damp rather than sopping, though her boots still squelched with each step. Malachi suggested they rest and regroup, but Oz rejected the idea. Grubs explained that the doors to the Hole shut at nightfall and didn't open until dawn. No matter who was locked outside.

The thought of a night at the mercy of Bleeders, Walkers, and wild animals made Auri shiver.

Thankfully, the Scavengers' farmland soon came into view. Oz hadn't bothered blindfolding Auri or Malachi this time. She moved with single-minded focus toward one of the structures—a blockhouse, she called it—and pulled a hidden switch. A door creaked open, and they ducked inside. Farming equipment, weapons, and clay pots crowded the narrow building, some fixed to walls, others stacked in strategic towers along the floor. The space smelled strongly of dirt and old wood.

Beyond the blockhouse stretched a trail cut through tall grasses. Auri's shoulders sagged with relief. The Hole contained its own dangers, but it was safer than the streets.

"Oz!" a familiar voice called from the Hole's entrance. Auri squinted in the darkening light. Greenie sat with her back pressed against the the partially shut doors. Two different guards stood just inside. Greenie pushed to her feet and ran toward Oz. A few stragglers on their way into the Hole turned to look back to see what was going on.

As Greenie drew closer, her footsteps slowed until she stood, frozen. Her gaze swept the group. Once, twice, a third time. Her lips parted to ask a question, but it was as if she couldn't form the words.

"He's gone," Oz murmured with her eyes lowered. She took a slow breath and strode past Greenie, hailing the two guards at the entrance. Grubs nodded his sympathy to Greenie as he passed.

Greenie lowered her head and clasped a hand over her mouth to muffle a sob.

Malachi was already moving to follow Oz and Grubs, but Auri stopped near Greenie. She hesitated, not sure what to say.

"He wasn't in pain," Auri finally whispered, just loud enough for Greenie to hear. Birdie pressed her forehead against the back of Auri's thigh.

Malachi paused at the entrance to the Hole and looked back. Shadows moved across his face from the flickering lights inside. Behind him, Oz had her arms crossed as she spoke to one of the guards.

"How?" Greenie rasped. She met Auri's gaze and a tear rolled down her cheek.

"Crossbow bolt to the thigh," Malachi answered as he approached. "He passed out from blood loss, but before he did, he murmured your name. I was carrying him, at the end."

"Malachi, Auri!" Oz called. Greenie straightened, hastily wiping at her eyes. "We have a problem."

Oz's panicked tone made fresh fear pulse through Auri. Malachi and Auri hurried over while Greenie slipped back inside the Hole. She only turned back once, her gaze darting to Oz, before she vanished down one of the halls.

"What is it?" Malachi asked. His gaze moved from Oz to the female guard beside her.

"Weapons first," Oz said. She held out her hand. Malachi and Auri exchanged a look before they relinquished knife and machete. When Oz had both weapons, she said, "Chieftain has your friends."

———

Oz explained the situation as they rushed down the Hole's central staircase. Surprised Scavengers pressed against the railing to avoid being plowed over.

"When I didn't report to Block Tower Two," Oz called, "they signaled the Hole. As hours passed without word, Chieftain had Castor and Tsuna dragged to the prisons."

"Did he put them in a cell?" Auri asked, trying to understand the panic tightening Oz's voice. Birdie's claws clacked against the metal steps in time with Auri's fluttering heart.

"No." Oz rounded a corner and they hit the landing of the final staircase. She hesitated a beat before speaking in a ghostly whisper, as if dredging up memories she'd shoved to the recesses of her mind. "My mother was tortured to death after being captured by the Alliance."

Oz let the words hang in the air for a beat before continuing, "She was the daughter of the Walkers' leader, so when the Alliance captured her, we asked for their help. But in the end… it didn't matter. Chieftain likes to repay the favor when given the opportunity."

Dread seeped through Auri's veins.

"How long has he had them?" Malachi asked. The rage crackling through his quiet tone made Auri look at him with a different kind of fear—fear he would do something they'd all regret.

"Half an hour," Oz said.

They barreled down the dark prison corridor. The walls seemed narrower than Auri's memory claimed. At the end of the hall, two guards waited outside a shut door.

Oz came to an abrupt stop a few meters away, and Auri bumped into her. The guards shifted to peer down the dimly lit passage.

"Oz?" one called. "That you?" Birdie growled in response.

Oz yanked at the hem of her shirt and tore a strip off. "Wrap this around your arm," she hissed through her teeth, passing the fabric to Auri. "Don't let Chieftain see your wound."

Malachi glanced at Auri. She quickly yanked the dirty strip around the bite marks in her synthetic skin and Malachi helped tie it off. Satisfied, Oz strode up to the guards.

"Oz!" the guard said, smiling. "We thought—"

"Frack off," she interrupted. "I don't kill that easy. Wait outside." She shoved past the guards and slammed the door open.

A lit bulb dangled from the ceiling by a thick wire. It illuminated Tsuna and Castor where they were bound to two chairs. Tsuna's fingers were splayed across the arm rest. Her thumb and forefinger were swollen and bent upward at a horrifying angle. Tear tracks glistened around a wad of cloth shoved into her mouth. Beside her, one of Castor's eyes was sealed shut and dried blood coated his nostrils. Chieftain hunched at a nearby table, back to the door, pointed instruments laid out on a strip of leather.

A whimper escaped Tsuna's gag.

The door slammed behind them. Chieftain turned with a growl as if he expected a guard. His eyes widened at the sight of Oz. "Daughter, you—"

Malachi darted forward. A knife flashed. He grabbed the back of Chieftain's shirt and pressed the blade against his neck. Chieftain attempted to grab one of the sharpened tools on the table but caught the leather underneath them and they clattered to the floor. Oz reached for an empty sheath on her belt and swore.

"You *dared* touch my crew?" Malachi growled. A droplet of Chieftain's blood slid down the knife's edge. "I'll saw your head from your shoulders."

Oz watched Malachi, one hand on the hilt of her machete. But she didn't call for the guards.

"You're safe, daughter," Chieftain rasped, ignoring Malachi as if he was nothing more than a mosquito. "I thought the Outsiders…"

"It was Walkers," Oz said. "Walkers attacked us in no-man's-land. We fled into the sewers and encountered Merks." Her gaze shifted to Tsuna and Castor. "Let them go."

"Don't move," Malachi warned Chieftain. His voice was calm, collected, and Auri realized he must've been planning this on their race to the prisons. "We have kept our side of the agreement. My people worked on the shuttle, we helped with rotations. But you…" He shifted the blade. This time Chieftain winced as blood dripped down his neck.

Oz closed her hand around her machete handle. She drew it a few centimeters from the sheath. "Outsider," she warned. "Don't make me choose between you and my father. You'll lose."

Malachi looked to Oz. "So will your father. It's time for new terms."

"I can call the guards," Oz reminded him.

Auri's muscles tensed for a hand-to-hand fight. Birdie hunched forward, her teeth bared, ready to pounce at Auri's command. There was no way they'd escape the Hole alive. Malachi had to know that. What was his plan?

"Go ahead. Chieftain will be dead before they open the door," Malachi countered.

Oz gritted her teeth. "What are the terms?"

"You know more about the Merks than you've shared. Chieftain tasked you with your tribe's future. You're an explorer. You're innovative. What you turned on at that old military base wasn't an accident. I saw the tech. You had to *read* to turn the right systems on. What else do you know?"

Oz's expression shifted. "There's—"

"Oz," Chieftain warned.

She avoided her father's gaze. "There is a lab. In Walker territory. Their people are technically mine, through my mother's blood, so we didn't violate the treaty."

"What's so special about the lab?" Auri asked. She placed a steadying hand atop Birdie's spine.

Oz tongued her cheek. She glanced from Chieftain to Auri. "At the end, communication between other parts of the country and world was very limited. But my mother said the last of Earth's scientists worked in the city, up until they were overrun."

"Why would we care about scientists?" Castor spat a wad of blood. It splashed crimson across the floor. Beside him, Tsuna took a shuddering breath. She shifted against her wrist bindings. She winced when the movement jarred her wounded fingers.

Oz shoved hair from her face. "They were a Merk taskforce."

"A taskforce for what?" Malachi asked.

"Stopping them. But we never discovered if they succeeded—my mother died before we figured out the technology." She shook her head. "We haven't gone back since. I planned to tell you about it when I knew you could be trusted."

"They will never be trusted," Chieftain spat. "If they are who they claim, they left our ancestors, *our world*, to rot when we begged for aid. They turned their backs and cut us off like a limb ripe with rot."

"*We* did nothing," Malachi corrected him. "A commander from decades ago made that choice without our knowledge or consent. But we plan to change things when we return. You have my word on that, if it means anything to you."

"I don't have the same prejudices," Oz whispered. "Legends aren't doctrine. You didn't have to resort to this."

"Neither did he."

"Frack you," Chieftain snapped. "I'll order your executions. No one—"

"Chieftain." Oz's voice was just barely audible. "I owe a life debt."

He sobered, gaze darting from Malachi to Auri. "Who?"

Oz gestured to Auri. "She saved me from a sewer Merk. We should welcome her as one of our own. Like we did for Grubs."

Chieftain took a slow breath, wincing as his neck touched Malachi's blade. He remained quiet for a few beats. "What do you propose, daughter?"

"I take them to the lab in Walker territory. Let them look for the information they need."

"That lab is the biggest Merk nest for a hundred kilometers!"

She nodded. "The Northeast Quadrant is dangerous."

"I've known you would lead the Scavs into the future," Chieftain murmured. "I just didn't expect it to be so soon."

Oz smirked. "I'm older than you when you became Chieftain."

He inclined his head. "True."

"And recompense to my crew?" Malachi asked. His grip on the dagger and Chieftain hadn't loosened.

Chieftain considered Malachi's question. "Medical treatment." When Malachi still didn't release him, he spat, "I will allow you free roam of the Hole."

"So you can kill us after?" Castor grunted as if it hurt to speak. "Or you just planned on killing us all along."

"It crossed my mind."

"Join us," Oz said, looking at each of them with sincerity, hand shifting away from her machete. "Join the Scavs."

"Oz," Chieftain snapped, voice laced with warning. "Enough. Be satisfied with what I have given. You are at my mercy."

"I'd disagree," Malachi reminded him. He started to say more, but Oz gave a slight shake of her head. Malachi hesitated then said, "Very well." He pulled the knife back and released Chieftain. Auri rushed to Tsuna and eased the cloth from her mouth. The hacker sighed in relief.

"Tell the guards they're relieved from duty." Chieftain wiped at his neck, smearing the blood. "Have one of them send a doctor to treat the Outsiders' injuries."

"Wait, Chieftain," Oz said. "The treaty."

Malachi and Auri worked to untie the bindings around Castor's and Tsuna's wrists and ankles. Birdie whimpered, butting her wet nose against Tsuna's knee.

"What about the treaty?" Chieftain asked, watching Castor and Tsuna rub at their tender skin.

"The Walkers violated it," Oz snapped. "Didn't you hear me before? They fired at *us* in no-man's-land to herd us into an ambush. High Top…" Her voice cracked, and she took a steadying breath. "They killed High Top. We need to retaliate."

"I know how much he meant to you. To Greenie." Chieftain ran a large hand over his bleeding neck. White scars crisscrossed his knuckles. "But the treaty has kept us at peace for the last five years. They could have been rogue Walkers."

Oz gritted her teeth. "Rogues! I'm no dit. One of them was my uncle."

Chieftain crossed his arms at Oz's outburst, and Auri watched the woman try to reign in her emotions. "I will double the soldiers at the Block Towers," Chieftain compromised, "but I'm not going to disrupt our peace because of one skirmish. You were a child during the war, Oz, and your mother protected you from its horrors. Besides, *you* are preparing to break the treaty by bringing these Outsides into Walker territory."

Oz's voice wavered. "They *killed* one of our people."

"And I'm sure you killed many of theirs."

"Not enough to avenge High Top," Oz whispered.

A flash of pain moved across Chieftain's face. "You are the perfect balance between your mother and me. You are the future of the Scavs, but you have a lot to learn. There are times to fight, but even more often, there are times to cling to peace. This is one of those times. You know it to be true, as brash as you are, my fiery daughter."

Oz's hands curled into fists. Auri thought she would yell or refuse to obey her father. To her surprise, Oz turned and eased open the door. "Chieftain says your dismissed," she told the guards outside. "But stop by medical and send a doctor to the Outsiders' quarters."

Chieftain watched Oz turn to face him, his brows drawn with concern. Auri helped Tsuna rise. The woman stumbled as if she'd lost feeling in her legs. Castor groaned and then swore as Malachi supported him.

"Oz," Chieftain called.

She turned to look at him. "Yes?"

The wrinkles around Chieftain's eyes and mouth deepened as emotion flickered across his face. "I am proud of how you handled yourself in no-man's-land." He cleared his throat, returning to his role as leader. "You leave for the lab after the first night of Harvest. Choose three of our people to accompany you. Bring this *captain* and one other Outsider. The others remain behind." His gaze flicked to Malachi. "If you do not return after two days, I will finish what I started."

CHAPTER TWENTY-SEVEN

---

15 Nov 3319, 22:01:21
Milky Way Galaxy, Earth,
Scavenger Territory

The walk back to the crew's quarters was somber after the encounter with Chieftain. Auri had one arm around Tsuna's hunched shoulders. The hacker cradled her injured hand to her chest, eyes fixed on the twisted fingers as if her will alone could heal the damage. Castor's face was fixed in a permanent seething glare in Oz's direction. Auri glanced at Malachi, but his gaze was ahead, expression unreadable. Birdie sniffed every door they passed, clearly unbothered by the melancholy mood.

Oz stopped in the hall between the crew's two rooms. "What just happened was unnecessarily unpleasant." She turned to Malachi and her mouth twisted in a frown.

"I agree." He crossed his arms. "The torture of two of my crew was unnecessary."

She arched a brow. "I meant with my father."

Malachi let out a humorless, dark laugh. "Don't pretend you wouldn't have done the same."

"No, I wouldn't have done the same," Oz said, her smile oozing cold malice. A chill that had nothing to do with the Hole's temperature washed across Auri's skin. "I would've done *worse*."

A growl rumbled low in Birdie's chest, and Oz shot the poodle an uncertain frown.

Tsuna shifted away from Auri's supporting arm, and Auri stepped aside to give her space. The hacker tilted her head. "Ever been tortured, Oz?"

Oz's lips formed a thin line. She shook her head.

"If your father is going to resort to such measures, his daughter should have a taste of it, I think."

"I'm not my father," Oz snapped. Her eyes cut to the still seething Castor. "So stop looking at me as if your gaze could melt my flesh from my bones."

"Give it a few more seconds," the cook hissed. "It might work."

Oz huffed. "Suit yourself." She returned her attention to Tsuna. "We need to discuss your progress with the shuttle, but that can wait until you're bathed, treated, and fed. I understand your concern about your fingers."

The thought of a shower nearly derailed Auri's question. She forced her attention on the present and not the promise of hot water and clean skin. "How long has it been since you went to the lab? War or no, it seems your people's best chance."

Oz peered down the hallway behind the crew. Even though they were alone, she shifted closer. The smell of blood and sweat rolled off her wrinkled clothes and metal armor. "My father is mostly content to survive. But I want my people to *live*. I'll be chieftain one day, so he allows me a short leash, but he won't readily risk Scavs without guarantees.

"After years of searching, my mother"—her voice wavered, and she swiped at the grime on her face, only smearing it further—"found the lab back when she was a Walker. Her own grandmother was a scientist there and had told stories of Archillean's last hope, but many believed it was a legend passed on by a half-mad woman. When I turned thirteen, she took me there, hoping I would support her vision for the future. We had begun to convince Chieftain of its importance, but soon after…"

She cleared her throat and rested a hand on her machete. "Chieftain is right. It *is* a Merk nest. My mother thought they were protecting the lab. Returning wasn't worth the risk, not even with the full force of the Scavs, because I don't know how to work the machines. But with your knowledge, you can help me understand—help me *do something*."

"Chieftain said we would leave after Harvest," Malachi said. "When is that?"

"Tomorrow."

"I see." Malachi leaned against a wall, eyes shadowed with exhaustion and the weight of the crew's lives.

"What's Harvest?" A spark of Tsuna's usual curiosity and fervor had crept back into her voice.

"We celebrate the harvest before the cold season. It's held every night for a week so all Scavs can attend, regardless of their shifts." Oz looked like she wanted to ask a question of her own, but footsteps down the hall drew her attention.

A man in a plain gray shirt and black pants approached, a duffel bag slung over a shoulder. "Where are my patients?" he asked.

Castor glared at him. "If you can't tell, you aren't much of a doctor."

A flush colored the man's cheeks. "It was just a polite…" He trailed off at Tsuna's arched brow. He shifted his bag higher on his shoulder. "If you don't let me take a look, I can't treat you."

Oz opened the door to the room Tsuna shared with Castor. "Simon, they bunk in here."

Tsuna glanced at her twisted fingers and swallowed hard.

"Tsu…" Castor began, his brows drawing together in concern. One of his eyes had swollen so badly, he could barely see. It reminded Auri of a *dango* fresh from the oven.

Tsuna cleared her throat. "Come on, Castor. We don't want to spurn Chieftain's generosity."

Oz sighed at the blatant sarcasm.

As the doctor examined Castor and Tsuna, Auri felt a sudden pang of loss for Ferris. She stole a look at Malachi and saw the same longing on his face before he noticed her staring and hid it away.

"Once he's done," Oz said, "I'll get you fresh clothes and show you to the bathing chambers."

If Auri didn't think Oz would stab her, she would've hugged the woman.

———

The Scavengers' bathing rooms reminded Auri of basic. Two benches spanned the middle of the rectangular room. Spigots emerged from the walls about a meter apart with handles at chest-level. Across from the entrance, three full-length mirrors helped reflect the light of the few bulbs hanging from the ceiling.

Auri had not missed the communal bathing of basic. But at least the Scavengers separated males and females.

Tsuna strode forward and plopped the towel and change of clothes she'd been given onto a bench. Her two injured fingers had been splinted and bound with linen. The doctor declared them dislocated, which was better than a break. Tsuna's relief had been palpable.

The hacker tugged her sleeve gingerly over the bandage, then she promptly stripped her jumpsuit off.

Auri lowered her gaze to the brick floor as heat rushed to her organic cheek.

"How does this work?" Tsuna asked. She stood in front of a shower, bar of soap in hand. Oz came over and demonstrated. She cranked the handle in a full circle. Water shot from the spigot in a thick stream that was more like a hose. The handle immediately started clicking as it spun.

"You have a minute per crank," Oz said.

"Just so you know," Tsuna murmured, "if my fingers had been broken, Oz, I would've told Castor to kill you." Her voice was colder than Auri had ever heard it. She was reminded that Tsuna had a past Auri knew nothing about, a past that had gotten her a death sentence in Attica.

"You don't like getting your hands dirty?" Oz crossed her arms. In the silence between them, the patter of the shower and tick of the crank echoed.

Tsuna's lips twitched. "On the contrary. My skillset just isn't as useful on Earth. I'll consider us at a truce, but your father is a twisted, broken man. And I've known a lot of twisted men."

Oz glanced down and whispered, "I know."

Tsuna stepped past Oz to restart the shower. She submerged herself under the spray with a groan.

"What is that?" Oz asked, pointing to Tsuna's forearm. The barcode was barely visible against the hacker's dark skin.

Tsuna glanced down as water droplets caught in her eyelashes. "They're identification markers in our galaxy. We have technology that scans them."

Oz glanced back at Auri. "All of you have them?"

"We do," Auri answered, thankful she was clothed for this conversation. She had no idea how Oz and Tsuna could be so casual about it. Just the thought of stripping made heat creep up the back of Auri's neck.

Oz pursed her lips. "Interesting." She moved to the spigot beside Tsuna. "Dog," she called. "Over here."

Auri slipped off Birdie's harness, procrastinating the removal of her own clothes. The dog shook with pleasure. Oz cranked the handle and Birdie plowed into the stream of water with a happy bark that echoed off the cement walls.

"Thanks," Auri told Oz as she approached. Oz nodded and left to find her own spot on the bench.

When the supply of water cut off, Auri knelt beside Birdie, soap in hand, and lathered up the dog. She turned the handle once more to allow Birdie to rinse.

While Birdie played in the water, Auri returned to the bench to find Oz sitting there, slowly unlacing her boots. Auri eased a few meters down for the illusion of privacy. She stripped quickly. When Auri looked up, Oz was already underneath her own shower across the room. Tsuna's water had run out and she paused, hair sudsy, to twist the handle again. Birdie had finished and was busy shaking droplets from her damp curls.

Auri chose a spigot in a shadowy corner of the room. The water wasn't as hot as Auri hoped, but it was warmer than the humid air. And at this point, she would've showered in an Arctic waterfall.

Auri kept her broken synthetic skin out of the spray, just in case. There were no warnings on her c-tacts, and there didn't seem to be exposed circuitry, but it was better to be safe. Her barcode, bare for the first time in days, glistened in the dim light. She wondered what her c-tacts would find if she was connected to the grid. Was she still considered MIA? Or had the GIC finally declared her dead?

Auri planned to wash quickly and dress, but she couldn't resist twisting the handle a third time. She closed her eyes and let the water run in rivulets over her skin. The temperature had gotten colder with each twist, but the robotic parts of her weren't bothered by the chill even when her organic skin prickled with goosebumps.

The attention of someone's gaze plucked at Auri's nerves. Her eyes snapped open as the flow of water stopped. Oz stood with her back to the mirrors, a wooden comb halfway down her hair. It was as if she'd seen Auri's reflection in the glass and turned for a closer look.

A flush banished the goosebumps on Auri's skin. In her mind's eye, she could see what the Scavenger saw: the faint lines where human connected to robotic. The scars bubbling and twisting skin. Auri darted for her towel.

At the bench, Tsuna's barcode cuff was back in place. She wore a linen shirt and was tugging matching pants over her hips. Her braids were damp and clung to the front of the material. Birdie danced around the woman, tongue lolling.

Auri peeked out the corner of her eye, but Oz had returned to the mirror to brush her hair. Auri quickly dressed in a pair of black pants and a high-necked tank top that had a small hole at a side seam. The color contrasted with her pale skin and made her freckles stand out like flecks of flame.

"What are you?" Oz murmured.

Auri shifted as Oz approached. She stopped a meter away and watched Auri with her brows drawn together.

Oz had already seen Auri's arm. She also helped keep it a secret from Chieftain. That alone earned her an explanation.

"I'm a cyborg," Auri answered. When Oz stared uncomprehendingly, she added, "I'm part machine. When I was a child, I was in a Bleed—Merk attack. To keep me alive, some of my organs and limbs were replaced with robotic ones."

Oz pressed her fingertips to her cheek, still rosy from the shower. "Even your skin?"

Auri nodded. She looked down at her robotic arm, as cleaned of mud and blood as she could get it. The teeth-marks stood out like knife marks in dough. "Though it tears."

Oz stepped closer as if she wanted to reach out and touch Auri. "Your eye?"

"One is robotic."

"I thought it looked different," Oz murmured. "Frack, Auri," she breathed. "You're impressive."

Auri almost laughed. She had never thought *impressive* would be used to describe her conglomeration of parts.

"What do you mean?" Auri asked.

"You've got a second chance at life, the way you've been so artfully put together." Oz held out her comb and her long, dark hair, still wet from the shower, slid over a shoulder. "What a world you must live in."

Auri thought of the lies and secrets that fortified the life she had known. Oz was right. Though not for the reasons she thought.

CHAPTER TWENTY-EIGHT

***

16 Nov 3319, 00:00:01
Milky Way Galaxy, Earth,
Scavenger Territory

After showering, Oz and the entire crew gathered in Auri and Malachi's room for a late dinner, according to the tolling bell. Auri was so hungry, the stale roll, chalky potatoes, overcooked carrots in brown sauce, and hunk of unknown meat tasted like a lavish spread.

Once their plates were clean, Oz broke the silence. "Auri, you need to use my life debt to petition to join the Scavengers."

Auri glanced at Malachi to see what he thought. He watched her from the opposite bunk, gaze roving over the black fabric against her skin. She fought back the blush creeping over a cheek and raised her brows. He shrugged, annoyingly content to see what she decided.

Auri cleared her throat as she looked back to Oz. "Why?"

"Chieftain's going to have you killed," Oz said honestly. "He doesn't trust Outsiders, let alone those claiming to be from the galaxy that abandoned us."

"That's no surprise," Castor grumbled. "Seeing how quick he is to start torturing *guests*."

"A life debt changes things," Oz continued, ignoring the cook. "As Scavengers, you'd be safe." She pulled down the collar of her shirt to reveal a pointed *S* tattoo with a crossbow bolt bisecting it. The lines were crude, and Auri wondered at how tattoos were done without a robotic arm with its needles shaped in the chosen design. By hand, one prick at a time? She winced at the thought.

"You'd be one of us," Oz was saying. She released her collar.

"I understand, but…" Auri shook her head. "We need to return to our galaxy."

"Lies are being spread," Malachi added, "and someone needs to answer for them." He shifted and Birdie groaned where she'd curled up next to him, much to Auri's surprise. It seemed their time in the sewers had tilted Birdie's scale in Malachi's favor. The poodle had been so relaxed, she looked on the verge of falling asleep.

Oz sighed. "I suppose I'll find another way to make it up to you then."

"I want our weapons returned before we leave for the lab," Malachi said.

Oz nodded. She stood and gathered the metal bowls from everyone. "I know what Chieftain said, but keep to your rooms. Meals will be brought. I'll return with clothes appropriate for Harvest tomorrow evening." She started to leave.

"I'm sorry about High Top," Auri said in a rush, unable to hold the words back.

The Scavenger paused, gaze on the door. "We lose people all the time," she whispered. "But he and Greenie…" She shook her head. "Rest well."

When the door shut behind Oz, Malachi leaned forward, steepling his fingers against his chin. "It's all my fault. This cluster—"

"*Urusai*," Tsuna cut him off. The frame above Auri creaked as Tsuna hopped to the floor where she'd shared the upper bunk with Castor. "This isn't your fault. We knew there would be danger, especially after Roanleigh." She toyed with a loose thread along the edge of her bandage. "We came anyway."

Malachi shook his head. "I got us captured. You've trusted me with your lives, and I screwed you over. Tsu, you could've lost your fingers."

"Didn't you hear her?" Castor muttered. "We chose this, you blathering sop. We aren't your little minions, even if you like to prod us into a direction you find favorable."

Malachi raised his brows. "*Minions?*"

"We all know you manipulate us," Tsuna added. "I thought it was attractive when I first met you."

"You were married, Tsuna," Castor snapped. "You only found your husband attractive."

Tsuna smirked but didn't reply.

Malachi looked down at his open palms before tightening them into fists. "I will get you all back on the *Kestrel* again. I promise."

Before his mind could slip into more guilt-ridden thoughts, Auri asked Tsuna, "Speaking of the *Kestrel*, how did things go today?"

Tsuna's eyes lit with excitement. "Their tech is very similar to Roanleigh's. I was able to reroute the solar energy to charge the shuttle. We even powered it on for a few minutes." Her eagerness fizzled and she grimaced.

"And?" Malachi asked. "What's wrong?"

"Thrusters are down," Castor said.

Malachi cursed. "How bad?"

"Fifteen percent operational," Tsuna answered. "Not even close to what we need. We'd barely get airborne, much less break the atmosphere." She glanced at Castor, and he nodded for her to continue. "But we do have good news."

Castor eased off the bunk and shuffled to the door. Tsuna shot him an appreciative smile and reached down the front of her shirt. When she drew it out, nestled in her palm lay the *Purloin*'s scavenged radio. The wires had been retwisted and rearranged into a tight braid.

"I charged this too," Tsuna murmured. "I haven't had a chance to test it. I wanted to save that honor for you." She held it out to Malachi.

Malachi grasped the radio so gingerly it might've been a young child. He took a slow inhale and exhale. Then he pressed the button on the back reserved for manual broadcasts. A red light flashed at the bottom before switching to a steady glow. Low static emitted from the speaker, and Birdie's head popped up where she'd fallen asleep beside Malachi.

"Malachi to *Kestrel*," he whispered. "*Kestrel*, do you read?"

Static resumed. Auri held her breath.

"Akki-tan?" Marin's familiar voice, somewhat hoarse, made tears prick at Auri's eye. "Akki-tan *bzz bzz bzz*. Is... that... you?"

"Yes," Malachi answered. "Are you alright?"

"We are... fine. I did as... instructed. Where are you? *Bzz bzz bzz* what happened?"

"I don't have a lot of time." He glanced at Castor, and the cook raised his thumb in a silent *go ahead*. "We were captured by Earth's survivors. They are bringing us to a research lab in two days. It should have more intel about the Bleeders."

There was a five-second delay in Marin's response as Malachi's words were relayed through air and space.

She replied with a dubious tone. "But how... are you going to... get back? Is the *Purloin* space *bzz bzz bzz* worthy? Do you even... have access?"

"*Purloin* is off the table," he said. "We're going to figure out something else."

"That brings up the question," Auri began, "who is going to Walker territory with Malachi?"

To Marin, Malachi explained, "We have to decide who is coming with me to the lab. Our captors want two to stay back as leverage. One second, Marin."

"I assume *bzz bzz* you mean longer than one second," Marin said. "I will wait."

Tsuna looked down at her bandaged fingers. "He tortured my dominant hand," she murmured. "I'll slow you down. I can't hold my blaster or use a knife with any proficiency."

"I'm not leaving Tsuna," Castor said, shifting away from the door.

Malachi inclined his head. "Noted. Tsuna, how complicated do you think the tech will be?"

"The black site was almost identical to the Hub on Roanleigh. You saw me power up both, so you'll be able to figure it out."

Malachi looked to Auri. "That leaves us."

She hesitated, peering down at the blue veins along the inside of her wrist. "My blood is a liability. Oz might want me to stay here."

Malachi's voice was harder than the steel hull of a Komodo class ship. "We aren't going to give her a choice. I need you."

I need you. Auri's belly flipped at the three words. She looked to Tsuna before her expression revealed her emotions to the captain. "What do you suggest for storing the data we find?"

"Without my gear on the *Kestrel*, storage won't be possible," Tsuna said, her forehead wrinkling as she considered other options. "I doubt the Scavengers have the tools either. You'll have to memorize what you see or take pictures with your c-tacts. Though the internal memory is limited, so don't go overboard."

"Marin," Malachi spoke into the radio, "Auri and I will be going to the lab. Castor and Tsuna will remain behind."

"How are you going… to escape once you have what… you need?" Marin asked. "I can bring *Kestrel* down, *bzz bzz bzz* but if

I don't know where… you are, if you can't reach us, there is… no point."

"Not to mention if you don't come back in time—or at all—we'll be tortured to death," Castor muttered.

"The radio cut out. What did Castor say?" Marin asked a minute later as the radio relayed the cook's sarcasm.

"Nothing," Malachi said, glaring at the cook. "We'll come up with a plan and reach out when we have something. Stand by."

The next few hours were spent discussing how they would escape if everything went according to plan…

And how Castor and Tsuna would get out if things went to *kuso*.

Both options left too many variables at play to satisfy Auri, but they didn't have many options.

If all went well, they'd radio Marin, and she would land outside the Scavengers' blockhouses east of the Hole, the closest area big enough to accommodate the ship.

If things went to *kuso*, Castor and Tsuna would alert Marin, decide on a meeting place, and work their way to the *Kestrel*. Once safely aboard, the three would wait in atmo for twenty-four hours, monitoring the rendezvous point for Auri and Malachi. If a day passed, and they didn't return, Marin would leave.

And all the sacrifices, everything the crew lost and fought for, would mean nothing.

ELINOR JAYRE
VIDEO LOG #05
February 27, 3277
Location: Planet 08: Roanleigh, Owari Settlement

"It's been a while." Marnie moves about her small kitchen, facing away from the camera drone. She reaches for a cup only to realize it's empty. Her mouth thins with annoyance, and she tosses the container into a shallow sink. The cup clatters against five others. "Things have been…" She opens a cabinet removes a plate but then shakes her head and returns it to the shelf. "They've been hard." She turns around, revealing a deep purple bruise circling one of her eyes. As if self-conscious, she prods it with gentle fingers. "Tempers are high.

"At first I blamed it on the stress of getting settled and losing comms." She reaches for an empty cup from the pile of discarded ones, turns on the sink, refills it, and takes a long swig. When she continues, her lips are wet with residue. "But almost two weeks in… I think it's something more."

The camera shifts as it detects motion. Elodie enters the kitchen, her hair in a messy ponytail. The green jumpsuit she's wearing is a few sizes too big. The cuffs of the sleeves and pants are rolled up.

"Mommy?" she asks. She rubs her eyes as if she's just woken up. "Where's Daddy?" A yawn splits her lips apart.

Marnie's fingers flutter to her bruised eye. She takes another sip of water before replying, "He got called for an overnight shift at the Hub, but he'll be home soon."

Elodie opens the fridge. It is mostly empty except for a container of apple juice, premade meal packets, and a few small eggs. Elodie grabs the mostly empty juice container and gives it a shake. "Can I have some?" she asks.

"We're almost out," Marnie says, her voice sharpening. "Drink water like everyone else."

Elodie crinkles her nose. "I don't like the way it tastes."

"Your juice is mostly water now anyway," Marnie snaps. "I didn't bring an endless supply from Earth."

Elodie looks down at the juice container, lower lip protruding with disappointment. Then she slides it back into the fridge. "Well, can we water the plants together?"

Marnie pauses, her cup halfway to her mouth. "When was the last time I even checked on them?" she murmurs. "It's been over a week." She strides into the living room where a few potted plants have been deposited in various corners. They appear to be saplings, likely destined for a replant at the Hub once they mature.

"How…?" she breathes in surprise. Marnie kneels next to a plant that reaches up to her knee. The leaves on it are lush and green. They practically glisten with vitality and new life. "They're flourishing."

In the kitchen there is a loud crash and then a cry of dismay. Marnie straightens and bolts into the room. Elodie stands atop a chair at the sink, spattered in water and mouth open in surprise. A watering can lies on the ground amid multiple cups and a large puddle.

Marnie grits her teeth and hurls her cup down to join the others. "Aghh!" she cries. "You are impossible, Elodie! No matter what I do, it's never enough!" She grabs one of the kitchen chairs and hurls it across the small room. It slams into the fridge, denting the metal. Elodie hunches atop her chair as Marnie approaches.

"I'm going to teach—" Marnie cuts off abruptly as she sees her daughter's face. Fear burns bright in Elodie's blue eyes. Marnie sucks in a horrified gasp. Tears well and spill down her cheeks. She holds her hands out. "Elodie, love, I'm so—"

"I'm sorry!" Elodie slides off the chair and throws herself into her mother's arms. "I was just trying to help. I'm sorry. Please don't be mad."

"It was just an accident," Marnie rasps against Elodie's messy hair. "You did nothing wrong." More tears roll down her cheeks. "I am so sorry. I will never hurt you. I love you. I love you, my sweet girl." As she cradles Elodie against her chest, a small droplet of blood seeps out of Marnie's nose.

CHAPTER TWENTY-NINE

---

16 Nov 3319, 18:05:31
Milky Way Galaxy, Earth,
Scavenger Territory

After a day confined to their small room, Oz finally returned that evening. Auri gaped the Scavenger. She had swapped leather armor for a short leather dress, and her black hair curled down to her hips, freed from its usual bun. A red sash looped around her waist with bits of smoothed metal sewn on the edges. It made tinkling sounds as she stepped into the room and passed out bundles of clothes to each of the crew. She looked beautiful in a ferocious, I'll-cut-your-throat-out way. Auri studied the dress in her hands. It was almost a twin to Oz's, sleeveless with a V-shaped neck, and a hem that would brush her upper thighs—if she was lucky. Castor and Malachi had leather pants with homespun shirts in a matching color.

"What's with the leather?" Tsuna asked, staring at the dress she'd been given. Hers had a square neck with thick straps at the shoulders.

"It's tradition," Oz explained. She ran her fingers over her hips, accentuated by the fitted nature of the dress. "We wear clothes made from our animals. It commemorates what we've been given and celebrates what we've earned." She smirked. "It's a time of harvest and fertility. Many make their life vows this week. And consummate them." She winked at Malachi and something icy stirred in Auri's belly.

"Hurry and get dressed," Oz continued. "The first night of Harvest will start soon."

They separated, Tsuna and Auri in one room, Castor and Malachi in the other. Oz left to wait in the hall.

Embarrassment washed over Auri once she'd adjusted the dress to lay against her body. Her muscled thigh, and closely matching robotic one, were barely covered. Auri tugged at the hem. The material slipped against her fingers. She'd never worn something so short before.

"Flaunt it," Tsuna said, drawing Auri's attention. The dress she wore fit like a second skin. It was even shorter on her taller height and accentuated her every curve.

"Castor is going to lose his mind," Auri replied, resisting the urge to tug at her hem again.

Tsuna ran her hands over the leather and glared at her bandaged fingers. "Maybe I can use it as an advantage to get to know more Scavengers. Nothing like a woman to loosen tongues. And I know the game well." A shadow flickered across her face before she banished it with a sultry smile.

Auri rewrapped her robotic arm with fresh linen, tucking the fabric to ensure it wouldn't come loose. "Are you sure that's a good idea?"

Birdie pressed her nose close to Auri's dress and sniffed. Auri swatted the dog away.

"We aren't married," Tsuna said.

"But aren't you…?" Auri hedged, not sure what word even described Tsuna and Castor's relationship. Or lack thereof.

Tsuna pursed her lips. A knock on the door ended the conversation, and Auri moved to answer it.

"If I didn't know better," Oz said with a grin, "I'd mistake you for Scavs." She gave Auri and Tsuna a once-over before shaking her head and pointing. "No shoes."

"No…?" Auri looked at Oz's feet and suddenly noticed the woman was barefoot.

Castor and Malachi stood just behind Oz, also shoeless. Malachi's pants fit him snuggly across his hips and thighs, the leather accentuating parts of him she hadn't noticed before. Her mouth went dry. She hurried to slip off her shoes to hide the expression on her face, holding down the hem of her dress with one hand.

"I tried to get your captain to shuck the glove," Oz muttered. "But made no headway. You look ridiculous."

"Says the woman wearing a sash with metal scraps hanging from it," Malachi countered.

Auri looked up to find Malachi's eyes on her. They didn't stray even when Tsuna sashayed out into the hall.

"Do I look ridiculous?" Auri asked him as she joined the group, laying a hand atop Birdie. The dog walked between them as they lingered at the rear. The hallways were surprisingly empty, but the delicious smell of roasting meat, vegetables, and something sweet lingered on the air.

"No," Malachi whispered as they moved up the stairs. "I can't take my eyes off you."

A spark of heat shot through her.

The main level of the Hole was a bustle of activity. Long tables in the eating area were decorated with arrangements of flowers and grasses. Two were pushed together to create a buffet with massive amounts of food. The stone fireplace crackled at full blaze, illuminating more Scavengers than Auri had ever seen. It was like a sea of brown leather crested at the heart of the Hole.

Chieftain stood beside the fireplace. When he saw Oz join the back of the crowd, he beckoned her forward.

The Scavengers parted as Oz strode to the fireplace. Oz squeezed a woman's hand as she passed. The Scavenger wore a black band around her upper arm, blonde hair twisted into hundreds of braids down her back. It took a moment for Auri to recognize Greenie. Misshot stood beside her and looped an arm around her shoulders as Oz left the pair.

When Oz reached Chieftain, his mouth spread in a grin. "Welcome, Scavengers!" he called.

His exclamation was met with applause and a few whoops of excitement.

"Old Earth has turned again, and we have reached Harvest week. Not all of us have made the journey together." He paused as if to honor the Scavengers they had lost. He folded his fingers into a gun and pressed it against his chest. "To madness and ruin!"

"To madness and ruin!" the Scavengers repeated. The sound of thuds echoed through the room as hands met chests.

A male Scavenger slipped from the front of the crowd. He positioned himself beside the fireplace, opposite Oz and Chieftain, and raised an instrument to his chin. It was different in style and material than the ones Auri knew, but it distinctly resembled a fiddle.

He raised the bow and looked to Chieftain.

"Oz," Chieftain said, waving a hand out to the crowd, "choose your partner and start our first Harvest dance."

"I'll take her!" Misshot cried.

Oz thumbed her chin at him. "You've got sweaty hands, Misshot."

The gathered Scavengers roared with laughter. Oz moved through the crowd, and they once again parted. Auri realized, with sudden dread, the woman was headed toward the crew. She stopped in front of Malachi and extended a hand.

One of her brows quirked up. "Do they dance in your galaxy, Captain Malachi?"

Malachi's lips quirked as if the two of them were playing a game he enjoyed. "Too often for my taste."

Some of the nearby Scavs whistled.

"He must not have rhythm!" someone heckled from the crowd. "Drag him out there, Oz!"

Oz smirked at the insults. "Are you going to dance with me? If the answer is no, I'll be very disappointed."

"Good thing my answer is yes." Malachi wrapped his fingers around hers and led her back toward the front of the room.

Auri felt her throat tighten at the sight of them together. She bit her cheek to keep the emotion from her face.

"This I've got to see," Castor said. He elbowed his way through the crowd. Tsuna cast one worried look at Auri before following. Auri moved too late and lost sight of Tsuna and Castor amongst the throng.

The fiddle played the opening notes of a slow, sensual song that sent prickles racing down Auri's nerves. It picked up speed and the Scavengers began to clap.

Someone in the crowd whooped. Another person whistled.

"The Outsider can dance!"

"Enough watching!" Oz called around a laugh, voice echoing in the dining hall. "Scavs, fall in!"

The crowd shifted as people moved onto the makeshift dance floor. Suddenly Auri had an unobstructed view of Oz and Malachi. The Scavenger was flush against him, her tanned cheeks red, firelight glistening off her exposed skin. Malachi smiled at something she said, moving with Oz as if he understood the very essence of the woman.

The dance was primal and intoxicating. Malachi and Oz ebbed and flowed as water, the other Scavengers moving around them like flickering shadows. Tsuna had even joined the dancers, sashaying around a man with long brown hair. Castor was nowhere in sight.

Despite the food, music, and freedom for the first time in days, Auri couldn't tear her gaze from Oz and Malachi. The woman was beautiful. The scars that glistened on her skin told a story of struggle and victory. Oz threw her head back and laughed at something Malachi said. Usually reserved, so concerned about her people and their future, she seemed finally able to let herself just *be* in Malachi's arms. And judging by his smile, he seemed to enjoy her company.

Oz and Malachi were two characters torn from the same book, born a galaxy apart.

Auri dropped her gaze. Her throat felt horribly tight, like she'd swallowed a stone. Birdie pawed at Auri's leg.

"I'm okay, Bird," she rasped. "I just need something to drink."

The people who hadn't joined the dance clustered around long tables on the other side of the room. Some ate while others puffed from long pipes. The emanating smoke smelled spicy with an underlaying sweetness that coated the back of Auri's tongue. She spotted Castor with a pipe of his own, a few Scavengers gathered around. Despite Castor's appreciation of whatever he smoked and the questions that garnered him attention, every so often his gaze strayed to the dance floor. Tsuna had already moved to another partner.

"You look like you need this." A woman with a thick streak of gray in her hair handed Auri a wooden cup. A murky liquid swirled inside topped with red berries.

Auri took a tentative sip. It reminded her of a sweet cider with a bitter undercurrent. She bit into one of the berries as it rolled onto her tongue, and the tartness melded with the taste of the drink, amplifying its flavor.

The drink eased the tightness in Auri's throat. She swallowed its contents. Her belly warmed as it filled. "Thank you," Auri said.

"Are you really from another galaxy?" the woman asked, looking down at Birdie as if not sure what to make of the poodle.

"I am," Auri answered.

"Is it much different from here?"

Auri considered the best way to respond. "At our heart, we are the same. We're just fighting to live a life we can be proud of, cherish our loved ones as fiercely as we can, and protect those in need." *Some of us, anyway.*

The Scavenger raised the pitcher in toast and refilled Auri's glass to the brim. "Good answer." Then she moved into the crowd to pass out more drink.

Birdie released a low *woof* that made her desire clear. Auri visited the food table and got a helping for the dog. Her own stomach clenched at the thought of eating. She led Birdie to an out-of-the-way corner and lowered the plate. Birdie ate while Auri sipped her drink.

There was a lull in the music, and Auri couldn't help but look to the dance floor. Oz and Malachi were no longer in the center. Instead, Oz had taken up the fiddler's spot. She raised the bow and began playing a cheerful tune.

People clapped in time as the dancers formed two lines.

A hand wrapped around Auri's wrist, and she gasped as Greenie appeared from the shadows. "Don't hide in the fringes, Outsider," she said, towing Auri toward the dance floor.

Auri just managed to deposit her cup on a nearby table before she was plunged into the dance. Greenie gave instructions as they moved, turning in circles, then shifting aside to their next partner across the line.

Auri faced a tall woman who had opted to wear pants and shirt. She was patient as Auri stumbled through the steps. The warmth in Auri's belly spread through her organic limbs and made it easier to move without feeling ridiculous.

The tune ended and the lines broke apart. The next song began, slower and deeper than the two before it. Greenie started to leave, but Misshot appeared at her side. "Don't run, Green," he said. "He would want you to be here. Dance with me."

Auri shifted to retreat to the tables but bumped into someone's chest. "Excuse—" Auri looked up into Malachi's multi-colored eyes. An image of Oz and the way she fit so perfectly in Malachi's arms flashed through her head.

The warmth of the dance and the drink vanished. Auri stumbled away from the captain even as he reached for her. She fled the eating area to escape the emotions warring within her. Malachi was her captain. She shouldn't be jealous of him dancing with someone else. And running away? She was being childish.

Auri found herself alone at the top of the staircase. The intense heat of the dining hall eased, cooling the sweat on her skin. She moved down a few steps until she stood on the first landing. A ragged breath escaped her lips, and she covered her eyes with her forearm. "*Baka*," she muttered to herself. "You *baka*."

"Aurelia?" Malachi's voice reached her, and she froze. His bare feet moved almost silently down the steps. He stopped centimeters behind her. She could feel the heat of his body. Smell his sweat and the scent that was all him, even on another world.

"I was getting hot," she murmured. Which was the truth. *Technically*. "I just needed a break."

"Will you look at me?" he asked.

"No."

"Why?" His hands found her shoulders, easing her around to face him. Moonlight shone through the skylight to cast silvery shadows across his skin.

"Oz is beautiful," Auri whispered, dropping her gaze. "I can understand why you like her." She tried to pull away, but Malachi's grip tightened.

"Oz is…" He trailed off. Auri jerked to look at him, desperate to see the expression on his face. When her gaze met his, he smiled, as if that had been his intention all along. "Oz is playing a game," he continued. "Which is why she danced with me. She was showing her people that we aren't a threat. I doubt Chieftain is pleased."

The words didn't help assuage the pain in Auri's chest. She had seen the way Oz smiled at Malachi. "It looked like more than that. And you didn't seem to mind how close she was."

"*Kuso*, Auri. No." He shook his head, all traces of humor leeching from his face, replaced by hard resolve. "My heart is stone until I eradicate the Bleeders and see the GIC punished. Love would only get in the way." He paused. "But if I loved as I wanted? Oz would not be the one I chose." His words hung in the air, and Auri refused to allow herself to hope. His grip on her arms tightened as if he feared she would disappear into the darkness.

Auri shook her head. "She wouldn't agree."

Malachi's brows drew together. "Who? Oz?"

"*Katara*. She would tell you to love while you can."

"Oh?" He gave her a sad smile. "Is that what she would've said?"

"Something like that," Auri shrugged.

"I doubt it would've sounded as eloquent." Malachi chuckled. "There would've been an insult in there somewhere. Definitely some swearing."

Auri rested her palm on Malachi's chest, just over his heart. "Malachi, your heart isn't stone. It's flesh and blood. You deserve a love that lines your scars with gold. That makes you stronger, happier, and more *you* than you have ever been."

Malachi stared at her for a beat, as if letting her words slip under his skin. "*Kuso*," he rasped. "You're beautiful." His hand slipped up her arm to knot in her hair. He slammed his lips against hers, backing her against the railing. Her mouth opened to him and she moaned at the way her belly seemed to plummet and soar.

His fingers traced the knotted scars on her shoulder. She tensed to shift away, but he held her in place.

"*Beautiful*," he repeated, eyes meeting hers. "All of you." Then his mouth was on hers again. The kiss deepened. Hunger grew between them. Auri ached to be closer, closer, closer.

Malachi's palm skimmed down her arm, along her hip. She pressed into him and he groaned.

"Aurelia," he said, voice husky and deep. He shifted to press kisses along her neck, making sure, as he always did, Auri realized, to touch the parts of her that she could *feel*.

"Can you give me that love you spoke of? Scars and all?" he whispered in her ear. His voice was rough with need. A delicious chill skittered down Auri's spine. "Do you want to?"

Yes. Auri knew the answer without pausing to think. She wanted to give Malachi all of her.

But she had wanted to give herself to Ty too. *You love too freely and forgive too easily*, Ty had said to her after the revelation of his treachery. She had loved Ty, despite the now obvious signs he didn't deserve it. Malachi was no Tyson Peri, but love also came with pain. Ferris's absence was proof enough of that.

Fear of giving her heart away kept her from saying the word she desperately longed to say.

Instead, she kissed him again while his question hung in the air, to be answered at a time when she was ready. And Malachi let it.

Let her simply feel, and be…

Beautiful.

CHAPTER THIRTY

17 Nov 3319, 05:55:19
Milky Way Galaxy, Earth,
Scavenger Territory

When Oz retrieved them the next morning, the crew was already dressed in borrowed patrol gear: patched cargo pants, t-shirts, and jackets with metal shoulder coverings. Despite the tight space, they had bunked in the same room again. No one wanted to separate with the dangers ahead. Auri quietly feared it would be the last night they spent together.

"Morning," Malachi said to Oz. He swiped a hand over his beard. The memory of it tickling her jaw the night before made Auri's face warm.

Tsuna eyed her with a knowing grin. She shifted closer to whisper, "Something happened, didn't it?"

Auri tried to pretend she hadn't heard Tsuna's question, but her cheeks flushed hotter.

"I'm surprised you're all ready to go," Oz said, stretching her arms overhead. "It was a rough wake up after Harvest. The first night is always the most… celebratory. Who's accompanying your captain to Walker territory?"

"I am," Auri answered.

Oz lowered her arms. Her gaze cut to Malachi. "Even with her blood?"

"We've dealt with Merks hunting her before," Malachi said.

"The Merks we'll encounter are different from those in the sewers," Oz warned. "They aren't half starved and half crazed. They have armor, and they have weapons."

Auri tried to picture Bleeders toting the Scavengers' machetes or crossbows and winced. "What kind of weapons?"

Oz glanced at her. "Harpoons. It isn't pretty. We'd normally bring shields, but we need to move fast."

"Auri is coming," Malachi said. "It's not up for discussion."

"Very well," Oz relented. "But if you endanger the lives of my Scavs"—she turned a hard stare on Auri—"you will be left behind."

Auri swallowed. "Understood."

"What about our weapons?" Castor asked.

Oz inclined her head, all trace of the carefree Scavenger from Harvest gone, neatly tucked away like her hair, now wrapped in a tight bun. "I keep my promises. I will give all of you weapons." She hesitated then met Castor's gaze. "I have every intent of returning. But if things go awry, my people will help you escape. Consider it the fulfillment of my life debt to Auri."

Castor's eyes widened in surprise. The cook was speechless, which was no small feat.

Oz jerked her head toward the door. "Let's get your weapons."

The hall outside bustled with Scavengers, a few returning from duty while others staggered from their rooms. Their stumbling gate and green-tinged faces hinted at too much fun the previous night. The bells chimed the six o'clock hour as Oz led them around a corner.

Oz's room wasn't far from the crews' quarters. She opened her door, painted with swirls of green and flecks of purple, and led them inside. The room was double the size of Auri's. But that wasn't what made her jaw drop.

The bulb in the ceiling illuminated posters covering every space of wall: long-dead musicians, far-off planets, and tranquil nature photos. Oz's sheets were a rumpled mess at the bottom of her bed. The fiddle from last night leaned against the footboard. A small dresser was pressed against one wall with a small stack of books. Auri recognized the top one as an Earth classic: *The Wizard of Oz*. Taped against the spine was a worn sticker with only a few words legible: *One More.*

"That's how my mom picked my birth name," Oz said, noticing Auri's interest.

Auri looked away from the stack. "I haven't seen books anywhere in the Hole. I'm surprised you have some."

"That isn't saying much," Oz countered, "since you haven't seen much of it. But you're right. We don't have many books." She shrugged, shoving her hands in her jacket pockets. The metal at her shoulders and chest winked in the light. "It's been almost fifty years since the world fell apart. Most of us didn't consider reading necessary to survival.

"My mother disagreed. She taught me when I was young." Oz rested her hand against the stack of books. "My mother was labeled a *progressive* when she was alive. When my father married her, it caused a fracture in our people. But Chieftain didn't care. I suppose he's progressive in his own way. He has to be, with a daughter like me." She cleared her throat. "Enough sentiments. We have a job to do."

Oz crossed over to her bed and shoved aside a pile of dirty clothes. She stooped over to pull out a long metal box. When she hoisted the lid, Auri recognized the crew's weapons nestled inside among thick animal furs. Auri's fingers itched at the sight of *Ganbaru.*

Malachi knelt and extracted his belt holster and coil guns. Once they were secure, the ever-present tension in his shoulders eased slightly. He rested his palms atop his guns and let out a breath. "Much better."

Auri grabbed *Ganbaru* and her laser knife, leaving the useless blaster gun behind. Malachi gave her a knowing look, which made her roll her eyes. She strapped the boomerang to her back and the knife around her upper thigh. Birdie sniffed at the new additions. Her tail wagged once in recognition.

Tsuna's injured fingers slipped when she attempted to secure her oversized blaster. She winced, and Malachi helped her loop the weapon around her hips. Castor gave him a nod of thanks, halfway through adjusting the dart gun around his wrist. Oz slid the bin back under her bed.

"I'm surprised *you* have the weapons," Tsuna said after thanking Malachi. "I thought your people would've studied them."

"Our military head isn't interested in this kind of advancement," Oz answered. "We wouldn't be able to replicate any of it with what we have in the Hole. You should be glad that's the case. Otherwise, getting them back would've been a challenge." She stood, wiping at her pants. "Castor and Tsuna, I recommend you stay close to your rooms. I'll have someone come by with meals."

Castor grimaced but, after an elbow from Tsuna, nodded.

Oz gestured at Malachi and Auri. "Let's move. My people are waiting at the exit."

Tsuna and Castor accompanied them to the Hole's top level. Oz slowed when she saw three Scavengers gathered at the ramp. Backpacks looped over their shoulders and crossbows were strapped to their backs. Auri recognized Misshot and Greenie, but the third man was a stranger.

"How in the…?" Oz murmured with a frown. "Greenie!" she called as she charged over. Passersby paused at the commotion. "How are you here?" She stopped in front of the group, arms crossed. Oz's gaze cut to Misshot, who was studiously examining the belt that held his machete. "Misshot, did you tell her?"

Misshot cleared his throat. The crew joined the group as he answered, "Not willingly. She beat it out of me."

"I'd believe that if I actually saw bruises," Oz muttered. She rounded on Greenie. "How did you really find out?"

Greenie raised her chin. Her blonde hair was slicked back into a braided bun at the nape of her neck with a deep blue kerchief wrapped around her forehead. "I overheard Misshot bragging about entering Walker territory at Harvest. All I did was corner him, pretend to cry, and ask what he was talking about."

"Traitor!" Misshot glared at Greenie.

"I don't know why I bothered bringing you, Misshot," Oz muttered.

"Because I'm the best shot in the Scavs, that's why."

"Well, your ability to keep your mouth shut definitely has nothing to do with it." Oz pointed to the man Auri didn't know. He was tall, taller than even Castor, with a patch over one eye. Scar tissue in the shape of human teeth bubbled around where a pinky finger should be. "This is Nibs," Oz said. "Short for Nibbles."

Nibs inclined his head.

"He's mute," Oz said. "And he's a hell of a sneak."

Nibs winked at the compliment. Something behind him let out a low *meeeeh!* Auri started and Birdie growled. Nibs shifted to reveal a short creature munching on the remains of a cabbage leaf. A thick rope was looped around its neck and attached to Nibs's belt. Two curled horns extended from its skull and its shaggy white coat was stained under the belly by mud.

"What's the goat for?" Castor asked.

"Bait," Misshot said. "We're going into a Merk nest, so we need to lure them out."

At Auri's horrified look, Oz raised her brows. "Unless you want to volunteer your dog?'

Auri laid a hand on her knife by reflex, and Oz smirked. "I thought not." She gestured to the goat. "We've bred his line to have more Ambrosium in their blood. They are raised as bait. No different than being raised for meat."

"Except how they die," Castor muttered.

Nibs gestured quickly with his remaining fingers and Oz translated, "Nibs says they lure the Merks away about seventy-five percent of the time. The other twenty-five is how he almost lost his hand and *did* lose his eye."

Nibs shrugged as if it wasn't a big deal, then itched at the skin under his eyepatch. The gesture reminded Auri of High Top. She glanced at Greenie, but the woman's face was resolute.

The main hall grew more crowded as Scavengers lined up to exit. Oz gestured for their small group to gather closer.

"Our journey will take a day there and a day back," she began. The goat snuffled at her jacket and tried to nip at the hem. She gave the animal a dubious look and swatted its nose with her hand. Nibs pulled out another cabbage leaf and the goat's attention shifted.

Oz continued, "Chieftain has ordered we uphold the truce"—she glanced at Greenie—"even after their treachery. So, we don't want to be seen in their territory. We're going to travel by day and find somewhere safe to hole up at night. Using the goat as Merk bait, we'll get in the lab, get out, and get back to the Hole. Got it?"

Everyone nodded just as a deep voice called, "Oz!"

Chieftain strode toward them through the crowd. Oz detached from the group to meet him. He cupped her cheek with his palm before wrapping his arms around her. Auri read his lips as he murmured, "Be safe, daughter."

Malachi shifted closer to Tsuna while the other Scavs were preoccupied watching the sentimental moment. He placed a hand around Auri's waist to draw her nearer. Castor leaned down to listen.

"You have the radio?" Malachi asked.

Tsuna laid a hand over her chest. "Yes."

"Don't let it out of your sight or let them see it. You know what to do if you and Castor get into trouble?"

"It won't come to that," Castor insisted.

"You *know what to do*?" Malachi repeated.

Tsuna nodded.

"Good."

Oz returned to the group and Malachi shifted away.

"Let's go," Oz said.

Auri wrapped her arms around Tsuna in a hug. The hacker squeezed tight and whispered, "Be safe." Castor rested a hand atop Auri's head. He didn't speak, but in his eyes, Auri saw his concern and fear for her safety. He was rough around the edges, but he cared about her. She nodded to show she understood his sentiment.

"We stick together," Oz said. Her gaze drifted to where Chieftain had been, but he was already gone. "We get done what needs doing and try not to die on the way."

"Why are you being so difficult?" a woman snaps. Her familiar voice is muffled and the camera lens is dark. There is external chatter as if a crowd has gathered.

A man mutters a few expletives under his breath. "You're not the easiest person to live with, Elinor."

"Well, maybe you should move out."

A snort. "To where? Someone else's igloo? You're the one who dragged us to a cursed ice rock."

Marnie's voice rises in pitch. "It was better than being eaten alive!"

The darkness clears as Elodie shifts and the camera is freed from the confines of her coat. The drone wobbles into the air, everything blurry before it focuses on Elodie as she hugs the legs of her parents.

"Don't fight," she pleads. "We're supposed to have fun." She clutches a doll garbed in ornate red robes and sewn in a cross-legged position. "This is supposed to be Girl's Day. *Hina...*" Elodie stumbles over the Japanese term for the holiday.

The view shifts as the camera scans the rectangular room. The Dayre family stands in a corner, and two rows of tables and bench seats extend away from them. On the other end of the room sits a table laden with food and drinks. A large crowd extends from a sink where people wait in line to fill water cups. The sign above the food table is written in *kanji* and reads *Hinamatsuri*, or Girl's Day.

Several people are shouting angrily, and others sit in sullen silence. Three boys are gathered in a circle, shoving one another between gulps of their drink. Two girls stand in front of a pedestal where fabric dolls similar to Elodie's sit. One girl grabs a figurine and bites it, ripping it in half with her teeth.

The camera finishes its sweep and refocuses on Marnie.

"How did you get here?" she mutters, swatting at the drone. "I haven't activated your recording in days."

Elodie glances at the camera and swallows. She looks around as if to draw her mother's attention elsewhere. Her eyes catch on something and she begins to wave. "Hello, Mr. Niel! Happy *Hina... Hinamatsuri!*"

The drone shifts to show Othniel approaching, hands in the pockets of his jumpsuit. Faded stains mar the knees of the white fabric. His gaze sweeps the agitated crowd, then Marnie and Aldin, before settling on Elodie. His smile is tense but genuine. "Hopefully it is the first of many for you, little El." His expression falters and he clears his throat. "Do you know the song for today? I heard your class practicing."

Elodie opens her mouth, but Aldin cuts in. "I'm thirsty." Without another word, he storms off to the sink. The bottles of wine and soda sit unopened.

Marnie's hands curl into fists, and she looks like she wants to yell after her husband. But her gaze shifts to Elodie's concerned blue eyes and she takes a breath before forcing a smile. "I'm sorry—or *gomenesai*," she says to Niel. Then to Elodie, laying a hand on her daughter's shoulder, she asks, "Would you like to sing the song for our friend?"

Elodie nods. She straightens her coat and adjusts her hair, a single braid down her back. She sings the traditional song first in halting Japanese, then in more confident English:

Let's light the lanterns on the tiered stand.
Let's put peach blossoms on the tiered stand.
Five court musicians are playing flutes and drums.
Today is a happy—

Elodie cuts off as someone screams. The camera spins, turning the room into a dizzying blur of color. The lens refocuses on the line of people at the sink. A woman hurls her cup into the basin, water spattering the walls and floor, and charges a man headed away from the front of the line. When he turns to face her, she swipes at his face with her fingernails. Blood bubbles from the scratches, and the man stumbles back with a roar of fury. Some of his water spills onto the floor.

"Mine tastes different!" she snarls, stalking toward him. "You took the last of it and thought you could just sneak off!" She lunges, but he shoves her back. She slips on the puddle and falls backward. Her temple cracks against the floor, and she lies still. Red begins to stain the tile in a spreading circle around her head.

"What does she mean?" someone calls from the line. People shift closer to the sink, ignoring the woman bleeding on the floor. Aldin is the first to fill his cup. He takes a quick sip, then hurls his cup against the wall.

"What happened to our water?" Aldin whirls, eyes wild. He moves toward the man with the scratches on his face, except, as the camera focuses, the wounds have already begun to knit closed. A drop of blood rolls out of the man's eye like a tear.

The man cradles his cup against his chest. "This is mine!" He chugs the last of the water and flings his cup away. It rolls along the floor and stops beside the woman who fell. She has managed to push herself onto her elbows, hair matted with blood.

Marnie places a hand on Elodie's shoulder and pulls her closer, as if to hide her daughter from view. Niel looks at Marnie from the corner of his eye.

"We switched to Roanleigh's supply this morning," Marnie murmurs. "I'd completely forgotten. It was automatic. Scheduled a week ago."

Someone nearby hears her and cries, "Was anyone going to tell us?"

Another person yells, "I would've rationed mine!"

"I'm so thirsty," a little boy whines, pitch deepening into a growl.

"You took the last of it!" The injured woman launches herself into the legs of the man she scratched. He falls and she scrabbles her way up to him until she reaches the bare skin of his throat. She sinks her teeth into his neck. He screams, and the sound seems to last an eternity before it dies off.

The woman shifts upward. Red coats her lips and stains her white jumpsuit. "So thirsty," she groans. "I can taste it… the *water*."

Everyone in the room freezes, then glances at each other. Marnie catches Niel's eye and gestures at the door behind her with her head. Niel nods in understanding.

The woman licks her lips before turning back to the man who has begun to groan. But two colonists creep up behind her to clamp their jaws around her half-closed head wound. She screeches in agony.

The room dissolves into chaos. People attack each other, teeth tearing into flesh. One of the children laps at the puddle of blood on the floor. Marnie stumbles for the door, yanking Elodie behind her. Niel throws it open and they, with a few other fleeing people, hurl themselves inside.

Niel goes to close the door, but Marnie pauses in the doorway, peering into the mass of bodies, looking for someone. Her gaze lands on Aldin. He runs toward Marnie. Relief washes over her until she notices the blood smeared across his face and chest, matted in his hair. His eyes are wild and he reaches out, face contorting in hunger.

"Marnie!" he yells.

She slams the door and twists the lock.

CHAPTER THIRTY-ONE

---

17 Nov 3319, 19:25:56
Milky Way Galaxy, Earth,
No-man's-land

The waning sun sank into the depths of the river, painting the rushing water in its dying hues of gold and crimson. Which Auri could clearly see through the missing slats of wood beneath her feet. She bypassed a particularly large opening.

"I hate this bridge," Misshot muttered. He followed at the rear, keeping an eye on the dilapidated street they had left behind.

Auri had to agree. The pedestrian bridge had likely been beautiful—once. The thick wooden beams were fairytale-esque, the way they arched to form the supports. But those supports had rotted with age and lack of maintenance, further weakened by the tendrils of ivy covering almost every spare centimeter.

"Small Way was the best choice, and you know it," Oz said from the front of the group. Auri and Malachi followed just behind her. A few meters back, Nibs had the goat slung over his shoulders, Greenie beside him. "After the Walker attack in no-man's-land, I wasn't going to risk Gordian Bridge. I know a safe place to camp once we cross." In a quieter mutter, almost to herself, she added, "Well, it was safe when I was last here."

"How long ago was that?" Misshot asked.

Oz pointedly ignored him.

Nibs chuckled as the goat sniffed the man's braided top knot.

They had made good time through the Scavengers' territory and into no-man's-land. Ahead loomed the Walkers' swath of land: a much larger city already fading into dusk. The buildings were mainly skyscrapers, reaching at least twenty stories into the sky. But despite its height and sprawling size, the area seemed quiet. The grass-covered road beyond the bridge was empty. The toppled cars shoved to the sides were still, reminding Auri of metal carcasses. She suppressed a shiver of unease.

Beside her, Malachi kept his gaze on a swivel, one hand on his coil gun. His profile, the crooked nose and resolute chin, brought back memories of the night before. Auri could hear the whisper of his questions: *Can you give me the love you spoke of? Do you want to?*

Their kiss had awoken an ache inside Auri. She hungered for his closeness, in whatever form that took. She cared less about protecting her heart and more about taking advantage of the time she had with him. His eyes caught hers when he took in their perimeter again. Her stomach flipped.

Birdie had made a game of crossing the bridge. She bounded over some holes and stuck her nose down others. As long as the dog remained quiet, she could have her fun.

"Have the Walkers always been your rivals?" Malachi asked Oz. They had reached the halfway point in the bridge.

Greenie answered, "We don't agree with the way they operate. We worked together once"—she glanced at Oz—"but only because Chieftain felt he had no other choice. It didn't go well in the end."

Oz didn't look back. "They're a cult," she said. "My mother managed to escape. She never would've wanted Chieftain to treaty with them in exchange for help. They left us alone before they learned about our resources."

"What do you mean, a cult?" Auri asked. She thought of the militias back home, groups of dishonorably discharged or drifters to who had nowhere else to go.

Oz shifted her backpack higher on her shoulders, crossbow in one hand. "They live in Merk-infested territory, but rather than go on the offensive, they steal supplies from others. They use prisoners, or people who hope to become Walkers, as bait."

Auri's brows drew together. She glanced at the goat.

Oz chuckled dryly. "They chain people together, cut their palms open, and lead them through the streets while their scouts loot the surrounding buildings. If their captives or initiates survive a fortnight, they are set free and brought into their fold."

"Do any survive?" Auri asked, unable to keep the disgust from her face.

"Enough to keep the Walkers' numbers high. The experience makes their people brutal. Blood thirsty. Willing to do anything to survive."

They lapsed into silence for the remaining trek across the bridge. Auri found herself thankful that Scavengers had found the *Purloin* and not Walkers. She couldn't imagine what their fate would've been.

They weaved through a desolate parking lot of some long-abandoned shopping mall. Carts were turned on their sides, cars upended with smashed windows and dented bumpers. Auri's footsteps resounded painfully loud, and she breathed a sigh of relief when they crossed a weed-infested street toward a row of three-story townhomes. Oz directed them toward an end unit that faced the city.

A row of cracked cement steps led to the front door. The oak, stained glass cutout, and surrounding siding had been spray painted with a large, ominous red *X*.

Oz strode through knee-high grass to a dead flower bed tucked under a bay window. Broken bricks stuck up from the mulch, some in danger of dissolving if touched. Oz crouched, nearly disappearing from view. When she stood, she brandished a metal object between thumb and forefinger. As she drew closer, Auri recognized an old-fashioned key.

"You'd be surprised how successful a locked door is at keeping people out," Misshot commented, guarding the street behind them. "Breaking in is loud. It's also the best way to make sure no one has come in before you."

Nibs lowered the goat to the ground as Oz hurried up the steps. She slid the key into the door and turned the handle.

"Misshot," she whispered, looking back. "Keep your eyes on the street. Nibs, check around back."

Misshot nodded without turning. Nibs gave a thumbs up and passed the goat's lead to Malachi. He drew his machete and slipped around the rear of the building.

"Greenie, with me." Oz raised her crossbow as Greenie moved up the stairs. "Auri, Malachi, you wait here." Then she and Greenie disappeared inside.

Night descended while they waited. Auri thought she heard the faint echo of footsteps, but even with her robotic eye, she didn't detect movement between the buildings or streets beyond.

Something snarled in the distance followed by a dying whimper. Misshot raised his crossbow and took a step away from the townhouse.

Malachi had drawn one of his coil guns. He shifted close to Auri and the steps, making sure his back wasn't vulnerable. Auri kept one hand on *Ganbaru,* ready to yank it free. Birdie sniffed the air and whined.

The anxiety of being hunted made the hairs on Auri's skin stand up. Even the goat paused trying to chew a hole in Malachi's pants. Quiet settled on the streets once again, but Misshot didn't relax. Auri whirled at the sound of footsteps behind her.

Greenie emerged from the doorway; her crossbow strapped to her back. "All clear."

Misshot nodded. "I'll get—" But Nibs was already trotting back to the group. He tapped at his ear with a smile as if to say *I heard her.* Malachi returned the goat's lead to Nibs.

Greenie waited at the threshold as everyone hurried inside. She eased the door shut and locked the deadbolt.

The hallway beyond was shrouded in a musty darkness. On Auri's left, a flight of steps emerged from the gloom with a small room on her right. The bay window there was covered with thick boards that kept even the meagerest light from entering—or exiting.

The Scavengers cranked their flashlights and details emerged. In the center of the room was a piano, keys splashed a disconcerting pink. The carpeted floor was riddled with patches of old stains.

"This way," Greenie whispered. She led them up the staircase, the steps creaking under their passing, to a landing. The second-floor hallway branched into rooms in the same state of disrepair as downstairs.

They took another flight of steps to the third level, which was one large loft. Two king-sized mattresses covered in folded blankets were against one wall. A table and chairs sat in the center of the room with a few books on top. Oz had already dropped her pack on it. Compared to the rest of the townhome, this room looked almost lived in.

Auri understood why Oz had chosen the building. It had been hard to see in the darkness of the street, but this upper room had windows on every outward facing wall. Matted drapes could be pushed apart to allow for sightlines. They would be able to see whatever was coming.

Oz moved from the table to the drapes of the front window. "Go dark," she whispered. The other Scavengers stowed the flashlights in their bags before the illumination revealed their location. In the sliver of night through the parted curtains, the full moon painted the landscape in a silvery sheen. Oz went to each window and eased apart the drapes a handswidth, allowing enough moonlight in to see the shapes of the objects in the room.

"When she was a Walker, my mom used to hide up here," Oz explained. "The last time I was here with her, she was so full of hope and life." She pressed her fingers against the dusty window-pane, as if reaching out to grasp a fond memory. "It's a good vantage point. Any volunteers for first watch?"

Nibs raised a hand. The goat had wandered over to the blankets, and he tugged on the lead to pull him back.

"I'll take watch with Nibs," Greenie said. "I haven't been getting much sleep anyway."

Guilt flickered across Oz's shadowed face, but she nodded and moved away from the window. "Malachi, you're on next rotation with me. Auri and Misshot will take the last shift."

Greenie and Nibs settled into their guard positions, Greenie at the front of the house and Nibs at the back. Misshot passed Auri and Malachi strips of jerky before he joined Oz in a hushed conversation. Auri sat with Malachi at the table as they ate their meager dinner in silence.

The moon rose higher and the temperature in the home dropped. Auri found herself shivering. She wrapped her arms around herself and eyed the two beds. Across the room, Oz and Misshot had laid out their weapons and contents of their packs on the floor.

"Come on," Malachi said to Auri. He nodded at the blankets. "Let's get you warm."

Auri rose with him, and they approached the beds. She wanted to kick off her boots, but knew that if they needed to flee, she'd regret the decision. Instead, she slipped *Ganbaru* from its holster and placed it beside the bed. Auri pulled the blankets back and gave them a subtle sniff. They smelled of old fabric, but nothing like sweat or blood. Malachi chuckled beside her.

Reassured, she settled onto the mattress. A spring creaked and dug into her back and her metal shoulder plates pulled on her jacket, but she had never been so thankful to be horizontal. Auri held her breath as Malachi moved to slide in beside her. His arm looped around her, and she rolled against him so his chest pressed against her back. The heat of him, trapped by the blankets, banished the chill in the room. Malachi's lips brushed her ear, and Auri's body hummed with awareness wherever they touched.

Then Birdie loped onto the mattress and plopped herself between their legs, her head resting on Auri's hip. Oz looked up at the commotion and saw Auri and Malachi together before quickly returning to her conversation with Misshot. Auri couldn't see clearly in the darkness, but Oz's shoulders seemed to hunch around her ears.

"Birdie," Auri grumbled. "Get off."

"She's fine," Malachi said around a chuckle. "More body heat, the better." He lowered his voice. "And I still get to be close to you." He raised a hand and ran the tips of his fingers down her neck. "Anyone ever tell you your hair looks like poppy blossoms in the moonlight?"

Heat unfurled in Auri's chest. She turned to look at him. He'd propped himself up so he could look down at her.

In the darkness that cloaked the room, with the low rumble of Oz's and Misshot's resumed conversation, Auri found courage to ask the question that had wound through her mind since last night.

"Malachi," she began. "I know now isn't the time—"

"You want to know what we are." His breath tickled the skin behind her ear, and Auri ached with wishing they were back on the *Kestrel*. Safe and alone.

"Considering you never answered my question," Malachi murmured, "should I answer yours?"

She wriggled in frustration and Birdie let out an annoyed groan. "They're two very different questions."

Malachi caught a tendril of red hair between his fingers. He studied it before letting it slip free. "You deserve more than I can give, Aurelia."

Auri held her breath, afraid of his next words. Already her mind swirled. *He doesn't really like me. The kiss was a mistake. I should never have—*

"But you're my sun." He lowered his lips to her hair and inhaled as if breathing her in. His mouth skimmed her lobe as he spoke. "Even if I don't look at you. Even if I tell myself that you aren't for me—*can't* be for me. I feel the heat of you. Your warmth, your way of brightening even the darkest places." He pressed a kiss against her temple and then shifted, rolling onto his back.

"I would want to learn more about you," he murmured. "Work toward a life with you. But Auri…" He trailed off until she turned to face him, making Birdie groan again. The dog stood, stretched, and then plopped down at the bottom of the mattress, safe from human conversations.

"But what?" Auri prodded. She could only see the outline of Malachi's bearded jaw in the dark.

"I can't have that," he said. "Not yet."

Auri let his words linger in the air. Then she ventured, "We could make something from what we have now. I was afraid of losing you, but now I'm more afraid of losing *time* with you." Her words were half desperation, half hope. In the darkness, it seemed easier to confess. "I could love you, Malachi Vermillion. Peter Treatis. If I let myself. If you let me."

"You *could* love me." Malachi was silent for a beat. "I'm not Tyson Peri, Auri."

Her breath caught at the anger in his voice, the way he'd unearthed that lingering fear. "I didn't say—"

"I hate him for fracturing the trust you have in yourself," he said. Then he sighed. "Let's get back to the *Kestrel*. We'll decide what to do about us then."

"If we—"

"Outsiders," Oz called, her tone abrasive. She stood beside the other mattress, Misshot beside her. "If you two are done discussing your feelings, we could all get some sleep."

Embarrassment flushed Auri's back. How much had she heard?

Misshot dropped into the mattress with a sigh of pleasure. Oz hesitated, her gaze moving to Malachi's. "In my experience, Malachi," the woman advised, "it's best to take what you can while you have it because it may not be there tomorrow. In this world, we are promised nothing."

CHAPTER THIRTY-TWO

A hand squeezed Auri's shoulder. Her eyes fluttered open as she grabbed for *Ganbaru*. She was halfway into a seated position before Malachi whispered, "All's well. It's your turn at watch."

Auri took a slow breath to steady her racing heart. "Any Bleeders?"

"A few, but they haven't ventured close. Oz said Bleeders here use scouts to scope the area for prey. So we may be in for a herd closer to dawn."

The thought made Auri's grip on *Ganbaru* tighten. "Night-walkers?"

"All clear."

Oz was easing back onto the other mattress, now occupied by Greenie. Nibs lay in bed beside Auri. He'd rolled a spare blanket between them to give her privacy.

Misshot already sat on a chair facing the rear of the house, crossbow on his lap. Auri vacated her warm spot and Malachi settled in. Birdie still lay at the bottom. The dog's snoring didn't pause even as Auri slipped away.

The air in the room brought goosebumps out on her organic skin, and Auri wrapped her jacket more tightly around her shoulders. At least shivering would keep drowsiness at bay.

Auri slid into the vacant chair facing the street, *Ganbaru* on her lap. She palmed a yawn and peered through the opening in the drapes. The moon had moved closer to the horizon while she slept. Its light was barely visible behind the skyscrapers. The heavens lightened, the darkness of night shifting to a hazy purple. Auri found herself wishing for the grid and her c-tacts to know the time.

Minutes passed. Auri's thoughts wandered, but her gaze remained fixed on the empty street. The only sounds were the staggered breaths of those sleeping. Even Malachi seemed to be resting peacefully.

The captain's nightmares had been one of the things that first drew her to him. It was an agony they both suffered. Though Auri's dreams had changed since Roanleigh.

Now, her nightmares transformed her into a Bleeder, feeding on those she loved, hunting the innocent. Other nights she dreamt of Aldin and Marnie. She watched them shift into cannibalistic monsters and found herself clutching a gun and facing a horrible choice.

When Auri woke from those nightmares, she found comfort in the fact that Marnie was already gone before Auri even knew her significance. But Aldin…

The Bleeder he had become…

Would she have to face her father as she had faced her mother?

The creak of a floorboard made Auri shift. Greenie had snuck out of bed, careful not to disturb Oz. She moved over to Auri's window, rubbing her arms as she peered between the drapes. The light from the sinking moon cast shimmers of silver on the woman's hair.

"All quiet?" she asked.

Auri nodded. "Can't sleep?"

Greenie tucked her hands into her armpits. "I would almost prefer nightmares to sleeplessness. Every time I close my eyes, I see High Top's face. Sometimes I wish I could forget what we had so I wouldn't know what it was like *not* to have him. Sometimes I'm terrified I *will* forget." Greenie's gaze wandered to the empty street. "Sometimes I hope that I'll die too."

Auri ached for Greenie. She could see Ferris's agony reflected in the woman's eyes. Were the doctor here, maybe he would know how to help the Scavenger grieve. Auri felt inadequate but whispered, "You have so much more life left to live."

"Doesn't seem worth it without him." She let out a staggered breath. "Don't tell Oz what I said. She would take the blame. She already carries enough deaths around her neck. She doesn't need the weight of the living." Greenie glanced at Auri. "If you think I blame her, you're wrong. Every time we leave the Hole, it's a risk."

"She's more than just the next chieftain to you, isn't she?"

"She's change. She's hope." Greenie allowed herself a small smile. "And in a world like this, we need hope more than anything. I'd follow her anywhere. Everyone in this room would. Probably even the goat."

Auri smiled and opened her mouth to say more, but movement caught her eye. She shifted, nose almost pressing against the glass. Her gaze swept the street, filled with more shadows thanks to the setting moon and pre-dawn sky.

"What is it?" Greenie hissed.

Something darted from a building on the other side of the road. It leapt across the street and paused at a tuft of grass sprouting from the asphalt. Auri let out a held breath, recognizing the slender legs and large antlers.

"Just a buck," she answered.

"We saw Merks on our shift," Greenie said. "Scouts. A herd usually follows."

"If one passes by, will they try to get in here?"

"As long as we keep our blood in our veins, we'll be fine. They'll be going back to their nest to rest for the day. But if they haven't had any kills, they'll be hungry."

Auri's stomach clenched. After a few minutes without movement outside, she gestured to the beds. "You should try to get some sleep at least."

Greenie started to move away, but Auri caught her wrist. Auri rose halfway out of her chair, her other hand fisting around *Ganbaru*.

The buck had straightened from its early breakfast, antlers proud and curling as he sniffed the air. The small tail atop its rump raised halfway to show the white underside. He took a few steps toward the building across the street and stomped his front hoof.

Auri knew in the depths of her bones what was about to happen. "Run," she whispered, as if the creature could hear her warning. "*Run.*"

Hulking shapes hurtled from the darkness. The buck bolted but only made it a few leaps before three Bleeders tackled it. Waning moonlight flashed across metal weapon strapped to the creatures' backs—the harpoons Oz had mentioned. They didn't draw them, instead seeming to prefer their hands and teeth to bring the buck down. Blood splattered across the asphalt and the buck's keen of agony split the quiet night.

Auri clasped a hand over her mouth to keep herself from screaming. "Wake the others," she rasped as more Bleeders emerged from the building. Greenie slipped away. Auri watched as the monsters congregated around the deer. They moved in almost a pack order, each taking a turn at the twitching carcass.

"How many?" Oz asked as she approached, voice low. She shifted the curtains to provide more visibility.

"At least twenty," Auri answered.

Oz frowned as Greenie, Misshot, Nibs, and Malachi clustered at the window. "They must be desperate to attack a buck like that. Deer don't typically have much Ambrosium."

"We'll be going into a hungry and desperate Merk nest," Misshot grumbled. "Fantastic."

Nibs's fingers moved in fast circles as he signed.

Oz nodded in agreement. "We'll be using the Walkers' bridges once we get to the city."

"Bridges?" Malachi asked. He kept his gaze on the Bleeder frenzy below, one hand on his coil gun, the other curled around the back of Auri's chair.

"That's how the Walkers avoid the Merks at night," Misshot explained. "Swinging bridges between the skyscrapers. It bottlenecks any Merks who get up there while keeping the Walkers safe from ground-level dangers."

"Doesn't that mean we might run into Walkers?" Auri couldn't help but point out the obvious.

"It's too hot during the day so they usually move around at night, except their new recruits. But rather Walkers who die from a bolt," Oz said, "than a Merk that requires a few lucky shots to the head."

CHAPTER THIRTY-THREE

"**B**irdie, *come*," Auri commanded so sharply her K9 drill sergeant would've been impressed. But even the sharp order wasn't enough to entice Birdie across the bridge.

The poodle trembled at the entrance, tail tucked between her legs. Auri waited halfway down the bridge's length. The supporting cables stretched between two skyscrapers, only secured by a few bolts drilled into the roof. Wooden slats comprised the walkway, fixed in place by pieces of rope. The bridge appeared sturdy enough—much sturdier than the bridge they crossed to reach Walker territory—but the structure swayed with the slightest movement.

Auri forced herself to keep her gaze on Birdie, ignoring the way the ground yawned out, hundreds of meters below. "Birdie, come on. You can do it."

Birdie whined, her tongue sliding out in a nervous pant. Auri didn't begrudge the poodle's refusal. This was the sixth bridge they had crossed this morning. And for Birdie, it was just one too many.

A breeze gusted through the skyscrapers and the bridge swung. Auri grabbed the cables on either side in a death grip. Her heart slammed against her chest.

"Birdie," she said, trying for soothing. "Please. Just go across really fast. We're almost there."

The Scavengers waited on the other side. Malachi had stopped a meter beyond her, waiting to see if Auri needed help. Even the stupid goat had made it across the bridge.

"Auri!" Malachi called. She looked back to see him gesturing for her to hurry up.

They hadn't run into any Walker recruits this morning, which made Oz wary. Normally bands would be scavenging buildings. Though maybe the attack in no-man's-land signaled just how little their scavenging turned up. Maybe they were getting desperate. The Merks were quiet too, though Oz had no explanation there other than "They usually hunt at night."

Auri eased along the bridge back to Birdie. "You're not going to like this," Auri whispered. She held out her hand to her dog. Birdie was well trained, but terrified animals were unpredictable. When Birdie nudged Auri's palm with her nose and whined, Auri said, "I'm going to carry you across. I'll keep you safe, Bird. Trust me?"

Birdie whined again, followed by a yawn.

Auri moved behind Birdie. The sun reflected off a window and flashed in her eye. She grimaced and blinked away black dots.

"Here we go." Auri slid one arm under Birdie's chest and the other around her legs, just under her tail. Birdie's body was so rigid, it made lifting her even harder. Auri steeled her nerves and leaned into the robotic parts of her body for added strength. *Kami,* she prayed, *please let there be no sudden breezes.*

Auri took a deep breath and stepped onto the bridge. It wobbled, then steadied. She took another. Birdie started to squirm, a growl of protest building in her chest, claws catching skin, and Auri hissed through clenched teeth, "Stay!"

This time the poodle listened. She rested her head on Auri's shoulder as her entire body trembled.

Malachi shifted backward across the bridge to the other skyscraper, timing his movements with hers to reduce the bridge's swaying. "You're halfway!" he called in encouragement.

Birdie's bulk and the struggle of keeping balanced made Auri's human parts tremble. She clenched her jaw. The Scavengers, and now Malachi, gathered on the rooftop grew closer and closer until suddenly Auri stepped off the bridge onto solid concrete.

Birdie leapt down and shook her entire body. Auri stretched the cramping muscles in her arm and back. She buzzed with adrenaline and fear.

"You made it look easy," Auri breathlessly teased Nibs.

He shrugged, smiling.

Oz peered over the side of the roof down to the road.

"Any Merks or Walkers?" Misshot asked.

Oz shook her head. "We're good." She looked down at Birdie who had dropped her chest to the asphalt in a deep bow. "We're done with the bridges, but we need to jump from a building to reach the research lab." Her gaze met Auri's. "Can you do it?"

Auri nodded and quietly prayed Birdie would make the jump, because if she didn't, there was no carrying her.

As they hurried across the rooftop that spanned two blocks, bypassing skylights and vents, Auri realized what Oz's question really meant.

Can you keep going, even if you have to leave Birdie behind?

They reached the end of the roof and Oz pointed at their target. The building was one story lower with a narrow alley bisecting the two structures. Fixed in the center of the roof was a dragonfly-shaped vehicle with sleek propellors and hooked landing gear.

Malachi raised a hand to block the sun. "That looks like a helicopter," he said." He turned to Oz. "Have you ever turned it on?"

Oz shook her head. "My mother never dared, the Walkers avoid the lab, and I was only thirteen the last time I was here."

Malachi pursed his lips. "And that?" He pointed at a rectangular building attached to their target. It was only two stories and opened out into a large, fenced-off area of asphalt.

"There are spaceships inside," Oz said. "Some bigger than yours, by my mother's description. But she didn't take me down there. Too many Merks." She pointed to a square structure atop the roof, near the helicopter. A door was fixed in the center. "There are steps that lead inside. The rooftop is the best way to enter. Last time, the Merks were congregated on the lower levels so they could leave quickly if they saw something worth hunting."

Oz turned to Nibs and then the tethered goat. "Time to say goodbye to our hairy companion. Misshot, give Nibs the rope."

Misshot pulled a thick bundle of rope from his pack and handed it to Nibs. Auri watched Nibs loop it around the oblivious goat and knot it atop the animal's shoulders. Then he drew his knife.

Auri snatched Birdie's harness and turned the dog away. Nibs grabbed the goat's hind leg and sliced the tendon in one quick motion. Blood sprayed across white hair and the goat let out a pitiful cry.

The sight made Auri's stomach roll. Malachi threaded his fingers through hers. "It's just a goat," he reminded her.

A goat that could've easily been Birdie.

Nibs lifted the protesting goat and moved to the edge of the roof. Greenie grabbed the slack and looped it around a pipe sticking from the asphalt.

"Drop it," Oz ordered Nibs.

Nibs lowered the goat over the edge as he and Greenie slowly released the rope. The goat kicked and wriggled as it moved closer to the street while blood oozed from the slice on its back leg.

"Frack," Misshot swore. He nodded at Greenie who held the burned end of the rope. "We're out. How far?" he asked with a grunt.

Auri looked down. There was at least another story between the goat and the street. The impact would—

Oz strode beside Nibs. She took the knife from his hand and brought the blade against the taught rope. It split.

Auri cried out as the goat hit the ground. She whirled to press herself against Malachi's chest. Birdie whined where Auri still held her away from the roof's edge.

"Is it still alive?" Greenie asked. She dropped her end of the rope.

"Broken legs," Oz answered. She handed the knife back to Nibs who sheathed it. He cast a glance over at the goat and wiped a single tear from his remaining eye.

"Auri, tuck it in," Oz called. "We just rang the dinner bell."

Auri pulled away from Malachi. She looked down at Birdie as the goat's pitiful brays echoed in her ears. Auri dropped to one knee. She caught Birdie's face in her hands and pressed her forehead against the poodle's. "Follow me, Birdie. Like you always do." She placed a quick kiss between the dog's eyes and stood despite the worry twisting her gut.

"On three," Oz called. Everyone lined up along the other side of the roof. "One… two… Three!"

Auri ran, Malachi and Oz on either side. The edge of the building loomed closer and closer. Her mind screamed for her to stop. But she shoved reason away. She couldn't hesitate. Not for a second.

Auri leapt. For a moment, she seemed to hover above the alleyway, frozen in time and space.

And then the lower edge of the building rose up to meet her. She tucked her shoulder and hit the cement in a roll before rising to her feet. Malachi straightened beside her, rubbing his shoulder where it had taken the brunt of the impact. Greenie, Misshot, and Oz were already grabbing their crossbows from their holsters. Nibs peered onto the street below, looking for the goat.

Birdie stood on the other rooftop, watching, head tilted. She barked at Auri as if to say *Come back!*

Auri stepped closer to the edge. "Birdie," she called. "Birdie, come!"

Birdie's tail gave one quick wag.

"*Please,*" Auri begged in a whisper. Her fingers curled into fists.

Birdie took one step back and another. The dog barked again and darted forward. She bounded into the air and hit the rooftop a few paces in front of Auri.

Auri fell to her knees, arms outstretched. Birdie pranced up to Auri and licked her across the face. Auri buried her face in Birdie's warm neck. "Good girl," she rasped. "That's my good, good girl."

"Shat," Oz muttered. "Where the pit are the Merks?"

Auri pulled away from Birdie. Everyone else had gathered at the edge of the rooftop, laying on their bellies.

Auri joined them, keeping low.

"Don't let yourself be visible from the street," Greenie warned Auri. "Remember, the Merks have adapted to the Walkers and their bridges. They use harpoons to tow down their victims. Nasty way to go."

Auri shivered at the thought. The goat had dragged itself to the center of the street, leaving a trail of blood. Its front two legs were twisted at a horrible angle and one horn had snapped off.

"Come on, come on," Oz whispered. "Smell the blood. Come eat."

Birdie shifted beside Auri. Her nose twitched as she sniffed the air, and a low growl built in her throat. Moments later, the first

Bleeder crept onto the street, his head outfitted with a strange metal helmet that flashed in the sun. More armored creatures followed heartbeats behind. At the sight of helpless prey, they charged.

There were so many, they looked like a wave of hunger and death crashing onto the road. The goat disappeared underneath the frenzied mob. The poor animal let out one final scream before it went silent.

"Let's move." Oz eased back from the edge.

They ran past the helicopter, Malachi giving it a lingering glance as he passed. They stopped at the stairwell door. Oz laid one hand on the surface above the gaping hole where the knob had been torn out.

"There may still be Merks inside," she warned. "Move fast, move soundlessly and"—she looked at Auri—"keep your blood under your skin."

CHAPTER THIRTY-FOUR

---

17 Nov 3319, 11:08:41
Milky Way Galaxy, Earth,
Nightwalker Territory

The corridor leading to the lab was eerily quiet. Light filtered through the tinted windows revealing a few turned over benches and potted plastic trees. A single metal sign on one wall read *Research Labs* with an arrow pointing to the left.

They hurried down the hall to a pair of double doors with two thin panels of glass on either side. As they got closer, Auri saw one was broken. Oz stuck her arm between the protruding shards, grimacing as she reached for something. Moments later, a lock released and Oz puffed a satisfied breath before pushing the door open.

Auri stole a quick glance down the hall, but only saw dust motes dancing silent spirals in the air.

The research lab was a long rectangular room. Beside the entrance, rows of cabinets and a few refrigerators were bolted against a wall. Beneath a lens mounted to the ceiling rose a circular platform, wider than Auri was tall.

The setup reminded Auri of a rudimentary holo projector. Across the room, desks coated with dust were positioned underneath grime-covered windows. Most of the monitors were cracked or had toppled over, but three looked functional.

"Misshot, Nibs," Oz instructed, "eyes on the door."

They nodded, adjusting their crossbows and moving to peer through the slits of glass.

"Do you remember what your mother did when she brought you here?" Malachi asked Oz.

Oz approached a long row of switches fixed under a row of cabinetry. She hesitated as if uncertain, but then flicked one in the center. Seconds later, the three monitors lit to a pale blue. A buffering circle appeared. Everyone but Nibs and Misshot hurried over to look.

The buffering completed and a computer desktop loaded, files and apps covering most of the screen. Auri and Malachi scanned through the available folders, many of which had abbreviated labels that made no sense to Auri.

"How far did you get on these?" Malachi asked. "Is there something specific we should look at?"

Oz shook her head. "My mom wasn't able to open any of them." She tapped a random document and a password prompt appeared. "And we didn't have time to go through each file. We just read as many names as we could." She pointed at one folder in the lower right corner. "I saw Ambrosium and figured they were Merk related."

"*Maitta na*," Malachi muttered, running a hand through his hair. "They must've left something behind. Something not password protected."

"Whatever you do," Oz said, "do it quick. We only brought one goat."

"Try a keyword search," Auri proposed. "Like Tsuna did with the Roanleigh intel."

Malachi was already pulling up the prompt. It took a painfully long time for the search bar to appear. "Suggestions?"

"SOS," Auri said. "If society was falling apart, maybe they logged a final call for help."

Malachi keyed in "SOS" and, to Auri's relief, a single hit loaded. It was keyworded with a varying list: *help, unlocked, open me, cure...*

At *cure,* she looked to Malachi. For the first time, hope seemed to brighten his face. He used the mouse to double click the file.

The monitor winked out.

Malachi slammed his fist on the desk. Auri almost wailed with despair until she saw a single red button tucked back on the wall behind the monitors labeled *emergency backup power*. She slammed her palm against the button.

At first, nothing happened. Then the floor seemed to tremble under their feet. The smell of ozone drifted from the vents above as air blew, hot and dusty. Auri sneezed.

The lights in the room flicked on. A surprised gasp from Misshot made it clear the ones in the hall had turned on too.

"*Kuso,*" Auri swore. The monitor flashed back to life. The refrigerators along the wall began to hum. "*Gomen.* I didn't..."

"We need to move fast," Oz said. "The Merks will have seen this entire building light up like a flash bomb."

Malachi retraced their steps through the search command. He tapped the SOS file and it opened, filling the monitor with a black image. Words pulsed in the center.

Hologram loading... Hologram loading...

Behind them, the circular platform exploded with blue light. The lens in the ceiling flickered once, twice, then powered on. A figure appeared atop the pedestal: a man with more gray hair than black, though shrunk down to be half the size of Auri. He wore a lab coat with a bloodied handprint on one shoulder. His fingers trembled as he pushed his glasses higher on his nose.

"If you found this video," he began in an accent Auri recognized from her mother's video logs, "then you're the last hope for Earth."

Birdie leaned against Auri, cocking her head as the man continued.

"The drug Ambrosium was intended for *good*. You must know that. And it did good. *So much good*. The FDA rocketed it through human trials and put it straight on the market. Then the government added it to the public water supply. Cancers, cured. Birth defects, gone. Even the common cold was something of the past.

"Imagine breaking your leg and going for a run the next day. Or giving birth and recovering within hours instead of weeks. It was heaven on Earth." The excitement in his voice faltered. He looked down at his hands then wrung them together. "Until it wasn't."

The man pressed a fist against his mouth as he struggled to find the words.

"Move it along," Oz muttered, her awe of the holo dissipating the longer it took to watch it. She glanced at Misshot and Nibs. They had managed to resist the allure of the technology and were still watching the hall.

"But as time went on, there were… *signs*. What started as irritability became violence. Vessels in the brain burst, healed, burst and healed. People bled from their noses and eyes. Nothing we did helped. When we realized what was happening, we recalled the drug. Removed it from the water, from *everything*. But that only made things worse. Hours after withdrawal began, people started attacking each other—cannibalizing each other. Those with Ambrosium in their blood who hadn't undergone a full transformation became targets. The monsters were like addicts seeking their next fix."

Auri's eyes widened in realization. "Roanleigh," she breathed as the man rambled on about guilt and how he wished he could change the past. "The people there must've been dosed with Ambrosium somehow." She recalled the video logs and wanted to sob with understanding. "The water. Oh, *Kami*. I only wanted apple juice." She looked to Malachi. "That's why I'm the only one who didn't become a Bleeder. I barely drank any of the water. Only what my mom used to cut the apple juice."

What if the Ambrosium in her bloodstream was why she survived coming out of cryosleep in the first place? Her mind spun. When the colonists couldn't get more of the drug from each other, they had escaped the planet and turned on the rest of Ancora Federation.

"But he just said they removed it from the water," Malachi countered Auri's earlier conclusion. "Unless…" His brows drew together. "It was added without the colonists' knowledge.

Auri shook her head. "Who would do that?"

"We've discovered a cure," the scientist continued. Auri's head snapped up. *A cure.* She could find her father, she could—

"Of sorts. Nothing can undo what has been done," the man said, unknowingly crushing the castle in the clouds Auri was building for herself. "But we have made a drug that stops the regenerative abilities of the Marked. It will give the humans left on Earth, give *you*, a chance."

He glanced over his shoulder as if someone was shouting at him. He turned back to the camera, eyes wide. His next words came out hurried. "We were only able to generate four samples. We're evacuating and taking two with us, but I'm leaving two here, in case we fail. You'll find them taped beneath the desk by the wall." He shifted forward, as if to end the recording. His image glitched. "Good luck."

As if the backup power only remained to play his message, the electricity died in a loud *ba-dum*. Auri moved before her eyes even adjusted to sudden dim. Malachi and Oz were steps behind. Auri knelt beside the last desk, moving a toppled rolling stool out of the way.

Taped against the underside were two glass vials the size of Auri's pinky, black caps twisted on top. Auri raised a trembling hand and pulled them free. They clinked together in her palm. There couldn't be more than a mouthful of amber liquid in each. She gaped at Malachi who stared back at her, emotions flashing in his eyes before settling on one that warmed her blood: *hope*.

He raised his brows in an unspoken question, shifting his gaze to Oz, who had gone tense. Auri read his mind and nodded. He took one of the vials and held it out to the Scavenger.

Oz grasped it between thumb and forefinger, staring at the contents with lips parted and eyes wide. "This was here the whole time, and my mother had no idea. Frack."

"Frack!" Misshot echoed, his tone a panicked contrast to Oz's wonder. "We've got Merks!"

CHAPTER THIRTY-FIVE

17 Nov 3319, 11:56:01
Milky Way Galaxy, Earth,
Nightwalker Territory

"Sitrep!" Malachi called, fisting his coil guns and striding toward the doors. Auri slipped the vial into a pocket of her cargo pants and drew *Ganbaru*.

Misshot glanced back at Malachi with a furrowed brow. "The pit does that mean?"

Auri moved around Nibs to peer through the glass. A Bleeder prowled about the middle of the hallway, back to them, face up-turned. Its metal helmet was sharp-edged and appeared likely to slice skin if the creature was careless in its movements. Strapped across its back was a long, barbed weapon attached to a rope coiled at the hip—a harpoon.

As if sensing Auri's attention, the Bleeder peered over its shoulder. Auri, Nibs, and Misshot ducked in unison.

"Just one," Auri reported to Malachi, stepping out of the windows' sightline.

"There will be more," Oz warned.

"Malachi." Auri caught his shoulder. "The Bleeder is protecting its head with some kind of metal covering."

"I warned you," Oz muttered. "Our bolts can pierce the coverings after we weaken it, but there isn't time for multiple shots. We need to get to the staircase."

Oz rested her hand atop a side pocket in her backpack where she'd stored her vial. "I'll try a close-range attack. Get its helmet off. Misshot, you—"

Malachi cut her off with a shake of his head. "Their defenses are for your weapons. Let's try mine." He raised his coil gun and crept to the door, sliding the barrel through the broken panel.

The Bleeder growled and shifted as if to barrel toward the doors. Malachi pulled the trigger, and the gun recoiled. A barbed bullet whirled through the air to puncture a rounded hole in the Bleeder's metal helmet. The creature staggered sideways with a halting snarl. One clawed hand swatted at the wound in its head as if confused.

Malachi fired another two bullets in the span of a heartbeat. They struck centimeters away from the original shot, slicing through the Bleeder's skull and pinging across the floor as they exited. The creature stumbled, then hit the tiles with a *bang*.

"Go," Oz hissed, shooting Malachi's coil guns a jealous glance.

They bolted from the lab, easing around the Bleeder's corpse where it blocked the door to the staircase. The ichor from its blown-out skull spilled onto the tile. Auri's boots slipped in blood and she fell to one knee, hand splashing into the crimson pool. She fought the urge to retch.

Greenie pressed an ear against the stairwell door. She frowned and pulled back. "I hear movement."

The Scavengers drew their machetes.

Auri disconnected *Ganbaru* and activated the blades.

"On three," Oz said. "One, two… *three*."

Greenie yanked the door open and they charged into the stairwell. The enclosed space echoed with grunts and heavy breathing that turned into roars of excitement at fresh prey. A glance over the banister showed swarming Bleeders only a handful of floors down. Every creature bore matching face coverings and barbed harpoons.

The Scavengers fled up the steps with Auri and Malachi acting as rear guard, Birdie loping behind them. Oz slammed open the rooftop door and daylight shone into the stairwell.

A growl sounded just behind Auri. She turned, and the sharp nails grabbing for her hair slipped through the short strands. Auri struck out with *Ganbaru* and felt the satisfying slice of steel through flesh. A Bleeder roared and stumbled back.

And then she was fleeing through the opening. Oz closed it and slammed her machete through the slit between the door and the rooftop. The metal frame buckled as the Bleeders shoved against it.

"Jump!" Oz was yelling. Greenie was already almost at the roof's edge, Misshot and Nibs meters behind.

Greenie skidded to a stop at the ledge and whirled around, eyes wide and panicked. A breeze gusted, catching an escaped curl from her blonde bun. "Merks on the str—!"

Something slammed into Greenie from behind, cutting through the front of her chest and sending her staggering forward a step. She glanced down at the spike poking through her sternum. Crimson dribbled from her lips as they parted around a surprised whimper. Then her body was yanked backward like a demented marionette and she disappeared over the side of the building.

"No!" Auri screamed. She scrambled to where she had last seen Greenie, keeping herself low. The Scavenger lay prone on the street, limbs twisted. Bleeders surrounded her broken corpse. Another harpoon flew up and Malachi yanked Auri back. It clanged harmlessly on the rooftop. Auri sliced at the connecting rope with *Ganbaru*, stranding the harpoon tip.

"*Kuso*," Auri wheezed. Her mind reeled to Katara as she dropped from the *Kestrel*, her body hitting the snow, Malachi raising his gun...

"Aurelia," Malachi snapped. He grabbed her shoulders and shook her hard. "Focus."

Oz fisted her hands in her hair, gaze darting from the roof to the buckling door. "Shat, shat." She looked to Misshot, then Nibs, finally to Auri and Malachi. Tears glistened in her eyes, but she tilted her chin so they wouldn't fall. "We still have to jump. Odds are some of us will make it. There are two vials."

There was a loud *squeal* and everyone whirled to the door. The metal had buckled at the top. Only the lower section held together. The machete handle scraped the rooftop as it was shoved forward. Auri glimpsed the snarling faces of Bleeders, the metal of their protective gear flashing in the sun. It reminded her so much of the attack on the vault that she might as well be back on the Spire, back in Ancora Galaxy.

"*Some of us* are not good odds," Malachi said in response to Oz's command. He strode beside the helicopter and detached a thick cord that connected the vehicle to an outlet the size of Auri's torso. Then he swung himself up into the windowless pilot seat.

Auri hurried over. The inside was bare bones. There were only two seats in the front, the back just a hard metal floor. There weren't even any doors. But if it flew, there should be enough room for all of them.

"Can you fly it?" she asked.

Before Malachi could answer, the staircase door flew off its hinges.

"Buy me time!" Malachi called.

Auri ordered Birdie into the back of the helicopter. Then she tightened her grip on *Ganbaru*'s baton and positioned herself in front.

"Tell me how these are better odds," Oz grumbled as she and Nibs joined Auri. Meanwhile, Misshot launched himself up into the back of the chopper and drew his crossbow to provide cover fire.

Bleeders swarmed from the open doorway like spiders darting across a web toward trapped prey.

Auri crossed the batons of *Ganbaru,* blades pointed toward the rooftop. She sliced them up in a lethal curve as the first Bleeder lunged. The blades disemboweled the creature in one stroke. As its guts spilled over Auri's boots, she stabbed one blade through its exposed mouth at an angle. The stench of rot and *wrongness* swept over her as crimson sprayed across her face. The Bleeder fell.

Another replaced it, but a crossbow bolt slammed into its throat, courtesy of Misshot. Auri stabbed through its gaping mouth, the best way to access its brain without taking off the helmet. The Bleeder collapsed atop the body of its comrade. Auri looked up in time to see Oz a meter away, drenched in blood. The Scavenger held a knife in each hand. Nibs had lost his machete and knife and was now using two crossbow bolts to deadly effect. Panic spread through Auri. But she only had a moment to fear. More Bleeders poured onto the roof.

One bolted toward her, eyes wide and bloodshot in the depths of its metal helmet. Auri struck out, but the creature dodged. *Ganbaru*'s blades caught on the side of its helmet. Sparks flew and a sharp edge sliced the back of Auri robotic hand. She reversed the stroke and brought her blade back, piercing the monster's eye. The Bleeder stumbled back with a roar.

Something yanked on the back of Auri's jacket. She resisted the instinct to jerk away and moved with the attack. A Bleeder towed her against its naked chest. Its jaws extended inhumanly wide, and the stench made spots dance before her eyes. Auri stomped down on the Bleeder's instep, simultaneously stabbing *Ganbaru* through its vulnerable chest, straight to the heart.

The creature collapsed, revealing Nibs meters away and surrounded by Bleeders. He'd fallen to one knee, his other leg caught in a creature's mouth. Blood oozed from the wound, stirring the surrounding creatures into a frenzy.

Auri reconnected *Ganbaru* and threw it with all the strength in her robotic arm. She ran as it swept a destructive path through the Bleeders. It slammed to a stop, blades sinking into the back of the one chewing Nibs's leg. The Bleeder toppled face-first onto the rooftop. Auri yanked *Ganbaru* from its back and tore off its metal helmet. Pain sliced across her palm but she was already decapitating the Bleeder. She grabbed Nibs and hauled him upright.

The battle suddenly stilled and an eerie silence descended as the Bleeders paused in unison, their heads tilting, noses sniffing the air. Oz stood near the helicopter, barely recognizable beneath the sweat and ichor. Three Bleeder carcasses lay at her feet. Her gaze swept the Bleeders, brow furrowing, before her eyes widened in realization. "Auri!" she screamed in warning.

Auri looked down to her hand, still wrapped around Nibs's waist. Fresh blood trickled from the deep scratch along her pale skin.

The Bleeders shifted toward Auri as if they were androids programmed to hunt her down. At the same instant, the helicopter powered on with at loud *whoosh*. The propellors spun, kicking up a breeze that nearly knocked Auri off her feet.

The Bleeders roared as they staggered back. Auri dragged Nibs toward their only chance of safety.

Oz was already swinging herself into the back of the chopper. She drew her crossbow and joined Misshot laying down cover fire. Malachi's coil gun resounded from the pilot's seat as he helped keep the Bleeders back.

Auri and Nibs ran, Bleeders reaching for them with contorted claws. Birdie's panicked bark was an undercurrent to the chaos, a sound Auri could barely hear over the spinning blades.

Nibs reached the opening. Auri hauled him up, Oz and Misshot helping to get him inside. Auri moved to jump in when a shape slammed into her from the side. Her robotic leg took the impact as she hit the ground at an awkward angle.

An alert flashed across her c-tacts, but she blinked it away as claws swung down, slashing into her malfunctioning robotic leg. More alerts flashed. Auri tried to stand, but the limb gave out. She hit the roof. Human teeth closed around her shoulder but glanced off the metal armor. The Bleeder pulled back, fury contorting its face. Auri stabbed *Ganbaru* through the exposed flesh under its jaw all the way to the grip. She yanked it free. The Bleeder fell to its knees with a gurgle.

Auri staggered to her feet using her organic leg. The helicopter was only a few steps away, but as soon as she put weight on her robotic leg, it crumpled. The Bleeders swarmed, braving their fear of the chopper where it hovered a meter from the rooftop. Auri fell forward, only to gasp as Oz caught her, hauling her toward safety. Auri jumped and Misshot and Nibs caught her. Oz was seconds behind, a Bleeder grabbing for her boot. She kicked it in the face and bone crunched.

The chopper shot upward so fast, Auri found herself pressed against the floor. Her hands scrambled for a handhold, closing around a metal rung to keep from sliding out the open doorways.

Malachi swore and adjusted the controls. The vehicle hurtled forward a few meters before it plummeted toward the street and more waiting Bleeders. This time Auri screamed as her body lifted from the floor, Misshot's cry of terror joining hers. Malachi stabbed a button among the conglomerations of switches on the dashboard and yanked on the steering. The helicopter gained altitude meters from the street.

Everyone let out a collective breath as the chopper leveled off and the swept over the city, the only sounds the whir of blades overhead. Their volume even drowned out the panicked thump of Auri's heart. The heat of someone's gaze made her look up to see Misshot gaping at her. She followed his gaze down to her leg.

The Bleeder who attacked her must've torn the fabric of her pants, because a large chunk of her thigh was visible. Except it wasn't her thigh anymore. The synthetic skin hung in tatters to reveal the bent metal rod, twisted valves, and torn robotic muscles that allowed her to walk. Which also explained why she hadn't been able to stand.

Misshot opened his mouth, but an ominous beep chirped from the front of the chopper. Malachi swore.

"Oz," he called, "get up here. We're almost out of power and I need to get close to the Hole. Bleeders are pursuing."

Auri didn't risk a glimpse at the ground to confirm Malachi's warning. She was too afraid she might fall out.

"Frack," Oz swore. She shoved herself into the co-pilot's chair.

Moments later, the chopper veered hard to the left and accelerated. Skyscrapers zoomed past before the shorter buildings of no-man's-land replaced them.

Auri closed her eyes and Greenie's face rose in her mind, the woman's shock as the harpoon sliced through her chest. Greenie was another casualty to add to the growing list.

But the bloodshed would come to an end. They had hope. Auri slid her hand into her pocket. Pain flashed up her fingertips, and she tugged her hand out with a wince.

A glass shard impaled the tip of her index finger. She pulled it out and a drop of blood bubbled to the surface. The pain was quickly swallowed by mind-numbing panic. Auri shoved her robotic hand into her pocket, the glass scraping harmlessly at her synthetic skin. She closed her fingers around the shards and eased her fist free.

The remains of the vial rested in the center of her palm.

ELINOR ƆΛYRE
VIƆEO LOG #0ꓱ

February 28, 3277
Location: Planet 08: Roanleigh, Owari Settlement

Marnie sits with her back pressed against a wall. Her jumpsuit is stained with splotches of red, face caked with grime, except where tears have washed it clean.

Elodie huddles beside her in a wool blanket. The girl is asleep, now dressed in a pair of oversized pajamas Marnie discovered in storage, but she twitches as if in a nightmare.

Marnie places a trembling hand atop her daughter's head. The woman swallows visibly and groans as if her throat is dry. The heartbeat at her jugular is rapid. Her gaze darts to the camera, looking straight into the lens. "Whoever finds this, you're no longer witnessing the settlement of Roanleigh. I don't know why." She swallows again. "Or how. But it followed us from Earth."

Behind the camera, someone growls.

"We are all infected," Marnie continues. "Except…" Her brow furrows as she looks down at her sleeping daughter. Her gaze returns to the lens. "Camera," she orders, "pan the room."

The droid bobbles as it shifts. Marnie and Elodie are hunkered in a small storage room with shelves of extra foodstuffs, blankets, and cleaning supplies. Four other people are with them. One is tied to a shelf. The woman's eyes are wide, blood rolling from them like tears, staining the gag in her mouth. Every so often she jerks and the shelf rattles where it is bolted to the wall. All the contents have already fallen from onto the floor.

Two other people huddle in a corner, whispering to each other. They have scratched the skin on their cheeks raw.

Othniel leans against the shelves nearest Marnie. He looks up as the camera moves over him then glances at Marnie. "We can't just sit here."

"I know." Marnie's gaze darts to the two whispering in the corner. "Either another of us breaks, or those outside find a way in."

Niel shakes his head. "I haven't heard anything in hours. We should get out while we can."

Marnie places a hand against her forehead, as if she's struggling to focus. "Get out to do what? Freeze in the snow? Wait until they break into our homes? Or until we snap next? I'm on the edge, Niel. The only thing keeping me—" Her voice breaks and she takes a slow inhale. "I need to get her safe. But I can't think." She shakes her head. "I'm *so thirsty.*"

Niel pauses, guilt flashes across his face, but Marnie doesn't seem to notice. "I have a plan," he says.

Marnie raises her brows in silent question.

"Our spaceship is down, but the shuttle is still functional," he said, speaking quickly. "I take that and get help from the nearest planet. Medea, I think?"

Marnie frowns. "You're willing to risk it even with the shuttle's screwy navigation?"

"We don't have a choice. We need help."

Anger replaces the dubious expression on Marnie's face. She clutches her daughter. "There's only room for one. What about Elodie?"

"I noticed you didn't ask about yourself," Niel murmurs.

"Too late for me."

Niel glances behind him at their companions. They've gone silent and are now openly staring at Marnie and Niel. Niel shifts closer so his shoulder touches Marnie's and turns so the others can't read his lips.

"The cryo chamber in your dwelling," he whispers. "Get Elodie there and when I get help, I *will* come back. I'll make sure she's safe."

Hope flickers in Marnie's eyes. She leans forward and grabs Niel's collar, towing him until he's nose-to-nose. "Swear to me," she says. "Swear you will protect my daughter with everything you have." Her spittle lands on his cheek.

Niel doesn't hesitate. "I swear."

"That means nothing," she snaps. "Swear on what means most to you."

Niel looks down. His mouth twists almost in pain. When he speaks, his voice is choked with emotion. "I swear on my brother's memory that I will protect Elodie with everything I have. I will ensure she lives."

Marnie locks gazes with him, searching his face. Then she nods and releases him. "When?"

"Now," Niel says. "Before the rest of our group turns mutinous."

Marnie nudges Elodie. Elodie's head flops forward and Marnie palms the girl's cheek. "Wake up, love," she whispers. When her daughter mumbles, Marnie shakes her. "Elodie," she demands, "wake up."

Elodie grumbles and then her eyes open, wide and horrified as if memories are rushing back. "Daddy," she whimpers. "I thought it was a dream. Where's—"

"Elodie," Niel murmurs, leaning closer to the terrified girl. "Your mom tells me you're a really fast runner. Think you can show me how fast?"

Elodie looks up at him. The blanket shifts to reveal her clutching the doll against her chest, too-long fleece pajama sleeves pilfered from the shelves rolled up over her wrists. "I... I think so."

Marnie brushes a tangle of red hair from Elodie's cheek. "Love, we're going to go back home, okay?"

Relief sweeps over the girl's face. "Really?"

Marnie nods. "But we don't have our coats, so it will be cold outside. We need to go very fast and very quietly. Can you do that? Hold my hand, run, and not look back?"

Elodie glances at Niel then back at her mother. "What about Daddy?"

Marnie shakes her head. "Daddy is… Daddy is working. He would want you to run home with me."

"Okay," Elodie hedges, not entirely convinced. "I can run. I promise I'll run as fast as I can. Even if I get cold."

"Good girl." Marnie looks to Niel. "Ready when you are."

He nods and stands. Marnie follows. She wraps the blanket tightly around Elodie's shoulders, knotting it across the girl's chest to form a poncho.

The two people in the corner jerk their heads up. "Where are you going?" the man asks.

"Somewhere better than here," Niel says. "I suggest you shut the door behind us."

The man looks at his female companion. She mutters something the camera mic doesn't pick up.

Niel slowly twists the deadbolt lock. He looks to Marnie. "Ready?"

"Ready."

He eases the door open and peers outside. "All clear," he whispers, beckoning Marnie forward. They slip into the room beyond. The camera drone just makes it out before the man slams the door shut and locks it. The sound echoes through the empty room. Smears of gore coat the floor with torn decorations and toppled tables scattered about.

Elodie gapes at the blood with wide eyes.

Marnie tugs on her hand. "Remember your promise, Elodie. *Run.*"

Niel sprints for the doors to the hallway beyond. Marnie follows, dragging Elodie along. Niel looks out first.

"Clear," he says.

They creep from the room. More blood and gore are splashed across the walls like macabre decorations. But like the room before, there are no bodies. A gust of wind rattles the Hub, emphasizing how quiet the building has become.

"Where did they go?" Niel asks when they reach the front doors without running into anyone.

"Probably looking for water," Marnie mutters. Her lips stick around the word *water* and she forcibly spits it out. "They'll only get so far attacking each other."

"The filtration center." Niel glances down the hallway to their right, the lights flickering with another gust of wind. "The same place where the shuttle is parked."

"Backing out?" Marnie asked, jaw clenching as rage darkens her face.

Niel held up his hands. "No, Marnie. I will get to the shuttle no matter what."

Marnie glances at Elodie, who stares straight ahead. "You better. For her sake."

"Good luck," he murmurs. Then he turns and disappears down the hallway. Elodie doesn't even register the man's departure, her gaze is fixed on the doors. Her shoulders tremble.

Marnie places a hand on her daughter's cheek to get her attention. Elodie jumps. "Shh," Marnie soothes. "Are you ready to run back home?"

Elodie nods.

Marnie yanks a door open. Frigid air slams into them and snowflakes rush through the opening. The sky above is a somber gray as if the planet is mourning the fate of its colonists. Elodie stumbles, but Marnie tows her into the snow. Even with the plow drones moving overhead, the snow is as deep as Marnie's mid-calf and reaches Elodie's knees.

"I'll carry you!" Marnie yells over the wind. Elodie's makeshift poncho flaps out behind her. The girl's eyes squint shut against the gusts. Marnie scoops Elodie into her arms and breaks into a frantic run.

Elodie tucks her head into her mother's chest while the drone is buffeted back and forth, barely able to keep pace. The view twists and turns, showing glimpses of snow, sky, and then Marnie's running form.

A row of homes appears as the camera manages to right itself during a break in the wind. But Marnie has stopped. The camera focuses on her panting silhouette. Her dwelling is only a few meters away, but four people block her path.

Marnie wipes a smear of blood from her nose. "Move!" she shouts.

One of the figures steps forward. Marnie gasps. Aldin's eye bulges in its socket. His clothes are torn and stained with blood. Despite the blizzard around them, he doesn't appear to feel the cold. He snarls.

Marnie's voice breaks in a sob, "Aldin, for the love of God. *Please.*"

At the sound of her father's name, Elodie's head pops up. "Daddy?"

"Let us through," Marnie says again. "Fight the need, one last time. Let me save her."

Aldin jerks to the side as if an inner voice fights for control.

Marnie reaches a sudden, painful realization. Determination wipes the horror from her face. She lurches from the group, toward a wide alley between dwellings. Aldin's internal battle ends in an enraged roar. He darts after them, faster than a human should move in such heavy snow.

Marnie reaches the rear of her home when Aldin slams into her. Marnie hits the ground, and Elodie tumbles from her arms. The girl's small body disappears into a deep drift.

Aldin looms over Marnie. She turns and slams her palm into his nose. He arches back with a hiss of pain. She scrambles toward where the tip of Elodie's red braid sticks from the snow meters away. Two colonists round the other side of the dwelling.

Elodie's head pops up, chunks of white clinging to her hair. "Mo—"

She screams and ducks as a colonist grabs for her. The woman's nails slice across the side of Elodie's face. The girl hits the snow, raising a shaking hand toward her face where deep gouges mar her pale skin. Her eye is bloodied and torn open.

"No!" Marnie roars, scrabbling to her feet. Aldin catches her leg and tows her back down. She slams her boot into his face as the male colonist pounces on Elodie. The girl releases a panicked shriek that turns into a wail. The snow around her becomes a red slush.

The woman grabs for Elodie's leg too and sinks her teeth into the underside of the girl's thigh.

Marnie is on her feet again. Crimson seeps from her eyes. She grabs the male colonist by the back of his shirt. She tears him away from her daughter and snaps his neck in one quick motion. He releases a gurgling wheeze before she tosses him into the snow. Marnie slams her foot into the face of the woman gnawing on Elodie's leg.

Elodie is half conscious, her body a tattered tapestry of torn skin and muscle. White peeks out from the traumatized flesh.

Aldin and the other colonists growl as they begin to heal, slowly working themselves to their knees.

Marnie scoops Elodie into her arms and runs. She skirts around her home before sliding open the front door. She slams it behind her, not stopping to take off her shoes.

Marnie tears through the house, leaving a trail of blood and melting snow. "Elodie, Elodie, Elodie," she whimpers. "Stay with me, love. Stay. Please stay." Marnie staggers in the hallway leading to the bedrooms. She braces a hand on the wall to catch herself, leaving a handprint and smear of crimson.

Elodie whimpers. Marnie stumbles to the final door. She keys in the code on the pad. It chirps.

Marnie opens the door. She shifts Elodie higher, and the girl cries out. The doll she'd managed to hold on to topples from her hand, two fingers bloodied stumps.

Marnie jams her thumb onto the cryo chamber's screen. Its beeping makes Elodie's eyelids flutter. Marnie taps the required specifications and the lid hisses open.

"Mommy," Elodie rasps. Her remaining eye shifts.

The sound of toppling furniture reaches Marnie, and her face hardens. She lowers Elodie's broken body into the opening.

Elodie seems to realize what is happening. Her eye widens with panic. *"Don't!"*

Marnie presses hard on Elodie's chest as she enters the final command. The machine lets out a series of beeps as a countdown begins.

Elodie's energy to fight dissipates and Marnie releases her hold. She runs her fingers over her daughter's cheek. Tears mixed with blood flow from Marnie's eyes. "I love you," she chokes, pressing a kiss against her daughter's temple.

Elodie murmurs something, but her words are barely intelligible. She reaches for Marnie's face, but her hand closes around Marnie's earlobe instead. Her missing fingers leave fresh lines of blood on her mother's cheek.

The cryo chamber chirps a warning as the lid begins to close. Marnie jerks back. Elodie's grip on the earring is strong and it tears from Marnie's ear. The woman doesn't seem to notice the pain.

"Don't leave—" Elodie's final whimper cuts off as the lid seals shut.

Marnie watches as liquid rushes into the chamber, sees the final panic in her daughter's eyes as she inhales. The cryo fluid, normally clear, is tinged red. Elodie's beautiful blue eye drifts shut.

Marnie's gaze finds the camera. Her entire body trembles. She huffs in and out and gags as if choking.

"Back up contents," she growls. "Stop recording." Then she stumbles toward the door. She pauses on the threshold and looks back at the cryo chamber one last time. Fresh blood seeps from her eyes, nose, and mouth. The expression on her face is volatile, hungry, and desperate.

"I love you, Elodie," she rasps, then physically hurls herself from the room, slamming the door behind her.

The scene goes black. A message flashes across the darkness with a growing percentage.

Back up in progress…

CHAPTER THIRTY-SIX

---

17 Nov 3319, 15:35:12
Milky Way Galaxy, Earth,
No-man's-land

The helicopter sputtered. Overhead, the propellor slowed. Malachi jerked on the controls, but nothing happened.

"Hold on!" he cried moments before the chopper dropped into a thicket of trees. The propellor blades sliced through limbs and underbrush before the landing gear slammed into the ground. The impact sent everyone in the back bouncing painfully against the metal floor.

When everything settled, Auri could only stare down at her fisted hand. Hopelessness hollowed out her chest. The only chance they had to save Ancora Galaxy and her *ketsu* had crushed it.

Oz was already hopping out of the helicopter. Misshot gave Auri's leg a final appraising stare before he slid out.

"Nibs," Misshot called, "this way. Oz and I will help you down."

"Auri," Malachi said. He stood on the other side of the chopper, hands held out for her. Birdie bounded out. Auri avoided his gaze as he encircled her waist and eased her to the ground. Flecks of dried blood flaked off her clothes and floated around them like a macabre snow.

He frowned, cupping her chin and bringing her gaze up to his. "Are you okay?"

Birdie nudged Auri's fisted hand.

"Malachi…" Shame burned hot in Auri's stomach. She forced herself to raise her hand and uncurl her fingers. The fragments glistened in the remnants of sunlight. Malachi stared, not comprehending. "It must've broken during the fight," Auri choked out. "When that Bleeder tackled me."

Emotions flashed across Malachi's face. His eyes flicked to where the Scavengers were taking stock of their weapons and injuries on the other side of the chopper.

"It's not the only vial," he murmured.

"We need to get back to the Hole," Oz called. "Those Merks were in pursuit. And with the Walkers so quiet… Something isn't right. I need to tell Chieftain. This vehicle"—she slapped her palm against the exterior—"will send both of them straight here."

Malachi gave Auri a final glance that seemed to say *I'll figure this out* before they fell into step with the Scavengers.

They moved through the trees. Auri's robotic leg seized every few steps, forcing her to lean on Malachi most of the way. Misshot kept an arm around Nibs as the man limped through the underbrush. Oz guided them through thickets, whispering warnings of hazards in the tall grass.

By the time they reached the blockhouses and patches of farmland, the sun had begun its descent. Dusk settled upon them while the pressure of time passing propelled them forward. They didn't see anyone as they hurried along the path that led to the Hole. When Auri asked why, Oz explained that Harvest ensured people were prompt with their rotations. They had just missed the last change of guard.

The sight of the Hole's entrance made Auri's beleaguered body sigh with relief. She leaned more weight against Malachi.

Oz strode to one of the guards waiting just inside. "Where's Chieftain?" she asked.

The man's gaze swept over the wounded group, fixing on Auri. His lips parted as he gawked at her leg. Auri shifted to hide her mauled limb behind Malachi, and Oz stepped closer to the guard to further block his view.

"Chieftain?" she repeated, her tone hardening.

"I… I heard he was helping in the kitchen tonight." He shifted, trying to look at Auri again.

Oz jerked her chin at the other guard. "Go get him. Tell him we are waiting in his council chamber with important news." She started to move past, then added, "*Run.*"

The beleaguered group shuffled along the empty corridor, the music, clapping, and excited chatter of the third night of Harvest echoing from the dining hall.

When they were gathered inside the council room, Oz closed the door and turned on a few of the mounted lightbulbs while Misshot eased Nibs into a chair behind the large table. In the dim light, the mural had a ghostly quality. Auri half expected to see phantoms weaving in and out of the painted trees.

"Chieftain should be here soon." Oz looked to Malachi and Auri as she settled against the door. "Don't mention the second vial. Get it back to your galaxy and…" She trailed off as Malachi and Auri looked at each other. Her brows drew together. "What's wrong?"

"Our vial broke," Malachi answered.

Auri forced her expression to remain neutral despite her surprise at his blatant honesty. "It broke during the fight on the roof. I didn't realize until we were in the air."

Oz's hand went protectively to her pack where her vial was stowed. "I see," she murmured.

The door opened behind her, and she stumbled backward, catching herself on the frame as Chieftain appeared at the threshold. Auri shifted her injured leg behind Birdie's bulk as Oz retreated farther into the room to make room for her father.

The huge man wore a stained apron over his shirt and trousers. His gaze swept the bloodied and wearied occupants, relief flashing in his eyes at the sight of Oz unscathed. He took a slow breath, removed his apron, and proceeded to fold it. When he finished, he faced his daughter. "Greenie?"

Oz shook her head, lowering her eyes to the floor.

Chieftain nodded slowly. "What happened?"

Oz relayed a condensed version of the day's events, only mentioning a single vial and finishing with the potential for prowling Merks in Scavenger Territory.

"You know they've never gotten close to the blockhouses before," Chieftain countered, waving off Oz's concern. "It's one of the reasons we keep our *secrets* so guarded." His stare turned cold as he frowned at Auri and Malachi. "And the vial?" he asked his daughter, extending a hand.

Oz slid it from her pack and passed it to Chieftain. It looked so small in his palm, the amber liquid nearly blending in with his dark skin. He shifted it between thumb and forefinger, peering at the contents.

"Is such a small thing really the key to our salvation?" he murmured. "Your mother was right all along. She would be so proud, my daughter." He cleared his throat. "Well done."

"The cure will only save us if we find a way to replicate it," Oz said. She glanced at Auri and Malachi. "We don't have the technology, but—"

"We're Scavengers," Chieftain said, not comprehending Oz's intentions. "We'll figure it out. We always have. Always will."

"Chieftain," Misshot added, "that's not all." He glanced at Oz, who nodded for him to continue. "The Walkers' activity is suspicious. We didn't see a single recruit while in their territory."

Chieftain lowered the vial and returned it to Oz with a frown. "I know why."

Oz cocked her head. "What are you talking about?"

"It's clear they've been planning something," Chieftain said. "Between the attack in no-man's-land and the arrival of our *interstellar* travelers." He spoke the word *interstellar* as if it was a joke told in bad taste. His steely gaze fixed on Malachi and Auri and he raised his voice, "Come get them."

Auri whirled as four armed Scavengers strode into the room.

Malachi's hands drifted to his guns, but Chieftain clucked his tongue. "So much as twitch, Outsider, and your two friends will pay the price. Weapons on the floor."

Malachi gritted his teeth. "We had a *deal*."

"I don't make deals with liars," Chieftain said. "There were no problems with Walkers until you arrived. I more than suspect you *are* Walkers, and the vehicle you crash-landed was a ruse. I've seen enough of the old relics in their territory. I will not be fooled." He turned his attention to Oz. "While this vial is a great victory, you have much to learn before you are ready to lead. Specifically, who to trust."

Oz lowered her head.

"This is the last time I'll ask," Chieftain snapped, taking a step toward Malachi and Auri. "Drop your weapons."

Nibs staggered to his feet in protest, but Chieftain raised a hand at him in a silent *stop*.

Malachi yanked his coil guns free and lowered them to the floor. Auri unclasped *Ganbaru*'s harness, her knife resting atop the sheathed boomerang.

As she rose, one of the guards grabbed her roughly from behind. Her robotic leg locked up and she nearly fell. The guard jerked her upward and the injuries from her fight with the Bleeders sent a fire crackling across her chest. She hissed in pain. Birdie snarled, but quieted at Auri's command. The guard bound Auri's arms behind her back with a thick swath of rope.

Auri looked up to see Chieftain watching her, his gaze fixed on her robotic leg.

"Chieftain," Misshot called, drawing his attention. "The Outsiders saved us in Walker territory. I don't think—"

Oz interrupted. "No, Misshot. Chieftain is right." She shook her head. "Everything makes too much sense. He's seen through their plan. They're only here to betray us." She spat onto the floor in front of Auri and Malachi.

Malachi jerked away as a guard grabbed him, but there wasn't much fight in the motion. Auri tried not to crumple in defeat as the third guard secured a rope around Birdie's neck, and they were dragged from the room.

CHAPTER THIRTY-SEVEN

"What's going on?" Tsuna demanded from the shallow depths of another prison cell as Malachi, Auri, and Birdie were shoved inside. The door slammed with a *bang*. A dim dankness engulfed Auri as the full weight of the Hole above settled over her shoulders. The only light emanated from a narrow opening at the door, cloaking most of the room in shadow. Malachi used his bound hands to help Auri stagger to her feet.

"Auri? Malachi?" Tsuna called. The darkness shifted as the hacker moved.

Auri peered into the shadows as her eyes adjusted. Castor perched on one of the beds set against a wall, Tsuna standing beside him. Auri was relieved to see the only injuries were those the two had sustained days prior. They both looked clean, if a little rumpled and frustrated.

Tsuna rushed to Auri, untying the wrist bindings before easing her onto a bed. "You're covered in blood." Her lips pinched together as if nausea threatened.

"Most isn't mine," she assured the hacker.

Castor made quick work of Malachi's bindings and then Birdie's. "You good, Captain?" he asked, tossing the ropes to a corner of the cell shared by an empty waste bucket.

"Mostly." Malachi rubbed his wrists.

Birdie hopped up onto the bed beside Auri and curled tightly against her side.

Once everyone was settled, Castor repeated Tsuna's earlier question. "What is going on? As soon as you left yesterday, we were dragged down here."

That revelation made Malachi scowl. "Chieftain thinks we're Walkers. Has the whole time."

Tsuna's brows drew together. "That rival group?"

Malachi nodded. "He claims we're here to infiltrate the Hole." He let out a slow breath. "The leap he's making isn't really that far. His concerns and our arrival do line up damn nicely."

Tsuna slipped Auri's jacket down to examine the wounds on her shoulder. She winced at the human-shaped teeth marks. "I'm guessing you ran into Bleeders."

Malachi nodded. "Auri put up a good fight. Katara would be proud."

Heat warmed Auri's chest as if the assassin herself had given the praise. "Thanks, Malachi."

"I'm just glad you made it out in one piece," Tsuna said.

Auri's smile faltered. "Not exactly."

Tsuna followed Auri's gaze down to her robotic leg. The hacker sucked in a breath. "Well, that's not good."

"Tell us everything," Castor demanded.

Malachi shared the past events in a similar manner to Oz, except he didn't leave out the second vial. And how Auri had accidentally broken it.

At the mention of the vial, Castor staggered against the cell door, bracing himself with both hands as if he might fall. Guilt knotted in Auri's belly, and she cursed her foolishness.

Tsuna took a shaky breath. "This isn't ideal, but let's tackle what's immediately before us, like looking at your leg, Auri." At Castor's pained grunt she added, "Don't be dramatic, Castor."

"It's not dramatic," the cook grumbled. "I'm mourning the usefulness of this entire mission."

Tsuna leaned over Auri's robotic leg and peered into the deep gash. Her brow furrowed and after a few moments, she leaned back shaking her head. "I'm sorry, Auri. Without my tablet or any kind of interfacing, I can't run a diagnostic on how to even begin a repair or patch." She rubbed at her forehead. "I don't know much about robotics. The dim light in here doesn't help either."

"It's okay," Auri said, fighting to hide her worry behind an appreciative smile.

"Castor, the door doesn't need your help to hold it upright." Malachi gestured for Castor to join them around the bed. "We're going to get the other vial from Oz. And we are going to get the hell out of here."

"How do you propose we do that?" Castor asked, easing away from the door as if not entirely convinced. "Considering we're locked in a cell. Again. *Maitta na*," he cried, slamming his palms together. "I just want some green tea!"

Tsuna rolled her eyes and caught his arm. "Cai probably has a backup plan for this failed plan."

Malachi took Tsuna's place beside Auri. His eyes met hers, ringed purple from exhaustion. "Oz will turn up. She has no way to replicate what's in the vial, and she's a realist. She knows it'll go to waste here."

Auri blinked, realizing Malachi was right, though a lot of it hinged on what he believed Oz *might* do. "Not much of a plan," she began.

"But a hope," Malachi finished. He gestured to her robotic leg. "I might be able to do something. Are there any error alerts on your c-tacts?"

Auri pulled up the command screen she'd minimized during their flight. "They're mostly gibberish error codes. But the description says something about a synthetic muscle jam." She closed the alert and looked to Malachi. "Not sure what that means."

"I think I do." He nodded at her leg. "May I?"

Auri swallowed. "Go ahead."

Malachi slid his hands underneath the tattered remains of her pants and tugged. The material made a loud ripping sound that sent fire crackling up Auri's neck. Castor and Tsuna craned their necks with interest.

"I'm not going to tear her clothes off with you two in the room," Malachi muttered, intent on his work.

Auri's skin burned hotter. She staunchly avoided eye contact with the other crew members and tried not to think about how Malachi was prodding around inside her leg. It somehow felt even more intimate than their kiss.

Which was also something she should *not* be thinking about right now.

"I'll update Marin," Tsuna said. "We haven't talked to her since last night. I'm trying to conserve battery power."

Castor assumed a position by the door. He squinted through the narrow opening that looked onto the hall. "You're clear," he said.

Tsuna removed the radio from her shirt and hailed the *Kestrel*. Marin responded moments later, and Tsuna quickly relayed what happened in Walker territory.

Malachi glanced up at Auri. "How's this?" He pressed something inside her leg. A green light flashed across her c-tacts, and an alert cleared.

"Better," Auri murmured. "One alert's gone."

Malachi shifted his hand and a warning slid across her c-tacts. Auri grimaced. "And it's back."

"There's some decent damage," Malachi said. He moved up to her head to brush stray red curls from her eyes. The strands practically peeled off her forehead. "You'll want to see a cyborg surgeon when we get back," he continued. "But I can patch you up enough so you can run." He hesitated. "It might shred your thigh muscle."

"Whatever you need to do, do it."

Malachi smirked. "I thought you'd say that." He raised his gloved hand. "I'll need to scavenge parts, but a working leg is more important than an articulate hand." In one smooth motion, he tugged off the garment with his teeth.

Auri's eyes widened as shadows slid over Malachi's skin. Except... She let out a startled gasp. The swirls of tattoos that covered his arm stopped at the base of his hand. And so did his flesh. Synthetic skin covered just his fingers, while the entire meaty part of his hand was robotic. As he flexed his fingers, Auri watched the mechanics move, replicating the tiny bones and muscles.

"You're a cyborg too," Auri breathed. "I never even suspected."

"Barely." Malachi squinted at his hand, moving the small pieces aside as if looking for something. "But I don't go around flaunting it."

"Why isn't there..." Auri trailed off, not wanting to be rude.

"Skin?" He looked up at her. "Because I got the machinery while in the Marines. Which means it's a piece of *kuso*." He waggled his fingers. "There used to be synthetic skin, but the thing jammed so often, and the VA has a nice long waiting list for those dishonorably discharged." He shrugged and looked back at his hand. "I learned the basics of how to fix it and just kept the skin off to save time. The glove keeps the machinery safe and free of dust. I'm not ashamed of it. You'd be surprised how many Ancorans are secretly cyborgs."

He pulled a piece of machinery from the depths of his hand, not much larger than the tip of Auri's pinky. The bare robotics twitched and his fingers curled in. Malachi forcibly straightened them with a frown. "Workable. Let's see if this helps you."

"Finally showing her your hand, huh?" Castor asked from the door, a lewd tone to his voice. Tsuna finished her conversation with Marin and slipped the radio back down her shirt. Castor raised his brows at Auri. "That hand's probably why he's been single so long."

Malachi forcibly flipped a rude gesture with his robotic hand. "I'd still have to use my arm, you *boke*." He tried to relax the gesture, but his hand had fixed in the position. Malachi sighed in frustration.

"Teach you to respect your elders," Castor goaded.

"Worth it." To Auri he said, "Take a few practice steps." He held out his functioning hand to help Auri off the bed. She gingerly lowered her robotic leg and stood. It didn't buckle under pressure, but an orange alert flashed across her vision. Something in her leg was on the verge of malfunctioning.

Auri took a few steps from one end of the narrow cell to the other. Her leg felt unstable, but it didn't collapse. She'd be able to run. Not far, but as far as they needed to reach the *Kestrel*. Hopefully.

"Good?" Malachi asked. He watched her progress with his arms crossed, studying her.

"Good," she answered with a smile. "Thank you." The two words didn't feel adequate. Malachi had given her a piece of himself, sacrificing his ability to use his coil gun. Just to give her a chance.

Even though the piece of him was robotic and lacked connection to her nerves, she could almost feel it tucked safely into her thigh. Warming her from the inside out.

Auri opened her mouth to say more when Castor hissed, "We've got company."

CHAPTER THIRTY-EIGHT

---

17 Nov 3319, 19:06:47
Milky Way Galaxy, Earth,
Scavenger Territory

"How many?" Malachi asked. His working hand went for his belt only to close on air. Instead, he fished into his mechanical hand again and removed a bar as long as her thumb with a pointed end.

"Just one." Castor shifted away from the door. "Oz."

"Earlier than I thought she'd be." He pressed the piece of metal against his organic palm. Castor sidestepped as Malachi pressed against the wall opposite the hinges.

The door rattled as Oz inserted a key. Moments later, it swung open. Oz stood at the threshold. She glanced over her shoulder before striding inside.

Malachi leapt from the shadows. He caught Oz around the waist, bringing his hand up to her neck. At the same time, Castor eased the door shut soundlessly.

"I hope my suspicion is true," Malachi murmured to Oz, pressing the point of his robotic innards against her neck. "And your betrayal in the council room was just a ruse."

Oz glared at him but didn't try to escape. "Obviously, you dit. I'm here to get you out."

Castor crossed his arms. "And why should we believe you?"

Auri eased onto one of the beds before she fell over. Birdie shifted closer, and Auri rested a hand atop the poodle's warm head.

Oz arched a brow in response to Castor's question. "Because you *don't have a choice*? I could leave you here to rot."

"Or," Tsuna countered, cocking a hip, "we could use you as a hostage and escape."

"But you don't need to," Oz repeated, clearly irritated. "Because I'm going to *get you out*—as long as you bring me with you."

Malachi chuckled darkly. "I knew there would be a catch." He let her go. Oz crossed her arms and turned to face him.

Malachi raised his hand and Oz, to her credit, didn't balk at Malachi's robotic enhancements. With a grunt, Malachi slid the metal rod back into place. His pinky and ring fingers twitched.

"What makes you think I want you on my crew?" he asked Oz.

Oz tilted her head. "Because I have the vial—your only chance to stop the Merks, Bleeders, whatever." She glared at each member of the crew. "Now hurry up and agree, we're wasting the little time we have."

Tsuna frowned. "What's going on?"

Concern flashed across Oz's face. "The Walkers invaded our territory and sent a runner requesting a meeting. Chieftain has taken a fighting force with him. War is brewing. I've been told to stay here in case..." Oz trailed off and cleared her throat. "The squadron left behind is loyal to me. I've told them to let us out so I can come with you to replicate the cure and return. Return to save my people."

"I'm guessing that is part of the deal to use your vial?" Malachi asked. He didn't seem concerned about the invading Walkers.

"Yes."

"Fine." Malachi held out his hand and Oz shook it with an excited grin.

"I've got your weapons and some extra supplies by the gates," she said, looking around the room as if checking to make sure there wasn't something else they should bring. "We can use the negotiations as a distraction to reach the shuttle at the darksite and—"

Malachi shook his head. "No need for us to go that far. We have an alternate means of travel."

At Oz's confused expression, Auri explained, "That shuttle is for short-range travel, Oz. And it isn't operable anymore. Our actual ship, the one we brought from our galaxy, is much bigger. Though not as big as some I've seen."

Malachi gave her an accusatory look.

"You don't insult a man's ship size, Auri," Tsuna teased.

Auri rolled her eyes. Now was not the time.

"Tsuna," Malachi instructed, "tell Marin we'll still meet east of the blockhouse—"

"No," Oz said. "You go that way and you'll run into the Walkers. Southeast is better."

Malachi's brows drew together as he considered her suggestion. Then he nodded. "It'll be tight, but Marin can make it work." To Tsuna he said, "Relay our meeting place to Marin. Have her try to pick up the radio's signal to hone in on our location. We'll stay in touch as we go."

"Got it." Tsuna pulled out the radio again.

Oz gawked. "Where the frack did you get that?" She stepped forward as if to examine it, but Malachi raised a hand to stop her. Marin's voice crackled through the speakers, and Oz paled. "What is it? Who is that?"

"It connects us with the pilot on our ship," Castor said. He watched Oz with narrowed eyes, clearly enjoying the upper hand. "That has plenty of fire power."

Auri resisted the urge to correct Castor's blatant lie. The *Kestrel* was far from a gunship. Transport ships were built for speed, not offense. Which was why they usually made such easy pickings for pirates lurking in Krugel's Curve.

Oz moved closer to where Auri sat on the bed. The Scavenger reached into the inner pocket of her jacket and removed a small wooden box. She extended it toward Auri.

"What is it?" Auri asked. She leaned forward to get a better look and disturbed a dozing Birdie.

Oz opened the box. Inside was a swatch of thick fabric. She eased it aside to reveal the vial, its amber liquid almost black in the dim light creeping through the cell's window. Auri nearly jumped out of her skin when Oz slammed the lid shut.

The woman grabbed Auri's wrist. "Keep it safe." Auri's eyes widened as the woman placed the box in Auri's palm and closed her fingers around it.

"Dumb to bring it with you," Castor pointed out while watching the display. "If we hadn't agreed and just decided to kill you, you *really* wouldn't have had anything to bargain with."

Oz snorted. "You assume I'm easy to kill." A knife seemed to materialize in her hand. It hurtled through the air and caught in the wooden door centimeters from Castor's cheek.

"Fair point," he said with a frown at the knife where it still wobbled from the impact.

"This is hope," Auri said as she tucked the box into a jacket pocket. She slipped her arms into the sleeves and drew up the zipper. "For both of our galaxies."

Oz's mouth twitched in a smile. "I had a feeling you would say something heartfelt like that. Which is why I trust you to carry it." Her voice lowered, so quiet, Auri could hear the static over the radio as Tsuna waited for Marin to pull up a surface scan. "And," Oz continued on a whisper, "to keep another promise."

Auri glanced at Malachi, but his attention was on Tsuna. "What promise?"

Oz took a slow breath. "If something happens to me on the way, or if Malachi changes his mind—"

"Malachi wouldn't—"

Oz held up a hand. "The future is unpredictable. Promise me you will return to my people with the duplicated cure and help rid our world of Merks."

Auri didn't hesitate. "Yes. I promise."

"Thank you, Auri." It could've been the shadows of the room, but Oz's eyes seemed to glisten with unshed tears. She curled her fingers into the shape of a gun and pressed them against her chest. "To madness and ruin."

Auri repeated the gesture, feeling as if her mother's ghost hovered at her shoulder. "To madness and ruin," she whispered.

"You would've made a great Scavenger," Oz said with a smile.

"We're all set," Tsuna called. The static quieted as she turned off the radio.

"Let's move." Oz strode to peer through the small opening at the hall beyond. Without asking if the crew was ready, she yanked open the door.

They filed out after her, Auri and Birdie at the rear. At first, Auri's leg felt like a rubber band ready to snap. By the time they reached the stairs, the feeling eased some, though it lingered enough to keep Auri careful.

True to Oz's word, the prison hall was empty, as was the metal staircase. Even glimpses of different levels revealed barren halls, shut doors, and dimmed lights. Only when they reached the main level and approached the ramp that led outside did Auri see faces she recognized.

Misshot held a large bag slung over one shoulder, chatting with Nibs and Grubs in low tones. When Misshot saw Oz, he whooshed a relieved breath.

"You're not dead," he said when Oz reached him.

Grubs cackled. "Looks like you're taking my kitchen duty next week."

Oz shoved Misshot in the shoulder. "You bet the Outsiders would kill me?"

"Of course not," Misshot grumbled, handing her the sack to rub his shoulder in mock agony. "I *bet* we would have to save you."

Oz pursed her lips. "That's insulting, Misshot." She tossed the bag to Malachi. His robotic fingers twitched but didn't bend to grab the strap. He caught it with his good hand before it fell to the floor. A glance in the bag made him grin. He passed the bag to Tsuna and quickly removed his two coil guns, returning them to their holsters.

Tsuna took her blaster and knife while Castor refitted himself with his dart shooter.

Auri was last and had to fish in the bottom for blood-encrusted *Ganbaru* and her knife.

Once everyone was outfitted with weaponry, Oz looked to her friends. "Stay safe, yeah?" Her voice cracked. She started to step away from them, but Misshot caught her and pulled her into a tight hug. He whispered something in her ear that Auri couldn't hear. Then pulled back.

Oz punched him in the arm playfully before she led the way up the ramp, the crew paces behind her with Nibs and Grubs following. The doors at the top were sealed and it took both Nibs and Grubs at either side to rotate the mechanisms that controlled them.

The doors opened slowly and soundlessly, creating a crack just wide enough for them to squeeze through single file. Darkness bathed the landscape beyond; whatever sliver was left of the moon barely illuminated the way ahead.

Auri crept outside first with Malachi bringing up the rear. The night was cool and quiet without even the shuffle of animals in the undergrowth. The silence made goosebumps pucker on Auri's skin.

The doors slid forward on silent rollers, and the warm light of the Hole grew narrower. Then the doors shut and the clang of activating locks broke the quiet of the night.

Oz stared at the sealed entrance, her face shadowed in the moonlight. She took a slow breath and then turned away. "There's no going back now."

Auri wasn't sure if Oz's words were to warn the crew or to remind herself of the consequences of her choice.

CHAPTER THIRTY-NINE

———

17 Nov 3319, 22:55:36
Milky Way Galaxy, Earth,
Scavenger Territory

Oz guided them away from the main path and into the underbrush. Without flashlights, they relied on the waning
moon and stars for light.

Auri tried to ignore the squeaking sound her leg made with
each step, barely masked by the crunch of leaves and grass under-
foot. She lagged at the rear, doing her best to dodge branches and
fallen logs. Malachi kept close, checking on her every few
minutes.

After what felt like hours, they came to a stop so abrupt, Auri
bumped into Malachi. He reached back to steady her.

"What is it?" he asked no one in particular. Oz had shifted
behind a tree, Tsuna and Castor just behind her. Sweat slicked
Castor's face, and he wiped at his brow with the edge of his

sleeve. Something about the moonlight on Tsuna's skin made her appear otherworldly, like a nymph from a fantasy story.

Oz pressed a finger against her lips. "Voices." She pointed just ahead. "Could be the negotiation." She frowned.

Malachi turned an accusatory glare on her.

She shrugged. "My father said they were meeting farther east. They must've moved."

"How far are we from our rendezvous?" Tsuna asked. Her hand strayed to where the radio was stowed, prepared to give Marin alternate coordinates.

"A ten-minute run," Oz said. "But if we're forced to go around it could take—"

"You have violated the treaty." Chieftain's faint voice from somewhere to their left made Auri tense.

Birdie growled a warning. A twig snapped and Auri spun, drawing *Ganbaru* in one smooth motion. The blades emerged, nearly pricking the neck of a woman lurking behind Auri. Four other figures waited steps behind the interloper. Judging by the mixture of metal and leather armor, they were Scavengers.

Malachi already had his coil gun raised. Oz strode past him, forcing the weapon down. She rested a hand on Auri's arm. "They're my people."

Auri slowly lowered *Ganbaru*, not entirely convinced they weren't a threat.

"Oz?" the woman asked, voice low, looking from Oz to the crew. "What are you doing out here? What are *they* doing out here?"

"Why aren't you with Chieftain?" Oz asked.

"We're moving around the Walker group to flank them," one of the other Scavengers said. "Chieftain plans—" His explanation was cut off by a scream.

Everyone whirled in the direction of the sound. "Chieftain," Oz rasped as if she'd been punched in the gut. Her machete was in her hands, raised and prepared to fight.

The sound hadn't even died before a bellowed war cry of a hundred voices rang out, followed by the clang of metal clashing against metal.

Birdie released a high-pitched bark moments before five Walkers shot from the underbrush on Auri's left, their skin stained green, brown, and black for camouflage. Auri blocked the swing of a bladed staff by crossing *Ganbaru*. If she'd moved seconds later, she would've lost an arm. While Auri trapped the Walker's weapon in place, Birdie lunged, grabbing one of their legs and yanking them to the ground.

The other Scavengers faced off against the remaining Walkers. Steel flashed and blood splashed black in the shadows of night. Someone grunted in pain.

"Oz," Malachi snapped.

The woman seemed to have grown roots, watching the battle in front of her. Then she came back to herself. "Forgive me," she whispered to her fighting comrades before she turned and ran.

"Oz?" someone called. Then louder, voice hardening in realization at the woman's betrayal. "Oz! What are you—?" The question cut off in a cry of surprise and pain.

Oz and the crew plowed through the trees, Malachi shooting any Walkers who got too close, still competent with his non-dominant hand. Moments later, they stumbled into a small clearing. Chieftain stood in the center, moonlight bathing him in a silvery sheen as he yanked an axe from the chest of a Walker. Oz gasped.

"Rally to—" Chieftain started but stopped as his head whipped around to follow movement at his left.

Auri squinted to determine what had caught his attention. Hulking shapes stalked from beneath the snaggled boughs of the surrounding trees, and terror crawled up her throat.

"Merks!" Chieftain bellowed. Both Walkers and Scavengers turned as the horde of Bleeders crashed into them.

Chieftain whirled on a creature, his axe blade flashing. As he hacked off the head of one, another pounced, slamming him to the ground. He disappeared underneath muscled bodies and flashing teeth.

Oz was trembling.

"Go," Auri whispered, grabbing Oz's wrist. "We will come back."

"Keep running that way," Oz choked out, gesturing away from the battle. "The trees will clear and you'll be at the blockhouse." Without a glance back, Oz dove into the fray. Her scream of rage and desperation overshadowed the shouts of pain and terror. Bleeders turned as she attacked, their attention flicking past her to the crew hiding at the tree's outskirts. A handful of the monsters stalked forward. The harpoons attached to their backs winked at Auri in a promise of pain.

"Run!" Malachi ordered.

They sprinted across the clearing into the next cluster of trees. The Bleeders snarled and pursued with an inhuman, horrifying speed.

"Get Marin down here, *now*!" Malachi cried.

Tsuna already had the radio out. "Bleeders in pursuit!"

Malachi dropped to the back of the group, just behind Auri and Birdie. He fired his coil gun into the shifting shadows. A flash of light from a bullet striking metal illuminated the Bleeders meters away. He swore when the guns clicked, their chambers empty.

A warning flickered across Auri's c-tacts, the orange alert turning red. Something in her robotic leg tore. She gritted her teeth. The limb gave out and she nearly tumbled into the tall grasses around them.

Malachi caught her shoulder, supporting her in a shambling run. Tsuna and Castor were steps ahead. A loud *woosh* and the purr of a well-maintained engine reached Auri's ears. The ground shook. Metal clanged as if a ramp was being lowered.

The trees grew sparse and then suddenly they were running onto farmland. The *Kestrel* had landed in the middle of a tilled patch of earth. The running lights were turned off, but scant moonlight glinted off the ship's exterior in a way that seemed to say *Welcome home. You're safe.*

But they weren't safe, not yet. Auri risked a look back. The Bleeders had paused at the edge of the trees, gawking at the transport ship. The sight made Auri's throat clench. Their expressions were far too human for such monsters.

Tsuna and Castor clanged up the ramp with Birdie on their heels. Malachi helped Auri limp upward. They reached the entrance to the cargo hold and a massive weight seemed to melt off Auri's chest. They were safe. They were *home*. At last.

Tsuna slammed her palm into the radio on the ship. "Onboard!"

The thrusters whined as they shifted into take off position. Auri leaned against Malachi's chest. His heart hammered against her cheek through his sweat-slicked shirt.

"Aurelia," he rasped. His hands came up to either side of her face, drawing her eyes up to look at him. The night sky glistened with stars behind him. "You were right before." He swiped away a drop of blood on her jaw. "I'd be a *baka* to wait until I've had my revenge before letting myself love you."

Auri gasped. The *Kestrel* trembled underneath them and began to rise. One meter, two, three. A light flashed as the ramp slid back and the cargo hold doors began to close. The ship climbed toward the starlit sky.

All the fighting, all the loss, all her fear slipped away as she stared into Malachi's beautiful eyes.

Before Auri could answer with feelings of her own, Malachi's mouth was on hers. She stumbled into him as the *Kestrel* gained altitude. At the same time, Malachi's body jerked forward.

Something hard and sharp pressed into Auri's chest. Pain throbbed just above her heart. She pulled back to look down.

Then she screamed.

A metal harpoon stuck from Malachi's torso. He looked down at it in surprise, then back up at her. Time seemed to slow.

Castor and Tsuna raced toward them, Tsuna shouting, Birdie barking.

Malachi was yanked backward. He tried to grab the edge of a door, but it was his robotic hand, and the fingers didn't respond.

"Malachi!" Auri screamed. She was running to reach him. Her leg buckled and she slammed into the floor so hard, spots danced before her eyes.

His gaze met hers for a brief instant—

And then he was gone.

A blur of white flashed in Auri's peripherals. Birdie bounded through the narrow gap in the doors after Malachi.

Auri slid forward on hands and knees. She reached the cargo hold doors as they closed. The warning light turned off. A stunned, horrified quiet settled on the ship.

Auri couldn't move. Couldn't breathe. Couldn't think.

"Go back," she rasped, clawing herself to standing, staring at the pitch black visible through the small window. Then in a wail, "Tell Marin to go back! Go back! Go *BACK*!" Her voice broke on the scream.

Tsuna reached for Auri. "Going back… It won't…" Tears streamed down her cheeks. "We were fifteen meters from the ground. The impact killed them."

But Auri knew the truth Tsuna hid with her lie.

By the time Marin turned the ship around and they landed, the Bleeders would've already killed—*eaten*—the ones Auri loved most in this galaxy and the next.

"Go back," she sobbed. "We are going back!" She staggered toward the intercom that would alert Marin, but Tsuna stepped in front of the screen. Castor shifted closer as if to help restrain Auri. Tsuna shook her head in warning.

"We can't," Tsuna said, voice breaking. Tears rolled down her cheeks and pattered onto the floor. "They're gone."

The ship's thrusters engaged, increasing in power so that the floor hummed under Auri's feet. As the *Kestrel* gained altitude, the ship keened in sorrow as if she too mourned the loss of her captain.

The stars visible from Earth turned into the dark clouds of upper atmo. And with the loss of the stars went Auri's chance of seeing Malachi or Birdie ever again.

———

OTHER BOOKS BY
Emily Layne

A centuries-old curse plagues the island of Viaii Nisi and an ancient enemy lurks beneath the depths of the surrounding water. When Annie makes a terrifying discovery, she must face her biggest fears to uncover the truth and save the people she loves.

These Wicked Waters by Emily Layne
available wherever books are sold.

ACKNOWLEDGEMENTS

After publishing *Of Starlight and Bone*, the thought of writing its sequel terrified me. I hadn't written something new since 2018 and was struggling to balance life as a sleep-deprived mom of two rambunctious littles and author dreams. But this acknowledgements page is proof—I did it!

Though I can't take all the credit. The creation of this book wasn't a solitary effort. Not by a long journey back to a postapocalyptic Earth. So many thanks are in order.

Thank you to my agent, Becky, and the team at Owl Hollow Press for helping this story go from rough draft to polished book.

Endless love and thanks to my family. Mom and Dad, thank you for watching my littles so I could write or nap—usually both. Dad, you finally got your dedication! Mom, get ready, you're next! Maddie and Sarah, I hope you know how much it means to your big sister that you read every book I write, regardless of genre.

Without the ear of my husband, this story wouldn't be the same. Jeff, thank you for listening to plot ideas after a long day or over our babies' shouts in the car. You battled my imposter syndrome on a weekly basis, and you were my champion at each stage of the writing process.

To my littles, Eloise and Wilder. You two inspire my creativity with your own imagining. I can't wait for the day I get to share my stories with you. And, as always, to God, without Whom none of this would be possible. Mark 10:27

Emily Layne grew up a proud Army brat with an Anne Shirley-esque imagination. She loves reading, eating too much pizza, and spending time with her husband—who loves books almost as much as she does.

When not writing fantastical stories, Emily can be found playing with her curious children, exploring the great outdoors, or concocting mostly-believable excuses to avoid socializing.

Her debut novel, *These Wicked Waters*, was inspired by her experience on a cruise ship (which proved to be quite flammable, unfortunately).

Emily is represented by Becky LeJeune of Bond Literary Agency.

Find Emily online at www.emilylaynebooks.com